12/98

To Sandy & Norman two
lovely persons I was fortunate
to meet while cruising
South America in 1998

Lotsa love

Andy

JUST
ANOTHER
MAN

JUST ANOTHER MAN

A STORY OF THE NAZI MASSACRE OF KALAVRYTA

ANDY VARLOW

Frog, Ltd.
Berkeley, California

JUST ANOTHER MAN
A STORY OF THE NAZI MASSACRE OF KALAVRYTA

Published by Frog, Ltd.

Frog, Ltd. books are distributed by
North Atlantic Books
P.O. Box 12327
Berkeley, CA 94712

Cover photo: German troops celebrate the capture of Athens by raising their battleflag over the Acropolis on April 27, 1941

Cover and book design by Paula Morrison

Printed in the United States of America

Library of Congress Cataloging-in-Publication Data
Varlow, Andy.
    Just another man / by Andy Varlow.
        p.   cm.
    Includes bibliographical references.
    ISBN 1-883319-72-2 (hardcover)
    1. World War, 1939–1945—Greece—Kalavryta—Fiction.   2. World War, 1939–1945—Atrocities—Fiction.   3. Greek Americans—Fiction. I. Title.
PS3572.A725J87   1998
813'.54—DC21   98-20804
                                                                              CIP

1   2   3   4   5   6   7   8   9 / 02   01   00   99   98

This book is dedicated to the victims of Kalavryta—
the dead and the living—
and to Climpt.

CONTENTS

AUTHOR'S PREFACE

Everyone has a story to tell, and this is my story, the story of
Just Another Man.

The writing of this novel has resulted in both a memoir of my early
life and a cleansing for me. Without revealing the twists of the plot, I
will mention up front that much of the high drama in this book is fic-
tionalized. My pursuit of such an involved fantasy will become clear
to you from the story's outset.

These events of my childhood are all too true, remaining vivid and
tragic in my memory to this day. The Kalavryta massacre is told as I
remember it, though some names have been changed. By expanding
that horrible experience of my youth into a novel, a fragile peace has
returned in me. *Just Another Man* is a catharsis that has abated my nightmares.

Most of my characters are based on real-life friendships that have
bloomed during my lifetime. I have endeavored to portray these rela-
tionships honestly and respectfully, just as I have honored my strong
family ties.

Though chronologically inexact, the romance I paint in this book
is genuine. I have had the good fortune of living out a storybook love
in real life. I only hope the tenderness and devotion I portray between
Yiannis (my name in the book) and Kathy (my wife) does justice to
our boundless feelings for one another. My novel aims to commemo-
rate and share this special camaraderie.

I hope readers will accept *Just Another Man* in the spirit it is offered—
a story that comes from the depths of a man's heart, as it tells the world
of the Kalavryta Crime.

Andy Varlow
San Rafael, California
April 1998

June 2, 1951. Whistles bellowed.... The mooring lines were cast, the umbilical cord severed, and Nea Hellas, *the steamship, was set free from her snug concrete womb to sail to the New World. I leaned against the deck railing and gazed down at the huge boisterous human hive on the quay below.*

Piraeus was hot and humid that afternoon. The air was heavy, filled with restlessness and sweat and many odors, and I was smothered by arms waving all around me. To my left a middle-aged woman squashed her breasts against my back as she shrieked at relatives somewhere off in the distance. When I edged away from her shoving, I smelled the warm breath and scent of a younger woman dressed in black. She appeared not to mind the intrusion and she smiled. I stayed, entranced, glued to the spot and crushed by the crowd.

The shouting, the commotion, the hollow stares, and the screaming cries on the dock that day strangely rekindled the same numbness I had felt deep inside my gut during that dreadful day in Kalavryta.

PART I

THE CRIME
AND
THE VOW

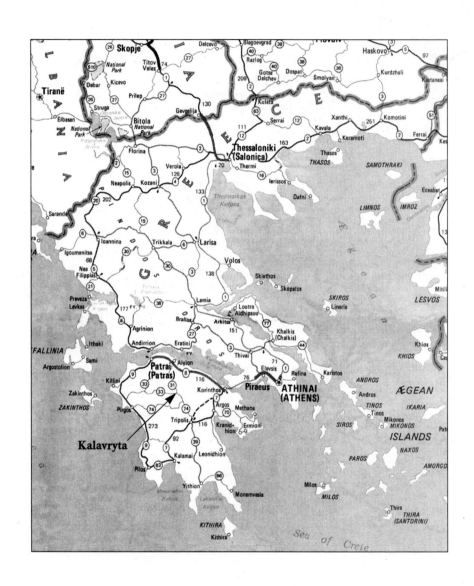

1

GOD'S BETRAYAL

waved my cap, acknowledging that someplace in the turbulent assembly on the pier lingered my mother and Betty, my only sister. It had been heartbreaking to see them weep and to feel their warm tears on my excited red cheeks as we embraced and kissed. Betty was nineteen, only one year older than I, and yet she cared for me as if she were my second mother. We were fond of each other, the three of us—no, more than that, we loved each other—and I'm not embarrassed to admit that I was profoundly spoiled by those two women.

I had sobbed, too, for leaving them behind without a man, and it felt awkward to cry in front of so many strangers. Maybe a man of eighteen who had seen and felt as much as I had no right to cry.

Besides, why cry now? At last my long-awaited dream was coming true. Uncle John, God bless his kind soul (provided there is a God out there who cares enough to bless someone who does a kind deed), had sponsored me on this exciting voyage. A distant cousin of my father, he had visited us briefly right after the war when we were finally settled with my maternal grandmother in Tripolis.

A kind, compassionate man in his fifties, well-fed and clean-shaven, Uncle John had taken an instant liking to me, casually asking if I would like to visit him in Davis, California, when I finished high school.

"And if you like it there, you could take classes at the local university, get a diploma and return home, or just stay on and work and settle as I did many years ago." He knew that as a displaced person I could immigrate to America the Great.

I was astounded by his offer and fearful that something might spoil his good intention. My grandmother, mother, and sister all sat there expressionless and gray as if they were made of marble, but I replied without the slightest hesitation, my voice quivering but determined. "Nothing in the whole world would make me happier, if it could be arranged and if it isn't too much of a burden on you."

He took in a long breath and scratched the lobe of his left ear. When he said, "Yes, of course, it would be just fine with me if you want to come," I felt like an anxious young hawk must when it is about ready for its maiden jump into space, to be free from the confines of its nest, to glide to liberty on the strength of its own wings.

Then Uncle John reached into his coat pocket and took out a couple of American silver dollars. He handed one to Betty and one to me, and I remember so clearly snatching the shining coin from his extended hand, planting a hurried kiss on his fat cheek, and zooming out of the house onto the streets, eager to tell all my friends, and indeed the whole wide world, that in a few years I would be traveling to California. At that very moment I was the happiest lad in Greece!

The deafening blasts from the ship's steam whistle shook my mind loose from those memories and I began to wave once again, more frantically now as I caught what I knew would be the last glimpses of Mother and Betty for a long time. And while I wondered about their thoughts and their feelings, my stomach tightened and my eyes grew moist.

I gazed absentmindedly at the slowly dispersing crowds around me and in the distance. The land grew removed and hazy but I stayed, leaning against the ship's rail, possessed by the past.

Kalavryta was where I was born, delivered at home by Doctor Hampsas sometime in the early morning on the 15th of September, 1932. My father, Theodoros, had been born in Kalavryta also, but not his father.

According to family lore, my Grandfather Yiannis was an adventurous young man who traveled to foreign lands and made his fortune in Egypt, exporting raw cotton. Then he roamed the African plains hunting wild game and finally returned to his motherland to search for his own Shangri-La.

During one of his horseback treks over the mountains of northern Peloponnesus, he rode through the grandiose Vouraikos Gorge. His route was unplanned. There was no urgency to his excursion. But the petroglyphs sculpted on the vertical rocky banks beside the rushing currents of the wild river mesmerized his soul. Farther up, he stumbled on the heroic Megaspileon (Great Cave) Monastery. Perched like an eagle's nest on the bare face of a sheer cliff, it was shielded by God's hand and never succumbed to the tyranny of the Turks during the Ottomans' 400-year slavery of Greece. This was God's country, the legend claimed. No territory for the devil to poke his spooky fork.

Welcomed by the reclusive monks, Yiannis was hoisted halfway up into the sky in a bamboo basket and stayed as their guest for two days and two nights.

He received the sacrament, and when he left that holy place, he felt closer to God than ever before. As if directed by a divine spirit, he followed his nose higher up, through the stunning rocky gulch. On one turn his heart stopped beating. Only the Lord knows how long he stood still in absolute wonder and reverence.

To his left, stretching out on the imposing slopes of Mt. Chelmos, lay a breathtaking jewel of a village. Mammoth plane trees shaded the square; older than Jesus they seemed to be. Streams of clear, cool spring water meandered along the streets and among the stone houses with their iron balconies and red tile roofs, and the air was drenched in scents of oregano and sage and thick pine forest moss. His heart was bewitched by Kalavryta, which means "crystal springs" in ancient Greek. Then and there he chose this site to build his home.

Kalavryta was a historic place. In the nearby monastery Agia Lavra, the gallant bishop Paleon Patron Germanos had raised the banner that started the revolution against the Turks in 1821. The town, as the provincial seat for sixty-nine surrounding villages, proudly displayed its courthouses and gymnasium. Moments after the newcomer's first visit to the National Bank, since nothing was ever secret in that town of two thousand souls, the place buzzed with rumors about this fine man and his riches.

As if he were some maharajah, Yiannis was offered his pick of the available maidens. His eye returned to Kalliopi, renowned for her angelic loveliness and grace, the daughter of Takis Kalatzis, the respected leader of a prominent clan. Othon, the new king of Greece, had slept in their home once as the guest of Takis' grandfather.

After constructing a fine dwelling that featured the first indoor bathroom and plumbing in that region, Yiannis wed Kalliopi in a ceremony and celebration that has remained a local epic. He settled down as a happily married man.

Yiannis, forty, and fair Kalliopi, just shy of twenty-one, were blissfully happy when my father was born.

But soon after Theodoros' birth, Kalliopi fell ill. She was bedridden for two years, and although Yiannis sent for the finest doctors in Europe, and some came from as far away as Vienna and Berlin, none could diagnose her strange illness, and she died.

Four years after Kalliopi's passing, my grandfather married a school teacher from Patras, a soft-spoken and gentle lady who cared for both her husband and his son.

At eighteen, my father left home to attend the university in Athens and to study law. Gifted with a fine tenor voice, he also took vocal lessons in the Academy of Music.

Eleftherios Venizelos, the prime minister at the time, envisioned a greater Greece with a kingdom extending to the Sea of Marmara and beyond. A daring Cretan with fire in his soul and an unshakable faith in the fate of the Greek nation, Venizelos ordered a general mobilization to combat the hated Turks. My father was called to serve his country and was dispatched to the fighting front in the northeast.

In the final push of 1922, while advancing Greek forces sought to liberate Constantinople, they met with a shocking defeat. The army sullenly withdrew, and this unexpected retreat brought humiliation to the highly nationalistic military forces. At the end of this great Greek military adventure many heartbroken young men were discharged and sent home.

My father returned with many memories and one treasured trophy, a defused Turkish mortar shell bearing a crude inscription, "Forever grateful to the hated enemy fire," scratched on its steel casing with his pocket knife.

That round projectile with its ugly tail had flown into his foxhole and lodged in the mud about thirty centimeters from his left foot. It should have blown him to shreds. But it had failed to explode and, defused, ended up as a decoration on the fireplace mantel of his home.

My father spoke of Venizelos with affection, since he had refused to yield to the Turks and had reclaimed from them the northern lands of Epiros, Macedonia, Thrace, and the eastern Aegean islands, territories which had been Greek for thousands of years.

In 1928, the country hummed with land reforms and the spirit of economic reconstruction, and my father returned to Kalavryta at the age of twenty-eight with a diploma in law. The government had appointed him the district recorder. He sang and played the guitar. He was a kind man, and he believed in God. The community honored him as the Right Chanter at the Assumption of the Virgin Mary, the main church. On Sundays and holidays people of substance came to listen to his caroling.

Quite tall by national standards at almost six feet, he was trim yet big-chested with a finely carved face decorated with a black mustache.

Theodoros was a humorous, honest, and fun-loving man, and a most desirable matrimonial catch.

Relatives, friends, and acquaintances were quick to recommend as prospective brides their sisters, daughters, nieces, and cousins. When he turned thirty, Theodoros chose as his mate the third child of five and the oldest of two daughters of a prosperous fur merchant from Tripolis.

Vassiliki, pet-named Vakoula— my mother—was not a great beauty, but her milky skin, bright blue eyes, pleasant disposition, and fine upbringing most certainly compensated for her plumpish stature. She was a graduate of the middle school and had been tutored in French and violin, great accomplishments for a young woman in those days. They were married just as worldwide depression was infiltrating an already-fragile local economy.

The subsequent devaluation of the drachma had a devastating effect on the health of the nation and my grandfather Yiannis' bank deposits and Greek bond holdings. He bore the loss of wealth in silence and the subject was never discussed, but he aged quickly and in six years died of cancer.

I remember him stretched out stiff and motionless on his bed; too young to comprehend such a moment of great family grief, I sneaked out in the middle of the laying out and wandered off to the town square. While I was searching for a playmate during a game of hide-and-seek, a stranger stopped to ask me how my grandfather was getting along. Smiling, I replied in a matter-of-fact way that he was fine and had just died.

The funeral procession was enormously long. Heading the parade were young altar boys dressed in long frocks, bearing silver and gold icons and banners on tall poles. Four bearded Orthodox priests in their glittering stoles and imposing black hats, chanting eulogies and prayers for salvation, followed the ornate casket carried on the shoulders of six strong men. Next marched some thirty-odd, semi-uniformed musicians of the town philharmonic who blew through their instruments

a slow and melancholy dirge. They preceded my grandmother and my mother, both veiled and wailing, dressed in black, and my father in his best dark Sunday suit with a black mourning band worn on his left sleeve.

Then followed our beloved nanny, holding Betty and me firmly by our hands, with many relatives and family friends, and lastly a great number of town folks who had come to pay their respects to a likable man.

He was buried in the cemetery

next to the chapel, and after the customary forty-day church observance that commemorates the separation of the immortal soul from the earthly body, my step-grandmother left us to return to her roots at Patras.

I missed her kind face. She had been tender and loving to me, and I had liked to sit on her lap, where she let me rub her soft ear lobe between my fingertips.

Betty and I were heartbroken when our first nanny left us to marry, but in no time we adapted to Pagona, a sweet old maid and distant relative who, impoverished, had been asked by my father to share our home and help look after the children. We enjoyed the best of toys, and our mother took extreme pride in dressing us in the finest clothes, which she bought during annual visits to Athens.

We lived in a large two-story stone house on the west edge of town, surrounded by two acres of neglected vineyard. The soil was rocky and poor and the vines grew untamed. Scattered throughout the wild vineyard posed a dozen almond trees, and the boundaries of our land were marked with the traditional wall of mortarless gray rocks.

The lower story of our home housed father's office and all the district records: huge stacks of massive, musty-smelling ledgers. All the entries of property transfers and other legal matters remained secure, neatly hand-written, stamped with the official seal and dated either by my father or my mother, who acted as his assistant.

The office was always busy and the financial rewards sufficient to care for our family in a somewhat affluent style.

The second story of our house was spacious, with many rooms, a large kitchen with cold running water, a bathroom, a parlor filled with sofas, and a dining room with a china chest and a table with six matching chairs—the usual furnishings found in any prosperous household.

Three large, framed, sepia-toned photographs hung on one wall of the parlor. The middle portrayed our parents in their wedding finery; to its right a picture of Betty at age four sitting on one of the carved armchairs, cute as a button with her light shining eyes and blond curly hair. On the opposite side hung a photo of me taken on the same day and roosting in a similar chair, my upper body covered with some sort of flimsy fabric to resemble a toga, purposely arranged so that my

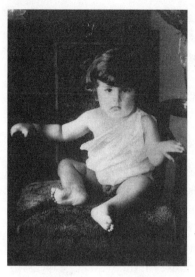

proud genitals were exposed for all the world to view.

Betty and I shared the same bedroom because we were afraid of the dark which often came unexpectedly, as the town's electric generator frequently broke down and we had to make do with oil lamps.

Dinner was served early to us, and we were usually finished by seven o'clock. Soon afterward we went obediently to bed, dressed in long flannel gowns, carrying our potties in hand, which we tucked under our beds for use during the night. Then we turned to face the Icon of Virgin Mary which hung on the eastern wall above a lighted oil lamp, kneeled, and in the presence of our parents whispered our prayers, respectfully asking her and God to protect our father, mother, and all our relatives from ill, and to help us grow up to be good citizens. I would add, "And please tell my mother not to force me to eat bread." We jumped into our beds and they tucked us in lovingly, told us stories, sang to us and kissed us goodnight. Our parents always went visiting unless one of us was sick. They mingled with their friends to talk and eat and serenade, but when they returned home, without fail, they sneaked in to check on us. In the morning, barely awake, we searched under our pillows for colorfully wrapped candies mysteriously placed there each and every night.

Their love and caresses tasted like the sweetness of the candies and our young hearts were filled with careless contentment as we licked and giggled, feeling treasured and secure.

Sometimes my father, towering above like Apollo or Hercules, lifted me up, placed me on one thigh, and bounced me up and down imitating a galloping horse. Other times he helped me climb on his back, and he crawled around on the floor, bellowing like a jackass, giving me "donkey rides." Then, a proud love flooded my insides and my eyes sparkled like two bright stars.

Time passes so slowly for children; a year seemed to last forever. In the summer, our town hummed with tourists enjoying the refreshing coolness of the mountains, away from the heat of the lowlands. It was a time for picnics and recreation. The various springs, where plane trees and poplars stood tall and graceful, were packed with fun-seeking families.

On Sundays after church, groups of cheerful friends and relatives often took a short walk to Alimbey, a patch of lush grass inside the grand ravine by the river's edge and alongside the tracks of our tiny train.

The area was surrounded by towering birches and lanky bamboo. Dressed in our finest, we carried ornate baskets filled with food and pastries, fruits and huge watermelons, which we placed in the frigid spring water to cool. We stretched out on blankets and ate and sang, or swayed from swings that hung from the sturdy branches of a giant mulberry tree.

My friend Stavros and I walked forever, like two seasoned acrobats high on the wire, on the skinny rails of the two-car train which linked us to the coastal village of Diakofto.

On occasion our family destination became the beach, twenty-two kilometers north and half kilometer below the heights of Kalavryta. At the railroad station my father purchased round-trip tickets from our station master, an imposing and pompous fellow in his gold-beribboned hat and spotless blue uniform with epaulets, decked out as if he wished to outrank even an admiral in glitter.

We rode the "Tooth Train" for two and a half hours, nicknamed for its ability to climb and plunge with the help of a geared wheel that grabbed onto the teeth of a rail laid between the tracks. We listened to it groan and moan as it strained around sharp curves, crawled through dark scary tunnels and over frightening bridges, all the while spitting out streams of dense black smoke and scattering lignite ashes in its wake, and we gloried in its lively whistling during the short straight stretches.

And how can I ever describe the exhilaration that flooded my young insides at the sight of the sea with its mysterious bluish-green color rippling, its immense expanse, and its invigorating freshness, an invitation to splash and play?

In the autumn, when the dirt roads and the square of Kalavryta were blanketed with crisp golden leaves, my group of friends' favorite pastime was racing wooden matchsticks down the rushing waters of a puny creek that sped alongside the main street, the proud winner rewarded with pieces of candy from the losers.

By December, the gigantic plane trees and the pine forests beyond looked sad and melancholic, their branches barren and bent, burdened by heavy snow. Except for traditional family outings to church and the occasional expedition to our front yard to build a snowman, Betty and I remained indoors, staring out through the foggy windows at the silvery flakes that twinkled as they fell, like two young sparrows tucked inside their feathered nest.

Finally, the warm April sun forced the white to melt. As another cold season withdrew and spring green gradually spread vivid color to the fields, the days began to grow longer. Here and there poppies bloomed and displayed vibrant red petals. Inside, Betty and I chattered with excitement at the coming thaw, shivering at the thrill of forthcoming adventures and endless hours of outdoor play, our smiling faces reflecting fantasies of imminent fun and games.

One late spring day our parents returned from their annual trip to Athens and presented us with the most startling gifts. Though Betty eyed her doll stroller with disappointment and resignation, my gleaming black racer was a thrill to us both.

It was a convertible with a comfortable leather seat, pedals to power it, and headlights that turned on and off just like a real automobile. Trimmed with chrome, it looked mighty flashy. When word shot through the town that I was the owner of a spiffy vehicle, all the children came to look and drool.

They touched it with reverence and pleaded in vain for a spin, while I nonchalantly drove around our front yard. Betty sat on the hood, legs dangling, the only place for a second person to ride.

Occasionally I gave the wheel to my best friend Stavros, while Betty adamantly refused to forsake her place on the hood, which she had claimed as her rightful stake. But I remained regally in complete control, letting the other children provide the pushing muscle. Since they were willing to supply the power, I hardly ever used the pedals; in fact,

I scorned them as if they were a chore.

We were a couple of spoiled children, my sister and I. Feeding us was a daily ordeal for my mother and the nanny. We seldom asked for food because we were never hungry, and pleas for us to eat were almost always ignored, unless, of course, our wish to have company was fulfilled. Then they would invite the brood of some less fortunate neighbor to share with us so that we might be influenced by their hunger.

Bread, the staple of all Greek tables, I emphatically refused to place inside my mouth, unless the slice was cut so thinly that peeping through I could see the sun during the day or a light bulb at night. However, when my friend Anna was our invited guest I ate heartily, and my mother's frustration subsided. Anna was five, one year younger than I, short and plump, and I liked to play hide and seek with her. She liked me, too, because one late summer afternoon when we were playing and I found her hiding behind some rocks in the vineyard, I asked her if she would pull down her pants and show me "hers," and she agreed, as long as I did it first. After I did it, she did it.

My world in Kalavryta was comfortable in those days. Oh, there is never clear sailing forever, and occasionally an event would upset the tranquil rhythm of my growing up—like that one July evening at the end of second grade when I was part of a bunch of schoolboys shooting the breeze on the steps of Agia Kyriaki, the tiny chapel in the square. A fat and rather nasty boy started talking about fucking. We all listened intently since he was older by two years.

I didn't understand much about fucking, except that fucking was a very bad deed performed only by prostitutes. Sensing my innocence, the fat boy turned, looked at me, and singled me out of the entire group. With a sneer, he asked me if I knew that my mother had been fucked by my father and I had been born because he had fucked her, and since I had a sister my mother had been fucked by my father twice!

I was so shocked and offended by his filthy revelations that I rushed away from the gathering as fast as I could to hide my tears. For a long time my young mind was tormented with awful, upsetting thoughts— I had always viewed my mother as a woman of saintly qualities.

During the warm summer months, the sun's stride across our narrow horizon seemed lazier, and we were allowed to play outside all day. My group of friends roamed the fields in search of crickets and butterflies and large golden beetles. Often Michalis, Stavros, Petros, and I drew a straight line on the dirt of a secluded road and stood in a row with the front edge of our shoes touching the scratch. Facing the same direction, we unbuttoned our flies, pulled out our willies, and competed to see who could shoot his pee the farthest.

After one of those contests, Michalis, who was a year older, produced a cigarette. He placed it between his lips and, with the bravura and suavity of a movie star, lit it with a match and puffed away, showing us the proper way to inhale. He even blew smoke out of his nostrils. We took turns trying to imitate Michalis, our new idol.

Oh boy, did I feel important after such an accomplishment! And when Michalis contemptuously ground out the butt I quickly retrieved it and tucked it inside my trouser pocket for safekeeping. Feeling that my participation in such a mature ritual had boosted me one more step up the ladder of adulthood, I arrived home confident and conceited.

But early the next morning, at the urging of my disciplinarian mother, my compassionate father, with his belt in hand and folded in two, yanked the covers off my bare legs. With Mother standing next to him to supervise the due punishment, he started to whack them. "Your mother found a cigarette butt in your pocket!" he shouted scoldingly. "So, now you want to smoke?" Another whack cracked the air. But the slapping of leather against leather delivered more racket than sting, and I minded more his anger than the pain. "Hah?" Whack! "You think you are a big shot already?" One more whack! "You need help to button up your britches, and you think you are old enough to smoke?" Whack! "You aren't going to touch any cigarettes again!" One more whack! "Are you?" Another whack!

"No. Never, my dearest father. Never, never, never! I promise," I cried. He stopped, and my mother's blue eyes gleamed as she stormed out of the room, followed by my regretful father; it was the first and the last time he gave me a whipping!

The nights were mild and our parents often let us stay up and play into the late hours. Exhausted, we would join them and their friends at the tavernas or restaurants by the square and listen to their concerned voices talk of the war in northern Europe, debating which position Metaxas, our controversial dictator, admirer of both Hitler and Mussolini, would take if the conflict were to spread into the Balkans.

As young as I was, I felt reverence for our aging leader and his nationalistic spirit, his development of the youth movement, and his command to schoolmasters throughout the country that pupils wear uniforms— white shirts and dark blue short pants. A thrill passed through me when, on many occasions and most all holidays, we students proudly paraded through the streets of Kalavryta and sang patriotic songs.

One morning, suddenly and unexpectedly, the common word "NO" took on a strange sort of honor while it echoed across the valleys and bounced off every mountain peak to penetrate the ears of every Greek. "NO," Metaxas had shouted in reply to Mussolini's demand that Greece unconditionally surrender.

In October of 1940 the Italian army crossed the Greek-Albanian border and a war was forced upon us. In Epirus, the Italians pushed south, but the unprepared and totally inferior Greek forces humiliated Mussolini's troops and miraculously, with a counterattack, drove the *macaronades* (macaroni eaters, as we contemptuously nicknamed them) from the Pindos Mountains back to Albania and into the Ionian Sea.

Our pride reached immeasurable heights as young and old gathered to listen to radio broadcasts of inspiring speeches by our ailing leader, glorifying the heroic sacrifices of our gallant soldiers.

Alas, our intoxication with the bravery of our men in the front lines was short-lived. The following April, the Germans attacked Greece from Bulgaria and a dreadful gloom fell upon us all.

The Nazi invasion was swift and devastating. The nation surrendered, despair overtook the land, and the people rapidly resigned themselves to the miserable destiny of the conquered.

Soon after, the Italians established a garrison in Kalavryta and confiscated most of our grains, livestock, and olive oil. Suddenly we, the Greeks, were demoted to second-class citizens in our own country, deprived of all human rights.

My father's cheerful spirit was crushed. His lively and quick humor abruptly died. He withdrew into himself and passed his time writing interpretations of the Apocalypse of John the Apostle.

While the occupation forces stole our reduced food supply, the farmers made their inventories available to the highest bidders. Greek currency became worthless, and the daily printing of ever-larger denominations became a farce. Inevitably, bartering was resurrected as the means of exchange for even the most basic foods.

My grandfather Yiannis' gold watch, which my father inherited and proudly wore in his vest pocket, was the first family treasure turned over to a peasant—swapped for a meager ten-kilo sack of wheat flour.

Clients to the recorder's office grew scarce, and the few who came often paid with a piece of dried-up corn bread wrapped inside a napkin or handkerchief.

In that era of hardship and misery, the farmers, scorned before the war as backward in their thinking, found a chance to retaliate and hoarded essential staples. Soon our family jewels and our finest furniture were gone—exchanged for food.

Our nanny returned to her own village; perhaps existence would be easier there. My mother spent her days combing the fields for snails and edible wild greens. In the evenings she washed and mended our clothes as they gradually faded, grew threadbare, and were outgrown.

While time crawled by and our fundamental preoccupation was simply our daily survival, the wonder of an occasional miracle gave us a spark of hope.

One such event came early one morning in the spring of '42. Betty and I were still buried under our quilts when we heard Mother shrieking with excitement. We sprang up and raced toward the kitchen, where she looked fixedly out the window, facing west, her arms frantically waving.

We followed her stare and rubbed our eyes in total disbelief. Not far from the house, inside our vineyard and grazing alone, was a stray ewe.

"She must have separated from the Italian flock," Mother surmised, and without hesitation and still in our nightclothes, the entire family sped outside. After a considerable chase we subdued her and led her into our earthen basement, where we marveled at our God-given treasure. Father rushed to put on his street clothes over his pajamas and hurried off to fetch the local butcher.

The butcher came quickly since, for his skillful cooperation, he had been promised the ewe's head, intestines, and hide. The slaughterer performed his deed unwitnessed by any of us. Since refrigeration was nonexistent in those days, we boiled her immediately and stored her for future eating inside a big terra-cotta vat, its mouth sealed with the ewe's tallow to keep out the air. We hid it behind a large wine barrel in the cool basement.

The winter that year was hard. Snow on the streets measured at least a meter, and attendance at the schools dropped to a trickle; most children had neither the nourishment nor the warm clothing to brave the nasty chill.

Leather was unobtainable at any price, so everyone's shoes and boots were in sorry shape—decorated with countless mismatched patches; uppers deformed from mending; cardboard-box cutouts for soles.

On Christmas morning the church bells rang early. My father and I put on our warmest coats—mine tighter than the outgrown vest on Mr. Aristidis, our hefty local politician. We dared the falling snow and sub-zero elements to attend the holy services.

The church was filled with the faithful in tattered coats and thread-bare scarves and misshapen hats. Many came clutching worn-out blankets. A few stood barefoot. All prayed in silence to Jesus and God, pleading for our calamity to end.

Father took out his tiny La pitch pipe, gave it a soft blow as he always did, and in a hushed whisper sang, "Aaaaaa," offering us the starting note, to prepare the dozen young voices who stood around him like ducklings stretching their necks for a handout. Then, tapping his foot on the wooden floor in a beat, with a faint movement of his hand he led his choir to enjoin God: *"Kyrie eleison, Kyrie eleison, Kyrie eleison."* ("Almighty, show us mercy.")

The priest's voice, thunderous and full of heartache, soared to heaven, asking the Lord to send us hope and courage, while my father's choir continued its chant. The congregation appeared greatly moved. At the end of the liturgy we all embraced and lined up to receive the tiny cube of blessed bread.

The instant the good priest handed us the bite I was quick to devour mine, but my father wrapped his own piece in his handkerchief and put it carefully inside his overcoat pocket. We left for home in silence.

Mother and Betty had set the Christmas table—less our fine tableware which had long ago been exchanged for food. When the time came for the traditional early meal, we sat and bowed our heads in prayer and made the sign of the cross. Mother served us our portion of the boiled wild greens—short of olive oil, since we had none—three chestnuts and two tiny snails each. My father rose and left the room. He returned with the valued blessed bread in his palm. He carefully split the bite in half, placing the pieces on Mother's and Betty's plates. My mother was so moved by his selfless act and the scarcity of food on our table, particularly on such a special day, that she broke down and wept uncontrollably. Betty and I, unable to bear her sobbing, began to snivel. Father reached out and touched her, fumbling for words of comfort. At that moment another miracle occurred.

The brass knocker on our front door clapped sharply, and when Betty flung it open there stood the maid of a close family friend, the very resourceful manager of the Agricultural Bank. Hurriedly she walked into our dining room cradling in her arms something covered by a blanket. Mutely she placed this strange object in the middle of our almost-empty table and unwrapped it to reveal a marvel. An enormous steaming platter of spaghetti with hot tomato sauce and mizithra cheese sprinkled on top lay there before our dumbfounded eyes. Before we had a chance to utter a sound, she turned and left. Our crying stopped instantly and we four looked to Heaven, crossed ourselves in worship, and thanked God for His display of mercy.

With its tracks blown up, our tiny train had stopped running and Kalavryta, because of its mountainous location, was isolated from the rest of the country. Travelers often came from the lowlands on foot, bringing news of famine and death in Athens and the countryside.

The greed of growers and speculators brought on my father's constant wrath. He spoke of them as vampires and swains of Hell who had been brought to Earth in human form by Satan to suck the blood of the innocent God-loving Greeks.

Because the possibility of starvation grew, the Greek Resistance was born. Men took anything that resembled arms, grouped into bands, and hid out in caves, crevices, and on mountaintops.

"Freedom or death," the noblest of slogans for chained races throughout human history, became rightfully their motto. They increased in numbers daily and swelled into a fearsome force. Many bands adopted communism as their political doctrine, though some remained royalists or democrats.

When Mussolini fell and the Italians surrendered in September of 1943, the Kalavryta garrison was dismantled and our town was free.

The liberty fighters—"Andartes" they called themselves—were quick to descend from the mountains. Soon the streets were filled with rowdy, bearded, smelly men of all ages wearing antiquated rifles and strands of bullets around their necks. They seemed as undisciplined as their unruly hair.

Since their communistic beliefs alienated many learned Kalavrytans, and we feared possible repercussions from the Germans, our reception of the Andartes was cool.

One afternoon, my mother's shrieking cry came from the office. With my heart pounding, I rushed to discover the reason. The chieftain of the Andartes, known to us as a hard-core communist, was engaged in a shoving fight with my father, who was shouting, "I will not join your EAM! I don't share your political views, damn it!" The chieftain drew his pistol and waved it intimidatingly. My father screamed, "Go ahead and fire your damn gun; shoot me dead! I only have one life to give and you can take it! But I will not follow you, because I am not a communist! I'm a patriot but I don't trust your ultimate goals!"

Early in December, I overheard my parents whispering about rumors that the Germans were coming. Mother urged Father to hide in the mountains.

"And leave my family behind? Certainly out of the question," he replied.

The Andartes quickly vanished. The most respected townsfolk met in a council to discuss their choices, and they all agreed there was little to fear.

At first, some debated that the swarming of our town by the Andartes when the Italians had retreated could be misconstrued as our having harbored them; but then most agreed that against armed men we un-armed civilians had had no choice but to acquiesce—we had done so with the Italians before, and must do the same with Germans if and when they came.

Unquestionably, all Kalavrytans' efforts during these very difficult times were devoted to everyday survival.

The Germans, in spite of their reputations as austere and harsh, were well-disciplined soldiers. As members of a highly civilized soci-ety they harbored respect for law-abiding families. Since we local resi-dents had done nothing against them, we should not fear them. Therefore there was no sensible reason to abandon our homes and loved ones to run and hide like a bunch of guilty dogs. The council was in agreement and urged the men to stay put and await the arrival of the conquerors. We banked on German morality and, above all, in universal justice and the protection of God.

On Thursday the ninth of December the Nazis came, from the north and the south, in huge numbers. Callers were sent to the various neigh-borhoods, where they shouted warm greetings from our well-inten-tioned visitors.

Four soldiers appeared on our doorstep. One who spoke marginal Greek asked to look at the interior of our house. Satisfied, he told us that most of it must be made available to their commanding officers. Working quickly, they chose the rooms and brought in their superiors' belongings.

We moved our bedclothes to the west portion of the house, near the kitchen, and settled as best we could into the maid's room, unused since our nanny had left us.

Soon after, three officers in long overcoats and black cavalry boots climbed the stairs, followed by the original four soldiers. At the head of the group was a tall, thin, younger man, a cross hanging from his neck. He strutted about our terrace and gazed at the countryside like an arrogant rooster. One of the older officers—one with a kind face—clicked his heels, half-bowed toward my mother, and asked through the interpreter if either one of my parents spoke any other tongues. When my mother replied in French he asked her to please excuse the inconvenience they were forcing upon us and assured her that their stay was to be brief, certainly no more than a few days.

Throughout this short conversation the tall officer kept his piercingly cold gray eyes fixed on Betty, who stood by my mother's side holding her hand. He spoke in a coarse, thin voice, and in French he asked if Betty were adopted because she resembled an Aryan child. My mother smiled in a forceful way and answered, "No."

The three officers seemed civil. During that night Father reassured my suspicious mother, restating his strong belief that the Germans would most certainly be reluctant to harm defenseless civilians like us.

Confined to our crowded quarters we could hear them chuckling and whispering or singing, and shouting orders to their subordinates. When we bumped into them, they gave us smiles. The tall officer seemed infatuated with my sister's looks and took numerous photographs of her; my mother whispered her mistrust.

The town was saturated with armed men in uniform and armored vehicles with guns. In due time they torched the Hotel Chelmos along with a number of houses that informants had pointed out as belonging to families of Andartes.

Two days after arriving, the older officer with the kind face gave a Nazi salute, and when his arm dropped he took my father's hand and shook it. He said *adieu* to our family, moved out, and never returned.

On Monday, December thirteenth, before daylight, loud conversations and hurried movements awakened us. Mother, Betty, and I had made our places to sleep on the floor and Father lay on the single bed where, having buried his head under the quilt as he always did, he appeared to be asleep.

The commotion intensified. The outside stone stairway leading to the second story resounded with the hard pounding of black boots, climbing and descending. Harsh voices addressing Commandant Tenner shook the walls, and the tall younger officer's shrieking orders were frightful.

Mother squeezed us tightly against her, offering a shield of security. Our eyes stayed fixed on the dark ceiling and we listened in total silence. As suddenly as the turmoil had started, it subsided and then ceased altogether. Betty, who always seemed more daring than I, peeked through our door and into the hallway. In the faint light of dawn she saw the once-occupied rooms were now empty.

Still uncertain of the Germans' departure, Mother put on her thick robe and shook Father's foot before she tiptoed to the kitchen to start a fire in the stove.

When the wood crackled and hissed in force, my father stuck his head and neck out from under the covers, like a turtle from its shell, and the three of us rushed to join Mother. She told us they were all gone for certain, crossed herself, and sighed with relief.

My father was exceptionally quiet that morning. He drank his usual cup of mountain sage tea and leaned against the wall. Out the window he gazed to the east in the direction of the hill where the ruins of a Byzantine castle lay.

The haze was unusually thick, but his eyes stared intently and his lips moved. As if his soul had flown back in time and become a spectator at that familiar deed of ultimate courage, I overheard him whisper to himself words which at that time had no special meaning for me.

"Katerini, the handsome daughter of the local chieftain, long ago jumped to her death instead of surrendering to the beastly, besieging Turks. How thrilling when a spirit is free to act selfishly with no regard for the consequences."

While the stove grew red-hot and spat out its seductive heat, the four of us slid onto the stools around the table and sipped our soothing brew in silence.

The violent and irregular ringing of church bells startled us. Aware that such dissonance was not the ordinary signal for a holy event, we looked at each other in puzzlement. Mother told us of a horrible premonition she felt inside her heart. Since men were targets of roundups, once again she insisted that my father should reconsider and try to hide somewhere.

At that instant a caller shouted that the Germans were leaving and the commander wished to speak to all the hospitable residents of Kalavryta. We were ordered to congregate in the square; everyone must attend. Hiding would be considered an act scornful of the Fuehrer, and such enemies of the Third Reich would be dealt with mercilessly, shot on the spot when found.

The knocker on our front door sounded loud and rushed, and my mother opened it to the young son of our neighbor who owned the hotel by the train station. He stepped inside, wild-eyed and short of breath from running, and asked my father what his intentions were. His own father was considering crawling into the attic and staying out of sight.

And my father, as if he were the wisest of men, replied that our family would soon be preparing to attend the gathering, that he had every reason to believe no harm was going to be forced on innocent people. He strongly advised the lad's father to show up—he was risking death if he did not, so help him God.

Mother stuffed inside her bag a couple of family jewels, the last, saved for the ultimate need, while my father dug a shallow hole in the earthen basement and buried his treasured half-finished manuscripts. "Just in case," he explained, and the four of us set off on the road that led to the town center.

Both sides of the street were lined with armed soldiers. Soon we came upon other families and joined with them in a morbid procession. As the distance from our house grew, the crowd swelled—a herd of frightened, doubtful souls who walked in the cold morning mist, slowly and confusedly, with their heads bent like a bunch of sheep heading for the slaughterhouse.

By the crossroads where the elementary schoolhouse stood, the passage to the right which led to the square was blocked by barking, shoving soldiers who ordered us to turn left toward the school.

I felt my father's grip tightening around my hand, and when I looked up for his comforting reassurance I noticed for the first time that his face was pale and wrinkled with concern.

Surrounded by the threatening soldiers with their swinging rifle butts, we were driven through the iron gate into the schoolyard and the families forcibly separated. Men and young males were pushed violently to the right and the rest to the left. My father and I, still holding hands, edged to the right.

"No! No! Let Yiannis come with me," my mother shrieked, and her arm snatched me from behind and pulled me to the left. Perhaps my shorter-than-normal stature at eleven aroused no reaction from the soldiers. For the briefest moment our eyes found his, we three on the left and my father on the opposite side.

We followed the crowd up the wide schoolhouse stairs. The large rooms were empty of furniture and packed with frantic women and children. Some were crying, others prayed and kissed a circulating icon of the Virgin Mary with her young Son in her lap, while a few talked to themselves as if divorced from reason. Finally the main door was shut and locked.

The window ledges were high and no one could see out above the thick walls, but occasionally a woman stood on the hunched backs of others and peeked out.

"The men are being led away through the gate . . . some houses and the National Bank are on fire, and . . . the courthouses are engulfed in smoke," one voice bellowed. Such agonizing news forced an optimistic comment from my mother, who yelled at the top of her lungs that most probably, the men and boys were to be transported to a labor camp.

Moments later another woman, her voice low and somber, announced that she could see long columns of mules and horses loaded with carpets and furnishings following the road to Patras; many started to weep at the loss of their treasured belongings.

The same woman spoke again to tell us the post office and the church, Santa Barbara, appeared ablaze, and that hardly a house or building seemed to be spared by the ravaging fire. And while we listened intently to her every word, from the opposite side of the room a howl of horror pierced our ears.

"Fire! Fire! They are burning us alive! Fire and smoke are coming through the cracks of the wooden floor! They are burning us alive! Oh! Almighty Lord, help us."

The pandemonium was more frightening than Raphael's paintings of the condemned burning in the inferno of the underworld's deep crevices. The coughing from the choking smoke, the panic, the cries, the praying, the shouting and shoving, demoralized even the bravest hearts. A desperate instinct to survive possessed us all.

Some of the women lifted Stavros and me to the ledge of one of the tall windows. The hardware was jammed. Fearless of the visible soldiers and their machine guns, we kicked out the glass and leaped.

Many followed us, and then we saw women and children pouring out through the main door and from the other tall windows. Some who jumped squealed with pain as their legs snapped, but all ignored the guarding soldiers' threatening calls to halt. The horde headed down the street toward the station, and scattered into the open fields.

Numb and dazed, Mother, Betty, and I sat down by some rocks and gazed at the flaming town with the bloody setting sun beyond.

Our house stood about two hundred meters away. A soldier approached it, kicked in the office door, sprayed some sort of powder inside, took out his pistol, and fired a single shot. The office blew up like a bomb, all the books and ledgers fueling it. We witnessed our home go up in flames, yet at the time we felt its loss to be insignificant.

A column of Nazis, about a hundred strong, all singing and in goose-step, came near us, past the railroad station, heading north toward Diakofto and the sea. The tall silhouette of the man at the front of the column seemed familiar. Was he Commandant Tenner who had stayed in our home, I wondered? I stared until I became certain of his identity.

Conversations amongst the mob were wild. No one had seen or heard anything of the men. Speculations as to their whereabouts circulated and there were many, all different, and some ghastly.

My secret hope was that my dear father—and selfishly I thought little of the rest of the men—remained somewhere, alive. It did not matter where they were keeping him, as long as he lived.

When Mother and Betty walked briefly over to my father's cousins, to talk and comfort the six sisters Kalatzis, who drifted about in a sad mental state, pulling their hair and pounding their heads with their fists, I slipped behind some rocks in order to hide what I was about to do. I fell on my knees, and with the innocence and candor of my aching eleven-year-old boy's heart asked God to please spare the life of my beloved father.

When my throbbing insides pumped tears to my eyes, I brushed them aside with my sleeve. In my youthful awkwardness with those things that I perceived as belonging to the adult world, I wished my request to the Lord to remain a secret between the two of us.

The shadows of night came. All the Nazis vanished. Then a ghostly howl reached us. "They are all up there on the hill behind the cemetery, and they are all deeeaaad! All shot through the head by the dirty dooooggggggs!" A woman's cry chilled our intestines, and it was repeated by others, and then by some more, and finally by the entire crazed mob in the fields. I covered my ears with my cold hands, and a wry smirk wrinkled my lips while I thought of my appeal to the Divine Creator; I refused to become part of that raving madness—I knew deep inside my soul that my father was not dead. God had spared him, I was positive of that. The Lord would never allow anything so awfully unjust to happen to a good man who had worshipped His heavenly power, who had so often sung of His everlasting glory in our church. "Father isn't dead," I told Mother and Betty, who were weeping uncontrollably along with the rest.

The three of us nestled together for the night against the rocks. Endless wailing along with smoldering fires and wild thoughts kept us wide-eyed. When dawn came at last, we stood and followed the slow procession of women and children who had already begun their journey toward the "Hill of the Dead."

What had once been a spirited community of pleasant men and women and carefree children was now a deserted ghost town of smoldering, half-standing stone walls.

As we approached the road that led to the cemetery and the hill beyond, an old peasant woman told us that the Kalatzis house had survived the fire. The strength and authority of a grown man came to me, and I told Mother and Betty that they should head for our relatives' house while I alone would do what had to be done. They submissively accepted and walked straight ahead. I turned left.

From afar I observed great activity by the cemetery and its eastern stone wall. I walked slowly, hesitatingly. With every step I took, the buzzing of lamentation grew louder. Soon I saw wild women, their faces and hands and dresses smeared with blood and dirt. Some stood over the bodies of their loved ones, corpses on the shredded blankets used to drag them down from the hill.

Many, their minds demented, kept scolding the dead, as if they were alive and listening, for not having yielded to the women's advice to hide in the mountains, while others knelt next to the carcasses and caressed them and whispered words of love and comfort.

I passed among them and my pace quickened. I climbed the trail, mute but strangely composed. Hundreds of women and children, like programmed zombies, were descending, pulling behind them the precious remains of sons or husbands or brothers or uncles, wishing to bury them inside the cemetery.

Out of breath and with legs shaking, I reached the apex of a crude amphitheater in the hill and instantly knew we had been betrayed by our glorious God.

Blood had formed a gory creek that rolled down the slopes and saturated the hard earth. Where it stopped it had congealed into a large, grotesque pool. Hundreds of stiff corpses were scattered about, all stretched out in hideous positions. Some had intestines hanging out of their bullet-pierced clothes. Some stared fixedly to the sky, their skulls shattered and their brains splattered about. Some had one eye missing, some both.

Mrs. Hampsas, the wife of our family doctor and my school teacher, spat on the hem of her dress and kept wiping the blood from the faces of her husband and her two young sons who lay dead, embracing each other.

When I approached, I heard her talking to them but I couldn't understand her incoherent sounds. Her red, drained eyes met mine and in them I saw resignation and helplessness though she had no tears left to shed. I wanted to spend some moments with her, but I had no time. I vaulted over the dead, searching for my father, still clinging to a thread of hope that maybe, perhaps through a miracle, he would not be among the slaughtered. But, alas, my eyes fell on his gray suit in the distance and I rushed to him, my heart threatening to beat right out of my chest. There he was, his adored face immobile, with a hole through his forehead, and his eyes which had always sparkled with love now faced the sky, staring at the heavens.

An overwhelming turmoil seized my young mind and I blanked out. In a semi-conscious state I kept scratching the hard earth with a small stick. I remember coming to my senses when Stavros kneeled near me to help. Using our hands as shovels, we dug a shallow grave next to my father's body. We dragged him inside and covered him with bits of dirt. The sun was about to set, and we compacted the soil about him as best we could.

With our duty completed, we stood and clasped our bloodstained hands. "When I become a man, I will find Tenner," I said, "and kill him." "I will help you," added Stavros. We promised the dead fathers and brothers and friends and strangers, all one thousand of them who lay murdered by the barbarians from the north, that some day, as men, we would search the entire world, find Commandant Tenner, and collect the vengeance due us.

2

PICKING UP THE PIECES

The Kalatzis family provided us with a room in their house. A few patriots from the surrounding villages began to filter in. They offered us some bread, and helped with carrying the dead left on the hill down to the cemetery. We brought my father and buried him in our family plot.

Finally, when the snow melted and the weather broke, we packed our few belongings, said goodbye to the Kalatzis sisters, and paid a much-postponed visit to what once had been our home. A handful of half-scorched pages of my father's manuscripts protruded from the earthen hole. Mother picked them up with care and placed them inside her handbag, and the three of us left on foot for the seafront village of Diakofto.

We traversed the spectacular Vouraikos Gorge, as my Grandfather Yiannis had done so long ago, only we were returning to the lowlands instead of climbing up to the mountains. He had been entranced by Kalavryta's magic and made his proud home there. But fate had dealt us a vicious hand, and we, his descendants, abandoned forever what remained of Kalavryta. Now, with my father murdered, his God numb inside my spirit and soul, with my young dreams turned to nightmares, I walked through the spectacular gorge oblivious to its grandeur.

From Diakofto we took the short ride in the bed of a truck to Aigion, a pleasing city of twenty thousand on the southern Korinthian Bay. We stayed as guests in the home of my godfather.

My most vivid recollections of our short visit in Aigion are that of my stomach souring each time I happened to come across Nazis, and the scarcity of food. Mother, who sat between Betty and me while we shared skimpy meals with my godfather's large family, selflessly took her tiny portion of bread allowance, secretly split it, and placed half on Betty's lap and half on mine. My mother's plump figure was long gone, and she was thin and pale.

Three months passed. Unwilling to further drain the hospitality of the kind family, we took the bus to Athens to live with my mother's oldest brother Fotis, his wife, and young son.

Uncle Fotis' habits were strange. Even though Betty and I were enrolled in school and attended early morning classes, he insisted that we all remain awake, patiently waiting for his daily arrival from his shop, which never occurred before eleven, so that we could all eat dinner together like a God-loving family. This unreasonable demand wore thin my mother's composure. We soon took off for the town of Tripolis to settle with my maternal grandmother, who lived in her house alone.

Tripolis, built high in the heart of Peloponnesus in the midst of a fertile valley, is the capital of Arcadia province and home to about thirty thousand. We arrived in October of '44. The Germans had withdrawn and the Greek People's Liberation Army (ELAS) controlled the city.

At long last we were free again. The invigorating air of liberty filled our haggard lungs. Laughter and joy and patriotic exuberance reappeared everywhere, even in my injured heart. I joined celebrations as young and old carried flags of Greece, America, England, and the Soviet Union and marched through the streets shouting slogans of freedom.

On the immense Areos Square, the town philharmonic blared out our revered national anthem, and large groups gathered to sing along and dance to the exhilarating tunes of independence.

Grandmother Angeliki received us with about as much excitement and welcome as she would have offered a tax collector, and with the same sense of obligation. But then, no one ever claimed that Angeliki, in spite of her name of "female angel" in Greek, possessed a wealth of virtues. My mother's mother was frail, short, balding, and illiterate.

A cold woman in her sixties, she kept her bedroom locked at all times, as if it were some kind of vault packed with classified documents, and wore the giant key on a string around her neck.

On rare occasion spicy family tongues spilled the beans on Angeliki's mysterious background. She had been a maid in my great-grandfather's house. One tantalizing full-moon night, my young and amorous grandfather had slipped into Angeliki's room. When her belly began to swell as if she had swallowed a watermelon, his righteous father forced the unfortunate lad to face up to his sin, and Angeliki became my grandfather's wife.

Her house was comfortable and large enough to provide us with our own bedrooms and the choice of two bathrooms. The indoor one was located on the edge of a long glassed-in porch facing a courtyard with the other directly below it. The latter enjoyed all the accommodation and aromas of a doorless outhouse, but it was favored by my grandmother, who spent the best part of the early morning there, squatting and groaning.

Betty enrolled in the Gymnasium for Females, and I in the Second Gymnasium for Males. The following two years passed uneventfully. Most of our time was consumed with catching up on the schooling we had missed and cultivating new acquaintances and friendships. These new daily challenges helped push away the past as the horrible memories of Kalavryta ebbed from my mind like a dark tide.

Although there appeared evidence of political unrest and suspicion throughout the ravaged land, particularly in the mountainous regions in northern Greece, the various resistance factions, Left and Right, agreed to surrender their weapons. The pro-Right, with the support of the British and the Americans, elected a government and established an army. A garrison of regimental strength settled in Tripolis. With this security the city began to prosper once again as a successful trading center. A monthly pension from the lawyers' widows fund was awarded my mother. She also collected her share of rents from a couple of family-owned properties, so we managed to scrape an honest living.

On Sundays all students congregated on the school grounds and marched *en masse* to church. After attending the obligatory three-hour liturgy, my new friends and I rented bicycles by the hour and headed toward Agios Yiorgios (St. George) Park, about three kilometers out of town. On our way, we menaced the promenading crowd and zigzagged through bands of young maidens strolling arm in arm, some in groups of five or more.

Once we reached our destination, we sat in a bustling cafe by a little chapel under thick pine trees. Among wandering peacocks we spent our allowances on syrupy baklava, rich vanilla ice cream, or cool lemonades.

Occasionally our destination changed, and we rode north on the main road to Athens, passing by the infamous whorehouse discretely located at the town's edge. We smirked and giggled at the long queue of eager customers, mainly soldiers from the garrison, who formed a line seldom shorter than the full length of a soccer field, all patiently waiting their turn for the brief favors of the resident beauties.

The treacherous years of the civil war soon fell upon us, a power struggle between the government forces and the communists who took to the mountains once again. Entangled in a most depraved war for reign over our weary patch of Earth, Greece divided and suffered as brother murdered brother over their differing political convictions.

But our garrison was expanded in strength, and even though the communists retained influence over a number of remote villages, in Tripolis we lived in relative tranquillity. We did cope with the inconvenience of curfew, imposed on us during the late evening and early morning hours.

On a cold winter night in 1947, Grandmother Angeliki suddenly took ill and lay in her bed, grunting with anguish and pleading for a doctor to come and rescue her from imminent death.

Uncle Chrisanthos, my mother's second brother and my favorite of the three, whose gray eyes, trimmed mustache, slick black hair and impeccable dress made some of the opposite sex quiver with lust, had come from Athens for a short visit.

The curfew was in full force, and telephones in Tripolis were scarce. Neither Angeliki's children nor her grandchildren wished to live their remaining years with guilt-ridden consciences for having failed to fulfill her last wish, so Uncle Chrisanthos and I suppressed our reservations and just plain fear, and sneaked out of the house into the pitch-black darkness. He took one route and I the opposite in hopes that by contacting two different doctors at their homes we might convince one to respond to Angeliki's plight.

I tiptoed through the dead streets hearing only the wild pounding of my adolescent heart. When I reached my destination I rang the doctor's bell and listened for a sign of life. After what seemed to be a duration of eons, devastated, I ran back, only to face the inquisitive stares of Betty and Mother, and above all, my demanding grandmother, who howled even louder the instant she was told that my efforts had failed.

Almost ten minutes after my disappointing return, however, our front door opened. We heard whispering voices and our spirits lifted when we realized Uncle Chrisanthos had succeeded in fetching a physician. We all hurried to welcome them and were taken aback by the stench of alcohol that permeated the hallway. Upon looking closer we were discouraged, indeed, when we discovered that the much-anticipated demigod was only the mortal Mister Socrates, a known town drunkard.

Uncle Chrisanthos guided the unsteady and nearly incoherent visitor to our warm kitchen and forced him to drink strong black coffee; to mask Mr. Socrates' abhorrent body odor and breath, my favorite uncle drenched his valuable find with his own seductive shaving cologne and, after replacing Mr. Socrates' raggedy overcoat with his own stylish, tailor-made cashmere, handed him a couple of aspirins and gave him a basic lesson in impersonating a medical man. When the impostor entered my grandmother's bedroom, we followed, and Uncle Chrisanthos announced that the doctor had arrived.

My grandmother's delirious eyes focused on Mr. Socrates with a most pathetic look. "Hmmm," he said and stuck a flashlight deep inside her mouth. "Looks to me you caught that bad flu bug that's been going around," he garbled, assuring her that, as far as he and the Lord could tell, there was absolutely nothing seriously wrong with her. He helped her lift her head to take the two miracle pills, as a precaution, which she hungrily gulped down. Then, in a slow slurred speech, he promised her the following morning, or maybe the next, she should feel finer than when she was a young and beautiful filly. Angeliki's once-dead eyes sparkled with hope. She took Mr. Socrates' hand between her frail palms and hugged it and kissed it, thanking him a million times for his divine diagnosis. In two short days she was up and about, doing her daily chores as if nothing had ever happened, and I was amazed at Uncle Chrisanthos' genius.

Winters in Tripolis were cold. After school, six of us, the best of friends, gathered inside the warmth of Ermis pastry shop, where we played cards or backgammon or dominoes.

The well-to-do parents of friends and acquaintances gave parties for their sons and daughters on their name days and other occasions; I was invited because they approved of my family background and upbringing, the piano lessons (which I despised), and tutoring in the English language in a private school.

When I witnessed the protective glances cast on my friends by their fathers I cried silently in my innermost self. Gradually, though, I learned how to deaden my yearning for my own father, and only on rare occasions, such as holidays, did I break down and weep in seclusion. Still, I could not protect myself from my dreams. I had a recurring nightmare that I was running through mounds of corpses while praying to God that my father would not be one among those slaughtered. It played havoc with my sleep as I awakened in the night drenched in cold sweat, only to face the tormenting reality. I wished that somehow my adolescence would accelerate into adulthood so that I could pursue Tenner.

During the chilly fall, the cold winter, and the spring months, the customary endless evening promenading up and down a favored stretch of ground—a pastime treasured by all Greeks—was transferred from the breezy Areos Square to the shelter of the central Square of Agios Vasilios (St. Basil). The large church stood on one side, and restaurants and coffee shops on the other three. On Sundays and holidays the bulging crowds flowed down to the five blocks of the main street where rows of shops exhibited enticing wares in well-lit display windows.

The two indoor movie theaters were located on the main drag too, and when films about Tarzan the Ape Man or those incredible fast-draw cowboys came to town, our excitement reached its zenith. Lines for such performances swelled, and we fought for a seat in the first row.

In my fifteenth year I grew like a weed. My mother bought me my first pair of long trousers, and her visiting younger sister, Aunt Marika, furnished me with a Schick razor to shave my whiskers.

Girls became the dominant topic of daily conversation and gossip within our group. In the evenings we strolled six abreast in the hope of crossing paths with equal numbers of females of similar age or younger. We tossed frivolous, swift, flirty glimpses at them, and when the girl fancied by one of us responded by meeting his eyes, he would vault, ecstatically declare his eternal love, audaciously stake his claim to her, and daydream of her as being his very own.

One evening during Easter recess we were congregated inside our favorite pastry shop when my friend Fanis' brother Vironas, older by one year and a devilish prankster, strolled in with a bounce in his step and a smirk a kilometer wide. He announced his intention to make a second visit to Kazamias, the house of ill repute. While he acted out how he had done it with a whore we all became excited. He moved his hips and made noises as he relived those lustful moments of his recent first encounter. Then he told us the cost of his call and joked about how, by impersonating our friend Papagalos whose father inspected the brothel as part of his duties as the county doctor, he had fooled the madam. His ruse had gained him access through the VIP entrance in the alley, thus eliminating the embarrassing risk of being seen waiting in the long line out front.

Vasos and Lambis gleefully asked Vironas if he could take them along through the secret back door and, when he had assured them that it was a done deal, the two reached deep into their trousers for enough drachmas to pay their own fares, their faces shining with agitation and eagerness for such a tantalizing maiden expedition.

When Vironas asked me if I intended to join them (without words but with a question from his sparkling eyes), I shrugged my shoulders and told the group I couldn't. Suddenly a flash came to me. I asked for time to straighten out my finances and sped off for home.

As I had hoped, Grandmother Angeliki was in the kitchen helping my mother with the evening meal. I had known for some time where she hid her cash because I had followed her, spied, and seen her take the old black sock from her apron pocket and bury it deep under her freshly laundered long britches inside the chest. Playing a long shot, I took from the drawer of an old desk a rusty ring through which an assortment of old keys was threaded. Quietly, I tried one key after another on her bedroom door lock. To my utter astonishment it clicked on my fifth try. I sneaked inside, closed the door behind me, and with my fancy flashlight's powerful beam (with which I could have illuminated the dark side of the moon), I found the sock. From it I pilfered two twenty-thousand-drachma notes, each worth more than I needed for that afternoon.

My friends faithfully waited for my return, and the four of us set out on the long walk. On the way Vironas did all the talking. He jumped up and down like a rabbit; he hissed and whistled, barked like a dog chasing a bitch, and grunted like a jackass in heat. As our friend promised, he spoke to the madam, who was fat, short, and looked like a made-up clown. Snickering loudly, the lady manager allowed us entry and led us into the salon, where she called her girls to come and look at their novel customers.

The ladies rushed to inspect us youngsters, tender and shy as we were, and began to bicker among themselves as to which one of them would take which one of us. An older bleached-blond woman, dressed in a colorful robe, with a big provocative smirk on her bright red lips, walked toward me. She must have been roughly nineteen or twenty. While she advanced she moved her hips just like the pendulum on my grandmother's wall clock, and her smooth white thighs peeped through the slit of her robe. Taking my hand, she ushered me into her realm, a small room with a bed and two chairs, a mirrored chest, and a sink.

She asked me to undress and I did it reluctantly, because I was thoroughly frightened. When I was nude she took a step or two back and appraised me just like a farmer casting his eye on a mule before he shells out his hard-earned dough to buy it. A gleam came to her and suddenly she spat on me and mouthed something to ward off the evil spirits. Then she led me to the sink, where she washed my limp dick with cold water and soap. The cold water certainly did not help any, but she took it in her hands and petted it gently, cooing to it with baby-talk just like nannies do to infants. Then she dropped her robe, pulled me to her bed, and helped me get on top of her. She said in a seductive whisper, "Come, come, my little pigeon, stick it to me," and the warmth of her soft flesh and the sight of her large tits aroused me so that once I was inside her my body tightened. I pumped hard and fast while she made some strange sounds, and in what seemed only an instant I felt my being exploding. When the divine spasms of ejaculation subsided and I realized that I had finally acquired the credentials of manhood, an exalted serenity fell upon me, and I was very content and gratified, and proud.

The pockets of communist resistance in Peloponnesus dwindled. The fierce fighting had been concentrated in the wild northern mountains where the "Democratic Army" enjoyed supply routes from the leftist regimes of Albania, Bulgaria, and Yugoslavia.

Government forces remained in absolute command of Tripolis and the surrounding area. Eventually the curfew was lifted and our lives returned to a more normal, tranquil existence.

At age sixteen, I transferred to the First Gymnasium, where more science subjects were offered. Much of my day was spent in classes, and I lived for the evenings when I met with my precious clique of friends. We thrilled to each other's elaborate fantasies—to intercept our wished-for girlfriends in some dark corner and let the torrents of our pent-up sweet feelings gush out; to capture their first kisses. Hungrily we licked our lips, hoping the nectar from such virgin pecks would last forever.

Elva, the daughter of a local surgeon who operated his own clinic on the ground floor of his gigantic house, became my love. We met at a friend's Halloween party. At fourteen, she was curvy and well developed with long blond hair in pigtails. When I spoke to her, she responded in a coquettish way, her big green eyes radiating warmth. She surprised me by addressing me by my first name.

The words we exchanged that first evening were few, but I followed her every move. That night while I lay in bed I saw her vividly in my mind's eye, heard her melodic laughter a thousand times over, and knew that what I was feeling was profound love.

In the evenings I waited for hours at the corner by her school, hoping to catch a glimpse of her walking past with her friends on her way home. When she acknowledged my presence with a smile and a nod, my insides quivered and I yearned for that ecstatic moment when I would hold her precious body in my arms.

With my friends' encouragement, I made plans for intercepting her in some dark spot where, unseen by the snooping glances of passersby, I could tell her of my heart's passion. I hid behind some overgrown, thorny rosebushes near her house, but Elva proved elusive. I stayed out of sight, taking deep breaths, trying to muster enough courage for that moment when I would sing to her the rhapsody of tender love songs which I had composed and rehearsed a million times. But Elva appeared only in the company of friends, or brothers, or sisters, or nurses. It was indeed a frustrating and exasperating period!

I was filled with delicious, impatient passion, and I endured merciless agony. My hallucinatory state started to play havoc with my well-being, and my school grades fell faster than Sisyphus' rock.

After months of diligent guard duty inside those inhospitable bushes, my perseverance was finally rewarded. One evening Elva walked alone. I sprang from the blackness. She bolted like a frightened doe, until she realized there was nothing to fear. Then, as if she had been anticipating the encounter, she quickly found refuge inside the shadows. My heart palpitated and my breathing accelerated, and when I drew near her, I saw her long lashes quiver with anticipation. Intently she watched my lips. But, alas, those ardent and tender phrases that I had recited by heart became hazy, their sequence confused. It was only with the greatest exertion that I managed to declare, "I love you." To my amazement, Elva's bosom lifted in a deep sigh as she whispered that she loved me too. Then she looked startled, concerned that someone might have witnessed our meeting, and quickly asked me to call her at home.

"Don't say a word—just click the button on the telephone twice. I'll know it's you." She gave me a soft kiss on the lips and leapt away.

Wings would not have given me greater speed to reach my friends, who listened to my detailed report and shared my bliss. "I love her. Oh, yes, I love her and she loves me," I shouted radiantly again and again. Fascinated that one of their bosom buddies at long last had a true commitment from one of our imaginary sweethearts, they clung to me as if I were an irresistible charmer, a modern-day Don Juan.

The following evening when I called Elva's number, a deep male voice answered. I was petrified and quickly hung up. I called later. A woman picked up the phone. I clicked the button twice, but she did not respond to my signal. The third time I tried, I recognized Elva's sweet voice instantly. I clicked twice before she murmured, "Hello, Yiannis." I melted. Anxious to see her alone, I urged her to meet me somewhere soon; she responded that she would somehow find a way, although her parents were very strict. I suggested my grandmother's garden, a huge lot fronting another street and separate from our house. With its tall stone walls and private entrance it would be a perfect place for our secret rendezvous. I would be waiting for her behind the solid wooden gate to let her in. No one would ever suspect us being there. She agreed to come at seven the following evening.

Neither sleep nor appetite came easily that night. Even during those short moments of napping, my dreams overflowed with images of rapture and joy, and kisses and love.

The snow was falling fast when I returned home from school the next afternoon. I was fidgety and kept an eye on my watch, infuriated that the minutes were dragging. Betty noticed my agitation.

"What's wrong with you? You're pacing back and forth like a tiger in a cage." I brushed her off with no response.

Finally at six-thirty I announced I was going to meet my friends, and walked out. When I turned the corner, I sneaked in through the garden gate, which I had previously unlocked.

The dark street was deserted, although footsteps of a lone pedestrian could be heard in the distance. I stood in total concentration under the tiled overhang. My gloved hands and booted feet, which seemed to suffer always from poor circulation, soon lost all feeling; my ears—especially the right one, which stuck out more than the left—ached from the bite of the frost until I was forced to abandon all vanity and lower my cap to shelter them from the icy wind.

While I stood there, alert as an owl on a night hunt, I noticed the sound of hurried steps approaching. When I peeked through the cracked door, I saw Elva running toward me, bundled inside an overcoat and scarf with a woolen bonnet on her head. She plunged through the opening and fell into my arms. We kissed longer than forever.

The instant our lips parted, we spoke of our supreme love and whispered to each other pledges of eternal devotion. I complained of my numb hands and Elva valiantly unbuttoned her cozy overcoat, lifted her thick sweater and asked me to warm them between her upper arms and her bare breasts. I took off my useless gloves and obliged. And as my fingertips began to thaw and their sense of touch returned while they nestled, motionless but snug, against her velvety flesh, I thought I was in heaven.

Our separation was bearable only because we had agreed to meet again soon, perhaps in three or four days and in the same spot. She insisted that I call her daily, in case an unexpected opportunity arose. What a calamity indeed it would be if such a chance came and was lost, we agreed. We kissed passionately again and again until my Elva left me and disappeared into the darkness and the driving snow.

Every evening around eight o'clock I made my calls, but the telephone was always answered by someone else. After days of bafflement, I walked to the corner by Elva's school and made myself visible. I waited for her classes to end. When our eyes met as she walked by with her friends, she gave me a long gaze full of yearning and I became puzzled and confused.

I searched out my friends but I was too disturbed to enjoy them and withdrew to be alone with my thoughts. As before, I made my call at eight.

This time her voice came on, anxious and hurried. I clicked the button twice. She half-whispered, "Tonight," and the phone went dead.

The sky was clear, the moon bright and smiling and almost full. My Elva was late by a half hour, yet to my loving heart it felt like a century. When I saw her pale face in the gleam of the moonlight reflecting on the snow, I knew there was trouble.

We fell into each other's arms with warm, moist kisses, and in total rapture we stood tightly embraced in the freezing cold. She broke the silence to speak first, and her voice trembled with anxiety and despair and only a flicker of hope when she said, "Let's elope, Yiannis. Let's run away somewhere. I don't care where. Anywhere; away from Tripolis."

Turmoil overcame her and Elva began to weep. She told me how much she hated her father and mother, and everyone else in her family, because they had discovered our deep attachment. Her mother was furious and her father had threatened to cut off her hair and forbid her to attend school unless she agreed to end "all this foolishness." In spite of their threats, she had dared to dash out of her guarded room at an opportune moment to be with me, and only God knew the punishment awaiting her upon her return home.

The pain and suffering of her confused soul awakened in me an alien anger and a powerful hostility toward her parents, whom I had never met. I agreed, in the most chivalrous way, that eloping was the only solution but that we needed a few days to work on our plans. Her big green wet eyes responded to my assurances. Finally, with a half-smile she hugged and kissed me affectionately, brushed the tears from her face, and hesitantly parted from my arms. That was the last time I ever saw Elva.

Rumor had it that she fell ill with pneumonia, but her disappearance was absolute. My frantic phone calls were always answered by strangers and, heartbroken, I was soon resigned to patient evening walks past her house, with glances up at lighted windows hoping to catch a glimpse of her lovely face staring down, seeing me, and knowing of my faithfulness and yearning. But I never observed any sign of her, and my strolls became less frequent. After some months they stopped completely.

I returned to the company of my friends, and with renewed vigor we did crazy things. We devastated the chicken population of our back yards and indiscriminately wrung the necks of all the poultry we could get our hands on, from poor old tired hens to the proud, colorful, and cocky roosters. We took them for preparation, dead and unplucked, to Mitsos' taverna, a basement hole in an obscure alley.

Mitsos' taverna, with its earthen floor, lopsided wooden tables, and unsteady chairs, featured a giant dragon-like barrel which never seemed to run out of low-grade retsina, a charcoal cooking stove, and most of the poorest of the town drunks. Mitsos, the proprietor, who always

wore the same old dirty apron and a mean-looking droopy black mustache, plucked and cooked the chickens for the six of us buddies who congregated there, feasting and getting tipsy (and sometimes even nearly drunk) on his cheap wine.

It was inside the inspiring confines of this cave-like spot that our never-ending pranks were formulated, the tricks and jokes which we relentlessly played on our less respected and unfortunate teachers.

Kostas was the ceremonious head of our gang, and his past curiosity with a nasty hand-grenade had gotten the best of him. While he was toying with that armed thing it went "bang" and scattered the best part of his right arm into a million bits. Our "president" was forced to learn to write with his left hand, and while his effort was sincere, it appeared slow and unsatisfactory to our teachers. So he was held back one year and as a consequence had revolted against the scholastic system.

Our docile instructor of French, a man of gentle nature unprepared to be caged in a classroom with sixty rebellious students, often was Kostas' target. When our teacher turned his back on us to face the blackboard, exposing his balding pate as a target, Kostas shot dried peas through a tiny piece of bamboo with unerring accuracy. Then, with striking speed, he concealed his weapon inside his hollow wooden limb. The frail man bore this abuse with saintly tolerance, and only on occasion he stared to the heavens and muttered his disgust with the teaching profession he had chosen.

Then there was the short little guy whose esteemed duty was to tutor us on theology and religious subjects. Mother Nature had nastily amused herself by decorating his flat face with two beady black eyes and a nose similar in length to a medium-sized cucumber. These vast nostrils he compulsively scraped with his index finger. Just plain angry at everything and everybody, his eruptions of vulgar swearing were legendary. In our diabolic craving to amuse ourselves, we searched for ways to excite his wrath just to hear his eloquent tongue spit out diatribes which never failed to include God and the Virgin Mary, her Son, the Holy Spirit, and all notable saints. Lambis, a whiz at firecracker construction, at the most opportune moment lit the hissing fuse of one of his despicable paper-bombs and tossed it toward our teacher's feet. During the confusion that followed, we recorded in our minds a ferocious new repertoire of anathemas; mimicking him later, we remained in stitches for weeks.

One night, all of us were high and gay from having consumed several pitchers of the obnoxious-smelling retsina. Mitsos had placed his favorite blackened stewing pot on our table with the last of our president's mother's two egg-laying hens, and while their stringy parts were being equally divided among the six of us, we unanimously agreed that a strike was well overdue and certainly in order, to protest the school's enforcement of an antiquated short-hair policy.

DDT had long been in plentiful supply, and since lice were now a thing of the past, we concluded that the punishment of barring a student from all classes when his hair measured more than three centimeters was unwarranted and cruel. Tired of looking like a bunch of mean felons, we determined that a document should be prepared and presented to the faculty at once, demanding that the three-centimeter length be increased to at least six. The total student body was prepared to boycott all classes, we warned, if our ultimatum was not accepted within a week's time.

Vasos, the calligrapher of our group, wrote the document on a sheet of brown wrapping paper that bore numerous greasy finger marks. Signed by the Student Body Committee for Fair Hair Length, our instrument was entrusted to Kostas, our president, for delivery. He was to be our spokesman as well, if needed.

The school's staff disliked Kostas for his low achievement and bad attitude. When our delegate appeared in the administrative offices to demand a hearing with the headmaster, he was booted out of the building. Our committee declared a strike. The next day the six of us, along with an admirable number of sympathizers, blocked off the streets leading to the school grounds and physically prevented other students from attending. Except for a few who sneaked through, the classrooms remained deserted and the principal, a reasonable man at times, decided that six centimeters of hair growth on his students' scalps, instead of the standard three, seemed not too great a concession to make. Word of a truce was dispatched and we returned to our classes; a prolonged confrontation was averted and we celebrated our victory with a toast inside Mitsos' den.

With graduation finals approaching, panic overtook me. I set aside Dostoyevsky and Tolstoy, Dante and Kazantzakis—writers who captured my young mind—and made an earnest effort to cram inside my head as much learning as possible over the course of the last few weeks of the school year.

Because Papagalos was the best student in our gang he volunteered to shed a trace of light on the elusive complexities of calculus and trigonometry. He and I spent many hours in his home going over the same equations and exercises again and again, yet I remained unable to grasp the intricate mechanics of those outlandish subjects. While I was on the verge of surrendering to the idea of repeating the school year, a vision flashed through me.

I paid an impatient visit to my neighbor Pavlos, an outstanding student in our class who had widely diverse interests. He experimented with telephone equipment and possessed some old but still-functional ear pieces, plus microphones, batteries, and copper wires, and a lot of other gadgets.

Pavlos, whose social stratum was inferior to most because his father was part owner of a small, decrepit auto-repair shop and labored with his hands to earn a living, spent his time in what seemed to us a depressing world of books and contraptions, dreaming of higher education in engineering or science. I was perhaps the only one from our dashing bunch who never revealed his contempt for the poor bastard's suppression of his sexual urges in favor of his educational objectives, and he liked me.

I came quickly to the point.

"Pavlos," I said, "you have a great mind," and went on to propose my plan to bring into our classroom, from behind the tall stone fence of the school yard, a thin white telephone wire matching the color of the classroom wall, and lead it to the bottom of my desk. Of course such an undertaking was to be my total responsibility. On the day of our math exams I would wear an ear piece inside my left sleeve and, having secured it in place on the inner part of my wrist, its wire would travel down through my clothing and exit through the fly of my trousers. I would join the end of that wire with the one under my desk, and having secured such a link I would wait until Pavlos had completed his own paper, which he could do in a jiffy. He would then leave the room, rush outside to the deserted wall and connect one of his old mikes to the hidden wire, where he would relay to me slowly and in a very soft voice the solution to the problems. Naturally, in return for such a grand favor I promised him that as soon as I reached California (he knew of my travel plans) I would expeditiously send him whichever electrical devices his heart desired.

After a brief hesitation Pavlos agreed to undertake the project. Gradually, he became quite excited about our plan and started babbling about how we were going to construct the whole apparatus—with wires, batteries, and other paraphernalia.

On the dreaded day of the math exams our coarsely fabricated telephone line worked somewhat fuzzily but well enough. Thanks to Pavlos' persistent, patient repetition of those bizarre numbers and formulas, I did well enough to receive a passing grade, and although my honor was a bit soiled, my diploma appeared sparkling clean.

Well, let's face it. Our growing-up years were turbulent, to say the least. After two devastating wars, Greece lacked the funds to support sports to occupy our free time. Besides an occasional game of kick-ball, flirting with girls, stealing chickens from our own back yards, playing pranks on our teachers, and cheating at school a little seemed to release some of our pent-up energies and appeared to us pardonable acts then.

Betty, easily the more studious of the two of us, wished to take classes in the English College in Athens. Since I was destined for the New World upon my graduation, the three of us relocated once again to the capital, where we moved in with Aunt Marika, my mother's sister.

Her spacious house was located in Chalandry, a suburb of Athens about twenty kilometers north of downtown. Fifi, her daughter of six, was a sweet kid who stayed out of my way. Except for the constant bouts between Marika and her hard-core communist husband regarding politics and his addiction to horse gambling, our stay was pleasant.

Some of my friends from Tripolis had migrated to Athens, and while I waited for my travel papers to be processed, we spent most of our time shooting billiards in an infamous pool hall by Omonia Square.

The city was humming with activity, and the sufferings of the two recent wars seemed forgotten. Young women appeared to have undergone an evolution. In certain ways they seemed liberated from small-town inhibitions. Perhaps the city's vastness offered them a sanctuary from the horror of being detected on a date. So, young men and lasses mixed freely and were sometimes observed holding hands in public. Since I felt that my flirting technique had been elevated to a well-disciplined performance, I was elated to discover that it worked just as well in the cultured Athenian world. However, I honored and obeyed Uncle Chrisanthos' fatherly advice; he, as the main source of spending money for my dating needs, insisted that I always show regard for a young woman's virtue.

Finally my passport was secured. About a month before my departure, I traveled to Kalavryta to pay my respects to my father. The instant I saw his grave I broke down and cried for a very long time.

I lit the *kandili* (oil lamp) over his headstone, placed a few wild white daisies on the mound of soil that covered his remains, and told him good-bye. I searched for my childhood friend Stavros, but found only his surviving brother. He told me that their mother had been unable to cope with the loss of her husband and three sons—she had lost her mind and was in an institution for the insane. Stavros had immigrated to Florida and now lived with an affluent uncle, his father's brother. He gave me Stavros' address in Miami.

I stayed overnight with my Aunt Elleni Kalatzis, and early the next morning I kissed her sweet smiling face before I left that half-dead town, whose inhabitants now were mostly women dressed in mourning black.

3

THE VOYAGE

At sea the sun had taken its daily plunge and the dusk was golden and serene. Fluffy whitecaps broke gently and the breeze refreshed my skin. Except for the splash as the vessel's bow split the water, the deck had grown quiet and empty.

I came back from times past, feeling drained and fatigued and hungry. I turned to move away from the ship's rail. The sight of a lone female seated on a bench less than three meters from where I stood jarred me.

She wore a black sleeveless dress and black sandals and her face bore a faint smile. Her features looked familiar, and I was searching my memory to recall her when she spoke.

"I've been worried about you, spending so much time leaning there half-bent over the rail—four hours maybe or more. You know the sea can seduce you if you listen long enough. And you've had enough time stretching against that darned rail!" She stared at me with pitch-black eyes and in them I detected a trace of relief. Her dimpled chin was strong, her eyebrows bushy and unplucked, and she sported no makeup, not even lipstick. Her very black hair was braided and up in a bun.

She spoke with a firm voice and the distinct twang of Epirus, the mountainous northwestern territory of Greece whose inhabitants shorten their vowels. I placed her now. She was the woman who had stood on my right as the ship was leaving Piraeus. I remembered feeling the warmth of her face and her moist breath when I moved closer to her in my attempt to avoid the shoving and shouting, and the armpit stench of that annoying middle-aged woman.

"You had me worried! Everybody is having a grand old time pacifying their growling innards with good food—but I stayed here, even though I'm starving like a hungry wolf."

I gave her a questioning look but she went on.

"As I said before, I thought that something might snap inside your head—who knows what; the wars have put crazy notions inside the brains of many of us. So, you might jump over the rail, and 'pouf,' that would've been that." Her arm brushed the air with a snap of her fingers to illustrate how quickly my undetected plunge would have ended my existence.

From her speech I surmised that her schooling had been limited. I smiled back, thanked her for her concern, and assured her that suicide was the last thing on my mind.

"Come and sit here and tell me your name and where you come from. My own name is Paraskevoula, and I'm engaged, and I'm going to New York to get married and live there and be an American myself—all in due time, naturally."

Slowly I walked over to the bench and sat next to her. I told her my name and, briefly, my background.

"I wear black," she said with a bit of confidentiality in her tone, "because my oldest brother died in the civil war." Her two older brothers and three younger sisters all lived in a small mountainous village near Yiannina, and she was twenty-two years old.

"I dropped out of school before the end of the fourth grade, because being the oldest of the girls, when my mother died of cancer, I had to step inside my mother's shoes, cook for the family, attend to our seven sheep and all that, you understand. I'm curious, though, and I've read some books. *Romeo and Juliet* is my favorite. And oh, how I cry each time I read that story! And I've read it so many, many times. Maybe a hundred. I never kept track really, but I took my book with me and read parts of it every time I wandered around my village with the sheep searching for what little grass grows in that rocky soil."

When I asked how she met her fiancé, without hesitation and in a serious way she explained that her betrothal had been arranged by her father and brothers. She met him only once; his name was Stelios; he was part-owner of a small restaurant in a town called Astoria somewhere in New York, and she hadn't the foggiest idea where that might be. She only hoped Astoria was a nice place, as it should be, being in America and all.

"After we exchanged pictures and I agreed to take him, he came to our village and we talked and spent some four days together, properly and always in the presence of my brothers and sisters. We got engaged in the church and he gave me this ring. Do you like it?" She placed her middle finger near my face so I could view the small stone set on a simple gold band and looked curiously into my eyes.

"It's very nice," I replied, all the while contemplating how unjust these arranged marriages were to dowryless young women, forced to choose between spinsterhood and poverty, or committing their lives to strange, sometimes abusive men and bearing their children.

"Well, what are we waiting for?" She sprang up, reaching out to take my hand in hers and yanking me up from my seat. "Let's go and fill our empty bellies with the good stuff before they run out!"

She was of medium height, small-waisted and full-hipped, solid and strong as she strutted up front, pulling me along as if we were long-lost buddies.

I, having been brainwashed by a mother whose obsession with personal hygiene bordered on hypochondria, believed that the mirror of a person's overall cleanliness is their nails and toes. So, the instant this woman opened the door and we entered the lighted hallway, to appraise my new friend, I inspected her and was relieved to discover that her fingernails were clean, and so were her toes that protruded from her sandals.

The large dining room was stuffier than a hashish den, though portholes were ajar, inviting the breeze to pour in and dilute some of the thick smoke. The noise level was almost unbearable; Greeks tend to talk loudly, and all at once.

We sat facing each other at the end of a long crowded table. Sweating middle-aged waiters in dirty white shirts and greasy black trousers served us.

Large half-empty clay bowls of tomato-cucumber salad with chunks of onions and an abundance of oregano, platters of sliced feta cheese swimming in strong-smelling olive oil, hefty loaves of crisp brown bread, and jugs of pink retsina were strategically placed so they could be shared by groups of four. The waiters brought us individual plates of roasted chicken with potatoes in rich tomato sauce. As before, Paraskevoula did all the talking, only this time with her mouth full.

I considered myself worldly. I had seen Verdi's *Aïda* at the *Liriki Skini* (Singing Stage-Opera House) in Athens and had read the *Savoir Vivre (Book of Good Manners)* long before my seventeenth birthday, and I had acquired the skill, through painstaking practice, of course, to debone expertly with knife and fork any order of fowl. Now I sat silently observing Paraskevoula use her hands to pull apart the chicken and place it in her mouth, while simultaneously tearing large bites from a sizable portion of the crusty brown bread. With her soiled hands, she raised a short glass full of wine and gulped it all down in one great swallow, and I felt embarrassed to use my utensils in her presence.

A delight flooded me while I watched this peasant woman eat with gusto. I listened to her unravel the secrets of creating the thickest of yogurts and the art of baking the tastiest of breads, and I refrained from interrupting her. Her breasts danced from laughter when she spoke of her Aunt Vasilo, an exorcist who performed her village's medicinal duties by tossing a dozen magic pebbles onto her enchanted carpet in the presence of the ailing. By reading the shining stones she then prescribed the befitting remedies. Paraskevoula giggled heartily, relating her aunt's reply when she had questioned the stern widow's abilities to perform such miracles. Puckering her lips and striking a solemn pose, Paraskevoula mimicked her Aunt Vasilo as if she were on stage.

"There she stood, straight and foreboding, dressed in her long black skirt, her head hidden inside her black kerchief. Her mean lips under a black mustache twitching, she raised her hand to strike me for my disrespect. But then she had second thoughts and, with an air of authority, as if she were Jesus' mother, she said, 'Listen to me you saucy little rebel. So long as the afflicted believe in my Lord-given abilities, that's all that counts.'"

Paraskevoula seemed thrilled to see me amused by her tales, and when finally we shook hands and parted for the night, we confessed to each other our joy for having made friends.

The following day I bumped into Dinos, the older brother of a schoolmate of mine. Dinos, a brilliant student, had been accepted at Harvard University's School of Medicine. I thanked my lucky stars for meeting up with him. The meager sum of twenty dollars legally allowed by the Greek government for my twenty-day voyage to America and to Davis could not have lasted me long, and Dinos was willing to give me a loan. He flashed his wad and explained how he had courageously stashed it inside his left shoe before he passed through our frightening Greek customs.

Since the probability of running into me again in the vast land of the New World seemed remote, I was puzzled by his generosity when he handed me a twenty and two tens, even though I promised to mail him the precise amount the instant I sat foot in California.

We chummed together and met other men and women of similar age and background, mostly students heading for the various American universities.

Time passed leisurely. In the mornings we gathered in the lounge. After the traditional breakfast—a tiny cup of Greek (Turkish) coffee along with a *koulouraki* (cookie) to dunk into the hot thick brew—we played backgammon, dominoes, card games, or chess. Some of us became absorbed by political and philosophical discussions punctuated only by short breathers at lunch and dinner. These continued into the late evening hours.

I met Christos on our third day at sea. Dinos and a deacon named Gregorios were engaged in a ferocious game of chess, made more intense by an audience. The deacon, up to that point enjoying the advantage, was about to make a careless advance with his queen to check his opponent. While he was hesitantly lifting his fingers, a strong voice shouted, "NO." When I looked up I saw a stranger.

A dozen travelers of both sexes and all ages, some standing and some seated in a circle, watched the match develop, a few with keen interest, most out of boredom. The deacon, who refused the stranger's advice, quickly lost his queen. Upon the conclusion of the match, the stranger glanced at the loser, pointed his finger in a scolding fashion, and said, "I told you so." Uninvited he took a chair, wedged it between two spectators and introduced himself as Christos.

His hair was long and his thin face bearded. He looked much like an unkempt Andartis who refused to discard his rough appearance, although both World War II and the civil conflict had ended long ago.

Christos' hollow black eyes appeared strong-willed. They zeroed in on the deacon, who seemed to be several years his senior. Casually, Christos asked the deacon where he had done his theological studies. "At a very young age I became a disciple of our Lord at the Monastery of the Holy Conception. Then by special permission I entered the seminary."

Christos' face brightened as if alerted to an enchanting vision.

"How interesting indeed," he exclaimed. "Then you must have studied under Abbot Vasilios."

Now the deacon lit up.

"Yes. Yes, of course. But how do you know of Abbot Vasilios?"

Christos swept the audience with a reminiscing look. Then his eyes rested on the deacon. His reply came out slow and crisp as a bell.

"My father was killed fighting the Italians on the Albanian front. Then, my mother was raped by enemy soldiers. Soon after these devastating events, unable to feed us children, she arranged for my admission to the Monastery of the Holy Conception."

The deacon's face clouded briefly, then its shine reignited. "God never closes one door without opening another," he said, and by moving his head up and down encouraged Christos to continue.

"In the winter of '42, at age thirteen and a three-month novice, I accepted the Abbot's invitation to his cell 'to discuss extensively my slow progress in the study of the Lord's teachings.' When I arrived after supper, he welcomed me with open arms and kissed me on both cheeks. Toward the conclusion of his lengthy religious lecture he told me that in order to receive God inside me I must be prepared to make immense personal sacrifices. 'God, my son, demands not only your spirit and your soul, but also your body. Are you prepared to accept God as your absolute ruler?'"

The deacon's head kept up its encouraging signals.

"'God's will shall be done,' I replied."

"'Then, let us pray together to the Almighty and beg Him to cast His enlightenment on you, my child,' the Abbot said with excitement in his face. He asked me to kneel.'"

"A Christian on his knees sees more than an eagle in flight," commented the good deacon wisely.

"When I did, the Abbot came and stood directly over me and placed his hand on my bent head. Then he started gently to massage my hair. As he stroked it, he slowly pushed my face against his cassock until I felt his hard prick protruding from under the garment."

The color of the deacon's skin suddenly turned red hot and his long whiskers seemed to change shade.

"When I realized what was happening I jumped back and saw his eyes were half shut. A wild satanic smirk had lit his face and he was steaming with sweat.

"As I sprang up to flee, a barrage of incoherent prayers spewed out of his foaming mouth: 'God be praised. No, don't, my son. *Kyrie eleison.* No, it's God's will. Thy will be done. God needs your soul. God needs your body.' He chased after me. He cornered me and was about to rip off my britches. He kissed me on the lips. I kicked the bastard in the balls, ran out of the monastery as fast as my young legs could carry me, and joined the Andartes."

The good deacon's face stayed flushed. He said nothing, but the audience suddenly came to life because we sensed that an intriguing discussion was about to unfold.

"What you have just said is most blasphemous, my son," the deacon finally declared piously. "I urge you, for the salvation of your soul and its acceptance into the everlasting life in Heaven, to stop spreading this slander against the highly regarded Abbot."

Sparks flew from Christos' black eyes. He sprang up and shouted, pointing angrily toward the deacon.

"I am not your damned son! And I resent being accused of spreading slander. Here the Abbot preached celibacy to his disciples as the state of purity in which a devout messenger of God must spend his entire life, yet he himself preyed on young students' innocence and fear—poor children who never suspected that part of the holy education they would receive included sodomy and rape."

Except for the faint lyrics of a popular old serenade that reached us from some distant source, silence fell. All stares rested on the deacon. But he remained red and silent so Christos continued.

"I only wish I could believe there was a God somewhere out there who, being the most righteous of all judges, as you religious fanatics advocate, would punish degenerate pedophiles like the Abbot by tossing the fat prick on top of a heap of burning coal and frying his ass. And that God would demand that such skewering be witnessed by all of you chaste souls as a warning that a similar fate is in store for anyone who corrupts His gospel."

The deacon's lips trembled. He appeared confused. Miraculously, though, he recovered and raised his head proudly.

"So, you do not believe in the Lord," he announced, slowly running his hand through his beard. "It's such a pity that your association with the communist Andartes has warped your mind and you have distanced yourself from God's embrace. Now, you are doomed to spend the rest of your life wandering and searching for answers—asking questions which I assure you shall eventually lead you back to our divine creator." The deacon spoke with a dignified serenity and seemed pleased by his well-chosen words. He continued. "And, if for some satanic reason you fail to recognize God's absolute dominion over man, may I remind you, my friend, that hell is not a fine place to send your soul, for upon judgment day there will surely be no room for you in heaven."

Christos seemed driven now. He raised his right arm and pointed his finger, preparing to reveal a significant point.

"On the second day of my admittance to that good school, I respectfully asked his holiness the Abbot for his interpretation of my father's senseless, premature death. He simply replied that it was God's will. I could not accept his answer. Fearfully, I pressed on with the most logical question: 'Why would God want to harbor such an unjust will? Why would God wish my father killed when the poor man had been a fine Christian, God-fearing and God-loving?'"

Christos and the deacon were locked in a struggle that had been my own since the 14th of December, 1943. From that dreadful day on, in my heart and soul, the beneficence of the God I inherited and accepted blindly had been reduced to an outrageous deception. I waited for Christos to tell us the Abbot's answer. Christos smirked scornfully and spat on the floor.

"'God often acts in mysterious ways, ways we mortals can never comprehend,' the Abbot said to me, and I knew then and there, as young as I was, that the holy man was either a liar or an idiot. After I ran away I spent a lot of time, along with many comrades, hiding in caves waiting for the chance to ambush Italians or Germans. While I waited, I searched for answers. And, by now, I have concluded that the whole religious manifesto is just plain self-serving priestly imagination. Although many of the teachings of ancient philosophers have provided us with building blocks for shaping obedient societies, theological beliefs are mythical fabrications and certainly unacceptable by the intelligent contemporary man."

"You are insane!" Gregorios shouted with all his might. He raised his arms to the sky. "How dare you question the existence and sovereignty of God?" He crossed himself. "May He have pity on your soul— which, surely, is heading for the blazes of the underworld."

"There he goes," snickered Christos, dismissing the holy man with a gesture of his hand. "Enforcement of church teachings through intimidation is a long-standing practice. When one questions their power structure and livelihood, the men of God are quick to excommunicate you, call down His curses, and terrorize you by condemning you to hell." Christos paused and a shine came to him. "But I am not frightened, deacon, because . . . ," he stared about in a vacancy and as if he were speaking to himself, he whispered, " . . . because I am a god myself."

Now the deacon sprung up with a furious glee. Beaming, he broke out in contemptuous laughter. He took a quick full turn and made contact with all of us who remained focused on him. "So you are God?" he shrieked. He rolled his eyes in mockery that implied Christos' allegations must be the hallucinations of a demented mind. "So you are the one who controls our existence and checks our deeds?"

Chuckles of ridicule and murmurs of disbelief arose from almost all the listeners.

Christos raised his arms and waved them up and down in an effort to bring the crowd back to order.

"Please, please, let me explain," he protested. "God is not this man-like image that the icons depict." Christos pointed above with reverence. "God, my friends, is that vast arrangement out there. The universe. The cosmos. That splendid, immense enigma of matter and energy, the mind-boggling power and order—and I harbor awe and humility for its mysterious purpose. Only simple minds believe that our tiny planet, tossed in the midst of millions, maybe billions of other dazzling bodies as it is, is the center of the universe; and that we, its inhabitants, are the only beings enjoying a privileged existence." He scratched the top of his head and lowered the pitch of his voice. "But, much closer to home, God is any noble spirit freed of religious inhibitions, like myself, who has the courage to reject the church's past violence and seemingly passive teachings. Anyone who commits to higher achievement through exploration and discovery. Coupled with the sincere practice of Moses' brilliant Golden Rule, 'Do unto others as you would have them do unto you,' man now is capable of establishing moral standards to create disciplined, orderly societies." Christos stroked his mustache with the air of a commander gazing at a retreating enemy.

"But we live by the Golden Rule. We do," cried the deacon loudly.

"You are wrong. You see the world through a set of religious eyes. You have no tolerance for the views of others. You are as rigid as the kings and emperors, the patriarchs and popes, rulers incapable of ridding themselves of their selfish motives, who have fought wars and committed mass murder so that through intimidation and fear they could impose their own will, and their own Gods, on the frightened survivors."

Bewildered, the deacon mumbled to himself, "Get thee behind me, Satan," as if by so declaring he could expel the anathema that had befallen him.

Christos, amused by the baffled holy man, continued.

"For one moment let us take the lighter side. Let us suppose your God is real and oversees our deeds. Since you and all His devoted spokesmen welcome the salvation of nonbelievers' repentant souls, why doesn't someone of contemporary saintly importance communicate with Him and plead with Him to pay us a brief visit? Well, we all know how busy He is, sitting on His lofty throne, passing judgment on us all. But surely, the Almighty Lord owes it to us to appear before his subjects now and then, even for just a flash; many of us down here very much wish to meet Him or simply see him. I give you my solemn promise that upon this revelation I will fall on my knees and offer Him my everlasting worship." Christos smiled and scratched his head. "Tell me then, my holy man, the real reason behind God's coy game of 'You can't see me, yet you must revere Me in perpetuity or else.'"

I could no longer control the stirrings inside me, and I burst out with a piercing cry.

"The Nazi dogs shot my father dead along with a thousand innocent men and boys!" I stared at the deacon. My chest was heaving. A hand reached out and touched me. "Where was your God then? Where was his mercy?" I demanded, aflame with rage. Through bleary eyes, I could see the deacon crossing himself, unwilling to yield to Christos' views and unable to answer mine.

The holy man sat exhausted and perspiring with his shoulders stooped and his head bent over his long gray cassock. Yet like a gallant wounded warrior he straightened up as best as he could and made one last effort to defend his God.

"But He does appear. God's almighty power and presence are revealed to us through His countless miracles," he muttered. Christos shone with confidence, readying to deliver his *coup de grace*.

"Hmm, miracles you say? Why is it that miracles always occur under the most obscure and dubious circumstances, witnessed by a very select group? In societies where the masses are ignorant, poor, and almost hopeless, and where sorcery, superstition, and demonology are highly developed?"

The deacon's chest deflated and sagged, though he kept crossing himself, reciting one prayer after another.

Christos went on. "The destitute have always been easy prey to promises of eternal life after death. The privileged voice skepticism. But then, most of those fall victim to their own vanity. Vanity overwhelms a prominent man's reasoning and renders him incapable of accepting his death as his end, as is natural for everything living. The pyramids of the pharaohs are a powerful testament to the favored man's inability to accept his mortality. So, the foxy religious fathers, recognizing the fears and hopes of man, provided him with wishful answers, and have succeeded in dominating him." Christos stood erect and imperial and finished with a deep breath, luminous eyes, and a strong voice.

"My friends, let me state here and now that neither God nor Christ will ever be my Lord, because I, Christos, am my own god and the master of my own spirit and soul."

At that very moment the loudspeakers blasted our approach to the port of Naples. I rushed to the deck for my first view of Italy.

When the ship was secured to the quay to pick up passengers, Dinos and I ventured ashore. Mobs of children, three and four years old, half-naked and filthy, raced up to us, encircled us, and stretched their tiny hands for handouts. They fought among themselves for Dinos' still-lit discarded cigarette butt and then puffed on it with all their might.

Beyond the harassment in the harbor I stood still, taking in the colorful Neapolitan street scenes while Dinos was busy listening to a fast-talking street vendor whose cunning eyes, mouth, arms, hands and even feet harmoniously orchestrated to persuade this unsuspecting tourist to purchase one of his precision watches. While I stared about in wonder, I noticed a well-dressed man briskly walking along, proud of his new straw hat, until he crossed the path of a barefooted fisherman carrying an enormous basket on his head. The instant their paths crossed, a youngster hidden inside the fisherman's basket lifted the well-dressed man's hat from his head. Before the well-dressed man realized what had happened, the fisherman, his basket with the child in it, and the man's hat were out of sight.

Two hours later, we returned to the ship with Dinos' newly acquired Omega chronometer. It had cost him only fifteen dollars. I had tried in vain to convince him not to be fooled by the watch's glitter—not that I was so damned wise, but having visited Uncle Nikos' basement shop in one of Athens' sleaziest districts, I had been exposed to numerous con men and unethical street merchants who peddled goods of dubious origin to naïve suburbanites and tourists.

Before the two of us separated for the afternoon, Dinos proudly glanced at his bargain Omega, only to find that it had stopped running. He wound it but it failed to respond, and then the winding knob popped out in his fingertips. He swallowed his pride to give me a blank stare but said nothing.

I chose not to mention my warning; renewing the theological debate seemed urgent to me, though.

"What do you think of Christos?" I asked.

Dinos shrugged his shoulders. "Well, he is a maverick, a communist, an atheist—obviously a disciple of Nietzsche. Have you read *Antichrist?*"

I had been fascinated by the book. Dinos looked out at the harbor.

"Even though I share your grief for your killed father, I'm at peace with my religion. No one pretends to have all the answers, but I do believe in Christ and God," he said, and began to edge away.

"How do you feel about the Athenians of the Golden Era?" I asked hurriedly, pulling on Dinos' sleeve to hamper his departure.

He turned and his eyes pierced mine. For the first time I sensed a touch of annoyance in his face. Perhaps he was stewing for having ignored my advice about the shining timepiece which still decorated his wrist.

"The Periclean period was a time of grand intellectual achievement," he said, his brows arching with pride for our ancestors.

"Don't leave yet, Dinos," I said, still holding onto his sleeve. "I have all these puzzling thoughts," I pleaded.

"What thoughts, Yiannis?" he asked mechanically. His face took on a dull mask; he had no interest in this topic.

"Intelligent as they were—the Athenians of that period, I mean— they made immense efforts to build temples and shrines to their Olympian Gods."

"The gold and ivory statue of the Goddess Virgin Athena inside the Parthenon was ordered by Pericles and sculptured by Phidias," he added in a smirky way to impress me.

"Clearly they were avid worshippers of their Gods and defended them if anyone dared attack them, like Socrates."

"Well . . . yes."

"Then, a few hundred years later, Christ emerged and preached his own philosophies and claimed that he was the Son of the one and only God."

Dinos puckered his lips.

"Well, yes again."

"And now, we Christians view the Gods of Pericles as products of wild imagination, pure mythological balderdash."

"For crying out loud, finish your thought," shot Dinos.

"Now, suppose somehow you and I were beamed back in time and found ourselves in the midst of the *agora* next to Pericles, and in so many words we told the listening crowd that their deities, those they worshipped with dedication and fervor, were nothing but a hoax, a fabrication of their ancestors' and their own zealous minds."

Dinos ran his fingers under his moistened chin and his eyes danced.

"Hmm," he said, and scratched his head.

Since I had finally captured his attention, I took my time.

"What if five hundred years from now, a man of magic, a communicator gifted with an eloquent tongue, comes forth. He senses the time is right for religious change and convinces the crowds that he has been sent from a distant star to deliver a message. All past earthly religions are hallucinations of wishful minds; all souls upon their demise, and indiscriminately of their earthly status, are transmitted to his homeland, a star of unimaginable proportions and beauty. Life there is neverending, filled with fun and song and dance and love; there is no sickness and pain; no aging or feebleness of the mind. Food is plentiful for all, and evil is nonexistent." I saw my friend taking my argument in.

"Go on," he said impatiently. I gave him a jovial pat on the back and shrugged my shoulders.

"There is nothing more to say, Dinos. The cycle seems to repeat itself."

My friend tossed me a foggy stare, yanked his sleeve free, and took off at a quickened pace.

As the days went by, I saw Paraskevoula less and less during the day. I was busy with my new friends and she was absorbed with the knitting of a sweater. Often she sat for hours on her bench toiling diligently and quietly with her needles.

Not that I hadn't asked her to join our group. Courageous as she was, she initially made an effort to become one of us, but her peasant stock haunted her. She was politely scorned and made to feel inferior by most of the better-educated bunch. She soon withdrew with as much pride as she could muster, and pretended that since she was busy with her sweater project she had no time for us.

But we always had dinner together, just the two of us, as we had agreed to do on that joyous evening when we first met. We waited for each other by the same bench, and her round face always lit up the instant our eyes met.

We had the greatest of times together. She taught me to whistle like a shepherd, opening her mouth to show how she lodged her tongue against her small white teeth to produce the shrieking sounds by which she had once controlled her dogs.

We developed a bond, a comfortable attachment, a fondness for each other. But as the voyage was winding down its fifteen-day duration and we stood anchored in Halifax, where a great many of the passengers disembarked, for the first time Paraskevoula's spirited chattering seemed subdued.

My small talk did not succeed in bringing out her usual broad smile. And while we faced each other inside the smoky dining room I could not help noticing that her black eyes looked pained.

The following day, our last aboard the *Nea Hellas,* the mood sizzled with excitement; the very next morning we would be entering the Hudson River.

Festivity and jubilation showed on every face. Even the crew seemed bubbly as they went about their chores and prepared our final meals. The evening was temperate and the sky cloudless, and the decks were busy with promenading passengers of all ages. Groups of children shouted with gaiety, chasing about and playing under the watchful eyes of their relatives.

I found Paraskevoula sitting on her bench beside a middle-aged couple; she was in obvious discomfort. The strangers had intruded into her space, and her face reflected her displeasure. She wore a crisp new black blouse and a long full black skirt, and to my surprise her cheeks bore a touch of rouge. Her hair was braided, up in a bun as it was always, but that last evening it was decorated with a yellow ribbon, and I must admit she looked the prettiest I had ever seen her.

When she sensed my approach, she sprang up and rushed to meet me, but she was fidgety and nervous—the light fuzz over her upper lip was moist with sweat.

"All these people," she snarled at the crowd. Before I had a chance to utter a sound she took my arm.

"Yiannis, come with me. I have something to show you." With an air of urgency, she led me through a maze of narrow hallways and stairs until we reached the end of a poorly lit corridor. She stood in front of a cabin, and with the key already in her hand and a tormented look, she assured herself there was no one in sight, unlocked the door, dragged me inside, and rushed to fasten the dead bolt.

The room was small, with two bunks and a dresser. An open porthole was the only means of ventilation. The air was humid. A framed photo of an old schooner hung on one wall, and in one corner, out of the way and half hidden behind a solid partition, peeked a small sink. On the dresser, wedged between the two bunks, stood an icon propped up by two water glasses—a seated Virgin Mary carrying her infant Son against her bosom.

"Paraskevoula, you never told me you were staying in such a fancy cabin," I blabbered in a lighthearted attempt to defuse her mysterious discomfort.

"The old woman who was sharing it with me got off in Canada," she whispered and pretended to study the traveling sea through the porthole. "Now, I'm here alone," she added, her voice faint and cracking. Then, still facing out, she asked. "Do you like it?"

"I think it's great, particularly now that it's all yours—at least for one more night," I said.

"The sweater, I meant. Your sweater. Do you like it?" Her voice was emotional, soft and gentle. She turned and pointed to the light blue sweater stretched fully out on one of the bunks. Her whole body began to tremble. She sat on the berth next to the sweater, crossed her hands in her lap, and let her eyes drop to the floor.

Moved and speechless I stood staring at the product of her frantic labor. Uncle Chrisanthos had told me once, "There are times in one's life when words do not come easily. Then, it is wiser that nothing is said." Now, I discovered for the first time the meaning of his teaching.

I knelt in front of her and took one of her hands and kissed it. Her breathing was labored and teardrops fell from her bent head.

"I ... I ... " She tried to speak but choking overcame her. When she raised her head her eyes looked into mine with a fragile, long gaze; then she stretched her neck and timidly placed her lips on mine. As worldly as I was, having played my share of games with women even though I was young, I was barraged by conflicting feelings while our lips touched. When Paraskevoula finally withdrew, her tormented look drifted toward the icon of Mary and her Son and, falling to her knees in front of the dresser, she untied the yellow ribbon and let her black hair fall onto her shoulders. Slowly she made the sign of the cross as the Orthodox do, then spoke directly to both of them with courage.

"You know well I've never sinned," she paused, breathing heavily. Time passed, perhaps in prayer or her search for the appropriate words to finish what she needed to tell them. "But for the first time I feel urgings very deep within me." She took another long breath. "And I'm prepared to pay for my sin ... when I'm brought before you or ... whatever."

Her head drooped and she stayed on her knees and crossed herself again. Then she slipped to the floor near me, stretched out, and delicately pulled me down next to her. As the moon's rays filtered through the porthole and we lay there still and mute, she reached for my hand, as she had done before, only this time she guided it under her blouse and up to one of her naked, firm breasts. I do not know how or when, but somehow our boiling young bodies united in what were divine moments. So intertwined, we fell asleep.

When I awakened in the pink light of dawn, her arm was draped over my bare chest. Her wide-open eyes were tired and teary, but she gave me a broad, intimate smile of absolute contentment.

The need to talk to her was strong but I suppressed it and instead pecked her eyes with my lips and stood up. I fetched my shirt and trousers and began to dress. From the corner of my eye I saw she was affectionately following my every move. Troubled as I was, pressured by a compelling urge to clear my thoughts, I grabbed the sweater she had made, turned for a glimpse of her half-naked body on the floor, unbolted the door, and rushed through the deserted hallway until I found myself on the deck.

I walked toward her empty bench, stood by the rail, and looked out at the gray water with the horizon ahead. There in the distance I could see faint lights on a not-too-far-away land. I was neither glad nor sad to observe the great old vessel racing to bring us all to the end of its mission.

As I leaned against the rail, desperately trying to clear my confused feelings, a brisk wind snatched the sweater from my hand; my mad dash to grab it failed. Distraught, I watched as it was dropping toward the sea and a bizarre vision came to me—the sweater was transformed into an imposing goddess who waved her magic wand to reveal two paths for Paraskevoula and me. I knew then and there that Paraskevoula was to remain a beautiful memory. Destiny had carved two separate routes for us to follow.

Out of the guts of the old steamer travelers began to stir, pouring out upon its deck, all shouting and pointing. I followed the direction of their waving arms. Coming up fast, as if she were striding to greet us, appeared the grand and gracious green lady. Tall and proud and regal, Liberty held high her torchlight to guide us. The gathered throng sighed with exclamations and joyous tears, for at long last the entrance to the realm of freedom lay ahead, immediate and real. And while most were charmed by the grand vistas of New York Harbor and the glittering skyscrapers beyond, my eyes remained on the face of Liberty, the matron of many promises.

After we docked, a dozen welcoming ladies wearing red and blue armbands came aboard to lend a helping hand to the passengers who needed assistance in arranging their subsequent travel, since many were trekking to places beyond New York City. My services were solicited at once because I spoke a fair amount of English.

I was kept busy translating as best I could, so I was one of the last to disembark. The custom lines at the processing center on Ellis Island were long. I climbed the stairs to the mezzanine balcony to search the crowd below for a glimpse of Paraskevoula. Suddenly I saw her, surrounded by a group of men, probably her future husband and his friends. She had cleared customs and was being led toward the building's exit. Ignoring threats from officials as I trespassed, I sped across

66

and reached the edge, hoping that maybe her eyes would drift upward and meet mine one last time. She looked frantic, darting glances from side to side, hesitating to pass through the door. Perhaps she lingered in hope that some miraculous salvation would come. As I was ushered away from my vantage point by uniformed men, I saw her head droop and her shoulders sag, like a beast encircled by predators that has just resigned itself to its end.

4

AMERICA—
MY NEW WORLD

The ferry took us across the river to Manhattan, and *en masse*, with yellow tags indicating our names and destinations hanging from our necks, we were herded to the railroad depot. At first opportunity I ripped my tag off and shoved it in my pocket. While we were being escorted to special wagons in the rear of the transcontinental train destined for California, I broke away and boarded a car in the middle, choosing a window seat facing forward so that I would miss little of the wonders of the vast continent called America.

This was to be a journey of four days and three nights, the fat black conductor said. I sat snug in my seat surveying my surroundings, feeling exhilaration for the adventures to come, but very sad about Paraskevoula.

A month before my departure from Athens I had composed a respectful letter informing Uncle John of my arrival date, carefully addressed it, added the correct postage and mailed it myself. Concerned about the efficiency of the Greek postal service, I also prepared a short cable, which I had safeguarded inside my zippered wallet, intending to dispatch it the very moment I reached New York.

One of the red- and blue-armbanded ladies had asked if she could do something for me since I had helped them, so I entrusted my important wire to her.

"Your telegram will reach your uncle immediately," she assured me and took it, refusing to accept the few dollars I was prepared to give her for the cost.

Other passengers boarded the train and stared curiously in my direction; I in return viewed them with much interest as they came and sat nearby. An old white-haired lady moved next to me and smiled. A young mother with her son took the seats opposite mine and both kept studying my clothing. Across the aisle settled a pleasant man with his wife and their ugly teenage daughters, dressed alike and giggling like a couple of playful puppies—since I could not tell them apart, I guessed they were twins.

The train clipped along with a rhythmic clink-clank and blew its loud whistle when it passed through small towns and large cities, bridges, and long dark tunnels. I was entranced at the immensity of it all, particularly the enormous parking lots packed with brightly colored cars. Since I could not fathom that all those vehicles belonged to ordinary folks shopping or working, I was amazed at what I envisioned as an infinite number of automobile factories. I kept shaking my head, dumbfounded by the wealth of America the Great.

We sped onward through the countryside and I saw farmhouses and cornfields, and infinite numbers of healthy cows grazing on the lush grass, with milk-filled teats hanging so low they seemed to touch the ground. And, just as my Grandfather Yiannis had wandered through the awesome Vouraikos Gorge and the towering mountains of Peloponnesus and decided to make Kalavryta his everlasting abode, I recognized (as clearly as my name is Yiannis Varelopoulos) that this fertile, vast land called America would become my home.

The afternoon waned and all traces of the sun withdrew. The train kept its steady clink-clank pace, and I sat behind my spiffy sunglasses feeling mysterious and important. I minded my own business and thought that perhaps the American passengers who kept eyeing me perceived me as some young private eye from abroad on a secret mission. While I viewed with never-ending interest the shadowed tableaus gliding by, the twin closest to me, freckled and pimple-faced, stuck her giraffe-like neck into the aisle and stared at me even more intently than before. Challengingly and with a smirk—in an unmannerly fashion, I may add—she addressed me. "Is there something wrong with your eyesight? Why are you wearing those dark glasses? The sun has set, you know?" From her smirk I surmised the little bitch knew darned well that my purpose for keeping my shades on was simply to add a bit of style and mystique to my looks, but since she had succeeded in embarrassing me, as everyone around found her remarks amusing and snickered at my expense, I took them off and never looked in her direction again until she and her family got off in Chicago.

My funds had been drastically reduced, so I ate sparingly, buying sandwiches from vendors who peddled their wares from large trays on the station platforms. By the second day my hunger for a decent meal was compelling. As much as I tried to ignore the frenzied storm of gastric juices growling inside my belly by thinking of unrelated subjects, I failed miserably. I discovered a mysterious dining car somewhere up front, and shyly I ventured into it and took an empty table. A Negro man whose skin was very black and teeth bright white approached me and politely murmured something that went completely over my head. I must admit that until I boarded that train I had never seen men who looked like they had just emerged from the depths of a coal mine, except once in Athens, when out of curiosity I peeked over the shoulders of a mob that had surrounded one, staring as if they had come upon a Martian.

It must have been about two in the afternoon and I was not at all versed in the American bill of fare; I looked up at this very tall, very black man staring down at me and panicked. I quickly pointed to some item on the menu and told him that was what I wanted.

He grinned and left. When he returned and placed under my nose a healthy plate of ham and eggs, with toast and butter and jams, I thought surely someone had played a nasty trick on me, and I almost fainted from fear that my funds would never cover the cost of such a bountiful order.

I did some quick calculating and reminded myself that Americans were famous the world over for their humanitarian hearts. Naturally I would plead my case to the authorities and tell them I was a stranger in their land, that I made an honest mistake, that in error I had asked the waiter for more food than I had money to pay, and that I was very, very sorry indeed. Most probably the police would take pity on me and tell me not to do it again and I would be horribly embarrassed. But since I could see no remedy to the situation, slowly I polished off every bite as if that meal might be my last. When the waiter brought the check and left it on the table, I hid my agony behind my dark sunglasses, picked it up with trembling fingers, and peeked at the total, only to discover that the cost for all those treats was two dollars and fifty cents! My jubilation was supreme. A thrill flooded my insides at having escaped humiliation, and I thought it very proper to leave a one-dime tip for my gracious server.

On the following day, at the same time, I went back and had my ham and eggs served by the same man. He must have sensed my predicament because instead of the customary two slices of toast, this time around he brought me a tall stack of six pieces. When he placed the goodies under my nose, he smiled and left me to my famished self.

Early on the fourth morning the train moaned and squeaked and finally stopped. I rolled up the window shade and read the bold black letters on the station marquee—Sacramento, California. Ornate lights were still burning, even though the night had begun to fade. Passenger activity was sparse; the train was nearly empty. I rubbed my eyes and yawned and calculated that we should not have too far to go to reach the town of Davis. I tried to picture in my mind's eye Uncle John waiting at the station, but since I had seen him only once, so long ago, I felt uneasy about recognizing him.

I sat counting, for the fifth time, my cash of six dollars and twenty-seven cents, when the now-familiar black conductor tapped me on the shoulder and finally made me understand that, according to my ticket, Sacramento was my destination and I should hurry to get off.

Bewildered, I scrambled off the train before dawn on that twentieth of June and found myself in the Southern Pacific station, sitting on my bags, scratching my head and contemplating my next move, since Uncle John was nowhere in sight.

Gradually the station became totally deserted, the only life in my view being a lonesome cabbie who leaned against his huge yellow taxi with De Soto written on its fancy grill, looking disappointed at not having secured a fare.

As time passed I mustered enough courage to approach him; I told him I wished to go to Davis and asked how much the charge would be for such a trip. He casually pointed to a mechanical fare box. "Probably ten to twelve dollars," he said. I thanked him politely, mentioned I had only six dollars, and went back to sitting on my bags.

The cabbie puffed on his cigarette and paid little attention to me. With his big round yellow hat cocked up high on his head he appeared nonchalant but, since we were the only two living souls waiting there outside the station we occasionally made eye contact. My face must have been hopelessly sad because he eventually raised his arms and motioned to me to come over with my bags.

We raced west on the highway toward Davis. The day grew bright and warm. Somewhere in the middle of the trip the cabbie pointed to the clicking money-measuring clock, and the instant it read "$6.00," he reached over and turned it off. Glancing at me, he mentioned how lucky I was to be getting such a long ride for half the regular cost.

We reached Uncle John's house on G Street, a modest, one-story, gray wooden structure. I peeled off the last of my cash and handed it to the charitable taxi man, took my bags out of the trunk, and walked across the street. Just as I was about to start up the five steps that led to the porch, my legs began a violent shaking and I broke into a cold sweat.

What if Uncle John had not received my letter and the telegram? What if he were unaware of my arrival? A bachelor (a divorced man actually—the rumor circulating back home had been that his wife left him for a younger man) with no children, he could be vacationing in Monte Carlo for all I knew.

My heart beat louder than the frightening, diving German Stukas. I made it to the door and pressed the bell in panic. The taxi had long since disappeared, and perspiration ran profusely down my back. I waited and waited for any sign of life.

Agonizing minutes passed and each seemed longer than the entire train ride from New York! Crazy speculations clouded my reasoning. At some point the door squeaked open and a nose peeked through the crack. Was it for real? Was I hallucinating? I stared intently. I broke into a nervous giggle. A full face came into view. Was the man who studied me with questioning, half-asleep eyes Uncle John or a stranger?

"I'm Yiannis Varelopoulos, your nephew," I announced with courage.

Neither the letter from Greece nor the telegram from New York had reached him. Bleary-eyed, he ushered me inside his home, all along crossing himself, distrusting his vision which showed him I was indeed there, standing in his presence.

But he led me to the kitchen and brewed a large pot of coffee. I made myself comfortable on one of the four chrome chairs with yellow plastic seats which surrounded a matching table. He busied himself preparing breakfast, whistling and humming old Greek tunes, then asked me to describe my lengthy voyage and questioned me about the health of our relatives back home.

At some point I told him, "I'm indebted to you for inviting me to America, Uncle John. I'm forever grateful for a chance to discover life outside the confines of Greece. I hate to tell you, but the wars seem to have taken the heart out of our country. It's all boredom, bribery, and corruption there now. Without your offer, my choices would have been as limited as those of all the young men and women I have left behind." He gave me the longest stare but said nothing.

Then we sat opposite each other and ate while he recalled events of his youth with a mixture of enthusiasm, nostalgia, and heartache.

"Yes, sir, my boy," he said in Greek, "not always was this country great. Those earlier days were hard. The work was hard and the conditions were even harder. I was thirteen when I came to this land of plenty. My oldest sister married an immigrant who had settled in Chattanooga. Back home I thought 'Chattanooga' had a nice ring to it. 'My sister lives in Chattanooga,' I sang with pride each chance I got. She sponsored me and I came to Chattanooga. I lived with them for a year, then I went and got me a job with the railroad laying the tracks across the continent. We labored twelve, thirteen hours a day, and then some." He took a sip of coffee from his steaming cup and continued reflecting.

"I remember one day in North Dakota," he scratched his chin. "Or was it South Dakota? Anyhow, it don't matter. Not a tree for three hundred miles maybe, except some dry sage brush covered with snow. Colder than a miserable winter night at the North Pole. Why, my breath, as soon as it came out of my mouth, froze into a goddarned popsicle. Well, what can I tell you. Petros, my buddy, and I say to hell with all this mess. We decide to abandon our damned jobs and get the hell out-tathere. So we sneak out of the compound, but the nearest town to the camp is a few miles south and there is this frozen river between the town and us. I had bought this new pair of boots and they were the most precious things I had ever owned; so I take them off and give them to Petros and I tell him, 'Okay, I'll go up ahead and try to cross the river first and if the ice don't hold,' I says to him, 'and I go under, you'll lose a friend but at least you'll have my good boots to be glad about.' And when we cross and reach the town, cold and miserable as we are, we look for a coffee shop to get us something to drink and defrost our freezing innards. It's a small town and we find the only diner there, and there is this big sign hanging over the door. Neither one of us knows how to read it. So we go inside, rubbing our hands with glee. And when we feel the heat on our cheeks we smile and I say a couple of happy words in Greek. But no sooner do we sit down at the counter, all the time salivating for a cup of hot coffee, or choco-late or tea, this big fat sonbabitch (I learned later that Uncle John read-ily used this expression whether he was speaking English or Greek) cook comes galloping over toward us like a crazed bear, swinging a great big butcher knife and shouting for us to get the hell outtathere, and fast.

"Horrified, we stampede through the door, stumbling over each other, and we fall on the hard ice. We curl up in the merciless cold, unable to understand what in good Christ is the matter with the prick cook, when the big bastard points to the fuckin' sign that hangs over the door." Here Uncle John's face twitched and his eyes moistened. "So, outtathere on the snow, cold and miserable, feeling like an aban-doned kitten I'm ready to cry. But instead I take out from my hip pocket my little dictionary, which I carried with me always, and sitting on my numb behind I manage to translate the meaning of the fuckin' sign. 'Greeks and dogs ain't welcome,' it read."

Uncle John made his living brokering hay. He bought hay from the farmers who grew it and sold it to ranchers who needed it to feed their stock. He worked out of his home and owned a sparkling, late-model, white Chevy, which he drove from town to town and farm to farm, visiting in fields and orchards men he knew by their first names. More often he socialized in the local saloons where he drank whiskey and chewed on big cigars and spat, aiming his saliva into those funny-looking brass spittoons, as did all the other patrons; they often missed and the spit ended up on the wooden floors but nobody seemed to give a hoot.

He was a sparsely educated man who cried as easily as he laughed, and he loved to hum songs he had brought with him from our homeland. Every Greek born grows up chanting those old folk melodies, and we often sang together.

I accompanied him on his daily travels and met a lot of leathery-skinned farmers in blue overalls who smelled of cow dung, puffed on long fat pipes, and shook my hand, enveloping it with palms twice as big as mine. Introducing his nephew to his friends gave him pleasure, and his face lit up every time he presented me to people of Greek ancestry, who communicated with each other in a weird, baffling mixture of Greek and English.

One day while we were trekking over backroads, Uncle John must have detected my yearning to learn how to drive, because he suddenly stopped his beautiful Chevy and offered me the wheel. After a few hundred yards of hesitant handling I assumed complete command over that monstrous, powerful machine. As I maneuvered it through the prosperous grasslands of Yolo County, I experienced for the first time the excitement and power of controlling an automobile. I felt very strong and happy and important.

We visited the giant redwoods in Big Basin, those majestic old creatures which for thousands of years have adamantly refused to stop growing taller and bigger. I gazed up in wonderment until the muscles of my neck ached and I was forced to return to my own humble level.

Uncle John turned out to be a good man. Once, on my account, he gathered a few friends and we drove to Santa Cruz to visit the playland on the boardwalk by the beach. When I stepped into the midst of the electrified splendor of that magical realm, bedazzled by the colorful neon lights, flashing gigantic wheels, and myriad games designed to entice and thrill, my fascinated heart pounded as if I had just run a marathon and won the crown.

When I heard the cries of joy and screams of fright from the young crowd who rode a tiny train that crawled up into the sky only to fall back toward the earth with freakish speed, I boldly voiced my desire to ride it. Uncle John and all his friends encouraged me to go ahead and do it.

At the end of a nauseating wild ride, I made a gallant effort to re-swallow my insides, which seemed to have fled through my clattering teeth. My shaking legs refused to lead me away from the diabolical little train. I sat stupefied while Uncle John and his entourage bellowed with laughter, greatly amused at my plight.

Three memorable weeks had passed since my arrival when, on a sizzling morning, while we were still sipping our morning coffee, Joe Ramos, the Spaniard, paid us a visit. Joe was Uncle John's close friend, a gregarious man full of smiles and jokes who owned a large almond orchard in the town of Winters. Uncle John and Joe, between chitchat and laughter, drank shots of Metaxa brandy to help the coffee slide down in comfort and, as the bottle emptied, their talk brightened until at some point Joe mentioned the upcoming almond harvest and the Mexicans he had hired for a forty-day hitch.

"Each a them gonna make four hundred bucks. Now that ain't bad dough for forty days' work, is it, Johnny?" he said. In my mind I rapidly converted four hundred dollars into drachmas, and when it turned out to be a small fortune, I slyly asked Uncle John if perhaps his friend would like to give me a job similar to the one he had offered the Mexicans. Uncle John smiled and said nothing, but Joe picked up on my interest.

"Now, the boy here, your nephew, he looks like a strong young fella to me. Don't you think he can do the job, Johnny? God bless him, to me he don't look like he shriveled up on account o' the hunger forced on Greece during the war. Go ahead and bring 'm on down to the ranch tonight. Why, we'll get us a bite to eat at the house and he can get started in the morning. For God's sake, Johnny, this young Yiannis fella here, he looks healthy and strong," Joe said, smacking me on the back.

When Joe, feeling his cherries a trifle, got up to go, I stuck out my chest and took his hand and shook it hard, and I commented to Uncle John what a great guy his friend was. Soon after Joe's departure, Uncle John drove me to a thrift store downtown and bought me a pair of jeans, a cap, and a sleeping bag. In due time we were off to Joe's place down Winters way.

Mrs. Ramos was gracious, their daughter and son quiet and polite, and after a nice meal of meat, potatoes, and lots of vegetables, I was escorted to a tall narrow dwelling whose upper floor could only be reached by climbing a tall ladder. The room had no furniture and it seemed hotter than a blazing August noon in Athens. I opened the window for some relief.

When I was alone, I spread out the sleeping bag and stretched out on top, naked. Then it happened! As if word of a newcomer's arrival had been broadcast throughout their network, mosquitoes of prehistoric size dove at my flesh in droves. I jumped inside the bag, my only available shelter. Since those hungry monsters mercilessly bombarded my head I covered it with the bag too. While the temperature inside the ventless bag rose higher and higher, I fantasized that I had been tossed inside the flaming community oven back in Tripolis where we took our Sunday meal to be cooked. Since I had never considered roasting an agreeable way to pass on, I crawled out from my shelter and prepared for a brave fight. Throughout the night I must have smashed one thousand intruders.

Before daybreak, someone came running halfway up the ladder and hollered, "Amigo, it's time to get up. Come down to the cantina for breakfast."

"Pity," I cried with a deep sigh, "isn't there any pity in this cruel world?"

The cantina was humming with activity. There were short wiry men, young and old, and women of various ages, all a shade darker than I, and bright-eyed. Unshaven and ill at ease from my exhausting night, I tasted some beans but couldn't make myself eat an undercooked, flat, round, doughy bread which everyone else was stuffing down their throats with speed and gusto.

At six-thirty, the foreman gave the signal. We rushed outside and were passed our weapons. All able men were handed a stick the size of a baseball bat but twice as long. While we virile fellows climbed onto the outer limbs of the trees, bashing heartlessly at their branches with our clubs, the women spread sturdy canvasses over the ground and encircled the trunks. The almonds, loosened by the sudden shaking and pounding, fell onto the tarps to be collected.

Three hours into this grotesque game, my legs stubbornly refused to respond to all commands. To climb one more tree and do my vicious number on its pleading branches was out of the question! The painful truth was that the aching in my arms was so severe, lifting the club a few inches would have been impossible even with the most chivalrous effort.

Completely exhausted, I stood oblivious to the urgings of the energetic muchachos who kept sneering and shouting, "Come on, amigo. You can do it."

But I knew better. For the first time in my almost nineteen years, I commiserated with all the overloaded Greek jackasses who stubbornly refused to budge one more inch, silently enduring the malevolent whippings of their masters. In this tragic state my delirious mind seized upon the idea of returning home, unionizing all those abused donkeys, and becoming their spokesman.

A horn sounded at noon and the Mexicans hurried to their midday feast, all giggling and gay, while I parked my limp ass under a tree and dumbly stared at the ground. The foreman came, helped me climb on his pickup truck, and delivered me to the warehouse.

During the rest of that dreadful day, demoted, I stood next to a crawling conveyer belt that carried scattered almonds. My new job was to pick out an occasional rotten seed and discard it into a garbage can, an assignment given to the elderly and feeble women.

Unwashed and humiliated, I kept one eye on the slow-moving belt and the other on the yard, hoping not to miss Uncle John's possible visit. Toward the end of the third day, his Chevy came into my view and his appearance seemed a miracle. Patiently, I labored until the end of the shift. Uncle John tossed a swift, almost careless look at me and asked in an indifferent way how things were coming along. I said nothing but I knew he knew I had had enough of Joe's almond harvest.

"Swallowing your pride won't give you indigestion," he said while he and Joe escorted me to the white Chevy.

As we sped away from Winters, heading for Davis and civilization, Uncle John admitted to me that he had known all along the almond-picking job was too harsh for someone who had never done manual work before, but he had hoped to teach me a lesson. When I tossed him an uncertain look he winked.

"My friend," he said wisely, "if earning four hundred bucks picking almonds was easy, everybody would be picking almonds."

A few days later, a disturbing telephone call informed Uncle John of the passing of Themistoklis, his friend; the funeral would be on Sunday, the following day, in San Francisco. The news saddened him and he cried a little. He sighed and crossed himself and told me that I should accompany him to the last rites for his buddy.

The death of this unknown man brought no grief to me, but the prospect of touring the beautiful city by the bay, known for its astounding charms, seemed golden. Although I deplored funerals and had refused to attend any since the Kalavryta disaster, I agreed.

The following morning, dressed in our best, we climbed into the Chevy and drove for three hours through a lot of towns of no importance until we came to Berkeley, which was known to me for its famous university.

When we were traveling the lower deck of a long iron bridge suspended by monstrous cables, I felt enraptured. From its lofty height I viewed the splendor of the brilliant city, the hilly landscape, and the magnificent bay below. A refreshing breeze whipped the azure waters; countless tiny vessels, sails flying, speckled the sea. They appeared like the bright unfurled wings of graceful gulls in flight. Those grand vistas excited me and I dared to announce, "I want to live here, Uncle John."

With time to spare, we drove by Union Square. While my stare followed the colorful cable cars laboring up Nob Hill I cried out with sheer thrill. We swung through the boisterous Chinatown and gazed at its strange-looking inhabitants as they rushed about like frenzied bees. Uncle John said it was the largest Chinese settlement outside their homeland. We crossed Broadway and wandered into the bohemian enclave of upper Grant Avenue in the North Beach district, a bustling

Italian community jammed with galleries, cafes, restaurants, and bakeries. Then we drove toward the sea and came to lively Fisherman's Wharf where vendors peddled crispy loaves of aromatic French bread and monstrous pink steaming crabs and bowls of some sort of hot soup, all in a carnival-like setting. Yes, by God, this hilly city by the Pacific with its myriad allures bewitched me, and I gasped as if I had drunk a cupful of magic brew concocted by Medea the enchantress.

At the Greek Orthodox Church, the corpse lay on display surrounded by wreaths and bouquets of seasonal flowers. A large crowd stood in silence while the priest sang, *"May he enjoy everlasting memory and life."* He swung his censer, spilling clouds of strong smoke in all directions, intensifying the stuffiness and unbearable stillness of the holy room. Some ladies coughed, some relatives cried, and one elderly woman fainted—from smoke inhalation, I guessed.

When the service came to an end we paraded, as is customary in our faith, to view and pay our last respects to the lifeless remains of what once had been a vital man of many accomplishments and maybe some failure. My turn came and I faced the corpse, laid to rest in an expensive coffin lined with satin-trimmed fabric. He had been made up with paints and powders, lipsticks and rouges. Themistoklis, the proud man he once must have been, now looked more like a sleeping old hermaphrodite, and I was overcome by distaste for our church's barbaric tradition—it procrastinated the disposal of the dead, perhaps to exploit the grieving.

After the burial at the cemetery, the entourage of almost two hundred mourners returned to the church and congregated at the hall to sample the customary meal offered by the survivors of the deceased.

The day certainly had been a trying one to us all, and somber faces showed deep sorrow. We took seats at big round tables. Uncle John and I shared space with his acquaintance, Mr. Pappas, his wife, their three teenage daughters, and his young cousin Tula, who appeared quite eager to display her sensual abundance.

Mr. Pappas was a huge man with Herculean shoulders and a bulldog face, who never tired of chattering about his financial achievements in the oil business, having acquired his fifth gasoline station within the past month, with the help of the Lord, of course. The very instant volunteer servers brought food to our table, Mr. Pappas discarded his coat, rolled up the sleeves of his dress shirt, and dug into the offerings with great vigor. Perspiring profusely under the arms, he kept diving into a heaping platter of large, fatty chunks of boiled pig, chewing loudly like a starving polar bear devouring a salmon.

But while the priest orated the standard compassionate promises, assuring the crowd that Themistoklis' kind soul had been accepted into the immortal realm of the heavens, and deservingly sat near our beloved and just Almighty, the crowd's sadness miraculously evaporated and a gala mood prevailed in its stead.

Mr. Pappas, wearing the confident air only success can bestow, with a mouthful of partially crunched swine swelling his cheeks, declared, "God without man is still God, my friends, but man without God is ... well ... he is garbage." The emphasis of disgust this large man placed on his last word forced a generous portion of his bite to spray over the rest of us who had roosted around the table.

While I toyed with a piece of meat frosted with cold lard, I observed my ordinarily complacent Uncle John assuming a courtly, adolescent pose. With his radiant eyes unusually inflamed and lustrous, he sat completely engrossed by the unruly, tantalizing, and enticing play of Tula, in her twenties, I guessed, who wore what appeared to me strong signs of her readiness to mate.

Her healthy bosom puffed, she sat straight, and tossed her pretty broad face about and flipped her long brown hair wildly like an untamed filly, appearing as if her sole aim was to tease everyone and everything around her, even the very air that embraced her every curve.

Since I aimed to achieve independence from my uncle's charity, meeting Mr. Oilman offered a unique opportunity. Calmly, coolly, and humbly I explained to Mr. Pappas that San Francisco had stolen my heart; if he were kind enough to offer me part-time work, perhaps pumping gas in one of his many service stations, I would be very grateful indeed, and that with the blessing and help of his friend, my Uncle John, I could immediately secure lodging and sign up for fall classes at a local college.

The big man tossed a swift glance at his stony-faced spouse, puffed out his big chest, and assumed a most judicious posture. With this melodramatic stance he coughed, wet his lips with his tongue, and voiced a statement—a potpourri of badly mispronounced English and peasant Greek.

"Somebody said once that a good young man can't keep his decency for long on an empty stomach." His prudent perception lit his face and he continued, "In this great land of ours called US of A, every Greek lad who wants to work must be given the chance to pump gas." Facing me he added, "When you want to start pumping, my son?"

My questioning eye found Uncle John's, who to my surprise took a brief reprieve from drooling over Tula, tossed me what I guessed to be a consenting nod, and mumbled, "In a coupla days." I thanked Mr. Pappas for his generous heart. He beamed, his wife gurgled, the daughters giggled, and Miss Sexy combed her fingers through the top of her head, spreading her glances about like a voracious spider in her web, then, with her pinkies raised, she proceeded to maul her third piece of baklava.

I surreptitiously kept one eye on Uncle John, his round face shining like a full moon on a sparkling night, as he sat on the edge of his chair taking in every suggestive hint the young seductress heaved his way.

Tula licked every inch of her syrupy fingers while she coyly and slyly darted her playful arrows toward his wishful heart, and, as a cat toys gleefully with a crippled sparrow until the helpless creature expires, she deliberately and cruelly tormented Uncle John until the party was finally over.

The Chevy purred. We headed back north toward Davis. Uncle John remained silent, lost in his thoughts. Then suddenly, as if a storm cloud on a very dark day burst wide open to let its cradled moisture fall all at once, he began to sing, loudly and with much vigor, zest, and sentiment.

He chanted wrenching verses of a frail old chieftain, who, during the Greek revolution against the Turks, had rested between battles in the shadow of an immortal plane tree, crying out the frustrations of his heart. He claimed that his mind was youthful and yearning for the caresses of a spicy maiden, but she scorned his wintry and feeble body for that of a *levendi* (brave young man) and he could no longer bear her rejection, so he welcomed the bitter bullet of a Turkish gun to tear his heart in pieces and give him everlasting peace, amen.

Uncle John must have recited the same lines at least ten times before he stopped. Quickly I took the chance to praise Mr. Pappas for offering me employment.

"Yeah, sure, Pappas is a good man, all right," he sighed and a wicked glow radiated from his round face, "but his cousin, Tula ..." Here he connected the tips of the first three fingertips of his right hand, brought them to his mouth, and smooched them with a loud kiss, a gesture of deep awe or desire. "She is a peach! A delicious peach! A peach full of nectar!" He smacked his lips and licked them as if he were taking a bite of that delectable fruit and the words seemed to spring from the inner depths of his craving.

Silently I enjoyed his excitement. His stubby neck stretched, his face glowed in the darkness.

"I read a poem once. I liked it so much I memorized it." Uncle John sat up straight and, like a poised Shakespearean actor, he unleashed his well-rehearsed lines.

"Across the door of my heart I wrote, 'No thoroughfare,' but love came snickering and said, 'I enter everywhere.'"

The capricious side of my personality pricked at me and urged me to lead him on.

"I don't follow you, Uncle John."

He took time pondering and finally said, "Don't you see, Yiannis? But, how can you? You are too damn young to understand the tragedy ..." He stopped, momentarily searching, "... the travesty of growing old. The fuckin' Devil must have prevailed in this one. God and the Devil must have had a fight on this one, and the Devil won!" He shook his head in disappointment. "A sensible Creator would have let us keep our youthful looks 'til *Charos,* the ferryman of death, came for us." The car was racing past Fairfield. Uncle John sneered in doubt. "Maybe God wasn't the one who made us after all, maybe it was the fuckin' Devil. And then again maybe, and most probably, neither one of them had anything to do with us being here." His fervor seemed to increase. "Just look at me, my boy. I'm almost sixty years old and wrinkled." He winked at me. Casting an impish grin he whispered confidentially, "But I'm able and willing. My mind is not wrinkled, and for sure my heart and some other parts of me aren't suffering from a case of atrophy either."

Up on our right from behind the defined crest of a round hill a red moon began to show us its profile. Uncle John's senses seemed keenly attuned to his driving. Traveling shadows passed swiftly. He sighed deeply and shook his head.

"Yiannis, my boy, tell me, why mustn't I look now as young as I was when I was your age, and hold onto those looks until my contract is up? Why must I get all wrinkled up and balding, and fat around the middle? Why must my tits sag soft like a milked cow's? Why must I look like a clown, laughable and undesirable to a delicious eager peach like Tula, when in fact my insides can still get inflamed and boil with the same explosive urges as the ones that burst my guts when I was sixteen?" He waved his arm in frustration. He expected no answer.

"Ah, you probably think your Uncle John has gone nuts. Well, I don't pretend to be an educated man; but I have spent a good share of my time searching for the unfathomable answers."

I sensed Uncle John's attempt to navigate the stormiest of seas. Discovering a slice of my compassionate relative's depth excited me.

"Please continue, Uncle John," I urged him on. "But what are the questions, first?"

"About man's purpose on this earth, if any, and who was the one who sent us here." He took his time, flashing side glances my way. I moved my head up and down in encouragement.

"I had an infidel cousin once. Older than me by many years. Pitch-black curly hair; the courage of an eagle; he spoke his mind. High school graduate. 'A heretic sinner,' the miserable faithful used to call him, fearful of his brave views. Adonis was his name, and he left our world early." Uncle John glanced at the sky in prayer. "Holy Mother of Jesus, please have mercy on his bones," he murmured. "Adonis told me this tale when I was a lad, eager to learn.

"God, who is a crafty artist, sat on the beach by the sea and built things. He picked up dirt and sand and sprinkled a few drops of seawater and made the mouse and the cat, the chicken and the fox, the deer and the tiger, the anchovy and the seagull. Every so often, when God's sculptures grew into a sizable pile, he spat life onto them and let them run free with orders to multiply. All these critters went about crawling, flying, or swimming, and God was ecstatic about all his creations. One day, while the seagull was gliding gracefully above in the light breeze, God cast his radiant eyes on it feeling proud of His ingenious conception. Lo and behold, at that very instant the silly bird took a crap, and the healthy dropping, like a well-aimed bullet, splattered God in the eye. Needless to say, fury possessed God. He thought of the ungratefulness of His humble toy and His madness grew to a wild vengeance. Here, the good Lord blows life onto one of his innovative trinkets, one which He gifts with wings to roam the endless skies in freedom, and the insignificant bird shits on its Master. So, the Almighty scratched his head. 'What if some of my other playthings misconduct themselves in a similar fashion,' he wondered. Wisely He came up with a quick solution.

" 'Since I got no time to bother with trivialities,' He says to himself, 'I'll build a foreman—someone who will keep an eye on all my breathing gadgets, hold them under strict control, supervise their actions.' So, He takes a chunk of dirt, sand, and water and molds a novel contraption: the DEVIL. But for reasons unknown to us, as His divine mind often works in mysterious ways, He names it MAN. The Lord spits on it and gives it life, but before He turns it loose He passes out his strict instructions. 'You shall reign over all my earthly creations,' He says. 'At will, you may enslave or murder any of my toys, including your very own descendants. In order to carry out this difficult mission, though, I must outfit you with a multitude of ... ha, ha, ha, ... abilities. You shall be cunning and merciless, greedy, selfish, vain, larcenous, and ferocious, to mention just a few. But because this exclusive power I'm granting you will most probably give you a big head, in balance I shall inflict upon you nasty illnesses and you shall grow old, ugly, and decrepit. And, after a short stretch of fulfilling your obligation to me, you shall pass your duties to your offspring and you shall return to dust.' "

Uncle John gurgled his throat and spat out the window.

"Well, man, cunning, sly, and selfish as the Lord had made him, wasted no time. He did his own speedy calculations. 'Almighty,' he says in a voice sweeter than honey, 'of course, I shall do as you please. As you are my Lord, I'll carry out your will with diligence and pride. But must I grow old and decrepit before I return to dust? I'll accept all your curses, including death, but must I age and grow ugly and senile in the process? Oh, Master of all, can't we strike a little deal here?'" Uncle John's eyes were twinkling. "God burst out in a coarse mean laughter. 'What an unpredictable swine you turned out to be. Of all the afflictions I cast upon you, vanity grips you the most, ha? How flat-out interesting,' says the Lord, His eyes glowing with mistrust. 'Let's make one thing very clear,' he says sternly. 'I intend to make no deals with any trinket I've created, especially a loony like you who notions vanity as the meanest of all my curses. However, to show you that I'm not a bad fella, I'll give you just one opportunity to rise above all my curses. I'll grant you the smarts to build a world nobler than the one I have assembled for you. And I give you my solemn promise here and now, if such a time ever comes, ha, ha, ha, YOU SHALL BECOME MY BROTHER.'" Uncle John chuckled and slapped my thigh mischievously. "And so, God gave the Devil-Man a shove and sent him off to perform his mission."

"A rather interesting tale," I grinned.

"So, here we are, you and I, the descendants of a nasty creature created by the Almighty solely because of the first seagull's bad timing."

The hot earth spilled the fragrance of onions swelling in the fields. We were approaching Vacaville, the self proclaimed world capital of the onion. Heat spewed from the rich soil of the Sacramento Valley. The breeze that blew in from the lowered windows brought us some relief from the scorching.

A barrage of thoughts bombarded my mind. Man's quenchless thirst to create idols, imaginary or breathing, set them on pedestals or thrones, and fight their blood-spilling war games. Tenner, marching in proud goosestep, careless of the poison he spread wherever his boot stamped the soil of innocent lands. Christos' claim that God was man-made, and that he, Christos, was the master of his own spirit and soul.

"This one chance God gave Man—to shed the curses placed upon him by his creator, I mean—do you suppose Man can ever produce a nobler world than God has given him?" I asked.

Uncle John spat his answer rapidly, as if he had anticipated my question.

"Can a young grapevine shoot straight up like a poplar?"

"What?" I missed the meaning of his parable.

"Adonis' tale got me thinking at an early age. You see, my boy, my father was a poor farmer. We lived no better than begging gypsies. As kids we had no toys. Since philosophizing is a poor man's game— nobody needs money to think—my cousin's story offered me a way to tolerate my young, aimless existence. God and man, man's spirit and soul, man's life on Earth and his thereafter, in Paradise or in Hell, are beans I've been soaking inside my head since those early days."

He scanned the mauve sky with wild-looking eyes. Uncle John now appeared driven and perspiring.

"You want to hear my own explanation of the whole darn thing?"

"Yes," I begged.

Uncle John moved about his seat as if coals were burning underneath it. The highway stretched ahead in a straight line. He took a deep breath and began.

"Well ... it's like this. Man has no purpose. None whatsoever. Nothing special in the way the churches and the good books claim. Man just happened to be. No different than a twig, or a piece of grass, a drop of water or a speck of dirt, a rodent or a wolf, a wasp or a canary. What lofty purpose could God have bestowed on man, when a radiant nightingale sings its tiny heart out spreading joy to all, yet my brothers thought nothing of felling it with a rock from their slings, then wringing its puny neck to snuff it forever?

"My uncle was a priest. Praxitelis, his old mule, tired and abused all its life, wanted to crawl inside a hole to die; I could see it in its sorrowful eyes, but my uncle, the priest, wasn't about to hand old Praxitelis such a final treat. No, sir. He kept the old mule laboring from sunrise to sundown, trekking from the fields up to the village and back, always overloaded. When Praxitelis hesitated for the briefest moment to catch his breath, the pious priest poked his long stick inside the old mule's sore asshole to make him jump and keep on going, reminding him that a beast's destiny is to serve man until its last painful breath. Ah baaaah," he bleated as Greeks do to say no.

"Once, I was invited by a couple of wealthy brothers to join them down in Baja, Mexico, for marlin fishing. I had no idea, then, what marlins looked like. Gus, the older of the fellas, hooked one. Throughout a two-hour struggle the creature tried to get rid of the hook. Finally, this most beautiful specimen of Somebody's handiwork was dragged alongside the boat and stared at me in a helpless, sad way. My gut turned sour on the spot. One guy, a crew member, took a hammer, reached over the side, and struck a blow to the critter's head and the spectacular being quivered some and gave up the ghost. They tied a loop around its tail, lifted it up inside the boat, and the three of us posed next to it for pictures to immortalize our brave deed. The torment of a living thing we know so little about, Man calls sport fishing.

"Yes, my boy, everything Man does, no matter how horrid, he cunningly justifies. Now tell me how can man change all that for the better? Ah baaaah, I tell you. Man is nothing but a hackneyed, accidental microbe inside the belly of a giant of unimaginable proportions. Billions of us humans cling onto our own little planet Earth, which is a speck of food inside this great big belly, the result of the giant's last meal. Millions of generations of billions of insignificant parasites, during this aimless, greedy frenzy, keep sucking away the nutrients from this grain of food as it travels a long, long journey of decomposition through the innards of our host giant. Finally, my dear nephew, after a time as great as this giant himself, our big fellow squats for that which is for you and me a daily need, only our giant's movement occurs every billion years, maybe. And then, oh, God have mercy; all hell breaks loose. Yes, the entire universe as we know it—the Earth and the Sun and all the galaxies up there, the ones we see and maybe some we can't see—everything, including the holy Patriarch's religious chronicles, and the Pope's ornaments and great collections of art, is extricated and floats into an abysmal hole, a huuuuuge"—Uncle John dragged the word until he ran out of breath—"outhouse so to speak, ... and ... and here is where my mind gets flustered."

He darted naughty glances all around.

"Gets flustered?" I pressed on.

"Yah! Flustered, my boy. Flustered because I can't come up with an end to my story. My mind gets all muddled up because it is unable to grasp this gigantic turd's destiny or purpose." His face shined with a dubious light.

"You paint a dismal picture of mankind, Uncle John," I said. He shook his shoulders indifferently, so I went on. "But during our inconsequential journey, mustn't we make an effort to create a nobler environment for ourselves, as in Adonis' tale?" I asked, wishing to engage him in a debate.

The rising moon had shrunk and brightened, and the air was heavy, scented with odors of French onion soup simmering inside a gigantic kettle. Uncle John kept sweating and failed to respond. Instead he whistled a Byzantine hymn, then crossed himself and murmured in prayer. "God have mercy on all infidels."

He lapsed into contemplation, as if he were petitioning for the absolution of his soul. Finally he turned to me.

"My boy, these thoughts of mine come and go. Actually I believe in miracles as much as the next foxy guy. So, I, too, play it safe. I keep sending my contributions to the church, attend the services regularly, and hope."

I thought of Adonis' and Uncle John's simplistic tales and marveled at their astounding association—that man's birth, existence, and end are, well . . . waste-related.

In less than a week, with Uncle John's help, I rented a clean room in a large green Victorian boarding house in the Ingleside district within walking distance of Mr. Pappas' service station. I began working four hours per evening (excluding Sundays), and registered for courses for foreign students at the nearby San Francisco City College.

On the campus, I observed people of all colors and tongues and ages, and I was intrigued by the uninhibited camaraderie of the young men and women who stretched out on the grass between classes and used each other's bodies as pillows, giggling and playing, naturally devoid of the constraints that plagued the Greek culture.

I was captivated by my favorite teacher, Mrs. Hayes, a handsome married woman who often spoke with pride of her three children. Her diction was perfect, and even though she spoke no other languages she communicated well with all of us—her foreign pupils.

Before Thanksgiving recess, Mrs. Hayes invited a bunch of us students to spend the holiday with her family at home in Berkeley.

"It'll be a fine experience for those of you who came from distant lands to share an important national holiday with an American family and sample some of our traditional foods," she had said.

When I arrived at the large brown-shingle house, surrounded by a sizable yard full of fruit trees and flowering plants, the door was answered by a young blond girl in braided pigtails who gave me a bright sweet smile. She said her name was Kathy and blushed, and I gave her one red carnation from the dozen I had brought as a gesture of appreciation for Mrs. Hayes' invitation. She took it with grace and half-bowed and kept on blushing. I told her my name, and she escorted me into the living room already crowded with family members and fellow students.

Mrs. Hayes rushed to greet me, and after accepting the carnations with an exclamation she eagerly introduced me to her husband Jack, who was tall, wiry, and a school principal; I met their two sons, Patrick and Michael, and was properly introduced to their daughter, Kathy.

Ethel, a much younger sister of Mrs. Hayes, was also there. She was tall and lanky, small-breasted, with short gray hair, enigmatic green eyes, and tanned skin. She lived in Southern California and had come up for a few days as she always did around Thanksgiving. Holding a large whiskey glass in one hand and a cigarette in the other, she sat in a brown overstuffed chair and looked bored, but grinned mechanically. Her face appeared to conceal a secret or two.

The small talk continued well into the afternoon, when Mrs. Hayes announced that dinner would be served. We took our seats around a large linen-covered table brimming with steaming foods, and all seemed strange to me except for the big roasted bird, which I was almost certain was a monstrous turkey. "Bigger than a spring lamb!" I thought.

Jack Hayes stood up and pointed to the various platters and bowls, describing in plain words the stuffing and the ingredients, the sweet potatoes with roasted melted marshmallows on top, the brown gravy and cranberry sauce. He began to carve the huge turkey and to place generous portions of the meat on the plates we passed to him. While we helped ourselves to the rest of the tasty spread, he told us of the first Thanksgiving.

As we waited for a signal to plunge into the food on our laden plates, Jack Hayes asked us to bow our heads and unite our hands in a fashion similar to starting a Greek dance. In a gentle voice, with closed eyes, he offered a simple grace. I was so moved by the purity, beauty, and closeness of this family, which reminded me of my own during the happier days of my childhood, that I began to choke with emotion.

I saw in Jack's tranquil face that of my own beloved father, whose absence during my painful growing years I had buried deep within my heart, and a wild river of bitter ache spread over me. I hurriedly excused myself and sped away from the dining room to hide in the chill dark shadows of the garden.

I walked about in a frantic state, needing to let go, to cry and weep and spit out the venom that polluted my gut. But I was too ashamed to be seen in a pitiful state, and felt guilty that such unpleasant emotions would surely spoil the gaiety of this fine gathering. Gasping for breath, I was alarmed by someone coming near me.

"Are you all right?" asked Kathy in a concerned whisper.

Avoiding her eyes, I coughed and gulped. "I needed some fresh air," I said. Slowly I led the way back into the dining room. To my great relief when I took my seat, everyone pretended they hadn't noticed my absence.

Jack Hayes spoke of his unforgettable six-year stay in Kyushu, Japan, where he taught English in the university in Oita in the early thirties. Along with a dedicated English professor, he had lived in simple housing without bathing facilities, sharing it with a live-in maid provided by the school.

Mrs. Hayes' faint displeasure at her husband's revelation about having cohabited with a Japanese woman was noticeable. Kathy, who sat across the table, lowered her head to hide her embarrassment but flashed tiny peeks in my direction.

After dinner, we were offered coffee and spicy pumpkin pie topped with gobs of whipped cream, and gradually, we drifted back into the living room. To my surprise, Ethel, who seemed slightly intoxicated, slid onto the piano stool and without the help of sheet music pounded the keys. Familiar melodies filled the air and the mood in the room became festive. Having recovered from my distress, I shared the group's excitement and was amazed at Ethel's ability to bang out all those tunes from memory.

It was getting late, so Mr. Hayes asked Patrick to drive us to our various homes. After the thank-yous for a memorable evening, we all piled into the family station wagon. I sat up front next to Patrick. He was attending the same school and promised to seek me out and introduce me to his friends.

Patrick and I became buddies even though our temperaments were different, he being the quiet and studious type in contrast to my more adventurous and less scholastic nature. Almost every other Sunday I was invited to spend most of the day with his family, and I became very fond of all the Hayeses.

I first became aware of Kathy's womanhood the following April. The Hayeses arranged for a gathering of friends to celebrate Kathy's fifteenth birthday. Patrick fetched me from the Berkeley train station, as he often did. While we were heading to the house, we made small talk about college and other trivial things but at one point, and with some seriousness, he said, "My sister has a crush on you." I was confused and looked it, since the meaning of this slang expression was beyond me.

"Kathy likes you a lot," he explained.

I felt somewhat flattered but not terribly inflated, because Kathy, almost five years my junior, seemed like a kid to me. She was so very shy; she blushed when I just glanced at her.

"Coming from a strange land and all, I must seem rather peculiar to her; oddity often enjoys a certain amount of appeal," I said.

Perhaps because of the seed planted by Patrick, or perhaps because Kathy looked unusually confident that afternoon, and beautiful in her black turtleneck sweater and long gray woolen skirt, my eyes became aware of her the instant I entered the house. I noticed her developing fullness as she sashayed about, chatting and giggling with the grace and purity of a butterfly just out of the cocoon.

Her deeply set blue eyes were playful and honest, her forehead proud and broad, and her blond hair had been brushed back from her temples and braided into two pigtails ending with ornate bows of shiny green ribbon.

Her warm smile was caring and bright. When she approached me I gave her the inexpensive cologne I had bought for her at my neighborhood drugstore. She beamed and blushed and gave a little bounce off the floor, thanking me with as much sweetness and sincerity as if I had given her the moon.

Back in Athens, my perceptive Aunt Marika had once pointed out how very dumb and slow I was in interpreting a woman's alluring signals. Now that Patrick had made his comments I became aware of Kathy's infatuation for the first time. Her gaze scarcely left me throughout the evening.

The April night was unusually balmy, and some of us drifted into the garden. The sky sparkled like a gigantic black platter full of diamonds. We gazed up at the eternal show. Patrick and I were surrounded by giggling young ladies, and I felt Kathy's presence next to me. I pointed up at the evening star—a large chunk of crystal hanging low— and started to tell a story that had been with me since my early years.

"Once upon a time, long, long ago, an enchanted land buzzed with preparations for the wedding of the lovely Princess Poulia to a neighboring prince. Poulia's heart, though, had been stolen by a handsome shepherd she saw by the well where he watered his flock of sheep. On the morning of the wedding, before anyone had awakened, Poulia, full of sadness and heartache, sneaked out of the palace and sped through the thick forest to catch one last glimpse of the young man she loved. Avgerinos, which means 'dawn' in Greek, was his name, and he was more handsome than a glorious spring morning; and he was very much in love with Princess Poulia, too. While his sheep quenched their thirst he leaned proudly against his staff, blowing through his flute a tune so melodious it enchanted even the stones and the trees.

" 'I came to tell you of my wedding to a prince, but I love you,' Poulia cried, and swiftly she turned and ran away, sobbing as she fled, because she knew that Avgerinos, being a commoner, could never, never be her husband. Avgerinos, despondent from the loss of his love,

94

plunged into the well and ended his life.

"All the local fairies, nymphs, and mermaids gathered in somber mourning. Between lamentations they decided that Avgerinos' handsomeness should be admired by all forever and forever. So they sent him up to the dark sky and made him the Morning Star. Poulia heard the horrid news from the fairies. Driven mad, she chased after Avgerinos. And she is up there running after him still. You see, Poulia is the Evening Star, and her tears have turned into tiny beads and filled the night sky."

Kathy appeared moved by the simple tale of tender love and ultimate sacrifice. Her moist, deep-set eyes sparkled. Her gentleness aroused a craving in me.

"Do you suppose it's a true story, Yiannis?" she asked with refreshing innocence.

"No one will ever know," I murmured and moved toward her, lured by a sudden powerful pull. Perceiving danger, though, I stopped short of reaching to wipe her tears. A yearning for Kathy was born in me, but I suppressed it at once and edged away.

At that time the Korean War was raging in all its madness, and many young men who had gone off to fight communism were returning in pine boxes. But I was committed to becoming an American citizen, and I felt strongly that serving in the armed forces during the time of need would be a gallant offering to a country I intended to call my own.

I approached the recruiting office on Market Street and told the sergeant in charge that I wished to join the army for three years as soon as my school semester was over. In late June of 1952, a dark green bus transported a number of us young recruits and volunteers to the training facility at Fort Ord in California to prepare us for combat.

I had concealed my plans. My mind was made up and I wished to be dissuaded by no one. While our training was in progress I wrote brief notes to Mr. Pappas and Uncle John apologizing for my sudden departure, and a thank-you card to the Hayes family. I sent a lengthy letter to my mother and Betty, explaining that I had joined the army and asking them to understand.

One evening Uncle John paid me a visit.

"I was passing through the area," he said, so we spent an hour talking. He never discussed with me whether he approved or disapproved of my enlisting, even though I knew that deep down he was a patriotic American himself, having joined the Navy during WW II.

On a sunny Sunday morning, toward the conclusion of our eight-week training, my Lithuanian buddy and I attended mass at the Russian Orthodox Church in Monterey. I went not out of religious devotion or need, but because Christian worship seemed the most innovative pretext for dodging Sunday KP, since every soldier who went to church services was automatically exempt from that much-despised duty. Kitchen Police was a dreaded sixteen-hour shift where the work consisted of peeling, cleaning, and preparing sacks of potatoes, carrots, and onions, and washing dishes stacked higher than the pyramids of Egypt.

Upon our return at midday, the company clerk approached me: There was a family waiting to see me in the recreation room. When I entered, I was bewildered to find the smiling faces of the entire Hayes family before me. They were on their way to Capitola to call on Mrs. Hayes' ailing mother, and it was a grand opportunity to visit. I was jubilant.

"Soon, I'll be leaving to serve my time overseas, somewhere near Frankfurt in Germany," I told them, and all seemed pleased with my news since Europe was a much safer place to be stationed than Korea, where the rest of my company was heading. "My language test scores— excellent in Greek, of course, and acceptable in French and Italian— got me this good fortune."

We chatted for several hours, and Patrick said he would be enlisting soon. As I was escorting them to their station wagon, at a snail's pace to make their visit last a bit longer, I mentioned that my new posting presented the opportunity to settle an old score, and that I was anxious to get going and grateful to be sent to Germany.

They glanced at each other in puzzlement, but I made no attempt to explain. I promised to drop them a card every so often and let them know how things were going with me and with army life in general. They all took turns shaking my hand and wishing me good-bye. Jack

Hayes placed his arm around my shoulders, and in a fatherly way began to recite a wise tale he had brought home long ago from the Orient.

"A wise man was once asked to describe life, and he readily replied that each person's life is a number. When you have your health you are in possession of number 1. If you are privileged with caring parents, you add one 0, and your number increases to 10. If you find a good wife, you add one more 0 to reach 100. When you bear a healthy child, you add one more 0 and your number rises to 1000, and should fortune smile on you, you add one more 0 and your number becomes 10,000—and so your number may keep on increasing indefinitely.

"Now, when your parents die your number decreases by one 0. And if you lose a child, your number again becomes smaller by one 0. But when at some point in your life you lose your health, what drops from the number of your life is that very first figure, that simple number 1. And without the 1, Yiannis, your life is reduced to a bunch of zeroes." He paused and looked deep into my eyes. "So, take care of yourself, son," he concluded, and patted me on the back.

They climbed into their station wagon and Jack Hayes started the engine. I stood waving to my handsome, smiling American friends. The rear door suddenly flew open and Kathy, who had until then stayed on the sidelines, ran toward me. She shoved into my hand a tiny crumpled envelope and just as quickly turned and sped back to her seat.

When their car drove away I unwrapped her gift. Inside the little pink wrapper was a note and a small locket. The locket's left side held a faded miniature picture of the Virgin Mary; on the right side was Kathy's radiant young face. The note read, "You don't have to write or anything but please keep this locket with you. My grandmother gave it to me and I want to give it to you. She told me that as long as I carried it with me I would be protected from anything bad. I just know it will work for you too."

Her gesture touched me deeply and I stood motionless, reading the note again and again in an effort to understand her young mind. Finally I folded it, placed it carefully inside my billfold, and then unhooked the gold chain which held my baptismal medallion around my neck and threaded it through the loop of the locket. And so the medallion and the locket dangled together and kissed against my chest.

Just ten days after the Hayeses' visit I flew from San Francisco to Newark, New Jersey.

During the flight, I wrote a lengthy letter to my childhood friend Stavros, explaining that the time had come to pursue and fulfill the sacred vow he and I had made when we clasped our young bloodied hands over the body of my father years before.

PART II

THE CHASE

5

THE YEARS
OF COGNIZANCE

amp Kilmer in New Jersey reminded me of Fort Ord, with its
two-story barracks of clapboard, its movie theater, chapel, mess
hall, and enlisted-men's club.

All of us GIs destined for overseas duty lay around bored, talking,
reading, writing letters, marking off our calendars the few remaining
days until the ship's departure. On the Saturday before embarkation,
we attended a customary bash at the enlisted-men's club.

The large hall was decorated with colorful banners and flags. Smiling lasses from Newark came, bussed over for the fun and dancing. As
the live band played tune after tune into the early hours of morning,
many couples paired off, held hands, and appeared to be deeply in
love, whispering promises of lasting devotion.

At last, the musicians put their instruments to sleep. The women,
unmolested but desired, took their seats inside the busses giggling and
murmuring among themselves, while their soft arms dangled from
open windows to touch some lonesome GI's hand for a few more precious moments.

But when the drivers revved up their noisy machines, shifted the
gears and slowly started to roll away with their festive cargo, the men
became fidgety, as their pleasant dreams began to drift away like a
string of loose balloons.

Two nights later, nearly two thousand of us boarded a troop carrier docked at Hoboken and, under the glittering lights of magical Manhattan Island, we slid slowly down the Hudson River and gradually picked up full steam east toward Europe.

The voyage was rough but uneventful, and after seven days at sea we disembarked in Bremerhaven. I was bussed to the railroad station and placed on a fast train heading southwest, first to Frankfurt and then to Idar-Oberstein, my final destination.

It was an all-night ride. The few Germans I encountered seemed somber, unsmiling, and poorly dressed. An indescribable gratification tickled me through and through as I tossed scornful glances at the ravaged remnants of the great Aryan race, those people who only a short time ago believed it was their birthright to devastate the world and become its master. Now, having succumbed to the twists and turns of fate, the conquered dogs appeared to have tucked their tails between their hind legs and, filled with bitterness, resigned themselves to their humiliations. Their once-frightening bark I remembered so well had turned into subdued whimpering—a subservient wail.

Idar-Oberstein was comprised of two unpretentious villages built inside a ravine connected by a paved road. Halfway through the mountains the train stopped briefly in Idar, where a dozen of us GIs got off; a waiting military truck took us to the base.

Our post consisted of numerous freshly-painted concrete buildings with red tile roofs, set on high ground overlooking the two towns. The truck driver stopped in front of one massive structure with a plaque reading "522nd Company." I tossed my duffel bag out onto the sidewalk and sprang over the gate.

A glass door led into an impressive hallway with an intricate border of mosaic tile. I climbed wide marble stairs and followed a corridor to the company orderly. Saluting, I passed my orders to a blond soldier, with one sardine on his sleeves, who sat toying with a typewriter. He handed them to a fierce-looking, black giant nearby, a master sergeant. The sergeant grunted and grinned when he inspected my papers. With a twinkle of amusement he said, "Follow me, soldier," and led me through an open door into the adjacent office.

In a bright corner room, where two large windows looked out to a forested hillside, behind a long brown desk, sat a stern man in his early thirties who wore the gold bars of a captain; I realized I was facing my new company commander.

I froze and snapped to attention like a proper soldier. The sergeant spoke with an authoritative voice, his upper lip twisting in a grin.

"Captain Karas, Sir, you may find this new arrival interesting. This is Private . . . ," here he stuttered and coughed and made three attempts to pronounce my last name before he gave up and I took over. Upon hearing my complicated surname the captain looked a bit puzzled, then his face broke into a pleasant query and he stood up. He was tall and fit, tanned and immaculate, and he had a spiffy black mustache. His black eyes shone as he walked around his desk and, to my astonishment, extended his arm, offered me a handshake, and asked me to sit. Unable to make heads or tails of the show as it was unfolding, I took one of the four available chairs. He sat next to me and asked, *"Ti kanis?"* which means "How are you?" in common Greek.

As if I were a preprogrammed machine, I replied, *"Kala, efharisto"* ("Fine, thanks"), and then he opened up to me. He was a second-generation Greek American who had grown up in Brooklyn; Karas had been shortened from Karavelakis, a Cretan name. Both his father and mother had come from Kalyves (Shacks), a waterfront village on the shore of Souda Bay in the northwestern part of the island. His parents, two brothers, and two sisters were still slaving away in the family bakery in Brooklyn, and he, being the oldest and most courageous, had managed to break away from his well-meaning but strict father. In 1941, immediately upon his graduation from West Point, because of his fluency in Greek, he had been dispatched to Chania. There he lived among Cretans and organized gendarmes, and had fought against the Germans alongside the resistance and allied troops, until the fall of the island. In May of 1942, days before the total loss of Crete, he and many others were evacuated by a British destroyer and ended up in Egypt.

Casually, he inquired about my background and schooling, and at the conclusion of the pleasant chat he told me his first name was Manny, for Manolis, and offered me the job of assistant company clerk, which I readily accepted. When we parted, I again snapped to attention and gave him a most respectful salute before he ordered the company clerk to take me under his wing, show me around the base, and outline my duties.

Later that day I found an empty, narrow, windowless room on the first floor of our building and, with the permission of the agreeable master sergeant, I moved a bunk bed, a foot locker, a small desk, and a chair into the tiny space and made it my home.

Before sleep took me that night, my fingers touched Kathy's tiny locket. Sweet thoughts traveled over mountains, oceans, highlands, and valleys until my mind's eye recaptured that brief moment when she hurried to hand me her good luck charm, a novel, selfless expression of her feelings. I threw her a grateful kiss hoping that somehow it would shoot through space to find its target, because, so far at least, the locket had emerged as a faithful genie laboring for my welfare.

The base was well laid out, originally constructed for German military officers, I was told. To my surprise, all the menial work was done by German women who staffed the mess hall, did all the cooking and serving, the laundry and pressing, and worked as sales clerks in the Post Exchange and attendants for the clubs and the theater.

The scarcity of local men was obvious. The *frauleins* who worked inside the post—practically all in their early twenties—were well-rounded, coquettish, and they appeared very willing, if the right GI came along to strike their fancy.

My work consisted of typing reports and running errands. Soon, I made many friends and everyone called me "Greek." After work I kept my mind busy shooting pool, reading, playing my harmonica and going to the movies.

The development of camaraderie among men in the Armed Forces is as indispensable as a flowing river to a mill's grinding stones. Out of all the personal alliances with which a GI encircles himself, one man usually becomes his special companion, his buddy and confidant, the one he trusts the most and upon whose support he can count under almost any circumstance.

It was on a cold evening in late November that chance brought Climpt and me together. I was practicing pocket pool shots alone, using one of the two tables available in the company recreation room.

The crowd was sparse, and this guy, a private I had seen before, was sitting alone by the wall watching me with interest. I had noticed him because he resembled a big ape more than a human. I was working the table, undisturbed, doing my thing, when two black soldiers dressed in civvies, with a spring in their step and chewing on big cigars, strolled in. The taller of the two tossed about a cocky stare and said in a very loud voice that he was looking for the Greek, some motherfucker who was supposed to be a pretty mean stick.

When our eyes met, I said I was the Greek. The dude puffed two clouds of smoke in the air, said his name was Jackson, and asked me if I would be interested in shooting a few games of eight ball.

"Sure," I said with a welcoming smile. Then he tossed his buddy a swift sly smirk, a sneer at my expense.

"For a few bucks a game, maybe?" he added.

"I don't shoot pool for money."

Jackson laughed contemptuously. "You're a yellow chickenshit motherfucker if you won't shoot me one game, for five bucks!"

My pride was wounded. "You're on! One game for five bucks."

Jackson broke first and ran four even balls before my turn came. I sank all the odd ones and the eight ball, and the game was over.

"You's motherfuckin' baaad," Jackson said. "One moah game, double or nothin'."

"I told you I don't play for money."

"Cause you know you can't do it twice?"

The adrenaline was flowing inside me. I was mad and wanted to kick his ass.

By the end of the next hour, Jackson had lost every game and owed me forty bucks. We were into our last game at eighty bucks or nothing. I had already sunk all the odd balls, so my next shot was the eight ball and it was smack in front of a corner pocket. My training back in Athens had been in billiards. By now the room was packed with lookers, the perfect climate to show off my superior stick. I told Jackson, in a loud voice, that I would sink the eight ball in the corner pocket with a three-cushion shot (instead of the easy straight shot which would have won the game, as well as the eighty bucks).

Everyone snickered in disbelief, most of all Jackson. "Go ahead and fuckin' do it, Big Stick." I prepared my stance and made my shot in total confidence. The cue ball was propelled from the tip of the stick with just the right English, traveled slowly around the table, and nicked the eight ball just enough to force it to slide into the pocket. I became an instant hero.

But while I drank the joy of the applause and the congratulations of the surrounding crowd, I noticed Jackson, sweating like a skinned porkie hanging over some sizzling coals, edging toward the door, intending to sneak out of the room along with his pal. But the door was totally blocked by the extended, strong, long arms of the gorilla guy. When I walked toward the soggy Jackson, in the midst of the commotion I could hear the private growling as he laid down the law.

"Jackson, cough up tha bread ya owe tha Greek fair an' square."

"Git outta my way, ya motherfucker ape," Jackson mouthed off. "I been hustled and I got no mind to pay up to no motherfuckin' Greek. 'Sides I only got me a ten and I ain't about to part with my last bread, the ten I got."

"I'll take the ten," I said, grabbing him by the arm.

Jackson stared at me, glanced at his pal, then took in the mob of soldiers from my company who had gathered around. He eyed his exit, shut off by the gorilla-private, then hesitantly reached into his pocket and took out a crumpled, moist, ten-dollar script note. I snatched it with disgust and retreated.

"Let them go," I said. The private dropped his arms and bashfully bent his head as he walked back toward his seat. I hurried after him to offer my hand for a shake.

"Thanks. My name is Yiannis, but everyone calls me Greek." He mentioned something, maybe his own name, but it went unregistered. Then he grunted, viewing me in a shy way.

"Shit, Greek, I hain't nevah seed no pool shot lak' that afore." He plucked up some courage and a wry smile. "Ya shoah done it good on that fancy-stepper coon Jackson. Ya made that fuckin' nigger sweat til he stunk lak' an ole bayou skunk." His honest eyes were pale, almost yellow. He was a loner. I had noticed his narrow forehead, flat nose, and harelip scar before.

"Collecting even a ten calls for a celebration." I asked him to join me for a beer and his dull eyes lit up as he readily accepted. We walked the one block to the club. The place was almost empty. I bought two Lowenbraus from the heavy-set German woman tending bar.

We sat at a small round table where, after sticking the bottle in his mouth and swigging down a big drink, he wiped his mouth on his sleeve and spoke first.

"Ya put it on 'm lak Grammaw's lye soap wouldn't get it off. That Jackson nigger needed a lesson an' ya shoah given'm a dandy one," he said, shaking his hairy head with approval. "Climpt Cook's ma full name an' I's an orphan, raise ba ma granny, me an' ma brothahs an' sistahs."

He looked at the floor and seemed uptight and preoccupied with shyness. He stuck his right index finger deep inside his right nostril, his face bent some to accommodate the probing.

"I joint up soon I come sixteen—lied 'bout ma age. Got tha fuck outta tha red clay o' Georgia an' all tha misery and fuckin' niggers. Ya hear?

"Ma ole man wadden much good, drunk an' mean all tha while I knowed 'm. He guzzlt tha darn whiskey lak' a hog after Sunday slop, an' whuppt ma mamma an' us kids sometim' shameful. Wall . . . tha likker taken 'm ta his last rest early."

Climpt twisted in his seat some and went on. "Ma momma wuz kinda sickly an' frail, an' sharecroppin' fer ole man Tompkins 'bout done 'er in, spittin' hern guts out, coughin' blood an' all, when she come home frum them fields. Wuz a goner long afore hern time, too." Unemotionally he took another swig.

I studied this Neanderthal in military clothing. He took another healthy swallow from the half-empty bottle, his face twitched, his shoulders drooped more, and he became pale and rigid as if he were about to pass out from pain.

"Fellers 'roun here don' talk ta me none," he stopped for a half-breath and half-sigh, "acuze I hain't smart an' all." He kept staring down and around like a carpenter examining the wooden floor for defects. After a long pause, in a whisper that seemed to come from the depths of his twisted gut, he added, "But I shoah 'preciate yer pool shootin' an' all that stuff." Then a heart-wrenching plea came out in the same hushed tone, "An' I kinda wanna be yer pal, if ya don' blame me fer axin'.""

I felt for this creature in his plight. Why is the world so mean to some and so good to others? That question had preoccupied me for many years. This miserable man who sat before me ached to be accepted. This creation of parents who couldn't have provided for a dog, let alone a slew of children, had crawled to me and extended his cup for a handout of tolerance. With fear and shame he was appealing for a chance to call someone his friend.

I spoke quickly to pacify his soul. "It'll be an ..." I began, but he interrupted me before I had a chance to tell him that, stretching the truth some, it would be an honor to accept him as a buddy.

"See, Greek, I appear kinda mean on accoun' o' ma bad lip an' all, but deep down 'nside me I got me ... I got me a good gut." His head was bowed as if in confession. "An' I hain't got nobody ta call me ma pal on accoun' all them fellers takin' me fer ugly an' dumb as a stump, I reckon." He let out a sigh, deep and soulful, while he played with his bottle. I sprang up, choking from a strange emotion.

"I'll get us another round," I blurted and rushed to the bar, needing a reprieve from his touching divulgence. I returned as soon as I regained my composure.

"I hain't fosterin' no bad feelins fer all them GI assholes, though, 'xeptin' o' course ..."—suddenly Climpt raised his ugly head and a meanness shone in his yellow eyes—" ... 'xeptin' all them shiffless niggers." His meanness grew. "Them's a bunch o' no-good cocksuckers, them niggers is, jist lak' that Jackson prick, an' I hold no goodness fer tha likes." He spat on the floor and his harelip twitched with disgust.

I knew something of American history, about the Civil War and the ongoing racial animosities, and it had always seemed to me the Negroes had more reason to hate the whites than the other way around. Climpt's hatred for Negroes made no sense to me, particularly since he himself was the product of deprived beginnings.

"I will be your friend, Climpt," I said. "But I have to ask, have Negroes done something terrible to you?"

"Lookahere Greek," he said matter-of-factly. "Down tha deep south where I's frum all right-thinkin' white folks hate all them jungle bunnies." He scratched his head furiously. "See, down 'n Georgia, white folks jist hain't got no patience fer them monkeys acuze they's a bunch o' motherfuckin' spooks—thass why we don' lak'm—acuze they's a bunch o' motherfuckin' niggers. Can ya unnerstan that, Greek?"

I stood up.

"Yeah," I told him, "but I don't think it's right. Not every Negro is like Jackson, Climpt. There are a lot of Negroes who are as decent as you are. They may be black but they have decency and goodness in their hearts, just like you have decency and goodness inside yours. Do you understand?"

We started back to the barracks in silence. The dark air was cold and a slice of the moon peeked from the partly clouded sky. The road was deserted, and when we came upon a steel lamppost Climpt gave it a fierce kick.

"Darn it Greek, fer shoah yer gittin' ma ass all fuckt up. Fist ya fuck up Jackson with yern fancy stick, an' now ya fuck up me with yern, here, preachin 'bout how sorghum molasses them motherfuckin' niggers coulda been." He was thinking hard. "Seem rightful ta me ya shouda been a preacher. Yessireee, I says, ya shouda been a preacher, a' right." We both smiled and said nothing, and when we were about to separate, his face seemed to reflect a peculiar serenity as he uttered his parting words.

"Needta doze off on what ya jist layed on me 'bout them motherfuckin' niggers. Okay, ma frien'?"

The anniversary of my father's death was approaching and, as in years past, around that time I withdrew inside myself. One day Captain Karas noted something was wrong so I asked if I could speak with him.

Once inside his office, I closed the door behind me, and while he remained standing by one of the large windows I poured out my feelings and told him in detail my recollections of the Kalavryta crime. At some point, I failed in my efforts to remain composed and I cried. I could see he was moved. At long last, I found the courage to ask him whether he knew someone who could help me in my pursuit of Tenner. The captain smiled encouragingly.

"My buddy Captain Rosenburg should be able to help."

"Who is this Captain, Sir?"

"Herb was my roommate at West Point. Now he is here in Germany with the Army Counter-Intelligence."

"How can I find him, Sir?"

"He is stationed in Heidelberg. Herb will help, I'm sure, not only because he is my buddy but, since he is Jewish, I know he harbors as strong a hatred for Nazis as you do."

"I hope Tenner has been tried and hanged, but if he hasn't, I want to find him," I said, my voice full of loathing.

"I share your hope, soldier."

"Should I take the train to Heidelberg to talk to Captain Rosenburg? I would rather see him in person."

"Herb and I get together the third weekend of every month. What is left of Heidelberg is still beautiful and certainly more interesting than these small villages around here. So I usually drive over there. It's a pleasant trip, a two- to three-hour drive. Many places to visit, more things to see and do down in Heidelberg." His black eyes shined and winked. "And lots of pretty *frauleins.*" He took a breath and observed me with some compassion. "How about riding with me on my next trip? In about a week from now. Think it over."

My good fortune was on a roll. I snapped to attention, gave him my best salute, and stood stiff like a statue.

"Thank you, Siiiiiiiiiir!" I shouted, and with a smart about-face I left the room.

A little red MG convertible swung around the corner, and Captain Karas motioned to me to get in. The weak winter sun was fading and the afternoon was cold. Under the expert handling of the captain, the four-cylinder engine hummed and purred as we climbed snow-covered mountains and swept through manicured valleys and quaint villages. Karas remained engrossed with his driving, and the muffler's loud throbbing prevented communication.

At dusk, after a leisurely jaunt, the captain edged his roadster next to the curb of a wide road and killed the engine. The sidewalk on my right followed a contour bluff that overlooked the dark waters of the broad river below. I crawled out of the confining space, stretched the muscles of my lower back, took in a deep breath of the chilly air, and exhaled steam.

Frail moonbeams filtered through snow-covered trees and bushes, casting shadows over scattered rooftops of the ancient houses below, which bore the punishment of the heavy snow with a stoic shrug. And just like a painter whose eye is seized by some wondrous tableau and who hungrily takes out his brush to promptly capture it on canvas, I marveled until the booming voice of Captain Karas startled me.

"Hurry up. Get your bag, and let's get going, soldier."

Throwing my knapsack over my shoulder, I followed him across the road. He unbolted the right half of a large arched iron gate and pushed it open. We climbed a moderately steep brick walkway which led to the broad staircase of a massive three-story brick mansion on whose facade ivy grew strong. The large windows of the main floor were illuminated with subdued amber light, and silhouettes played against the glass like in a shadow show.

As if an invisible eye had been monitoring our arrival, the heavy wooden door swung open the instant we reached it. We stood face to face with a tall man who wore a butler's mien and a black patch on his left eye, partly hiding a huge scar.

"Velcome, Captain Karas," he growled, taking our sacks while simultaneously handing each of us a business card with bold lettering scribbled on the back.

"Accommodations have been chosen by ze Baroness herself—ze captain vill be occupying ze lovely Baden-Baden suite, vile ze young man has been assigned ze cheerful Garmisch room. Ze names of rooms are on ze cards."

Through a short entryway we were ushered into a formal white-walled salon with an impressive chandelier. Both of us wore warm civilian clothes; the captain had on a sleek double-breasted, gray flannel suit, and I a pair of black slacks with a heavy gray woolen coat. Even though neither my pocketbook nor my rank matched that of my captain, at least I felt at ease that my appearance wouldn't cause him any embarrassment.

A matronly woman with an oval face and high cheekbones hurried toward us. Her silver hair was combed into a bun atop her head and braced with a gem-encrusted ebony crown; her long black jersey dress hugged her bouncy corseted hips, and she spoke in fluent English.

"Oh, my, my, Captain Karas. One of my most dear American friends. What a joy to have you with us again after so many months. At least four, or longer perhaps?" She raised a jeweled hand and pointed her finger. "I will scold you for staying away for so long, you naughty boy."

Captain Karas beamed.

"A delight to see you again, my respected Baroness." He bowed, took her hand into his, and kissed it.

"May I present my young cousin, Yiannis, who was reared in Greece and now resides in the most charming city in the world—San Francisco—second to Heidelberg, of course."

Unprepared to be presented in a ceremonial fashion to a lady of nobility in the midst of such an elegant setting, but taking my cue from my captain, I bowed deeply, pecked the Baroness' plump offered hand with the tip of my nose, and in a soft whisper expressed my gratitude at having had the fortune to meet her excellency.

The champagne was flowing as if the Baroness had arranged a direct hookup to the Moët et Chandon Winery, and all the guests, numbering about forty and equally divided in gender, seemed jovial. A few twinkled from light intoxication, I thought.

Captain Karas steered me toward a white sofa where a good-looking man with dark hair, large brown eyes, and eyeglasses sat wedged between two alluring young blond women. They were laughing heartily at his jabbering.

"Herb, this is Yiannis. I told you about him on the phone." With only that brief introduction I was left standing in front of Captain Rosenburg; my captain sped off to join a lovely creature costumed in a purple sequined evening dress. She kept tossing flirtatious glances in his direction as she sparkled and swayed like a graceful poplar tree in a light breeze.

Captain Rosenburg blinked only a flicker of interest, but waved me to an overstuffed chair nearby. He spoke in German, while both his long-gowned companions, their velvety cleavages daringly displayed, listened intently, giggling while they leaned against his broad chest.

Then, as if performing a well-rehearsed comical act, Captain Rosenburg pulled off his glasses, bobbed his fingers, rubbed the hump on his nose, and smacked his lips until the ladies bent to his face, choking with laughter.

I took in the festive climate of the refined space, waiting hopefully for the captain's slightest acknowledgment. At some point, maybe an hour after my arrival, the one-eyed butler emerged, sounded a gong, and proclaimed that dinner was served. The guests began to drift toward a large doorway. Uneasiness had crawled up my spine. Captain Rosenburg, well over six feet, stood up and unfolded his long, lean frame. I sprang up to attention. He drew close to me and brought his long arm down like a sledgehammer across my shoulders, then winked and whispered in my ear, "Tonight we have fun, tomorrow we talk. Loosen up, soldier." Then he shoved me to the front.

The shorter of his two lady friends came up next to me and with a casual move wove her arm through mine. In flawed English she told me I looked like a Frenchman, and asked if I were one.

We followed the smartly dressed crowd into a dimly lit mahogany-paneled dining room. The Baroness occupied the head of the longest dinner table I had ever seen, decorated from end to end with flaming silver candelabras and pink gardenias floating in crystal bowls. She sat

erect below the portrait of a uniformed, pale, serious but kindly-look-
ing man whose embroidered epaulets, shoulder patches, and breast
decorations were enough to fill half a dozen display cases in a military museum. Her ornate gold-leafed armchair of grand proportions
resembled a throne. To my astonishment, Captain Karas occupied the
honored position on her right, while his own right side was embell-
ished by that gorgeous lady with the swaying hips.

Rediscovering Captain Karas' whereabouts brought me a sense of
relief; he and his engaging companion had disappeared for a long time.
When his glance met mine, he winked and I saw his lips move before
the Baroness turned in my direction. Her eyes studied me in a most
motherly way.

Middle-aged female servers, in black dresses and sparkling white
aprons, brought us hot dishes of game and ham in thick brown gravies,
potatoes, steaming red cabbage and yellow rice, cheeses and breads.

When I was preparing to plunge into the foods carefully arranged
on a large gold-trimmed plate, anxious to introduce my taste buds to
the finest of German cuisine, the Baroness raised her crystal champagne glass and cleared her throat.

"May all of you, my dearest friends, who have gathered here to be
with us on this lovely evening, live a long, healthy, and prosperous life,
so that you may return again and again to sample my most delectable
treats." Her closing words carried a hint of mysterious giggle.

At once, as if the behinds of the seated had been zapped with a
powerful electrical jolt, all sprang up and lifted high their full glasses.
By now having accepted a state of obedience, I followed suit, and in
unison we all shouted, "Long live our Baroness." The Baroness' eyes
gleamed and Captain Karas, standing tall and wearing the same little
smirk beneath his fancy mustache, tipped his glass to me from across
the remarkable table in a private salutation.

I was seated between Sofia, whom I had escorted into the dining
room, and Camille, a very young and thin redhead with a long freckled face and hollow, gray, dreamy eyes.

Soft music filtered from the adjacent room and couples often abandoned their seats and disappeared; their absence was noticeably long,
at least to me, but they eventually returned and, even though I calcu-

lated it to be a strange and disrespectful practice, the Baroness did not seem to take offense.

I chatted with Camille, who spoke English as well as I, and she casually mentioned she was the Baroness' distant niece. When she proposed a dance, I declined and saw her subdue a flicker of puzzlement, but we kept talking and she told me all about her gymnasium classes and her aspirations to become a physician.

The champagne progressively drugged me while the background music seemed to pick up tempo. Camille's chitchat turned inaudible. I rose and excused myself. With bleary vision and a silly face, I strolled through the opening, ignoring the trio of musicians and the waltzing crowd. I hiked up the curved stairway and found a brass plaque on one of the baroque doors which read "Garmisch," pushed it open, slammed it shut behind me and fell like a sack of Greek dry beans onto the fancy soft bed, and passed out cold.

I came to from a deep sleep when I felt someone unbuckling the belt of my slacks. I vaulted up, ready to do battle with the intruder. I heard a giggle, and then I saw Camille standing in the gentle glow that flickered from a small pink lamp. Her bare breasts were no bigger than lemon halves, and dressed only in her white panties she pretended to want to hide her skinny nakedness as she jumped into my bed and under the fluffy quilt.

Needing the reassurance that what confronted me was real and not some well-executed mirror trick, I said, "Camille!"

"Yes."

"Camille, what are you doing in my room?"

Her head popped out from under the yellow cover and, sparkling, she studied me up and down while I remained confused and still.

"I came to keep you warm. Be nice to you," she teased in a kind of baffled voice.

Something didn't seem to jell. Had I become so terribly irresistible? Such a notion flashed through my dazed mind, but I dismissed it at once. Why should the niece of the respected Baroness take the risk of being seen sneaking into my room, sacrificing her reputation, and most probably an immaculate upbringing, just to make some U.S. Army private happy?

I bit my lips and shook my head, weaving back and forth on my feet, and Camille stopped jesting and asked, "You mean you don't know? Your Captain never told you?"

"Told me what?" I asked impatiently.

"Oh, poor child," she said, as if I were her innocent little brother in need of his big sister's compassionate explanation. "I just don't know where to begin."

Her eyes lost their playfulness and she paused, undecided about her next move. "Oh, Yiannis, for God's sake, don't stand there and tell me you have no idea at all that you have been spending your night in a . . . " She stared at me, her freckled face shining with disbelief. I must have looked pitiful because Camille mellowed and became almost benevolent.

"Well, look. It's like this. The Baroness, who is not a real baroness, has been running a fine house, you know, a bordello, for the past thirty-some years and my auntie, who isn't my auntie exactly, is the classiest madam in Germany. Her clients have been the biggest shots in Germany, and maybe the whole world. During the war even Hitler and many of his officers were entertained by the Baroness."

I was astounded but I hid it and instead cracked a grin. I only hoped the delivery of my next message could be serious and to the point.

"Captain Karas has played a trick on me." I needed a deep breath and I took one. "I'm only here because he promised to introduce me to Captain Rosenburg—I have important business with him."

"But your captain has paid us for your stay here," Camille protested, "and I'm ready to give myself to you and make you happy and . . . "

Her voice was lighthearted. She lifted the edge of the quilt and shook it in an inviting motion, revealing her nude, lanky upper body.

I was not in the mood for mating games. Tarnishing my lofty purpose by participating in a cheap overnight affair with this young German prostitute seemed inappropriate to me. Besides, even though I had made no promises, Kathy's genie had bewitched me, and I seemed to be spending much of my spare time thinking of her. Never did I go to sleep at night before reading her sweet note—except tonight, of course.

"Camille, you must go," I commanded.

"Oh! You don't find me attractive," she said, pretending to be hurt.

"It isn't that at all. I'm just not in the mood. There are too many things inside my head right now."

She viewed me queerly.

"Even though I'm young, I'm very good."

"Maybe some other time."

"You are a strange soldier, Yiannis," she said as she shrugged her shoulders. With a resigned motion she slipped from the coziness of the quilt, and, showing only a trace of pain from such an unexpected rejection, she draped her dress over her shoulders, picked up her shoes, and slid out of my room.

A soft knock on the door awakened me. I answered by squinting through the crack, and the one-eyed butler who seemed forever present handed me a folded note.

> *Yiannis, at ten o'clock be ready to be escorted to the Baroness' quar-*
> *ters. Captain Rosenburg and I will be there waiting for you. I hope*
> *you enjoyed the surprise.*
>
> *Your cousin, Manny*

At five minutes before the hour the same soft tap sounded. I grabbed my notebook and pen and silently followed the butler. We climbed a flight of steep stairs until we came upon a strong, solid wooden door which he tapped three times. The mellow voice of the Baroness asked us to proceed. The room was decorated in soft pastel colors, with thick embroidered curtains. On an oversized canopied bed the phony lady of nobility sat propped up on a sea of satin pillows.

"Come, come. Sit with us, young man," she said encouragingly, pointing toward a table covered with a starched pink cloth where captains Karas and Rosenburg sat sipping their morning coffees, clean-shaven but ashen-faced, obviously spent from their all-night activities.

Cheeses and meat cold cuts, crackers, marmalades, colored breads, slices of fresh fruits, and boiled eggs were arranged on platters on the table, and a large tray with similar goodies had been placed over the Baroness' lap; she looked bright-eyed, her powdered face cheerful and her hair hidden inside a decorated bonnet.

Both captains remained stone-faced, but the Baroness narrowed her eyes and spoke when I took a seat.

"Young man, Captain Karas has explained your situation to Captain Rosenburg and me, and we are indeed very sympathetic toward your quest." She took her time and threw her head back and a shadow fell over her. "However, I must encourage you to reconsider your vows. Your dedication to seek justice for the cruel death of your dear father is most honorable but from where I sit, naïve." She shuffled herself a bit and rearranged a pillow. "My optimistic young fellow, what makes you think that a lone GI will have a chance to locate Tenner? Nazis with pasts like his aren't easy to find. This is a Herculean task and your means are, forgive me for my assumption, very limited. The efforts of the allied governments with their inexhaustible resources have often failed." She brought her cup to her lips, took a sip, and then her voice slipped into a divine delivery.

"I know you came here for help but I'm going to offer you advice. Why not place this vengeance you have in your heart into God's hands and go on and enjoy your life? This Commandant Tenner you wish to chase is an extremely dangerous man."

As I listened my mind was racing. Who was this fake baroness, this madam who had gained the confidence of Captain Karas, and Captain Rosenburg too? If Camille was truthful in saying that her bordello had been patronized by the Nazi elite, why should the Baroness be willing to help me dig up the trail of someone who in the past may have been her comrade? I felt the urge to defend what appeared as a futile pursuit. My voice was soft and a bit trembling.

"On the thirteenth of December in 1943, my father and a thousand other helpless civilians were killed by a Nazi assassin. My father was a good man who loved his family and God, and his soul was filled with reverence for all living things. Every late spring, when the swallows returned to build their nests under the balcony of our home, he took his guitar and sang a simple serenade he had composed, welcoming the tiny creatures back."

There was silence. I watched three faces wrinkle as I revealed the deep admiration I fostered for the man whose genes I carried. I went on.

"This much is clear to me. Tenner has to be found and punished. He is cunning, elusive, and dangerous, and he mustn't be allowed to roam free. Besides, I believe that a crime committed on this earth must be punished here."

Captain Rosenburg glanced first at the Baroness, then at his friend, and finally at me. "I'm moved by your determination and commitment. I may have to step on some toes, but you can count on my help, soldier."

The Baroness gave a passing look at my two superiors and her eyes rested on mine. With a piercing stare, she strove to measure the quantity of steel in my heart.

"You'll be making an assault on Mount Blanc during a winter storm without snow shoes or insulated clothing, young fellow," she whispered hypnotically, as if she were reconsidering her thoughts.

"I must try."

For a few moments silence shadowed the elegant boudoir of that lady of enigma and riddle. Then her face brightened, and she spoke with the authority of a genuine baroness addressing her court.

"All right, then, let us begin. We know there are many war criminals who have been accused of inflicting revolting atrocities on the civilian populations in the Balkans, and particularly in Greece. Almost all of those who were tried by the Americans have been given a mere slap on the wrist. A whole roster of generals—Wilhelm List, Wilhelm Speidel, Hubert Lanz, Helmut Felmy—are already out of prison, either paroled because of failing health or because their sentences were reduced by the clemency board."

The Baroness stopped, her eyes darkened. Was she perturbed by the failure of justice?

"However," she went on, "there are others—General Karl Le Suire, the ruthless commander of the 117 Jaeger Division, the killer and torcher of Peloponnesus, and Colonel Hans Tenner—still at large. I entertained both these deranged executioners—that is how I remember their names. Not until much later did I discover their infamous past."

She gulped down a small glass of tomato juice and her mouth twitched. She frowned as if she had swallowed distasteful medicine. When she was done patting her red lips with her napkin, she continued.

"Sources have informed me that Tenner and Le Suire, along with many other killers, were smuggled out of Europe through Rome or

Genoa. Bishop Hudal, the Vatican 'Spiritual leader of the German people in Italy,' and Father Draganovic, the Secretary of the Croatian Confraternity of the College of San Girolamo, were very active in Nazi-smuggling. Reliable confidential connections have revealed to me that wanted mass murderers were given underground asylum by the Archbishop Andreas Rohracher of Salzburg, a longtime active Nazi sympathizer who placed the power of the Catholic Church at the disposal of any Fascist criminals who needed escape."

Admiration for this well-informed woman gradually won me over as I listened and sipped her strong coffee.

"It's no longer a secret, as Captain Rosenburg will vouch, that many Nazi killers stayed in hiding in Salzburg until about the end of 1945. Through the Church's elaborate channels, often dressed as Catholic priests, they obtained temporary shelter in Croatia, where they were given false identity cards. Bishop Hudal had access to Caritas International, a Catholic charity which provided travel money and general assistance to refugees. The Croatian priest, Father Draganovic, as the representative at the Vatican of the dreadful Croatian Ustashi, was very well connected with the Holy See. With the approval of the Pontifical Welfare Commission for Refugees in Rome, it became easy for these respected men of the cloth to obtain passports from the International Red Cross for refugees who claimed they lost their identification papers. Under the pretext the Church was offering a humanitarian hand to downtrodden refugees, the Church knowingly provided aliases, false nationalities, and cash to Nazi fugitives and helped them board freighters destined for the Americas."

Quickly I scribbled notes—Bishop Hudal, San Girolamo, Rome, Father Draganovic, International Red Cross.

"But why the Catholic Church?" I asked. "Why would it help such men escape justice?"

Captain Rosenburg spoke up. "Self-preservation. Survival. The Pope and his priests were horrified of Stalin. They feared that communism might spread throughout Europe. They calculated these escaped Nazi criminals would come in handy as recruits to fight the Reds if and when such a time ever came."

Captain Karas, who was listening quietly till then, cleared his throat.

"It's feasible then that this guy Tenner may be selling automobiles in America under an assumed name the Holy See has handed him."

"Let's talk about particulars, not generalities," said Captain Rosenburg, with the air of a professional. "Let's assume that Tenner is out of Europe. The chances that he has left a trail are high. No one has managed to vanish without leaving a mark somewhere. When the pursuer is indefatigable and relentless, a clue will eventually pop up and then other bits will follow, until eventually all the pieces of the puzzle come together." He rubbed his tired eyes from under his spectacles, turned to me, and continued. "I am committing myself to help you, as I said earlier. Perhaps the Baroness will make her resources available to us in our efforts to pick up this guy's scent. However, soldier, I want to make absolutely clear that the moment we pick up this fucker's trail ..."

The Baroness' nose quivered upon the delivery of such an offensive epithet, and she hurriedly picked up a giant white rose that decorated her tray and brought it up to her nostrils to hide a grimace of disapproval.

" ... the ball game will be left totally in your hands."

"I understand, and I wouldn't want it any other way," I said, and thanked them for their assistance.

The three of us stood up and offered our gratitude to our hostess for her ever-gracious hospitality.

As my captain and I were preparing to board the MG for our return to Idar-Oberstein, Captain Rosenburg strutted down the stairs of the bordello and intercepted us. I took the liberty of shaking his huge hand and thanked him for his help once again. Then I asked how the Baroness had entered into the intelligence game.

"It's a captivating tale." He smiled. "Someday she might reveal her story to you. She does disclose her past on rare occasions. One thing I can tell you with confidence. The woman has the memory of an elephant. She was one of the most resourceful agents we had during the war."

One Sunday morning in January, I was drifting around and in and out of the orderly room with little to do. The Holy Book sat on the master sergeant's desk as it did always. Out of boredom I flipped it open and began reading from the 82nd Psalm:

> *God stands up to open Heaven's court. He pronounces judgment on the judges. How long will you judges refuse to listen to the evidence? How long will you shower special favors on the wicked?*

The phone rang. When I picked up the receiver I instantly recognized Captain Rosenburg's voice.

"Are you alone? Can you talk without someone listening?"

"Yes, Sir."

"I went into our file rooms in the basement, where all our top-secret records are kept—copies mostly, you understand—and guess what! There is a folder on Commandant Tenner all right, but inside I found zilch, nada, nothing! An absolute mystery! Looks like someone who works for us took out all the guts and left us the cover. To get to these files a guy has got to have top clearance!"

"Somebody stole Tenner's file? I don't bel ... "

"Can you imagine how I felt, standing there with just the damn folder in my hands? Like that one time I was taking this fraulein in for interrogation. She was kinda cute and came on to me like gangbusters; so I made a stop at a hotel for a fast bang. She half undressed, then excused herself to go to the john and took a powder through the bathroom window and I was left there with her goddamn dress." For a Captain, Rosenburg was unpretentious and I liked him.

"Only Americans have access to these files, Sir?" I asked. Either he didn't hear me or ignored my question and went on.

"It smells; like someone has an interest in wiping this guy Tenner off the surface of the earth. So I get pissed, and I call Nuremberg, where all the main archives are kept and—get hold of this, Greek—they give me the run-around, like I'm some two-bit Chicago punk! When I finally get up the ladder to a major, he barks at me that strict orders have come down from the Congress of the United States; that anyone asking for any information pertaining to war criminals must first get a clearance through the OSS—you know, the Office of Strategic Services—a bunch of double-talking bastards who never give you the time of day! So I tell him forget it, and hang up. Our only chance is Berlin. I'm going there on business in a couple of months and I can work on it then. Say hello to my buddy Manny. Talk to you when I get something on this bird, okay?"

My friendship with Climpt continued to develop. Climpt may have lacked finesse and polish, schooling and looks, but in his veins flowed decency and honor. His loyalty was an unasked-for gift that brought out the same in me. I convinced my buddy to take some evening classes, and he appeared much happier, particularly after he started dating Brenda.

Brenda was a hefty, flat-faced fraulein who worked in the Post Exchange. Climpt had been spending extraordinarily long hours shopping and yet buying nothing of any consequence. The times we ventured into the PX together I noticed Climpt strayed in whatever direction a large healthy German girl was stocking the half-empty shelves. Even though he never gave me a hint that he fancied Brenda, it was comical to observe him seemingly engrossed in a random item—a sport shirt, a flashlight—while he stole adoring glances at Brenda's beefy bare thighs whenever her skirt rose as she reached the higher shelves.

So, to help things along, one day I had a little chat with Brenda and told her in simple words about my very shy friend's love for her, and that if she desired something good to come out of his crush she would have to help things along. Brenda, having a practical German mind, and bewildered and flattered by the thought that anyone might find her pleasing enough to want to court her, took my advice. When I pointed Climpt out to her she speedily approached him and casually asked him what his name was. One thing led to another and they began dating.

But misfortune knows no mercy, and Climpt's bliss with Brenda was short-lived. Six months into their peaceful courtship, she fainted at work while stretching up high to stock a top shelf. They rushed her to the hospital but it did no good; her heart was damaged and she never regained consciousness. Climpt was devastated; he cried bitterly, and for a long time he spoke to no one, except in monosyllables.

More than a year and a half into my army time, Captain Rosenburg phoned again. He hadn't forgotten his promise to me and was still pursuing the Tenner matter. By that time I had earned my second stripe, and when the company clerk left, his duties were passed on to me. Soon after that, Captain Karas received a promotion and was transferred back to the States. That was a very sad day for me indeed. But life goes on, and his replacement turned out to be an okay guy.

When off duty, I spent the bulk of my hours updating—mainly staring at, actually—the skimpy file on Tenner. The folder went with me everywhere though it held little, just my notes from several leads, and what I planned to do when I had leave and savings. On the outside I had written "Tenner" in bold letters. On the inside, the following notes:

> *U.S. War Crimes Office, Landstrasse 36, Linz, Austria*
> *Three letters, one reply.*
> *"We are looking into the matter. However no information can be given out without the written authorization of the United States Congress."*
>
> *Jewish Historical Documentation Center, Goethestrasse 63 Linz, Austria*
> *(Simon Wiesenthal)*
> *One letter, no reply.*
>
> *Centre De Documentation Juive Contemporaine, Paris*
> *Two letters, no reply.*
>
> *Allied Historical Commission, Munich*
> *Two letters, one note.*
> *"Have assigned a Mr. Karnoff to look into your request. Will advise soon."*
>
> *CIC (U.S. Army Counterintelligence Corps), Heidelberg (Capt. Herbert Rosenburg)*
>
> *San Girolamo, Rome, near the Vatican (Father Draganovic)*
> *Visit personally soon.*
>
> *Bishop Hudal, Pontificio Santa Maria dell' Anima, Rome*
> *Visit personally soon.*

When I wasn't mulling over my file I was comforting my buddy Climpt. And while reading, shooting pool, or playing my harmonica, I daydreamed lovingly of Kathy and remained faithful to the one who slept with me each and every night, hanging around my neck.

However, since she and I had never exchanged any everlasting vows, often I wondered whether my commitment to fidelity bore any roots. So, to assure myself, I took paper and pen and composed a short aria of love.

> *Kathy,*
>
> *Your locket has done miracles. It has kept me safe and out of trouble because it has enraptured me so that I dream of you continuously. Not one night have I gone to sleep without you. Yes, you and I sleep together, sort of, because your tiny picture, cozy inside the locket, has always been next to my heart.*
>
> *I'm sending you this photo of myself in the hope you'll keep it under your pillow always, for I had it sanctified by a local witch to frighten away all nasty spirits and make your dreams always pleasant and loving toward me, as mine are of you.*
>
> *Yiannis*

In less than a month came her reply. The envelope was pink, and I must have stroked it and sniffed it for at least two hours before I found the courage to open it.

> *My dearest Yiannis,*
>
> *I never dreamed that loving you could be so beautiful and fulfilling. The picture you sent me has replaced one of you I cut out of a photo I stole from my brother Patrick.*
>
> *Yes, you too are next to me, not under my pillow but by my bedside table, where I can look at you and talk to you and tell you of my love and kiss you good night before I fall asleep.*
>
> *Will you be here to take me to my senior prom? It won't happen for another year and a half but I would hate to go to it with one of my brothers. Please write to me and tell me you will come to take me to the ball.*
>
> *I miss you so very, very, very much,*
>
> *Kathy*

I fell in love with Kathy now more than ever.

After nineteen months in Germany I was nowhere near discovering the slightest trace of Tenner. Relying totally on the Baroness' connections or Captain Rosenburg's access to classified documents betrayed my pledge to the dead. With thirty days' accumulated furlough time I was ready to plunge into action. I planned to go to Munich by train, then hop a military plane to Linz.

I was packing my bag when Climpt called me to the phone. It was Captain Rosenburg with what initially seemed to be a report similar to the previous two. No accessible files on Colonel Tenner anywhere, not even in Berlin!

I was speechless.

"Are you there, soldier?"

"Nothing at all?" I murmured, unable to suppress my disappointment.

"Well, there is something, a short document in German. An investigator with a sharp eye led me to the file of Doctor Walter Blume, the Gestapo's liaison in Greece. Doctor Blume urgently requests of Himmler himself the assignment of Commandant Hans Tenner to the GFP—Gelheim Feldpolizei, the Secret Field Police, in Greece. Also some notes written by someone else—probably an intelligence caseworker." There was a pause. "Are you listening?"

"I'm all ears, Sir."

"Okay then. I'm translating from German.

"Blume, on behalf of General Karl Le Suire, the Commander of the 117 Jaeger Division based in Peloponnesus, demands 'a new face made of iron who could strengthen the division's intelligence network, raise morale, and supervise anti-partisan operations.' Blume says Tenner is such a man, having made his reputation as a young lieutenant at the Russo-Polish border, where the most brutal battles between Germans and Russians were fought. He was wounded there three times." Rosenburg paused again.

"Anything else, Captain?"

"There are some notes scribbled on this document."

"What do they say?"

"They are highlighted in red pencil on the bottom of the page. I'm sending you copies of this."

"Thank you, Sir. But please, Sir, go on," I urged him.

"'As a *Sonderaufgabe*,'—you know what that means, don't you, soldier?" asked the Captain.

"I'm afraid no, Sir. From the entire German dictionary, which I know by heart, this short word's meaning is the only one that escapes me," I popped lightheartedly.

"Well, in this guy's case, a mass terror, torture, and execution expert," he clarified, and went on. "Tenner's services were solicited by the puppet Croat state in Yugoslavia. He was awarded the Iron Cross 1st Class for single-handedly executing seven hundred Serbian hostages—some as young as seven years old, the note says.

"A man with such a military record was immediately needed in Greece because morale in Le Suire's division was extremely low after guerrillas in northern Peloponnesus captured seventy German soldiers and pushed them off a cliff. Le Suire, through Blume, therefore ordered the ultimate terrorist, someone who could scare the wits out of the Greeks in a manner no conquered races had ever witnessed."

"Sir, these notes, were they made by a German caseworker during the war, or one of our guys after this document was found?"

"These notes are written on the original request in German. I assume they were written by Germans."

"Any signatures other than Doctor Blume's?"

"Just his."

"At least we have an animal, a Commandant Hans Tenner, who served in Peloponnesus," I observed. "It's a start, Captain. In a couple of hours I'll be catching a train to Munich to do some searching on my own. Then I hope to grab a flight to Austria. I hear there's a survivor of the camps in Linz, Simon Wiesenthal, who is after Nazi war criminals with a vengeance. Maybe he'll have something to share with me on Tenner."

"The reason I haven't contacted Wiesenthal's group is because they are focused on Jew haters and exterminators, like Adolf Eichmann and his assistant—that bow-legged hunchback Alois Brunner—the Gestapo head Heinrich Muller, Josef Mengele, Franz Stangl, and the like. Tenner sounds more like someone who killed indiscriminately, anyone and everyone, for the sake of the Reich.

"You go to the Jews, though. Give them a shot. Something may come of it. Well, good luck, soldier. In a couple of weeks I'll be out of here. You can always reach me through my folks in Chicago, if you need to. Just remember the name. It's my father's name too. He is the only Herbert Rosenburg Senior in the Illinois telephone book. Dad is an important man in the community there. If you ever need anything, give him a call, tell'm you served with me in Krautland and that you are my friend. He likes Greeks."

"Thank you very much, Captain Rosenburg, Sir."

"My superiors tell me I'm needed in the Far East, so that is where I'm headed—after a short stop in the good old USA. I'll keep an eye open for any leads on Tenner. Sometimes the wind blows in from the least expected direction. Greek, understand the game I'm in, though. Help may come your way, and you may never know who sent it. Then again, maybe the Baroness will come up with some collectibles for you. You can't imagine her resourcefulness, and she never stops bragging about her perseverance. She is some lady. So long, soldier."

I felt depressed about losing one more friend, but I had a train to catch; no time for grieving.

In Munich I took a taxi to the airport. The sergeant in charge said a C-47 cargo plane would be taking off for Linz the next day. He secured a seat for me. Later on I stopped at the Allied Historical Commission and asked for Mister Karnoff. I was told he was on vacation and that he would not return to work for two weeks. Asking for someone else's help seemed an illogical waste of time to the middle-aged lady who spoke to me.

"Mister Karnoff has been assigned to look into this matter, so you must wait for Mister Karnoff's return," she announced sternly.

I took off for Linz.

From the air, Linz, a city by the Danube, didn't show much evidence of bombardment. I hitched a ride to the town center on an army truck. A church bell struck twelve times.

With the help of a map, I located the U.S. War Crimes Office on Landstrasse. I saluted a sergeant who manned the front desk. After I spilled my story, the chubby man gave me a compassionate look and advised me that the correct and perhaps only official way to pursue my search was through channels, like writing to my congressman and soliciting his assistance. I thanked him and went to Goethestrasse 63. At Wiesenthal's disorganized offices I approached a tall slender man with prematurely white hair.

"Do you speak English?" I asked.

"Yah."

"I am an American soldier. I'm a Greek actually . . . I mean, I come from Greece. Born and raised there. In '43 a Nazi killed my father. The Nazi's name is Tenner, Commandant Hans Tenner. I'm trying to find him. Some six months ago I wrote you a letter but I have not received a reply, so here I am in person. Can you help me?"

The thin man spoke in German to a small, balding, owlish man in thick eyeglasses who sat behind a desk and peered out through a sliver of an opening between stacks of folders. The thin man faced me again.

"Can show me identification?" he said in a coarse accent. I was in civilian clothes. I reached inside my shirt and stuck my dog tags out at him. He studied them, nodded, and extended his hand in greeting.

"My name Lowenstein. Vat is zis Nazi's name again?"

"Commandant Hans Tenner. In December of '43 he was with General Le Suire's 117 Jaeger Division in Peloponnesus, Greece."

"Greece?" he stared and pointed his finger at me. "Read German?"

"Some."

He shrugged and beckoned me to follow. We walked through a hallway packed with piles of papers, boxes with folders, transcripts, photographs, and every document imaginable. We entered a small, cluttered room. Against the wall a paper sign read "Griechenland." Below the sign, seven or eight boxes were stacked.

"Start there." He steered me to the boxes. "Careful, no tear anything. Place everything back same vay, okay?"

Three hours later Lowenstein brought me a cup of black coffee. I was searching through the last box.

"No luck?"

"Nothing."

"Vas zis man Tenner un SS man maybe?"

"Yes, I think. I remember he had a cross hanging from around his neck."

"Have storage room vit copies from Heinrich Himmler's SS files. Come, come vit me."

The storage room seemed organized, with folders and paper jackets filed upright and alphabetically on shelves. Lowenstein smiled for the first time and stood under the letter "T," searching.

"Tenner, Tenner," he muttered as he fingered through aged, discolored, and dusty manila envelopes. "Many SS men escaped to Brazil, Argentina, America," he said as he kept up his search. "Organisation Der Ehemaligen SS Angehorigen, ODESA for short—organization for SS veterans—zey helped each other escape from Italy." The room smelled smoky from cigarettes and musty from mildew. Suddenly from an upper shelf Lowenstein pulled out an envelope with a label.

"Von Tenner? Commandant Hans Karl Josef Evert von Tenner? Maybe him? Yah?"

Excitedly I agreed, even though I was not certain.

"I believe that's my man," I said, shuddering from the thought that Lowenstein held the key to Tenner's discovery. "Can we see what's inside?"

Lowenstein paced slowly toward an empty table; a strong light shined on its scratched varnish. He spread the file's guts out, picked up a handwritten letter, and began reading, mumbling to himself.

"Can you translate for me?" My voice was shaky and I was short of breath.

"Tenner's application to Himmler, beginning 1939, requesting he be admitted to SS. Ve have translated document to English language. Copies here. You see?" He held up a clipped stack of letter-size pages. "Ve make copies for you, if you vish, okay?" There were two wooden chairs nearby. Lowenstein grabbed one and sat down, motioning me to take the other. As soon as I did, he waved the pages in his hand like a conductor flourishing his baton for attention.

"Himmler vas genius," he said with an air of authority. "In deranged vay," he added as an afterthought. "Himmler, organizer unt leader of SS, adopted shrewd policy. Before von applicant could be considered for admittance to elite service of *Schutzstaffel*, SS for short, zat man must first reveal, under oath, some intimate secret about his life—some facts zat he never, never he shared vith anybody. Himmler promised such information, no matter vow abnormal . . . vow . . . vow . . . incriminating, ze SS vould keep in total confidence. Such revelations vere important components for consideration, qualification unt admittance to SS service, yes?

"Himmler vanted ze goods on all SS men unt control zeir ass, as Americans say, by having access to . . . to . . . vow ve say in English? to zeir most intimate secrets. Very smart vas zis guy Himmler, no? So, anyvay, Tenner wrote to Himmler unt here ve have it in translation. You can ask for copies ven finish, yes? I must go home now. My sister very, very sick unt I must go to sister." As I thanked Lowenstein and shook his hand, I gave him a scribbled note with my name and Uncle John's address in Davis, and pleaded with him to inform me the moment a document mentioning Hans Tenner passed his scrutiny. A profound sadness distorted his wrinkled face.

"Ve dismantling ze operation. Sending all files to Israel, soon. Ve have little money—unt ze Jews, Polish, Russians, Yugoslavs, Greeks— all vant to forget. No much interest to dig up murderers any more. But I vill keep address unt name in case." He left me and I began to read.

Mein Reichsfuehrer:

Dr. Wilhelm Braunsteiner, a first cousin twenty years my senior, was married to a younger, sophisticated Swedish-born woman educated in America, with limpid green eyes, long ash-blond hair and very, very beautiful.

When I was very young I remember sitting beside her and feeling awkward as we watched the Passion Play at Oberammergau. As Jesus was being hoisted onto the cross I found myself staring at my cousin's wife and her dazzling face, feeling mingled discomfort and attraction to her, plus a strange, strong envy and jealousy toward Wilhelm.

One sultry afternoon, when I had turned fifteen and my mother and I were on our annual summer holiday in Berchtesgarden, I knew that cousin Wilhelm had been called to Berlin to work on a secret project for his large petrochemical firm, and I rode my bicycle to their vacation cottage hoping to find Gretta alone.

Aflame from my peddling effort, the heat of the day, and my secret hopes, I knocked on the door. When she answered, she was dressed in a bathing robe; she flushed with excitement when she saw me and her sensual smile immediately aroused me.

'Hans, come in,' she said. 'What a pleasant surprise. Perhaps you are unaware that your cousin Wilhelm is out of town.' She opened the door wide but as I entered my arm brushed one of her breasts. I was nervous and thrilled, and tried thinking of ways to make myself look composed as I noticed her caressing me with her eyes. I had grown tall and slender and athletic, and she did not hide her pleasure at my being there.

'Well, since Wilhelm is out of town I should be going,' I lied. 'I had thought to ask him to go swimming with me.'

'No! No! You aren't in a hurry. Since you came all this way why don't you make yourself comfortable? I just took a bath and I was about to make myself some tea. You shall have some tea with me, Hans. Besides, I want to show you some lovely pictures of our last holiday on the Greek island of Corfu. Wilhelm and I had a marvelous time there.'

She went to fetch the tea while I sat on the large couch, stiff and nervous with the scent of the room making me feel wild and confused. When she returned she carried a tray and had an album wedged under one arm. She sat carelessly close to me where I could feel the warmth of her body.

'Look at these, Hans. Ha! Ha! I hope you aren't too embarrassed to look at nude photos of me. Wilhelm loves to photograph me naked on deserted beaches.' Her arm lay over my lap, pointing, and she was laughing.

The pictures were beautiful and provocative; and I could not take my eyes off her breasts as she was shown running in the sandy surf. And while I was engrossed viewing the pictures, from the corner of my eye I noticed her thighs part, soft flesh peeked through the opening of her robe, and I began to perspire from the titillation.

'Wilhelm has told me you are a very good photographer yourself, Hans. Have you taken any nude pictures of your girlfriends?'

She was toying with me, and I knew it.

'No! Uh . . . I mean I haven't . . . I don't have a girlfriend.' My voice was cracking.

'How about any other woman? Have you ever taken a photo of a woman totally exposed?' I tried to answer but couldn't.

'You haven't even seen a nude woman before, have you, Hans?' she asked, and stood up half smiling, while watching my trembling face. She slowly removed her robe, let it fall away from her wide shoulders, then slipped her fingers into the band of her lacy black underwear and gracefully pushed them down.

She took a step or two forward until she stood directly before me where I sat mesmerized. I gazed at her body, from her breasts down to the triangle of her torso and her two glorious legs as she softly placed her pubic hair against my lips, and she seemed enraptured watching me marvel at her. Then she unbuttoned my shirt and her hands gently squeezed my nipples while she kissed me as she helped me take off my short trousers. She guided me to mount her and when our bodies ignited I became lost in ecstasy and love.

Our affair lasted for an entire month until one afternoon I went to the cabin unexpectedly and found her in bed with another young man my age.

A madness came over me and I plunged my knife into them. The knife was given to me by the Fuehrer himself and I always carried it with me with the utmost pride. I felt like a wild beast hunting prey and, since the rest is history I enclose an article from the local newspaper, dated 6 August 1932. With your permission, Mein Reichsfuehrer, may I add that, if I am privileged to join the esteemed SS, I promise you that I will be as ready to plunge my knife into the hearts of all the enemies of my Fuehrer as deeply and with as much passion as I drove it into the hearts of those deceitful lovers on that summer afternoon.

The paper's description of the crime read as follows:

Frau Gretta Braunsteiner, wife of prominent scientist Dr. Wilhelm Braunsteiner, and her young lover Walter Felmy were found stabbed to death in a secluded vacation cabin owned by the Braunsteiners.

The unknown killer pierced the heart of Walter Felmy with one stab wound but Frau Braunsteiner's body had been cut and inflicted with multiple wounds. Her arms were slashed from wrist to shoulder. In a similar manner her thighs had been spread and sliced severely, and there were multiple deep wounds about the lower stomach area, her breasts and throat. Both victims were nude. No fingerprints have been found at the scene of the crime and no motive has been established. Dr. Braunsteiner is beyond suspicion with a foolproof alibi, as he has been on assignment in Berlin for the past two months.

Next morning I boarded a riverboat upstream to Passau, then Regensburg, where I caught a train to France, the land of light and human rights. I reached Paris on a Saturday, and since I was unable to further my business I toured the city on foot. I strolled the Left Bank, through the infamous Place Pigalle, and along the Avenue des Champs Elysées. I climbed the Eiffel Tower, and later marveled at a magnificent extravaganza inside the Grand Opéra de Paris.

On Monday, I paid an early visit to the Centre de Documentation Juive Contemporaine, where I soon discovered my French was insufficient to explain the importance of my mission. There, I quickly discovered that Parisians consider anyone who fails to speak their tongue fluently a barbarian. Feeling unwelcome, I moved on.

Finally, I called on the Eternal City of Rome with its incalculable treasures. I entered the colossal St. Peter's Cathedral, that towering golden temple of God, and I browsed through the revered Sistine Chapel, enraptured at the vastness of its wealth and statuary. I viewed frescoes painted by immortal masters that depicted the sovereignty of the omnipotent Popes, who sat unsmiling on their jeweled thrones, posing in their exquisite, brilliant attire while accepting the worship of the submissive faithful. With each breathtaking step I took I pondered the connection between humble Christ, the teacher, and his contemporary Lordly disciples.

Somberly I took a short walk to San Girolamo, the Croatian Confraternity. There I asked men in cloth who served as clerks and the hooded padres who roamed the yards where I could find Father

Draganovic, but they stared at me blankly. They muttered among them-selves sounds in a strange tongue and professed ignorance by shrug-ging their shoulders.

Suspecting a similar reception awaited me in Pontificio Santa Maria Dell'Anima, where I intended to search for Bishop Hudal, I dismissed the idea, and instead caught a plane to Frankfurt, then a train to Idar-Oberstein.

In the early spring of 1955, I hitched a military flight to Athens, spent some time with my beloved mother, and attended the marriage of my sister Betty to Kostas Katsouros, a decorated army major and the hand-somest Cretan I have ever met. I popped in on many of my old friends and, of course, I paid my respects to my father. While I stood at his grave, on this brief visit to Kalavryta, the pain of losing him was as strong as it had been on that cold winter morning in '43, when I found him slain, and I wept as much and as uncontrollably as I had then. Before I left him, I renewed my promise to find Tenner and bring him to justice. Then I strolled to the square.

Of the twelve survivors of the Nazis' killing, only four remained alive. I spotted one sitting with a group of men at a kafenion. Dimitris was a small, middle-aged man with a large scar in his neck, sad eyes, and a mustache. Upon hearing my surname he sprung up and embraced me.

"You are Yiannis? By God, you don't look like the little guy I remem-ber. What happened to your ear that stuck out like a donkey's? Did you chop some of it off?"

"I guess it just straightened itself out," I said, cracking a smile.

"I hear you live in America, now."

"Yes," I said.

"Visiting your mother and Betty in Athens?"

I nodded. He pulled over a chair, gestured me to join him, and promptly fetched the waiter. I ordered a lemonade and we talked about Betty's wedding and how the town had changed. Then with a somber heart I bent to his ear.

"Could you tell me about that dreadful day? I need to know the thoughts of the crowd—the Nazis' and Tenner's actions—everything."

His welcoming shine vanished instantly and he turned away. I knew I was trespassing. Perhaps asking him to relive those hours was cruel. To my surprise his voice, a whisper vibrating with grief, reached me.

"You remember how they divided us, all the men, from the women and children?" I nodded. He took a breath. "They marched us to the hill. The good priest Demopoulos, and the professor of French, Athanasiadis—both fearless men—walked up front. We followed. When we reached the amphitheater-like crack on the Hill they surrounded us with a dozen machine guns.

" 'Why did you bring us here? To kill us?' Professor Athanasiadis asked without fear.

"Tenner, the tall one, the one in charge . . . I still remember his eyes, cold as a snake's . . . shook his head.

" 'By my soldier's honor,' Tenner said in French while the professor translated, 'no harm will come to you. We have brought you here so you can witness the destruction of your homes. That should be a lesson to you for helping the Andartes.'

" 'Courage, children of God. The Lord is Almighty and his wishes are often concealed,' shouted the good priest. The words of the priest and the professor, two fine men, gave our snarling innards a potion of hope. Near me a handful of ex-military men, in whispers, calculated our chances if, as a mob and shouting like wild animals, we all at once stormed the machine guns. But even those brave men lost their courage when they realized the repercussions for the women and children who remained locked up inside the schoolhouse and guarded by soldiers. Many of us sat on the ground and the rocks. Others stood around talking, watching the ravaging fires below us in the town. Then the big church clock sounded noon. Soon after, maybe ten minutes or less, a green flare was shot over our heads.

" 'It's a signal from the Andartes. They'll help us for sure,' said the blacksmith. Doctor Hampsas, who stood near me embracing his two young boys, one lad snug against each of his sides, cracked a smile of optimism. Moments later a second flare blew up over us—this time its color was blood red. Tenner retreated a few paces and raised his arm. His machine guns began to spew their fire and death. As I hit the ground I heard Professor Athanasiadis spitting at Tenner. *'Ftou sou,* you barbarian. Where is your military honor, you savage beast?'

"Bodies fell on me. The howling of death is maddening. Many times each day I hear the last plea of the son of Adonis Demopoulos.

" 'Why are you killing me? I have done nothing wrong. I'm only a student. I want to live. I haven't done . . .' the boy's cry suddenly stopped. A bullet had shattered his head.

"The crying of the wounded was hell. The guns kept spitting for an hour maybe, though nobody was standing. I smeared my face with the blood of those over me and peeked through corpses. Anyone who seemed to breathe was dragged clear by the soldiers; then that animal Tenner blasted his face with a pistol shot. In due time they came around where I was buried. I felt someone grabbing my foot. They yanked me free from under the pile. I kept my eyes shut and held my breath. Tenner's bullet pierced my throat."

Dimitris started to weep. He took a handkerchief from his hip pocket and brought it to his face to hide his distress. Brokenly he added, "He left me for dead, and . . . and I don't know whom to thank—God or the Devil."

When he was composed again, I dared ask.

"Tenner—was he tall with a cross dangling from his neck and a piercing voice?"

Dimitris' red, sad eyes found mine.

"Yes," he said compliantly, scrubbing his face of tears. "I remember—his shouts and orders were in as high a pitch as the keening of a just-castrated swine." I stood, patted his stooping back, and left Kalavryta.

As I was preparing to say good-bye to Germany and Europe, counting down the last weeks of my stay in the army at Idar-Oberstein, anxious to return to America and to home at last, a much-anticipated note came from the Baroness. She assured me that her contacts were onto something substantial, but that it would probably take time to bear fruit.

Through a bit of my influence over our CO, being the company orderly, Climpt and I packed our bags together for our trip home.

Sweet thoughts came to me. The big bird's next stop would be on American soil, the premier patch of earth in the whole wide world. I heeded the master sergeant's favorite saying, "The Army gives a boy the big balls he needs to become a man." I was beholden to the Army.

My mind drifted back to when the military judge shortened my name to John Barlow and handed me my valued American citizenship certificate, in Frankfurt of all places. Indescribable ecstasy coated my tongue because to me that document was a priceless key to a chest stuffed with privilege and freedom.

Slowly I looked around me and wondered how many of these handsome American soldiers had ever contemplated the devastating change in their existence were they to be deprived of the most humble dignity due all people—the right to be born, to live, and to die free.

As the plane sliced through puffy haze like a giant stiletto slung from some mighty hand, the shadows resembled silhouettes of dancing ghosts. My speculations about my father's final whereabouts bombarded me once again.

I thought of his last tears and the droplets of his blood, those precious pearls and rubies that had decorated his face as he lay lifeless staring at the sky above the Hill, and I was spellbound by their transformation as I became certain of his immortality.

A serene contentment overtook me now. Yes, my father was alive somewhere, someplace; perhaps as a bead of sparkling dew decorating a budding lily, or as a speck of foam crowning a breaking wave in a distant sea, or as bits of vapor inside a lofty cloud.

While we headed west, I felt a great love for my new country yet regret for abandoning my family. Then guilt for having failed in my search for Tenner clenched my fists, and my teeth grinned from frustration and anger. "Butcher Tenner," I thought, "you may have taken a new identity. You may be hiding behind a respectable face, but the time to pay for your dreadful deeds will come."

"Ya hain't sayin' nutin' an' ya been shakin' lak' a dog shittin' peach seeds."

I gave Climpt an empty sidelong look and saw his yellow eyes searching mine. "Been jerkn' lak' a nigger spookt ba squealin' demons. What's eatin' ya, frien'?"

I remained quiet.

"Betcha I know whatsa troublin' ya—it's yern daddy, hain't it," he said with his gentle brotherly concern.

I nodded and returned to staring out the small window.

"Purty, them clouds outta there?" Climpt sighed reflectively as his eyes joined mine.

"Yeah," I agreed.

"Feelin' glum don' help none, frien'."

I let his philosophical comment pass.

"Got me this powerful notion, an' I betcha a month's pay, it hain't gonna be long now afore that ole Nazi snake gonna be crawlin' on his yella belly pleadin' fer mercy." He poked me in the ribs. "Feels it down deep 'nside ma bones. When it's time ta settle up, we's gonna hang' m frum a birch an' skin 'm lak' a squirrel—swear ta ma granny's grave I's ta be thar ta help ya send 'm ta tha devil, ya hear? Then, yer daddy gonna rest in peace."

"Yeah," I replied absentmindedly.

"Savin' up on ma furlough time an' when ya need me, ya jist gimme a holler an' awl be thar in two shakes o' tha pig's tail."

I stayed silent and Climpt poked me in the ribs until I faced him to see his whole being gleaming.

"Ya hear?" he asked excitedly.

Climpt and I, two souls from unmatched walks of life, had become devoted buddies, glued together by mutual respect and troubled pasts.

"I know I can count on you." I took comfort in his friendship, but my mood was somber and Climpt's craving for a dialogue seemed bothersome.

"Don' s'pose ya git what I's dyin' ta tell ya, but I's aimin' ta tell it ta ya anyways I can," Climpt persisted, his voice quivering with a strange yearning. "Been thinkin' deep. Ma brain been playin' tricks on me, best I can figger. See, frien', I got me this weird cravin', I shoulda been more lak' ya. Yessirreee, I wisht I'da growed up with feelin's fer ma daddy lak' ya got fer yern." His voice trembled and his lower lip hung loose.

"Must feel mighty good an' warm 'nside yernself ta love yer daddy." I turned to face him again. He bit his lips hard. The muscles of his jaw were tense and bulging. "Hain't got much feelin' fer mine. Hate meebe. Nutin' more, acuze o' tha way he whupped up on mamma an' us kids." He made a frantic grimace to hide his upheaval. "Waal . . . at times I git all fuckt up inside ma head. Wanna grab me a jugful o' likker an' git skunkt drunk an' stay thattaway fer a year er two an' fergit tha whole dern mess 'bout me growin' up an' all."

Climpt's breathing sounded heavier than the plane's thunder.

"When daddy drinkt hisself ta death, momma dolled up some, an' up ta ole man Tompkins' place she hiked." Climpt jerked as if a bullet had shot him in the gut. "She stayed up thar all night, sometimes. 'Momma don' ya go up thar an' stay all night,' us kids begged 'er. 'I gotta go. Winter's comin' an' we gotta git some needles an' thread ta make them flower sacks into quilts. 'Sides, who's gonna pay fer yern doctorin', granny's an' mine, ifen we git laid up?'" Climpt's gasping reached a crescendo. Swollen with distress, he looked ready to burst. But then gradually his puffing subsided.

"Said afore—feelin' low down don' help nutin'—'no use cryin' over spilt milk,' ma granny useta say."

"That's what they say; people do it anyway."

"S'pose so." Climpt suddenly threw his head back against the seat and looked at the ceiling. "But ya know somethin', ma frien? Jist acuze a man got 'm a prick an' a woman got hern a pussy don' give 'm no right ta keep pokin' an' humpin' an' poppin' kids." He brushed upward along one side of his face with the thick of his palm as he often did. "Ornery, a drunk and a cheat, Daddy, an' ma mamma, theyselfs, they hain't got but an ole rusty bucket fer a crapper, an' no window ta throw it out frum, but they gone on pokin' an' humpin' an' poppin' kids faster than a coupla minks. I wanna know tha prick who give 'm this, here, mighty right, Yiannis."

I looked at Climpt's stormy head. Diamonds and pearls, those glittering jewels come from coal and mollusks, I thought, and fondly put my arm over my friend's stooping shoulders, but Climpt became edgy and pulled away.

"Unfittin' folks who don' know one fuckin' thin' 'bout how ta be parents, pop them purty li'l critters an' leaves 'm ta fend fer theyselfs an' . . . an' it jist hain't right, darn it."

There we sat, survivors of social shipwrecks—two young soldiers entrusted to guard our nation's rights, while chasing to grasp fair God's wrongful world.

"Climpt, you're a Christian, right?"

"Ma churchin' been Baptist. Granny took tha slew o' us kids ta church, rain er shine, ta hear tha preacher deliver tha gospel o' tha Lord."

"There are a lot of people out there who believe in the Lord; but do you trust God to be righteous and all that?" Climpt seemed confused, unable to grasp where I was leading. He kept sneaking fearful peeks my way.

"Been 'ceptin' tha Lord as ma savior—take care o' tha good folks an' punish tha bad folks."

The story of a half-crazed Greek soldier, the lone survivor of a fierce battle between the Greeks and the Italians on the rugged mountains of Epirus, had long been a disturbing part of my memories, and I was itching to share it with my friend.

"Climpt, I've got a World War II story to tell you."

My eyes narrowed, searching. Then, as I looked straight ahead, a low, slow voice came from the depths of my past.

"Back in Tripolis, the town where I lived during my teen years, one cold evening my friends and I were bullshitting, breaking bread and drinking cheap wine inside a tiny basement tavern as we often did in the winter. A man in a filthy shredded army overcoat staggered down the stone steps and begged us for a drink. Mitsos, the proprietor, was about to boot him out, but it being Christmas week we took pity on the pathetic fellow and asked him to join us. He stank of stale sweat and urine, and he hadn't had either a shave or a haircut in years. His eyes were small and black and no one could guess his age. Snow had been falling for a week, and the stranger was shaking from the killing cold.

"We poured him a water glass full to the brim with retsina wine. He put it away in one gulp. After the third glass he began to defrost, and the stench came to life, and man, oh man, was it wicked! Anyhow, at some point as the evening progressed he began to feel at ease, the alcohol helped, and he told us about a specific clash between the Greeks and the Italians in the last days of 1940.

"He was with an infantry company that had dug in on a hilltop to stall the Italians advancing from the north. On Christmas Eve the Italians came and took over the opposing hill, and the Greeks could hear them loud and clear from where they were entrenched. The acoustics were spooky, and one Greek soldier, who had spent time in Sicily, talked to them from the Greek hilltop and the Italians responded from their own hill. Early on Christmas morning the Italians held Mass and the Greek soldier translated the Italian prayer. They begged the Virgin Mary to be with them and make them victorious over the Greeks because the Italians were Her servile worshippers and believed in Her Eternal righteousness.

"Not much later, the Greek priest held his service and asked for God the Almighty, defender of fairness and justice, to lead them into a triumphant battle. The battle came and it was ferocious. The Italians charged the Greek hill and the Greeks held their ground and men spilled each other's guts and slashed each other's throats; when dusk fell they were all dead except our man in the foul-smelling army coat.

"In a daze, our delirious soldier wandered about staring at the dead, and he began to gather the guardian crosses that had dangled from the necks of the young Greeks, and the Madonnas, the pictures of the Virgin Mary the Protectoress, from the breast pockets of the young Italians. With his booty he made a pile, and on top of the heap he placed the priests' vestments and their good books, and in the midst of the dead he set his collection ablaze. When the flame had consumed most all of the holy assortment, he took out his dick and pissed on the ashes."

In the Newark airport Climpt and I separated. Against my urging he had re-enlisted for four years and was heading for duty somewhere in the Far East.

"Th'army's ma life. Got me nowheres ta go. Nobody ta see." He coughed as he half-kicked straight out at a concrete wall, launching a hard strike at his cruel destiny through the tip of his boot.

"Brenda's gone. Ma brothuhs an' sistuhs scattert 'round tha country lak' tha darn wind had took them too, acuze I hain't seed hide nor hair o' none o' them since I signt up. Now that ma granny's in hern last rest I gots me nobody, 'xept . . ." He paused and stared about with aching uncertainty, avoiding looking my way.

I took him into my outstretched arms, a Greek's natural expression of grief between two parting friends, but Climpt showed his discomfort as he had before, yanking his body loose from my embrace. He stood near me, though, with the edges of his mouth dropped, his shoulders bent, and his teeth clenched, wearing a mask painted by a master whose genius excelled in capturing human suffering.

Climpt never looked up directly at me as we were readying to say good-bye. He kicked at the air like a little boy and mumbled half a dozen mutterings that could have been translated into a thousand feelings. Then, my friend hurried away and soon disappeared behind the many strange faces in the busy terminal, the man with the head of a simian and the heart of gold.

In Camp Stoneman while waiting to be discharged, I bumped into an acquaintance from my basic-training days in Company C at Fort Ord. As we chatted over a beer he broke some unpleasant news to me. From an old company book he pointed out pictures of men I had known and remembered well, who had drawn their last breaths on Korean soil—out of one hundred fifty-two soldiers in all, twenty-three would never return.

6

TWO LOVERS
WITH ONE SPIRIT

A week after my arrival in California, Uncle John came to fetch me. We embraced and pecked each other on the cheeks. He announced that he was itching to tell me some exciting news. When we piled into his brand-new white Chevy—he loved a white Chevy—he explained somberly that his bosom buddy had died, whose wife he'd always secretly fancied. Even though Tom had been his best friend, Uncle John, on occasion, had hoped that God would take his pal away, but in a decent fashion, so that he would have a chance to provide the mourning widow a lot of comfort and commiserating companionship.

"Well, lo and behold, about a year or so ago, my friend suddenly dropped dead, without complications. The divine Creator took pity on the poor fella and spared him from dragged-out suffering. Oh yes, the Lord is forever compassionate."

I was baffled by Uncle John's sudden acceptance of the Lord, but as a respectful nephew I kept my thoughts to myself.

"As you can tell, my feelings about the loss of my friend were kind of mixed. One hour I felt real bad, and the next hour not quite so bad. After the deceased had been put to rest, I called on his grieving widow to console her, because it was my duty having been her husband's best friend. I took some flowers to her and she made coffee and we chatted for some time, and even though Rosie was grieving, I courted her some—you know, a lot of agreeable smiles, polite overtures, and stuff like that. Nothing too obvious, you understand. I didn't want her to get the wrong impression of me, God forbid. So my sweet-talking and flower-taking went on for a month or two until one evening, while Rosie and I were visiting in her garden, just the two of us, poof, an apple falls on the ground from the apple tree. Now, Rosie bends over to pick up the apple and her big beautiful buttocks come up and stare me right in the face like two most delicious watermelons." Here, Uncle John's eyes widened with wonderment. For the briefest moment he turned to the heavens. "The Almighty may strike me dead if I am lying. Yes, yes. As if God had taken command of my hand and guided it against my own will, I pinched her in the behind." His round face glowed. "And guess what happened next, my dear boy?" He stared at me inquisitively with a smile a mile wide. "Rosie, instead of slapping my face, she giggles! So what do I do? I pinch her once again and . . . and what do you think Rosie does? She giggles some more." He crossed himself again as he prayed. *"Panagia mou, doxa nachis."* ("Holy Mary, may glory be eternally yours.")

"Well, naturally, after such a favorable response I start to court Rosie heavy and it wasn't long before I pop my proposal to her. 'Rosie,' I says, 'Tom's spirit will never rest in peace knowing you are in mourning and alone, without the solace of an understanding companion like myself, who was his best friend. Rosie, I must urge you, for Tom's sake at least, please, please accept my hand in marriage.' Rosie, being the proper woman she's been all her life, says to me that she needs time to think things over—which is only natural and befitting. Well, to make a long story short, after a couple of days my phone rings early in the morning. It's Rosie on the other end and she is all excited. She tells to me she just saw Tom in her dream and he urged her to accept me at once. Boy, did I jump up with joy. I was happy from head to foot. 'Tom, what a dear friend you are even now that you are dead,' I cried. And Rosie and I have been united in matrimony since three months after Tom decided to leave us for the better world."

He gaily whistled a few bars from an old Greek song and tapped his palm on his thigh to the tune's rhythm. Then he became serious and his face assumed the serenity of a bishop.

"Since Rosie and I married I have become a new man. Changed completely—well almost." He took in a deep breath, puffed out his chest, and went on.

"As I see it, every man has got two *trasta* (woolen peasant bags) dangling from around his neck. The one bag, which is stuffed with all his own faults, he conveniently hangs on his back where he can't see it, and the bag with everyone else's faults he hangs on his chest where he can go through it with a fine-tooth comb.

"Since my friend Tom died and I married Rosie, who is a saintly woman, I started to see things different. It isn't easy to do this, you understand. Tough to get rid of the devil and his little brats who dance inside your guts and force you to do weird things. Once that bastard sneaks inside your bowels and plants his seedlings you need a strong laxative to get rid of them all. So this is what I did.

"I start shifting my two bags little by little to the sides until they hang over my shoulders. Out of habit I keep on looking inside the sack with everybody else's faults—but sometimes, just once in a while, I take a peek inside mine. And when finally I find the courage to start shuffling through my own bag pretty thoroughly, in it I discover some not-so-very-flattering notes scribbled by the divine hand, and I begin to take notice. And as I'm looking through this bag, it shifts so that it's hanging under my eyes to see and examine, and to judge and make proper adjustments, and the bag with everyone else's faults I've tossed over onto my back. I try to keep it there on a kinda permanent basis."

I stayed as Uncle John's and Rosie's guest at their home. Rosie, whom I had met briefly in the past, turned out to be a classy lady and I was happy for their union and contentment.

The following day, with my three hundred dollars in mustering-out pay plus a portion of my saved-up cash, Uncle John helped me buy a used, green, '49 Chevy coupe, my first automobile. My intention was to enter college in the fall and take advantage of the GI Bill.

I drove to San Francisco, where, after checking about a dozen apartments for rent, I found a tiny sunny studio to my liking overlooking the west side of Stern Grove Park and settled in with my meager belongings.

Two days later, armed with a bouquet of pink carnations and a two-pound box of See's chocolates for Jack and Mrs. Hayes, and one healthy red rose plus a tiny gold bracelet (packed neatly inside a small lavender box) for Kathy, I climbed into my precious green car, full of anxiety and love, and took off for the Hayes compound in Berkeley.

It was a surprise visit. There appeared no sign of life about the house except Spunky, their feisty teacup poodle, who greeted me with excited barks, his tail wagging.

I passed through the low wooden gate and wandered into the familiar manicured yard. My gut tasted unsettled and jumpy in anticipation of the impending meeting.

The California sun was reaching the peak of its late May curve. I sat on a stone bench nestled under a purple-leafed plum tree. My eyes sluggishly drifted to the regal honeysuckle with its tangled trunks and branches cross-stitched through the weathered trellis. I watched two frail, bright green hummingbirds as they danced and sucked the nectar from the hearts of aromatic white flowers, and I relaxed and grew blissful.

While my thoughts drifted to memories of my hazy icon of Kathy, the American family I had become so very attached to arrived home from church.

Upon discovering their unexpected caller, both Jack and Mrs. Hayes sped toward me with warmth and commotion. From the corner of my eye I caught a glimpse of Kathy, fully grown and beautiful but surprised and shaken, running at full speed into the sheltering depths of the garden. When the parents realized their daughter's predicament, Mrs. Hayes' face clouded.

"Go to her," she said, giving me a gentle shove. "She doesn't know how to handle this—she is so young."

I found Kathy hiding behind the thick trunk of the weeping willow, her hands obscuring her lowered face, tears dripping down her wrists. Hesitantly, I placed my hands on her shoulders and felt her body quiver as she gasped for breath until finally, exhausted, she collapsed in my arms. I held her, tenderly stroking her fine hair. When her composure returned, she raised her head and brushed her blushing wet cheeks with her palms.

"I am behaving childishly." Her apology was gentle. "Please don't mind me, Yiannis, but I'm so very happy to see you. It's been three very long years."

I gave her a delicate kiss on each of her moist eyelids and handed her the rose and the lavender box.

"For me?"

"Yes."

She quickly dropped to her knees on the grass and buried her face inside the rose, then tore open the little box. At the sight of the glittering bracelet she brightened like a shooting star and cries of joy filled the garden's fragrant air. She slipped it on, and twisting and turning her wrist she raised her arm as if she wished to give all the flowering bushes and trees a chance to view her treasure. Suddenly she sprang up and jumped and hopped toward the house while she shouted her jubilation to her world. "Mother, Father . . . look what Yiannis gave me."

A blend of emotions flooded me. Admiration, affection and fondness, pride and longing, dominance and desire, all those caring and possessive feelings crisscrossed my heart, just as the twisted web of the honeysuckle branches crisscrossed its trellis. And while my eyes followed her skipping away into her home, I realized I wanted Kathy for me, and forever.

On a Saturday in June, the much-anticipated Senior Ball was held at the St. Francis Hotel in San Francisco. Excited and giggly couples proudly showed off their formal wear.

Young ladies wore the sophisticated airs of movie starlets, yet steadily stumbled and limped in their high-heeled shoes as if suffering from an affliction, while all the perspiring young men felt leashed by the stiff collars and bow ties of their rented tuxes and never stopped yanking at their ill-fitting trousers.

Kathy was dressed in a simple white evening gown belted by a blue lace sash to match her eyes. She hung from my arm as if our wrists had been chained together and glowed with pure bliss and refreshing pride when she presented me to her friends.

The band performed gallantly, but about midway through the night the singer lost his voice and the crowd lost its patience with discomfort. All the high heels were kicked off to the side and the bow ties stripped off tender necks and shoved into back pockets, squashed against sweaty buttocks, chided for the annoyance they had caused. The corsages and boutonnieres, so alive and fragrant just hours before, now appeared expired and forgotten.

As the adolescent throng began to exhibit signs of fatigue and the air was sprinkled with steamy whiffs of body odor, I, conscious of my advanced age of twenty-three, waltzed Kathy out of the hall and away. Soon her exquisite head was resting against my shoulder while the green Chevy headed down past the Cliff House to Playland at the Beach.

Laughing Sal, the grand mechanical welcoming lady, full of warts and scary teeth, was still doing her ha, ha, ha, guffawing song and, glued together, Kathy and I fed dimes into the fortune-telling and picture-taking machines while we strolled through the arcade of fun games and rides. Kathy tucked all the mementos carefully into her tiny purse. When we passed the enormous bubble gum machine she stopped as if a magnet had exercised its strong pull. Staring at the colorful little round beads, she dropped pennies into the machine. The instant the balls rolled out into the cup, she snatched them up and stuffed them in her mouth, chewing them rapidly, enjoying their sugar coating. Then she began her proud performance, blowing bubble balloons. Pointing at them as they grew bigger and bigger, she jumped with joy until, hanging from her lips, they eventually touched her breasts and blew up with a pop.

Jubilant minutes ticked away. The moon sneaked up on us, sending us its broad smile, and the fresh wind tickled our skins.

The roaring surf with its mighty rollers summoned us. We strolled toward the ocean front, discarded our shoes, chased and touched, embraced and hugged and kissed. No two other souls in the whole universe could have been blessed with as much rapture as my Kathy and I, her Yiannis.

Finally, out of breath, puffing, and full of love, we rested on a rock, breathing deeply, and I wondered at the deathlessness of the stars and the sea and my love.

"I wish time could freeze this very moment, capturing the love I feel for you—preserving it inside my heart like a bee in amber," I sighed.

Kathy squeezed my hand and stared into my eyes.

"I . . . ," she was choking, " . . . I'm madly in love with you, Yiannis." Her body pressed against mine. "The instant our eyes first met, I sensed I had known you all my life. Strange as it may sound, I felt that we had shared all our previous lives together and that it was only a matter of time before we were reunited once again."

I took her face into my hands and kissed her lips.

"You are the most beautiful *louloudaki* in the whole wide world."

"What does louloudaki mean?"

"A little flower; a most beautiful, genteel flower. I'm going to call you that from now on . . . Louloudaki, my Louloudaki," I whispered, holding her. I could feel her melting into my arms.

"And to me you are the sun. I will call you . . . sunflower, my Sunflower."

I stood erect, courageous and important, as if the sand under my feet were the world and I its master.

"Let us, you and I, make our vows here, tonight, and have the moon and the stars for our witnesses."

"Oh yes, yes, let's."

Her tender voice drove me mad. I could have devoured her, assuring myself of our unity in perpetuity. She was all I wanted. Life without Kathy would be insufferably empty; life without her love would be worthless; I would lack any and all reason to go on.

A seaweed frond lay abandoned at the foot of the rock. I tore a piece from one end and wove two rings. Then I took her hand and led her slowly to the water's edge where the crashing surf sprayed our bodies. Looking up to the moon, I shouted with a commanding voice.

"Moon. Yes! You! Monarch of all lovers, listen to the pledge of our hearts and give us your consent."

I faced Kathy, held her by her small waist and brought her near me, looking inside her through her big blue eyes.

I gave her both seaweed rings to hold in her open palm, then took the third finger of her left hand and threaded it through one. Kathy placed the other ring on my finger, and at just that very sacred moment a flock of migrating geese sailed between us and the moon. It was plain to us both that the monarch had winked his permission to us, and Kathy and I were united.

We became great lovers, inseparable companions, and best friends. We lived as a couple in the tiny studio by Stern Grove with plenty of room to spare since, to us, being one foot apart was one foot too far. We touched and kissed and hugged, possessed by a mighty hunger for each other's affection; I called her my Louloudaki and she called me her Sunflower. We babied each other and made our own tender language, one others didn't share.

The Hayeses, even though fond of me, frowned at our arrangement at first but soon became responsive to our euphoria and accepted us with grace. Their house in Berkeley, with the two boys away in the armed services, seemed empty; we visited often and stayed with them on Sunday nights.

One Monday morning, midsummer, upon returning from Berkeley I dropped Kathy off at the neighborhood market. When I entered the apartment, I found a note and two letters lying on the shaggy white carpet.

The message was a scribble from Uncle John; he had passed by to hand-deliver the two letters which had arrived at his post office box in Davis. Throughout my three-year absence in the military, I had used his box as my permanent address.

Both letters were decorated with postage from abroad—one was from Greece and bore my mother's instantly recognizable handwriting, the other came from a Swiss bank in Geneva.

Anxious to hear news from home, I opened my mother's letter first. When I read the first sentence I stopped with a lump in my throat and rushed outside. I found refuge in Stern Grove Park. A sunny spot called to me and I stretched out on the ground where I could smell the fresh earth and the breathing grass. I skipped through the rest of the letter quickly. Uncle Chrisanthos had died. I was choking.

Of my mother's three brothers, Chrisanthos had been far and away my most beloved and admired. As an adolescent he had been afflicted by the then-incurable syphilis virus, and I surmised that this illness was responsible for his early passing. He had died a bachelor.

My lips trembled. Recollections took me back. Uncle Chrisanthos had found time to fill the painful void left by my father's absence and passed on to me some of his own wisdom. And, besides my mother, he had been the only relative who recognized the needs of a growing lad and often handed me spending money.

"Wise is the man who knows when he has enough for himself," he said to me once while we sat at a sidewalk cafe by Omonia Square, observing the frantically rushing and ever-changing crowd.

Although he appeared stern, stiff, and aristocratic, his heart was kind and giving. He lived by the saying he taught me. One unbearably hot summer day in Athens, observing his sweltering employees, he closed the doors of his fur shop at midday and told them to take the rest of the day off. Since I was there visiting, as I often did, he asked me to join him for lunch.

A taxi drove us to the Old Falliro beach. The *meltemi,* the north wind, blew from the northeast, and it was markedly cooler sitting under an awning at a waterfront taverna.

While he was ordering our meal, I noticed his eyes, gray and expressionless and handsome as they were, dart to one side to focus on a passing boy of five or so, in patched clothing and ragged shoes. The child had been kicking a small smooth pebble that had somehow slid into a nearby hole and disappeared. With a frantic, devastating look the little lad kept searching for his pebble, perhaps the only toy he had ever owned.

Uncle Chrisanthos took a large note from his wallet. "Come here, little one," he shouted, waving his arm, unsmiling as if unaffected. When the child looked up, his large sad black eyes, on the verge of tears at having lost his plaything, were attracted to the note. "Here, take this, and buy yourself a real kicking ball." The child, confused and hesitant, approached us like a coaxed dog fearful of a sudden kick. When he was near enough he dashed in, snatched the note, and ran like a rabbit at first, then skipped and hopped happily until he faded in the distance.

On the eve of my departure for America, Uncle Chrisanthos visited to wish me good-bye. When he looked into my eyes I could sense him choking back emotions as he offered me his last guidance. "There are two kinds of men in the world—the doers and the students of the doers. Read, but do not become obsessed with other people's records. Instead, take time to create your own."

Half-heartedly, I opened the second letter.

> *Dear Mr. Varelopoulos (Barlow):*
>
> *The sad news of the demise of our late client Mr. Chrisanthos Konstantopoulos has reached us through a letter recently received from Mr. Panagiotis Karagiorgis, his attorney in Athens. Along with Mr. Karagiorgis' letter we have received a copy of Mr. Konstantopoulos' death certificate.*
>
> *Mr. Konstantopoulos has registered you as the sole beneficiary for account number 534561. Following Mr. Karagiorgis' instructions, we are providing you with a passbook for the account, and a booklet listing our U.S. affiliate banks. With proper identification you should be able to gain access to your funds at any of our affiliate banks.*
>
> *You may count on us serving your needs always.*
>
> *Sincerely yours,*
Pierre C. Freimuller
Vice President

The passbook showed a balance of four hundred and twenty thousand Swiss francs. Chrisanthos Konstantopoulos had left me, his nephew, only son of the older of his two sisters, financial independence. I'll never know why.

How can two opposing emotions dwell in a man's heart simultaneously? The sorrow of losing him tore at my guts, while joy at his final deed lifted my spirits. Perhaps the reason departing souls abandon their material possessions when they fly away is none other than to ease the pain of their loved ones left behind to grieve.

Kathy appeared in the distance. By some inexplicable stroke of nature Kathy retained some animal instincts most humans have long lost; she had sniffed out my whereabouts. Shining, she was on her way to join me, but some twenty paces away she stopped abruptly. Her smile vanished and her approach slowed.

"What is the matter, my Sunflower?" she asked, trying to read my face. She sat down behind me, took my head in her lap and began to stroke my hair.

She listened to the story of the two letters in total silence, and in her tenderness she sang to me her soundless sharing of my grief.

I handed her the letters and the passbook from the Swiss bank, but she put them gently aside. Instead she bent her head, kissed me, and held me.

As students our finances had been limited, and I had temporarily set the Tenner matter aside. I believed that with enough money, I could find him, so Uncle Chrisanthos' francs freshened my confidence.

"With Uncle Chrisanthos' bequest I will find Tenner."

"Who is Tenner, my Sunflower?" asked Kathy.

I told her of the Kalavryta killing and the circumstances of my father's death for the first time, and how Uncle Chrisanthos' periodic presence softened my father's early loss, and we both cried.

When we returned to our apartment, I wrote three letters, very similar in content: one to the U.S. Department of Justice's Office of Special Investigations, one to the World Jewish Congress, and the third to my congressman, each soliciting assistance in locating Tenner.

In the late spring of '62, the Kennedy era was in full bloom. The future and the spirit of America had been transferred to a much younger generation of political leaders, and Jack Kennedy, our enthusiastic president, was busy taking on the old boys in Washington, while the Beatles captivated lands around the world with their rock and roll ballads.

Kathy graduated from San Francisco State College with a degree in education and chose to work for the San Francisco Unified School District, teaching underprivileged children.

A hodgepodge of courses in business, finance, and law summed up my academic achievements. Since scholastic patience eluded me, I decided that acquiring a diploma would be fruitless. But my nibbling in real estate with the help of my inheritance was panning out remarkably well for us.

We made our marriage lawful by paying a brief visit to City Hall, then entered into a two-year option to purchase a cozy bungalow on

Telegraph Hill with spectacular views of the Golden Gate Bridge, Mount Tamalpais in the background, and Angel and Alcatraz islands. Our love and closeness seemed unlimited.

I maintained a small desk, seldom visited, inside Culeto Realty on Columbus Avenue in North Beach, and often sipped cappuccinos in an always-crowded bohemian hangout, the coffeehouse Trieste. One such morning, while two of my chums and I were visiting over our empty cups, Henry, who knew a great deal about the happenings around town, appeared, and we invited him to join us.

Henry excitedly informed us of a small, eight-story building for sale on lower Powell Street. The owner, a strange man, was falling behind in his mortgage payments. The building could be acquired for a reasonable price, and Henry asked if I would be interested in taking a look. I cheerfully agreed.

The building was in a great downtown spot, less than a block from Union Square, but only the storefronts were rented; a porno shop displayed its lewd paraphernalia in its two large windows, and next to it was a seedy hamburger joint. The upper floors were vacant and in a disastrous state.

The owner hadn't enlisted a real estate agent. Henry said the asking price was four hundred fifty thousand dollars, but the building could certainly be purchased for less. As the cable cars passed by, clanging their cheerful bells, I became eager to own this superb piece of San Francisco.

My gut urged me to ignore its liabilities. I quickly submitted an offer for three hundred sixty thousand; my proposal was countered by Mr. Baker, the owner, with a meager two thousand dollars more, but with an "As Is" clause. After only a day of hesitation and soul-searching Kathy and I signed the document.

The acquisition was pure joy for both of us. We spent weeks devising the transformation of our new property. The porno shop was the thorn in promoting the building as a respectable address; we decided to wait on our plans, hoping that the owners, AGG Entertainment Group, would not exercise their five-year option to renew.

I cleaned out and painted the second floor and within a couple of months moved my office there. I hired a four-hour-a-day secretary,

Mrs. Maria Moretti, a spirited middle-aged woman of Italian heritage from Texas, who spoke with a drawl and preferred to address me, for reasons I never attempted to know, as Bossman.

All was sailing along smoothly when, about six months into my purchase, a registered letter arrived from the real-estate division of AGG Enterprises, with an address in Palo Alto.

AGG Enterprises was involved in many ventures, I learned while I read through the letter, including ownership of the AGG Entertainment Group, which operated a number of similar "book stores." The parent company was interested in purchasing the building from me to ensure the continuous operation of their successful enterprise in its present location.

The letter went on to emphasize that the company found it prudent to pursue such an acquisition, as their intent was to secure their position beyond the duration of the present term and its five-year option period.

Instantly a depression overtook me and I crumpled the single page in anger. I was about to toss it into the wastebasket when I realized I had neglected to read the darn thing in its entirety. With a sour gut I slowly uncrumpled it and went on.

> *May we also inform you, Mr. Barlow, that Mr. Baker, the past owner of this building, is in violation of a witnessed verbal agreement between himself and our concern. The agreement was specific and unequivocal: Immediately upon Mr. Baker's wish to dispose of the above-mentioned property, AGG Enterprises was to be notified so that we could exercise our right-of-first-refusal option. Since Mr. Baker has neglected to recognize his obligation to us, we strongly believe the sale-transfer of Mr. Baker's property to your name is legally clouded.*
>
> *We wish to resolve this matter amicably by offering you $10,000 over your recent purchase price, plus all expenses you may have incurred such as sales commissions and closing costs; the total not to exceed $390,000. However, if you find our offer uninteresting may we caution you that our legal staff will be most anxious to litigate our legitimate claim in court.*

Immediately I phoned my lawyer, vented some steam, and discussed with him our legal course of action—I had become attached to the building, and a friend, a fine architect, had already begun to draw up plans to restore it. Giving it up for a miserly $10,000 profit was nothing more than a kick in the pants that I certainly did not deserve.

As I sat there fuming, listening to his advice, I caught a glimpse of three shadows passing quickly by the open door of my office. I quickly excused myself, hung up the phone, and listened intently to the steps while these mysterious visitors continued their climb up the wooden stairs. I decided to stay put and await their return; the elevator was keyed off and the only exit was the same stairs they had taken going up.

Barely fifteen minutes later I heard them descending and casually planted myself outside the door.

All three were middle-aged; two were tall and lanky, the third was short, balding, and pudgy. I introduced myself as the owner of the building. The two tall men tossed swift, contemptuous glances my way as if I were some dirty dog. Leaning against the landing railing they kept up a low-voiced conversation between them.

A warning light blinked on in my head, cautioning me that I had had a disagreeable encounter with one of the men—on the street, perhaps.

The pudgy man, with an arm whose loose flesh jiggled inside his sleeve, flipped his business card at me and told me his name, adding that he was the legal counsel for AGG Enterprises. He casually pointed to the two men and mentioned their peculiar-sounding names; those two continued to show as much interest in my presence as two giraffes for a fly.

Hmmm, I thought, these pricks waste no time!

"We took the liberty of having a quick glance at the building and its present—disastrous, I might say—condition. I'm sure you have received our registered letter by now, Mr. Barlow," the pudgy little lawyer said to me. I could have decked his ass right then and there! But, three against one are lousy odds, and Maria, though she came on as a true Texan swaggerer at times, didn't seem likely to offer me much support if it came to a real fight. I executed an about-face, sped into my office, and slammed the door.

When I reached home late that afternoon Kathy was in her garden doing what she loved to do most in her free time. Her flowering bushes were the envy of the neighborhood and often I found her half-hidden, either bending behind a hedge or concealed by a pile of manure and dirt, always preoccupied with her planting designs and often talking to her immobile friends.

She noticed me and, completely drenched in sweat, mud caked all over her face, her eyes peering through a mask of earth, she sped to give me a hug and a smooch. But I bolted, and my wife's face drooped and took on a most pitiful childlike pout.

"For God's sake, Louloudaki, don't sulk!" I snapped, annoyed, yet sorry for rejecting her. "You should see yourself. You are a total mess."

"But my lips are clean, and you can give them a *filaki*" (a little kiss, in Greek). She half-shut her eyes and puckered her lips, so I gave her a peck, turned, and somberly walked toward the house. She followed me in and disappeared into the shower.

Gazing out at the bay and the distant hills was a pastime I treasured. I sat on my special chair and did just that, though I was too depressed to cherish the breathtaking vista.

Quietly Kathy came toward me, fresh and beautiful and wrapped inside a dark green bath towel. She knelt in front and began to pull off my western boots and my socks.

Without the slightest sound or eye contact, she patiently removed my shirt by pushing my arms through the sleeves the way mothers undress their inexperienced children. When I was totally bare she led me to the middle of the room and gently pushed down on my shoulders. I landed on a large Turkish pillow.

As I waited, still and wondering, she sped away, only to return with a white sheet which she draped around my body. Then she wrapped a scarf around my head and tucked it in here and there until she seemed satisfied that my appearance was similar to that of a turbaned pasha. She rushed to the kitchen and reappeared with a tray of cheeses, crackers and other things and, still in silence, she uncorked a bottle of red wine and poured a glass for me. Finally, she dimmed the lights, lit some incense, and flicked on the hi-fi.

When the beat of a belly-dancing rhythm gave life to the until-then muted milieu, she left the room. While I sat there trying to guess what was next on her menu, a subdued "boom, boom, poof," reached my ears. I looked toward the noise. I saw one set of her toes wiggling out from behind the wall, then her ankle came into sight, followed by her lower leg, and she peeked to make sure the beginning of her performance wasn't being wasted.

Her right half emerged and her whole body jumped out in front of me with her arms raised, waving and swinging to the stimulating yet mystical melody. While the fragrance from the incense and the notes from the musicians' lute and drums permeated the room, she went on with her half-striptease, half-belly-dancing act, every so often kicking first her right leg to the front and then her left, as the can-can girls do, and each time she booted the air she shouted her "boom, boom, poof."

Sensing the finale of the composition, as she was very near me, almost against my nose in fact, she bent down, stared into my eyes, and with a sensual smile delivered the lines she must have memorized from some show seen in the past. "Is that a pistol you got in your pocket, my Sunflower, or you just like me too much?"

In her own intuitive way, by her concocted dance, she had labored to bring me out of the sadness I had brought home. She had vividly expressed the many blessings we shared together, subtly reminding me that the building on Powell Street was but a sliver of our whole pie of happiness. Feeling overwhelmed with contentment at having mated with such a special flower, my misery vanished and I buried my face in her delicate hair, hungrily inhaling her scent.

7

THE TALE
OF THE BARONESS

" 'll call you as often as I can," I told Kathy while she hung from my neck, inside my arms, full of all the anxieties our first separation as man and wife was dealing us. The Baroness' cable had been brief.

Yiannis, important discovery at last. You must come at once.

The last call for boarding the flight to Frankfurt had been announced yet Kathy remained tightly moored to me. When she sensed my arms dropping from around her shoulders she pushed them up, refusing to yield to the impending detachment. I kissed her adorable eyes, the tip of her nose, and her lips again and again. "No more than a couple of days," I said and rushed away just in time to slip through the door as it was closing. Our love seemed a bite of the most delicious cake created by a lofty baker.

Upon clearing customs in Frankfurt, I placed a long-distance call to report my safe arrival to my Louloudaki. She lifted the receiver faking deep sleep, then reminded me that half of my two-day trip was almost over, and that if I were planning to keep my word of honor, I should be preparing to board a plane heading back home. I cracked up and told her she was as insane with love as I.

Next I called the Baroness, who sounded pleasantly surprised to hear my voice. She asked me to meet her for dinner at the Cellar by Theodor Heuss Bridge.

I rented a Karmann Ghia with plenty of zip. A couple of hours of pleasant driving brought beautiful Heidelberg into my field of view and, because waterfronts have been alluring to me all my life, I took a room at a riverfront hotel. With time to spare, I showered to chase off a bit of the muscle ache from the lengthy flight, then headed out on foot to find the Cellar, anxious to see the Baroness and listen to her secret.

The stroll was invigorating. Locating the restaurant was easy with its massive facade of unfinished stone. Through a giant metal gate hanging from mammoth iron hinges, a worn granite stairway led down into a large hall. From the stone and brick walls of medieval texture and husky, rough-chiseled wooden posts hung flaming torches and stuffed wild beasts. This bizarre ambiance prickled me. An unsmiling gray-haired maitre d' in a black tuxedo approached me.

In my modest German I began to explain that I was expecting company.

"I speak English very well, Monsieur," he interrupted. He brought his white-gloved hands together and clasped them in front of his chest. "Are you perhaps Monsieur Barlow?" His sharp blue eyes searched me. I nodded. Wearing the same expressionless face, he motioned, "Please follow me. The Baroness is expecting you."

Under the ivory tusks of an enormous African elephant head, obscured from the entrance, sat the Baroness, alone and majestic. When she caught sight of us approaching, her brightly painted lips stretched into a wide smile. Then she extended her arm, offering me her pale jeweled hand for the traditional bow and kiss. She had aged; her generous cleavage bore numerous wrinkles and the skin on top of her plump hand was freckled with dark age-spots, but she remained gregarious.

"Come, come, my dear young Greek American. Please, have a chair. I have important news to tell you."

The maitre d' asked if I wished anything from the bar. When I declined, he suggested a bit of red wine, pointing at an uncorked, almost-full bottle in the middle of the large cloth-covered table. I agreed and he picked up the phial as if it were a most precious gem. Cradling and twisting it, he poured some of the ruby liquid into my glass.

The Baroness observed the ceremony with an approving grin and, having already begun to enjoy the fine qualities of this aged Rhine red, raised her glass.

"Let us drink to your ultimate success. Let us celebrate the beginning of the unraveling of the mystery of monstrous Tenner."

I lifted my glass.

A tall young waiter approached our table and asked if we wished to order. The Baroness asked for appetizers for both of us. When he was out of earshot, she leaned forward and whispered, "At long last, the break we have been waiting for came through. My sources have discovered the whereabouts of a woman who may be able to help us."

Her observant eyes danced. She studied my face and, responding to the respect and gratitude she saw there, she continued with zest.

"Young man, perseverance is a holy word. It is through perseverance that exalted states of human excellence are reached. Words such as achievement, perfection, fulfillment, would never have been invented if it weren't for perseverance. Perseverance is the drudgery, the toil, the sweat, but through it and it alone have we been granted a tiny, long-sought clue so that we may begin our passionate journey to discover the whereabouts of this elusive, repulsive man and bring him to a delayed justice."

"Please tell me about this woman. Who is she, where is she?"

The waiter brought two large plates decorated with pickled herring, smoked salmon and salmon roe, crudités and cheeses, and an assortment of crackers and breads.

The Baroness, whose stout appearance hinted at a weakness for the delights of fine cuisine, took up the correct utensils and, with pinkies raised and curved, as if she had been reared in the most prestigious European finishing school, began to taste the delectables with enthusiasm.

"Her name is Veronika Meier and she lives in the outskirts of a small town near Munich. Tenner was married to her younger sister, Ingrid. Veronika was living with those two in an apartment in Berlin. During an Allied raid Ingrid was killed and the apartment destroyed.

The story has it that, after gathering whatever she could salvage from the debris, Veronika went to live with her mother, and when her mother passed on, she vanished."

"And?"

The Baroness, with a twinkle in her eyes, tapped her index finger to her temple.

"Remember perseverance?" She winked. "It has been a frustrating journey of pursuit, but at long last, we have succeeded in locating her."

"Then I must be off to Munich at once. Tomorrow morning at the latest. Are there any direct flights from Heidelberg?"

She noticed my lack of appetite. "Oh, my, my, what a horrid waste. You haven't touched your delicious hors d'oeuvres. Are they too salty for you, perhaps? Do you wish something less tart?"

"Accept my apologies, Baroness, but my stomach is unsettled from the long flight."

Her face mellowed in a motherly fashion.

"Do you wish some medicine then? Maybe some soda will . . ."— cutting her sentence, she beckoned our waiter to the table and ordered a bottle of soda water at once.

"I have taken the liberty of reserving a seat in your name at noon tomorrow, since time is of the essence, of course." With her knife and a delicate touch, she scooped a bit of salmon roe, spread it on a rye cracker, sprinkled it with a bit of finely chopped chives, and placed it carefully inside her mouth.

"I have also arranged for Karl, one of my devoted confidants from Berlin, to meet you at the airport and be your driver and translator."

What an admirable woman, I was thinking all the while I sat across from this aged courtesan with the refined taste buds and unknown past. The Baroness was a riddle and I hungered for explanation. Who was this invaluable, efficient, and enigmatic madam?

"Baroness, I am as impressed by your proficiency as I am puzzled by your willingness to help me."

Dead silence fell. The Baroness cast her eyes on one of her rings, a gold one with a diamond of many carats. She turned it and stroked it with her thumb.

"You must understand that my reasons for helping you are not totally altruistic." She took a drink of wine and for the first time her whole face reflected pain. But her recovery was instantaneous and she smiled. She brushed at her gray hair with the palm of her hand. Her stare became vacant—her recollections filing back through the past.

"The tale is on the tip of my tongue and I'm in the mood to share it with you." Her eyes met mine, challenging me for assurance that her storytelling would be received by a worthy listener.

"It will be my honor to hear anything you wish to tell, Baroness."

She raised her half-full glass and with one motion the wine drained away. She rearranged her lower body and her dress to make herself a trifle more comfortable, and as a dignified breath lifted her bosom, she began.

"Long, long ago, a little girl was born to a very young woman whose parents were prominent and influential. To save the family from the shame and stigma of rearing an illegitimate child, the little girl was secretly given, along with a humble reward, to a childless roving laborer and his wife to bring up as their own. That simple man was called to serve his country and died fighting the French in the First World War.

"Destitute and hungry, the wife gathered her young daughter and the two traveled to Berlin. Food was scarce and Berlin was a ruthless place for a kind-hearted peasant woman with a child to feed, and soon—as it has happened countless times in the past and will occur myriad times in the future, I am heartbroken to admit—to stay alive she was forced to sell herself to anyone willing to pay for her favors. The take was meager and the abuse great, and within a few years she was afflicted with tuberculosis, an illness that devastated almost all the working prostitutes of the time.

"As the ill woman gasped her last breath, she revealed to her young daughter the truth—told her of the little she knew of her real parent-hood and handed her a tiny chain with a star. "I have been saving this for you," she whispered. "It is the Jewish star and it hung around your little neck when you were delivered to us, a mere puff of lovely flesh," and as soon as my mother handed me the star, she coughed and left me.

"Totally alone at twelve—alone and lonely, with no place to go—some of my mother's customers became mine. Then I became pregnant and my income stopped. The landlord asked me to go. To go— where?

"I took to the streets. As I was passing a synagogue, courage came to me and I walked inside. I saw the rabbi, a poor, kind old man, mumbled my story to him, and showed him the chain and the star. He looked doubtful at first. Then he took the time to explain to me that the star was the Star of David and that I was likely a Jew. He offered me shelter in the synagogue basement in exchange for some housecleaning.

"I lived there until my little boy was born; I named him David. At fifteen, fully grown, with the bits of savings from handouts, I rented a small room and began to take in customers, only this time I demanded more for my services and received it because I was well-developed, bosomy and curvy. David was almost two when one night a tall handsome officer, who later became one of Himmler's most vicious lieutenants, paid me a visit and asked me to do things I wouldn't. In a fury, he picked up my little boy by his tiny feet and flung him across the room, crushing his skull. I ran to the police, who came and took his little dead body away. . . . "

The Baroness lost her composure, her features tightened, her lips trembled. She let out a loud sigh and her head fell limp. When finally she revealed her face to me again, she looked much, much older.

"The following day I took a long walk along the river and contemplated ending it all. The world seemed irrational. I sat on the bank staring at the swift current. Then a man's strong voice came from behind me. 'I am Baron Von Hoffman,' he said. 'May I be of some assistance to you, my princess? You appear to be in great distress. There is an inn not far from here. So come, come along and share a meal with me and tell me your story if you wish.'

"He was very old. Through the bleary eyes of a fifteen-year-old he seemed ancient but he stood erect and dignified; he wore a tall black hat, held a cane in his hand, and his kind wrinkled face was semi-hidden behind his heavy mustache and a monocle.

"As if I were in a trance, I followed him to a small, almost-empty guesthouse and between sobs and sighs I told him my woeful story. His eyes showed great anger. Swinging his stick and threatening the air, he said he had friends in high places and assured me that the perpetrator would be found and hanged.

"Then he gently touched my hand and offered me one of the many vacant rooms in his castle, with no strings attached, he said. I accepted his proposal.

"We passed through the marketplace and the lowly peddlers ridiculed him—'Here comes the Baron!' 'Good day, Baron,' 'How is his excellency the Baron this morning?' They snickered and some jeered out loud, but he kept on walking with his pompous step, swinging his ornate cane, his proud head looking straight ahead, he in the front and I a few steps behind. We climbed a small hill and finally came to a very old, very large, and decrepit house.

" 'You will be happy living in my castle, my lovely princess,' he said as he ushered me inside the dilapidated front door.

"The huge wreck was in total disarray, but I began to tidy things up and after about a year the place was at least habitable. He taught me to read and write, and I listened to his stories of valor, such as when he was a young general and had single-handedly, with only his sword for backing, captured a thousand frightened, retreating Russian soldiers. While the days faded and the early nights came, his fantasies were agitated by the cheap port wine he loved, his dearest and only friend until I came along, and his stories became turbulent and confused.

"One morning he failed to come down from his room for his coffee. I went up to him and found him in his bed, ashen and trembling. I reached for his bony, listless hand. His cloudy sight rested on me. In a half-delirious state he mumbled that there were only a few breaths left in his lungs. Since he had no heirs he needed to make some arrangements at once. His castle and his title would be forfeited to the state at his passing and he did not wish that to occur under any circumstance. Then, the only logical step was for me to become his lawful wife, the baroness. When I agreed, his feeble eyes glowed with relief and he urged me to fetch the local pastor. The reverend came and married us. Not much later that evening my husband, the make-believe baron, perished."

Now the Baroness' old face frowned into a ghostly appearance, as if she were part of the wild animal exhibit. Minutes clicked by in utter stillness. She went on.

"During my short presence on this planet I had lived through a great deal of grief. Throughout all those losses I had cried a lot, but when the Baron died I wept for weeks." Her head tilted and she crossed her fingers in silent prayer.

The young waiter had been patiently waiting for an opportune moment to advance. He misunderstood her pause and came toward us, but I dismissed him with a wave of my hand.

"When I had no more tears to shed, I thought of the poor young wretches like myself in the not-so-distant past, who had nothing to sell except their unclean bodies. I began to visit my old neighborhood and offered many a place to stay in the castle. Some came and were grateful, some came and left, and some refused to come at all. Then, just as the Baron's money was running short, I had a dream."

Suddenly, as if a plastic surgeon had performed a miracle, the Baroness' contorted face relaxed, and her amiable smile returned to its full bloom.

"I pictured the castle restored, aglow, decorated with fine furnishings; my young women, outfitted in ball gowns, and their elegantly dressed customers—gentlemen, officers laughing, flirting, waltzing to the happy tunes of Johann Strauss, played by a small orchestra. Food laid out on long tables, only the best quality, well prepared and gracefully displayed.

"Upstairs, rooms decorated with antiques, canopied beds with fresh linen, to be soiled by only one man and one woman per room per night, as in all respectable hotels. Half-asleep, or semi-awake, I thought, why must these houses always be seedy, amoral, full of shame? Why can't this masculine drive, normal as sunshine, be appeased in a refined, genteel environment with music and dance, full of fun and games? Why can't the experience be more like an acted-out fantasy for both parties, enhanced and elevated to perhaps the same status as a joyful meal in a fine restaurant?

"Thus, my attentive friend, the castle was gradually refitted and revised and eventually became the most celebrated and distinguished house in Europe. I feel strongly that I have defended the Baron's title and his trust with dignity." I raised my glass to her.

"A very touching . . . fascinating story, Baroness," I said. She acknowledged my toast and went on.

"The second chapter of my life, the one you are probably wondering about the most, is rather brief. While the Nazis were overtaking the country, our clients increasingly became Nazi officers or party dignitaries. The most important training I provide, then and now, to hopeful young women who wish to learn the business is proficiency in listening. Much of the blabbering pillow-talk of our amorous and often tipsy clients was discussed and commented upon by the girls each morning when we gathered for our coffee.

"They chattered, innocently of course, about conversations they had had with their client-friends, and often, naïvely, revealed subjects of military importance which I passed on to Joseph, my old friend and confidant. Joseph, even though he enjoyed the rank of lieutenant in the SS, was an American agent. His frequent visits to the castle were known even to the Fuehrer himself. Joseph was considered by his colleagues as perhaps the most passionate lieutenant of the Third Reich. You met Joseph. He is the tall man with the missing left eye."

"Joseph, an American agent? And a lieutenant in the SS? How did he lose his eye?"

"In the latter part of the war during a confrontation with three Gestapo men. His spying activities for the Allies had been discovered. When the Gestapo men arrived to arrest him, he sneaked away. As he was being chased in the night, running for his life through a web of prearranged escape routes, a bullet ricocheted and pierced his skull. Luckily he was already within an arm's length of comrades who took him underground. He remained hidden until the surrender. Although he lost his eye and a small part of his left brain he has recovered rather miraculously, and functions fairly well." The Baroness made no effort to veil her special fondness for Joseph.

"To finish my story before I completely tire you out, I may be a Jew, but then, I may not. My deep hatred for the Nazis is only obliquely related to that question. David's death was just one of millions of grisly crimes they committed against children. In a way my little David was lucky; other toddlers were tortured, starved, burned alive, gassed. The Nazis had no respect for human dignity; they had no remorse. My efforts to bring men like Tenner to justice are all I can do for my son. It is the only true legacy he, or I, will leave."

The Baroness' eyes zeroed on mine and widened to convey to me the importance of her point. "The Nazis' most wicked crime of all, my young friend, is that which they have committed against us, you and me, living witnesses to their monstrous acts who must endure the nightmares of their atrocities until our deaths—the survivors of places such as Auschwitz and Buchenwald, Russia and Yugoslavia, and yes, Kalavryta and . . . and even Berlin."

The Baroness reached under the table for her large leather purse, snapped it open, and took out powder puff and lipstick to begin the ritual of freshening up her tired face. As she did so, staring into the tiny mirror, she casually added. "Now you know why I want to help you."

I nodded.

"You abandoned your castle in Berlin. Why?" I asked.

"It ended up in the Soviet sector, almost destroyed from the bombardments. My American friends relocated us to Heidelberg. This was my first choice."

8

THE MISSING LINK

The man who approached me as I stood by the newsstand at the Lufthansa air terminal in Munich had mussed hair, small sharp green eyes, and a red goatee and was dressed in a U.S. Army-issued green trench coat. After carefully looking me over, he stuck out his arm for a handshake.

"You must be Yiannis the American."

I smiled and shook Karl's hand. At a hurried pace he led me to an older Mercedes and we took off at high speed on a two-lane road toward the sun. We spoke little, but he placed a folder in my lap indicating that I should familiarize myself with its contents. Translated documents were stapled in an orderly fashion—descriptions of Tenner provided by various ex-Nazis who had supplied sketches of his physical characteristics along with his attributes and flaws, appetites and fetishes and obsessions—all those components essential to distinguish a human being—though in Tenner's case that categorization was high of the mark.

Certain descriptions of Tenner stood out. He was a tall man, up to three inches over six feet, fair-complexioned with blond hair and light blue eyes. His frame was lanky—devoutly hygienic, clean-shaven, and orderly. His right wrist bone protruded, as if at some point in his life it had been dislocated and never properly reset. Out of twenty-one persons interviewed, only four had noted this deformity, but it was a significantly unusual feature and Karl had highlighted it with red pencil.

Tenner was an avid photographer, very private, assumed to be married, even though no one had ever met his wife, and presumed to be childless. Stone-faced, for the most part, he maintained complete composure, yet on rare occasion violent outbursts of temper had been witnessed. His voice was high-pitched and piercing.

Forty minutes of sharp turning and tire-burning brought the Mercedes into a village centered around a cobblestone square with a round fountain in its middle. Four larger-than-life lions arched water through their mouths. A group of villagers dressed in lederhosen sat in the afternoon sun drinking beer from decorative steins.

Street signs were attached to the corner buildings, and Karl drove slowly around the square checking them before he took a left turn. Almost two hundred meters past some modest houses, the road became a narrow rural route and zigzagged up the slope of a mountain. Three kilometers or so from town Karl stopped in front of a secluded alpine cabin with a front yard and a low picket fence. A slim woman of medium size in her late forties, her gray hair in a bun, was busy pruning bushes.

She stood, half bent at the waist, staring at us inquisitively. Karl quickly told me to pretend I was an American writer doing research for a book on the war, but to trust him to do all the talking.

"Guten tag. We are looking for Miss Veronika Meier. Do we have the right address?" Karl's voice was soft and polite.

Uneasiness spread over her sad face. When she stood erect, her left leg was revealed to be noticeably shorter and her left shoulder drooped lower than the other. Her head appeared off center. After a moment of hesitation she wiped her hands on her apron and replied in good English.

"Yah, I am she."

"Good, good. You speak English."

"I majored in English in the university."

"You may have guessed that the gentleman, my companion, is an American," Karl said casually as he pointed at me. "I am Karl Weimar, a private investigator on hire to Mr. Yiannis, an American writer who is searching for material to complete his book on the war." At Karl's explanation and roundabout introduction I bowed slightly, and gave her my most luminous smile.

She limped forward, her eyes searching the two of us. As she opened the gate she spoke with a shrug.

"I don't know how I can be of any help to you since I have never been a Nazi and I had nothing to do with the war." She vacillated. "But since you have taken a long trip to come to my home please do come in, for a refreshment at least."

Karl and I sat on a spacious couch by a large front window. Knick-knacks were displayed on spotless crocheted doilies and lace-trimmed linens. A large, ornate porcelain clock with colorful figurines chimed as if pleading for attention. Veronika reappeared, carrying a silver tray with a steaming teapot, three delicate cups on saucers, and a plate full of assorted cookies, which she placed on the coffee table. Then she took a chair facing us and crossed her good leg over the weaker, perhaps to veil her deformity at least for the moment.

"Miss Meier, you are a very gracious lady and we both thank you for offering us a bit of your time, and your hospitality, of course. I would like to come directly to the point of our visit. What we are after is any information you can offer us concerning your brother-in-law, Commandant Tenner."

While Karl spoke, Veronika's eyes never left mine, scrutinizing me as if she knew all along that her sister's husband had done me wrong.

She addressed Karl but kept her eyes on me.

"Mr. Weimar, God hasn't been too kind to my limbs but he has compensated me with a keen mind. The American man, Mr. Yiannis, he isn't writing a book at all. What he is after is . . . the commander's head." She continued to observe me with intense curiosity. "He may be an American now, but his origin is Slavic, maybe Greek."

Pretense flew out the window. My heart took over and, ignoring Karl's coaching, I assured the woman that her second guess was accurate and that my ultimate intent was to bring down judgment on the commander, if and when I ever found the bastard, as long as he was the man I thought he was.

Veronika's large hazel eyes softened.

"He has hurt you terribly, I see it in your face." The ends of her lips drooped and so did her brows. "He is a vicious man. My sister Ingrid was always terrified of his temper. I lived with them in Berlin and I witnessed him intimidate her and humiliate her. He often slapped her and lashed her with his belt. Fortunately, he was away most always, at the various fronts."

Karl's face sparkled with anticipation.

"You have used the present tense, Miss Meier. Was it a slip of the tongue or is it a suggestion that you know for certain Tenner is alive?"

"I suspect he is alive—that man is like a cat, and cats don't die easily. He was wounded numerous times and has many scars."

"Any of them noticeable?"

"The one that instantly comes to mind was his right wrist. He always wore long sleeves to conceal it, but it was most noticeable if you looked carefully. And, of course the SS—you know, the lightning bolts—tattooed high on his left arm."

"Did you ever see him after the surrender?" asked Karl.

"No. Most wanted Nazis managed to sneak out of Europe. Anyway, he had no reason to contact me after Ingrid's death and the destruction of their apartment in Berlin. Don't you see? He despised me. To an Aryan purist, having an invalid as a sister-in-law was a disgrace. If he could have had his way he would have had me dumped in a well. Eliminated me, as the Spartans did with persons whose deformities rendered them unproductive."

"Any photographs, or his personal belongings? Did any of his personal effects survive the bombing?" I asked.

Veronika's memory flashed into action, and she brought a hand up to her lips.

"During the war, Ingrid received at least one package each month. Mostly Hans' photographs. On the back, all those pictures were dated. Each had a brief description of the location and the scene it represented. Most of them illustrated German soldiers performing despicable acts. I refused to view them but I did see a few in the beginning. Ingrid spent a great part of her spare time sorting and filing all those photos by date, as she had been instructed to do. She always did as she was told—as was expected of her, being the wife of a dedicated SS officer."

"Photos are difficult to destroy, unless, of course, there is fire. Did you try to recover any from the rubble of the apartment, Miss Meier?" Karl persisted.

"I was so heartbroken by Ingrid's death but, yes, there were some items recovered, and among them some photographs."

"Those photographs—are they available? Do you still have them?" I asked, my heart palpitating.

"They should be somewhere in the attic. Everything that was salvaged I have kept. Haven't thought of those photos for years. But why are you so interested in photographs of that war? What are you after, Mr. Yiannis?"

"I want to be sure that this Tenner is the man I am seeking—I remember him dimly—I was just a boy, but this man was tall and I remember him answering to the rank and name of Commandant Tenner. He lived in our house for a week in December of 1943. That tall officer took many pictures of my blond and blue-eyed sister."

"Your memory hasn't failed you. He is tall and an avid photographer, and he did serve in Greece."

"Could we impose on you to tell us what you know of the Commander, Miss Meier? Nothing lengthy, just the basics that come to mind, if you would, please." For a private eye, Karl was most polite, I thought.

Veronika resettled herself a bit in her chair and tucked her skirt under her knees. Her voice, somewhat muffled at first, soon came through crystal clear.

"Tenner's father, the late Colonel Heinrich von Tenner, and Hitler had served in the same company in the army. Fought side by side in the battle of the Somme. The then-Lieutenant Tenner and Corporal Adolf Hitler were both awarded the Iron Cross 1st Class for bravery, I was told. The colonel was killed on the Russian front in 1916, right after Hans was born. Hitler remembered his friend with reverence and he corresponded with Frau Tenner, who grew to be Hitler's ardent admirer.

"He invited her and her son to the historic gathering of Bavarian dignitaries in the Burgerbraukeller in Munich in 1923, where Premier Gustav von Kahr was to speak. Frau von Tenner accepted. She took her young son to meet Hitler, by then the leader of the Nazi party. Hans was barely seven years old. As Hans told the story, Hitler placed his hand on the child's blond head and said, 'You are the perfect specimen of our youth, Germany's pride, the future masters of the world. It is your birthright to rule the world, my son.'

"When Hitler pulled his gun and stunned all the attendees by firing two shots at the ceiling and shouting, 'The national revolution has begun!' Hans fell in love with Hitler and became one of his blind and ruthless followers.

"Hans' mother was insensitive. She always demanded, and had, her own way. She was a student of German history and she was filled with admiration for Germany's great past and dreams of German greatness in the future. Hans grew up in an environment of Wagner's creation—a romantic concept of German culture in the tradition of ancient Teutonic warrior gods and heroes. A staunch nationalist herself, she was deeply affected by Germany's defeat in the first war. She was one of those who expressed strong indignation at the terms for Germany's signing the Treaty of Versailles. Like the Frenchman Count de Gobineau, she believed that race was the root of all problems throughout the history of mankind."

Veronika took a sip of her tea and went on.

"Hans' secondary education was at the Royal Bavarian Gymnasium. There he joined the Hitler Youth. He was a delegate to the Nazi party congress in Nuremberg in 1929, where he carried the Hitler *Jugende* banner during a memorial celebration for the dead heroes of World War I. He witnessed the solemn consecration of colors where new Nazi flags were touched to the *Blutfahne* (Blood Banner), the old tattered flag drenched in the blood of those killed during Hitler's failed attempt to seize power in 1923. He loved all the ceremonies—the torchlight processions, the goosestep marches, the human swastika formations, and the fireworks displays. He often spoke of how he became captivated listening to a hundred and fifty thousand marching Nazi party members who sang along with a dozen brass bands the *Deutschland-Lied* (Song of Germany)."

She took one more sip, brushed her gray hair back from her face, and crossed her hands in her lap.

"He met with the Fuehrer during the congregation of sixty thousand young boys at the Youth Stadium in Munich. It was there he received the famed Hitler knife, the long knife with the inscription *'blut und ehre'* (blood and honor) on the blade. But Hans was most proud of the framed excerpt from the Fuehrer's speech given to him by Baldur von Schirach, head of the Hitler Youth Movement. He had it memorized and recited it at every opportunity. Do you know what it said? Have you any idea of its content? Dreadful! Sick! Would you like me to recite it to you? It hung in our salon in Berlin and I heard Hans and my sister repeat it so many times I still remember it by heart."

"Please, go right ahead," said Karl.

" 'In the New Germany that I will build, you young people will grow up who will frighten the world. I want a violent, arrogant, unafraid and cruel you who must be able to suffer pain. Nothing weak or tender must be left in you. Your eyes must project once again the aura of a free magnificent beast of prey. I want my young people strong and beautiful. I shall train them in all kinds of athletics, for I want young that are athletic, that is first and foremost. Thus will I erase a thousand years of human domestication. Thus will I mold the pure and noble raw material. Thus I will create the New Aryan, the master of the world.' "

"And thus he molded most of Germany's youth into beastly murderers," said Karl with disgust. Veronika gazed into her garden, while calling to mind still more of the past.

"He took courses in English, French, and Italian, all of which he was able to speak and understand, not fluently but well enough to communicate. When candid photography became popular in the early thirties, Hans quickly immersed himself in this new hobby. He owned various German cameras but his favorite was an American-made Kodak 620.

"He met my sister Ingrid, a very striking girl, at one of the youth functions at Munich University. Hans graduated with a degree in mechanical engineering, and they were married in 1939. He was twenty-three and Ingrid only twenty. He wrote a letter addressed to Himmler personally, asking to be admitted to *Schutzstaffel*.

"After two years of intensive training, my then brother-in-law graduated with honors, and in 1941 he was sent to the Russian front. There he was awarded the Iron Cross 1st Class for fearlessness in battle, just as his father had been during the first war. His visits to Berlin were very infrequent—seldom enjoyable or gracious—more often unpleasant and violent. If my sister dared to smile in the mere presence of another man, he would fly into vicious jealous tantrums. Yet he openly flaunted his admiration for other females, and even slept with them since it was the wish of the Fuehrer to propagate the pure race.

"Ingrid knew, but she loved him and as a dedicated Nazi herself, she accepted his amoral behavior. He served in Croatia and was awarded another medal, this one for exterminating hostages, and he spent time in the Balkans and in Greece."

"Thank you, Miss Meier, you have been a great help," said Karl.

"Would you mind our having a look at the pictures?" I asked impatiently.

"Well, the attic is dusty and you must be prepared to breathe a lot of musty air, but you are welcome to search through them if you like."

I stood up to indicate my readiness and Veronika, self-conscious of her limp, ushered us through a hallway and directed us to climb a stair with steep narrow steps while she followed. Through a small door we entered the large, dark, unfinished attic, but then Veronika turned on a light. She pointed toward a section filled with metal boxes.

"There they are, those two boxes on the right. That is all that was left of his photographs after the bombing. In Berlin there were dozens of these boxes completely full." She gave us a grin of encouragement and she hobbled away, leaving us alone. As the sound of her uneven steps echoed up the wooden stairs, Karl and I sat down opposite each other on two dusty pine stools and started our hunt.

In the pale light, we began our review of the documented moments of Tenner's dark path through history. It was a most disturbing task. Photographs of troops firing on civilians, their dying bodies falling to the earth, never to see the wonder of the next sunrise. Groups of Nazi officers wearing broad smiles while posing over piles of corpses, as if the dead were wild beasts. Men kneeling in agony under the smoking pistols of uniformed Nazis, frightened and pitiable faces still pleading, seemingly unaware that bullets had already left the pistols' chambers to shatter their skulls. Swastikas flying on top of the Acropolis while some gleeful Nazis gazed proudly at the captured Parthenon and the ancient lands.

Three hours into this grotesque chore, Karl's hand tapped me on the shoulder. "Take a look at this one. It was taken inside a house in Kalavryta in 1943."

My breathing quickened. I snatched the yellowed photo from his fingers. Three Nazis stood inside a room, grinning and arms linked. The men seemed to trigger a button of my mental camera. Was it for real? I sped to the light bulb for a clearer view.

"Miss Meier, Miss Meier!" I shouted, leaping down the steep steps. She came to me and I intercepted her in the hallway. I held the photo before her eyes and asked, "The tall man in the middle—isn't he Tenner? He has to ... I remember ... I think ... "

Her answer came quickly while her face froze into a mask of revulsion.

"Yes, that is Hans. That is Tenner." She looked at the writing on the back. "Is this picture taken inside your house, then?" Her eyes searched mine.

My excitement was so overwhelming that I leaned over and gave her a big kiss.

"Thank you, thank you a million times, Miss Meier. Yes, this photo was taken inside our home in Kalavryta. Do you see the picture hanging on the wall in the background?"

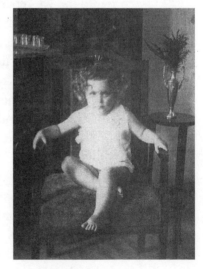

I could sense the presence of Karl behind me looking over my shoulder. "Can you see it, Karl? That is a picture of my sister Betty when she was four years old."

"You may have it, Mr. Yiannis, if you like," Miss Meier said.

Finally Karl took the photo away from me and walked slowly into the living room, where he sat on the couch, all the while staring at that very significant discovery.

"Half of the riddle has been explained," said Karl with some resignation while he scratched his goatee. As I edged near him, watching his face, I thought I could see a shadow creep over him.

"Miss Meier, has anyone ever in the past contacted you for information concerning Tenner?" His tone was calm and controlled.

"After Ingrid's death I moved to my mother's in Magdeburg and lived with her until 1949 when she passed on. I did receive a call there once, from someone who identified himself as an American intelligence officer, from the Office of Strategic Services, I believe he said. His call was brief, but when I mentioned the photographs he assured me that the unit investigating war criminals would contact me soon. Yet, strangely enough, no one ever did."

"Has there ever been an effort made by the commandant, directly or indirectly, to retrieve his personal belongings?"

"Only once, long ago. In 1947, a short letter arrived from Panama. The note was typewritten in German; it was a simple request from the German Archives of World War II of Central America expressing interest in any and all documents or photos that I might have. It offered a reward which would be forwarded to me immediately upon receipt of the materials."

"And what did you do with that note, Miss Meier?"

Veronika shrugged her crooked shoulders.

"I tossed it into the wastebasket, of course."

Karl darted a doubtful glance and promptly resumed his questioning.

"Why did you not pursue such a generous offer?"

"Because I knew, or let us say, I sensed, that the German Archives of Central America were Tenner himself, who hoped to get his awful pictures back into his own hands. I would never cooperate with him no matter what his monetary reward might have been!"

"Are you afraid of Tenner?"

"He is the reason I sold my parents' home in Magdeburg and purchased this remote cabin. I have lived a reclusive life. As long as I remain one of the, if not the only, person who can positively identify him, I am in some danger, yes. That is why I was so surprised when you called out my name. Frankly, the only visitor I ever receive, besides the milkman, is the local pastor."

"You have been extremely difficult to locate, Miss Meier, I must vouch for that. But let me assure you that your privacy will remain undisturbed."

"It's important to me," she said, her eyes filled with pleading.

"Much time has passed since, Miss Meier, but can you remember where in Panama that letter originated? Even the name of the city would help."

"Yes, I do. I remember it all." Her admission stunned us. With widened eyes Karl and I looked at each other and then at our hostess. "Simply through a coincidence. I remember quite clearly that the post office box number where I was to send the materials was the same as the last two digits of the year I received the note—1947—Post Office Box 47, Panama City, Panama."

Karl's face glowed.

"You are positive of the number? The post office box number, I mean?"

"Mr. Weimar, I have nothing to gain by feeding you inaccuracies. You are too young to remember that many Germans never supported Hitler's war. We opposed him from the beginning but we were in the minority. One of the reasons Tenner despised me was because I refused to accept his Aryan theories. I assure you it will be a great satisfaction to me if I can contribute to Tenner's discovery and punishment. Anyone who does wrong must be brought to justice and, as God is my witness, I know that this terrible man you seek has done many wrongs. I heard him brag a great deal about his atrocities."

She stood to show us our time was up. There were no parting words exchanged between us, but she gazed into my very soul and through her sorrowful eyes exposed her pain and offered me a silent, commiserating grief. When I took her hand and kissed it, she stepped onto her normal leg and reached up, stretching her neck, to give me a peck on the cheek.

We walked out through the darkened garden. But as Veronika shut the door behind us, we caught a muffled sound like running steps in the distance. I saw a silhouette disappearing in the murkiness of the night.

Karl's alert eyes glowed. They shifted about but he said nothing. We climbed into the Mercedes and raced to the airport. Once there he insisted on accompanying me to the ticket counter to check in for the next flight. As we walked together down a corridor leading to the customs hall, he unbuttoned his coat and felt for his revolver while he kept a sharp eye over our shoulders.

"Is there someone following us, Karl?" I asked in alarm.

He did not respond but instructed me to go directly to my flight gate and to refrain from wandering about the airport.

"You have enough to go on—the photo and, most important of all, the post office box and the date in Panama. You must pay Panama a visit soon. There's a good chance the records may still be around."

The moment I exited customs and before I even saw her, Kathy flew into my arms, weeping, and we plunged into a kissing and hugging orgy.

"My Sunflower," she cried. She kissed my face all over with the gleefulness of a cat washing her lost kitten. "Please don't you ever leave me again," she begged.

"I won't," I assured her and licked her tears with my tongue. I kept squeezing her body against mine, wishing her to become my second skin.

Blissfully embraced we walked to the garage. When we reached the Austin Healey, I was shocked to see the jump seats loaded with blankets, pillows, and belongings.

"What is going on, Louloudaki? Where are we heading? Are we about to join a band of gypsies—take off for the high mountains and set up house in a cave for a couple of years?" Looking deep into her blue eyes, I tried to read what my woman had up her sleeve this time. Though her lips moved no sound came out and her face seemed to choke a secret.

"I'll tell you as soon as we are out of here."

While we headed toward the garage exit, I noticed Kathy intently watching through the rear window by pushing her body up from her toes to clear her line of sight over the jumble of possessions that stood stacked high behind our backs. We paid our fee and approached the highway.

"Take the left lane and head south," Kathy said.

"Will you speak up, for crying out loud?"

"I'll explain, but please."

I took the left lane.

"Half an hour before I left to pick you up, I received a terrifying phone call from Germany from a detective named Karl. He said he had just been with you in Munich and asked me to tell you that Veronika Meier has been murdered."

I hit the brakes. "What?"

"Someone killed her after the two of you left her house last night. He said we shouldn't go home, temporarily at least, and warned us we should make sure no one is following you here."

I pulled to the side of the road; I was shaking and my tongue felt dry and numb. I flung the door open, sprang out, and looked to the sky with outstretched arms, pleading.

"God, talk to me! You can't be deaf and mute forever. She believed in you, damn it! Where is your fucking justice?"

Kathy pulled hard on my coattail and forced me back into the car.

"A premonition that something horrible would come of this trip has been with me from the beginning, my Sunflower," she whispered. She clutched my wrist, assuring herself I was indeed near her, alive and well.

"But why?" I cried, grasping the wheel with all my might, trying to shake it loose. "She didn't do anything to deserve such a fate! First, He gives her a tormenting disfigurement and now He takes her life— where is His fuckin' justice?"

"Would you rather I drove?" Kathy said softly. "It's dangerous to park in the middle of the road."

"Where in hell are we heading, anyway? You never told me."

"To Gran's house in Capitola. She is expecting us. Didn't tell her why we are coming, but it's not necessary. I'd rather have her believe we've missed her and would like to spend a few days with her. And we have missed her, haven't we, my Sunflower?" She forced a smile to cheer me up.

"Perhaps you have," I snapped and revved up the engine. We headed south on Highway 101 and Kathy kept up her vigilance toward the rear.

Guilt that Veronika's murder might be directly related to my visit tormented me. Kathy seemed to read my mind.

"I feel just as awful as you about this woman's death, Yiannis," her voice was solemn, "but you mustn't blame yourself for what happened.

They were after some pictures, Karl said."

"You didn't tell me that!" I barked. "Did Karl say the murderer took the photos from the attic?"

"Yes. Every one of them. As morbid as it may sound, he speculates that Lady Luck was with the two of you—you arrived at her house a few hours before the murderer did. He asked me to remind you of the shadow which disappeared into the darkness. Karl thinks that may have been the killer."

"What else did Karl say?"

"He expects you to call him at precisely eight our time tomorrow morning. I have written the number in my little book." She searched her purse to assure herself that her little book was there. "From a public telephone, which is untraceable—he was adamant about your using a public phone."

"Poor woman. Veronika was a . . . lady, Kathy." I shook my head in total perplexity and murmured, "I was talking with her only hours ago! Had she been tortured? Did Karl say?"

"No, he didn't."

Suddenly concern for our safety flashed through me.

"The Luger. Did you think to bring it along with all your junk?"

"It's in one of the suitcases in the trunk."

"How about ammo?" Kathy looked puzzled. "Did you think to bring the ammunition for the pistol?" She hesitated, but my fuse was short. "You know, the bullets—what a pistol needs to go bang, bang!"

"Boy, I've never seen you so nasty!" She tossed her head and stared straight ahead in protest. "To answer your snotty in-terr-o-ga-tion—yes. I did bring the bullets. I'm not as dumb as you think, Yiannis."

"I'm tired all of a sudden. Let's stop and get some coffee." Up ahead, lights on a huge sign blinked "SHELDON'S TRUCK STOP"; I guided the roadster off the highway, between two gigantic rigs. Within this temporary sanctuary, I reached over and patted the top of my Louloudaki's head, gently brushing her fine hair.

"I love you more than my life. It's stupid to take out my frustrations on you. It's just I feel we led Veronika's killer straight to her!"

She slid against me and kissed my cheek.

"It is only a matter of time," she said, her face glowing with warmth and forgiveness, "before someone who is hiding will be discovered. The world is too small, now. Karl found Veronika—after years of painstaking search all right, but he did find her. What makes you think Tenner couldn't have? You should be thankful that at least Karl located her first, and that you got to speak with her and get to know her before that Tenner did to her whatever he did. Oh, how I hate that man, Yiannis!"

"The thought that this animal is on the loose drives me insane."

"We will find him, even if we have to dedicate our whole life to it."

"You aren't just saying that to pacify me? Promise me you won't stop me from pursuing this prick!"

"I'll always support you." She was dead serious. "But I'm scared."

Her eyes fell with suspicion on three chatting truckers, and when she had assured herself of the absence of danger, she slowly walked to the rear of the Austin Healey. I followed her. She unlocked the trunk and produced the Luger in its leather holster along with a box of bullets, left them where I could see them, and withdrew. I loaded the clip, slipped the gun inside my shirt, and drove out from between the two trucks and parked in front of the restaurant.

With my arm draped over Kathy's shoulders, we walked into the place. Sheldon's was in dire need of paint, yet it hummed with men of all ages, sizes, and shapes. A few women, dressed in tight jeans and tighter blouses, stood around in various careless poses. Sheldon's appeared to be a decaying front for a whorehouse that catered exclusively to truckers. Since we didn't quite fit the norm of the patrons, many turned and looked us over inquisitively. We took a booth that offered us a view of our car.

A waitress wearing bright pink lipstick and a short black skirt came up to us, noisily chewing gum.

"Yup," she crackled while eyeing her pad, preparing to write the order.

"Hot apple pie à la mode with a double scoop of ice cream, and a chocolate malt," popped Kathy, all the while looking at me with a disarming innocence.

"Is your coffee fresh?" I asked.

"Yup. We make it every day," came the lady's reply. I shrugged my shoulders and ordered a cup. The moment she drifted away, Kathy said, "You know well when I'm nervous I like to eat sweets, and lots of them. And I'm scared, my Sunflower."

I smiled and she beamed. We sat facing each other. I reached out, took her hands, and held them inside mine. I told her all that had happened in Germany. During my reconstruction of the Baroness' sad biography, Kathy wept, using the paper napkins to wipe her tears. Then I took out the picture Veronika gave me, and told her what we had learned of Tenner's background.

Lastly I explained about the Panamanian postal address and suggested we make Panama City our next stop.

"Auntie Ethel has been telling me fascinating tales about Central America ever since I was a little girl," said Kathy as she inhaled the last drop of her malt through a straw. "Not so much about Panama and Costa Rica, but Guatemala. And how soon will we be leaving?"

"As soon as we arrange for your passport," I said.

"My passport is already in my purse. The school year was over last Thursday, and Friday the supervisor at the passport office took pity on me. I told him about my husband being ill and alone in Germany. I said I had to fly immediately to your bedside, and within two hours I had my passport.

"And since my intention was to join you in Munich, in case you were delayed there, I've also arranged to take a sabbatical for the entire coming school year, in case you needed me. Aren't you pleasantly surprised?"

"I'm elated," I said with a proud smile and meant it.

"But it looks as if we have become the hunted instead of the hunters," observed Kathy.

"Veronika couldn't have passed on to her killer any details about my identity, because she had none. Karl introduced me only as Yiannis, the American. The only information he could have extracted from her, if he tortured her, would have been that I'm after Tenner and that I'm from Kalavryta. There are a number of Kalavrytan survivors named Yiannis scattered around the globe, and I'm sure a few must have immigrated to the States. Karl is being overly cautious."

Kathy didn't buy my reasoning.

"Yes, but you're forgetting the picture! Veronika may have told them about the picture. Veronika knew that Tenner had stayed at your house in Kalavryta. Then, your identity would be obvious."

"Do you think Tenner would remember my family name? Almost impossible. But even if he does, which is improbable, my name is Barlow now. The judge in Frankfurt and I chopped off most of Varelopoulos and came up with Barlow. Hardly any relationship between the two. The name Barlow is British."

"You know, it would not be too difficult to look up records in the Immigration and Naturalization Service and match Varelopoulos to Barlow," she observed, with the air of a detective.

"Yes, they most certainly can do that, but—until they do all those things—we should enjoy our lives fully and stop crawling around in sewers like two rats afraid to be seen in public." With that statement I stood up, and we left the truck stop.

Gran Edith lived in a beach cabin with a neglected back yard next to a slow-flowing river. An old oak tree cast its shadow, and dried leaves lay scattered on the front lawn. The street was narrow and made of concrete. Two withered wicker chairs adorned the crumbling front porch. The wooden shingles showed their declining health, as if in sympathetic harmony with Gran Edith's aging. As long as I could remember, Gran had been old and sick and frail, but she lived alone and cared for herself, somehow dodging Reaper's call one day at a time.

I hoped, this time at least, that an angel might let her know we had a very trying day, and save me from having to face her favorite rhubarb stew. I detested the stuff with a unique passion. Yet to my total devastation, her simmering kettle was steaming on the stove, spreading its noxious odor as it had each and every time she expected us for a visit.

Before we even had a chance to exchange cordialities, I managed to whisper to Kathy, "I refuse to eat that garbage again! I just ain't gonna do it!"

"But we have invited ourselves, my Sunflower," she rightfully observed.

"Doesn't matter," I stubbornly insisted.

"Shhhhh. Please, be nice. She means well. And she is so old." Kathy placed her palm over my lips to stop me from getting saucy. I suppose at times my manners seemed a bit out of line and in need of a speck of refinement, but I had grown disrespectful of unchallenged conventional ways and often my objections, even though nonviolent, were loud.

Gran Edith came out of the single bathroom unsmiling, her wrinkled face powdered and pale except for her rouged, hollow cheeks. She was a rigid, proper Protestant woman who stood erect and always looked stately, and my intuition led me to believe that her tolerance for Mediterranean tribes was low-grade.

When my turn came to greet her, she extended her limp, shriveled hand and, since I knew she despised affectionate salutations, I bent and smooched her on the lips, causing her to bolt, withdrawing as if her chastity were in danger. Kathy pinched my behind. After fifteen minutes of family small talk, I excused myself using the pretense that my need to read a much-yearned-for newspaper was overwhelming. I left grandmother and granddaughter to visit with each other. The four-block walk to town along the riverside trail was serene and strangely mosquito-less. I found a phone booth and made two calls.

First I reached United Air Lines to reserve two tickets for Panama City. I am a firm believer in the old proverb that "fish and company begin to stink after the third day," so more than two nights of visiting with Gran Edith would be out of the question. Why tarnish a good relationship by overtaxing the patience of a loved one, I intended to explain to my Louloudaki.

Then I rang Maria at home and lied that I was still in Europe. I claimed that a very old but considerate auntie, aware I was on the Continent, to save her nephew the inconvenience of making an extra, costly trip upon her demise had expedited her biological end and passed on to heaven, and Kathy would soon be joining me to attend the funeral.

Maria, a perceptive sort, coughed into the receiver to warn me that naïveté wasn't one of her virtues. Then, efficient secretary that she was, she listened carefully to her Bossman and wrote down all the instructions to be followed during my absence.

"Let's see, now. Today it's good old Sunday, June the sixteenth— when should I expect you back? Or am I bein' disrespectful by darin' to ask?"

"Oh, in a week, two at the most," I replied half-spiritedly.

"Hmmm," Maria hummed and I could see her eyes gleaming with mischief. "Now, listen here, Bossman of mine," she added in her usual tinted-with-innuendo way, "how about givin' me a number over there in Europe, or wherever, just in case I need to get hold of you—in case of emergency, you understand."

"Maria, you can handle anything that might come up," I snapped and hung up.

I chose a dozen semi-withered white carnations, the best from the bunches available in a nearby grocery store, to present to Gran Edith in hopes that such an offering might cause her to look at me with some added valuation. Then, since she frowned at the mere thought of storing alcohol in her house, I purchased two jugs of table red—also the best from the poor selection—and a copy of the Sunday *San Francisco Chronicle*. With an unhappy gut, I headed back for the impending gastronomic torture. When I passed by a stranger's garden I clipped off one stunning ruby rose for my Louloudaki.

After sniffing at the stew, I ate a generous offering of Gran's apple pie and soon withdrew to the parlor to relax and read the paper while Gran and Kathy took to the coolness of the porch to continue their visit. The window of the parlor was open, and though I was hidden behind the heavy curtain where I sat in a comfortable old chair, I could hear them clearly.

"And when does this almost bare-chested husband of yours intend to give you a child?"

She was referring to my habit of keeping at least the three top buttons of my shirts free from their buttonholes, revealing some of the hair on my chest, obviously a primate state of nakedness and an unacceptable sight to Gran.

"Oh, Gran, Yiannis and I are too much in love with each other to want to share any of it with a child—for now."

"And what is that supposed to mean, dear?" Her voice sounded as if she were gargling with ice cubes.

"Simply that a child requires a lot of affection and, for now, I want to pass all my tenderness and caring to my husband and to no one else."

"Sounds selfish to me. He must be very selfish to have convinced you that he deserves all your attention and love."

"Please Gran, try to understand. Yiannis has been the only man in my life. I am crazy about him. In many ways, Yiannis is like a child, and I am too. When he needs me, I must have the time for him. I think couples grow apart because they forget the solemn vow they made. To love and to cherish are promises which should be taken very seriously. Those vows are sacred and should last a lifetime. I don't want us to be like all those men and women whose romance ends at their wedding ceremony—like in the movies."

"And what makes you think you and yours are made of different clay, dearie?"

"We have friends who beam with bliss during their nuptial ritual. Soon after, though, they toss their vows into the back of a closet, along with some of their least valuable wedding gifts, and close the door. They begin to take each other for granted, forgetting that marriage requires a lot of nourishment and effort. Can't you see how much we care for each other, Gran? And I want to love Yiannis as much when I'm fifty as I do now, and did when I was fifteen."

"That kind of talk is pure hogwash, child," declared Gran coarsely. "I don't know what has come over the younger generations. Seems to me you all talk strange." The pitch of Gran's voice had risen a couple of notes.

"Last winter Yiannis came down with a bad virus—he was so miserable. The high fever made him delirious. I was next to him ready to fulfill his every wish.

"Then a neighbor popped in unexpectedly and we chatted for a long time. When I returned, my husband had turned the TV on. He looked sorrowful and neglected.

"As mad as it may sound, a mixture of guilt and jealousy came over me. I turned off the darn TV at once. 'Nope, nope,' I told him. 'You're sick; if you need entertainment, you must talk to me. I'll be your amusement and your nurse.' I rubbed his feet, and his head and his arms, and I read from his favorite poet. I like to think that my nurturing made him well, Gran."

"So?" asked Gran, devoid of any tender feelings she may once have had.

"I just know that if we had a bunch of kids running around, demanding things as they do, I would have very little time for my husband, and I'm not ready for that yet."

"Fiddlesticks!" said Gran defiantly. "Children are a natural biological fulfillment for all women. You are spoiling this man; I can see it. Men usually grow tired of good women's devotion and start looking around for challenges. You'll be better off when you tie him down with some responsibilities, like a child or two. Take it from me, dear, I know." The tone of her speech allowed no further discussion.

"Besides ..."

"There is no besides," snapped Gran conclusively.

"Yes, there is," insisted my Louloudaki. "Besides, Yiannis and I are involved in something very important right now."

"Important! What could be more important than starting a family?"

"We are searching for someone, Gran. I'm sorry I can't tell you more."

My effort to read beyond the headlines had been futile. I took a proud, deep breath and moved to another chair, one away from the open window. Their voices became inaudible.

My sleep was short and packed with nightmares. I tossed and turned restlessly and was up before dawn, anticipating my call to Karl. I brewed strong coffee and sneaked out to the porch and the front yard. A rake lay half-buried under strewn leaves. The first sunbeams filtered through the oak branches. Wearily I approached the rake, lifted it, and started to scratch the grass, gathering the leaves into a pile.

"Morning." I was startled.

"Oh, good morning, Gran. Are you up already?"

"I'm always up before dawn."

I held up the rake. "Surprised?" I asked, itching for her reaction.

"I must say, I am. Never thought of you as the laboring type, particularly since you haven't learned how to button up your shirt yet."

I returned to raking.

"Too bad you live so far away, Gran. I could learn to like cleaning your yard."

At seven-thirty I cranked up the Healey and drove to the Shell station by the highway, and at precisely eight I asked the overseas operator to connect me with the number in Germany.

Karl picked up immediately.

"This man is determined to keep his identity hidden at any cost. He is ruthless and very resourceful. I'm positive he employs thugs. Until he is apprehended, your safety and your wife's will be at risk. Murder means nothing to him.

"Veronika may have been tortured before she was suffocated with a pillow. I think she may have been interrogated. Since there was no forced entry, we assume she knew her attacker. All the photos are gone. We were lucky on our timing, Yiannis. After all the years of tracing leads, we beat Tenner to Meier's house by an hour at most. I suppose her days had been numbered all along. Tenner had every intention of eliminating her. She was the only survivor who knew too much about him.

"It is a good omen that we got there first and found the picture, but you must be very careful. The Baroness is very concerned. She feels your wife must go into hiding. You see, we will never know how much information the wretched soul was forced to divulge. I would rather think that she spat on his face instead and told him to go to hell."

"Even if Veronika were forced to speak, she knew so very little about me."

"I agree with your rationale, but only partly," said Karl. "In my profession we learn never to underestimate the other side. What if he has kept a diary?"

"And carried it with him while he fled across the oceans with a phony ID? Extremely incriminating. What if he got caught with it? No, I don't believe Tenner would be so careless."

"Well, maybe you're right," he halfheartedly agreed. "However, under the circumstances I would bank on no more than one, at most two, carefree months. Within this very brief period, you must visit Panama City and find a safehouse for your wife. Call me at this number the same time and day two weeks from today—that will be Monday the first. You should be back by then."

"How about you, Karl? They can trace you through your vehicle's license number, which I'm sure they must have," I said with concern.

"Don't worry about me. When do you expect to hit Panama?"

"Our reservations are for Tuesday."

"Good. Be careful. *Auf wiedersehen.*"

"*Auf wiedersehen,* Karl."

9

THE PANAMANIAN
RIDDLE

Hazy emerald jungle flickered through patches of mist, the clouds were swept away, and the deep blue Pacific whirled beneath us. Through the airplane window I could see the Panama Canal like a shining ribbon splitting the earth in two. Kathy's hand gripped mine. Through at least the last half-hour of this bumpy journey, her eyes had remained shut, but every time the plane fell into an airless hole, her face tightened and took on an ashen mask. When the wheels finally thumped the ground and the turbulent flight came to its end, the crew and the weary passengers, mostly Panamanians returning from abroad, sighed and applauded the pilot's skills. A few in English, and the rest in Spanish, voiced their everlasting thanks to God the Almighty for having guided the large flying machine in one piece to its destination, crossing themselves and nodding their heads up and down in approval.

Even before we stepped on the ladder, humid tropical air hit us like a damp towel and our cheeks turned slick with perspiration. Since we had only carry-ons, we bypassed the baggage claim and easily cleared customs.

The waiting taxis appeared to have been assembled from spare parts collected in junkyards, but they were in abundant supply. A pleasant cabbie named Chino, a man of Spanish and Chinese blood who spoke marginal English, became our driver. His vehicle was in dire need of shock absorbers.

Simple wooden houses and fences shaded by banana and palm trees appeared in the jungle, with cows and chickens and pigs, and naked children playing in red dirt beneath clotheslines. The road ran below green hills until the Pacific suddenly burst into view, the heat left the air, and the distant buildings of Panama City glittered under the afternoon sun.

"Casco Viejo," Chino said and indicated a peninsula jutting out into the sea.

We drove along a street strewn with trash where men idled in doorways. Crowds promenaded on sidewalks in front of Spanish colonial buildings whose wrought-iron balconies, facades, and columns had long ago surrendered to time their details and paint.

The driver honked his horn, wheeled around a smoking truck filled with green mangoes, and headed toward the cathedral towers that loomed above the old city.

"Catedral Central, Oficina Central, Palacio Real."

Hotel Central was massive and gleaming white, with balconies and arches along the square. Two young men took our luggage, and after I paid Chino he offered me his card, assuring me that his expert services could be at our disposal within an hour's notice.

Our suite was air-conditioned and large. The instant the bellboy shut the door, I embraced Kathy and asked for her forgiveness—again—for having dragged her into this hunt. Her face close to mine, she reassured me she wanted to see Tenner punished too.

The balcony overlooked a plaza and we sat quietly, watching the sun's rays soften the stones of the square and the church to yellow and red and finally to silver and black. We studied the lovers, and the old men and women sitting on benches chatting, some dressed in black, others in bright festive colors.

"While I spend my time in some dusty warehouse checking through old records, you should be a tourist. I don't want you to waste your time tagging along."

Kathy's face grew animated. "If you think you're going to get rid of me, you have another think coming!" Her lips tightened with determination. "I'm sticking with you. Don't even try to dissuade me!"

"But these next few days may be very intense."

"My Sunflower, we didn't come here to go shopping for straw hats and bananas."

"Maybe we should hire a private eye to do all the searching for us."

"Hmmmmm."

"I value your thoughts. Tell them to me."

"What if Tenner has made his home in Panama? Up to now we've assumed that he used this place as a stepping stone, perhaps on his way to Argentina or Chile. But then, maybe, and I say maybe, this city—as the home base for international insurance corporations, shipping, and God only knows what else—has suited him fine. So he may have settled here and is influential."

"I'm missing your point completely."

"Reveal our mission to any old private eye who may run and tell Tenner that an American couple is here to uncover his Nazi ghost? No. I don't think it's wise."

"We will have to trust someone sooner or later, my Louloudaki."

"Yes, but why do it before we have to? I say the two of us should take it on. And we'll see the sights as we go." She squeezed her body against mine. "Besides, I enjoy the intrigue of being next to you." She gave me her most playful smile. "I need the stimulation, don't you see?" She planted her moist soft lips on mine and, tired as we were, we dragged ourselves to bed and slept soundly in the comfort of each other's arms.

The hotel manager received Kathy and me in his office with an overly-anxious-to-please smile. He was well-groomed and portly and appeared important seated behind his imposing desk. He ordered his assistant to bring two cups of Chiriqui, a highly regarded local coffee, into his office at once.

"So, you need someone to interpret for you?" he said to us, restating the obvious. "I would do it myself—for as you can see, and hear— I am well versed in American, or should I say English, but I am afraid my obligations will not permit me to extend such a courtesy."

I nodded, pretending to appreciate his "I would but . . ." offer.

"Could you point us in the right direction? Surely you know some reputable tour agency whose guides moonlight as interpreters."

"Well, yes, there are many. You might purchase our local newspaper, in the lobby. *The Panama America* it is called, and it is the most popular paper printed partly in English in the Canal Zone. There you will find listed numerous agencies. However, if you wish the services of a true professional, you should not hesitate to solicit the talents of Ricardo Rodriquez, or Ricky as we know him. I have used Ricky on various occasions and have found him to be most ...," he coughed, "... almost always, reliable."

"Is he available? How can we get in touch with him?"

The Señor's white teeth showed under his black mustache. He immediately picked up the receiver and dialed.

While he was waiting he said, "Panama City is cosmopolitan, of course, but like any other world-class city it has its neighborhoods and alleys that must be avoided. That is why, when one hires a guide, Señor and Señora, one must choose someone who is also strong and well-respected in the community. One who has many connections and can serve not only as a guide and interpreter but, should we say, as a protector as well."

I pretended to miss Kathy's concerned look. The manager chatted with someone in Spanish and nodded affirmatively, indicating that Ricky was free to help us.

"Could he meet us at the Central Post Office in an hour? We need to speak with the postal director."

He spat out some rapid sentences and when he hung up, he assured us everything had been arranged—Ricky would be looking for us at the entrance of the postal building at eleven.

"You will be meeting with Señor Hector Guerrero, the postal director? He has been with that service for a long time and speaks English fluently. Ricky would not be necessary there."

"How well do you know the director, Señor?" asked Kathy, with a disarming smile. "Perhaps a man of your stature will be more successful in obtaining an appointment for us."

"That should not be necessary. Bureaucrats are not as pompous in Panama as they are in other places. The director will be most gracious to receive you when you mention my name."

I shook the accommodating manager's hand firmly.

"Muchas gracias, Señor."

With my arm around Kathy's shoulders we walked out to the plaza. We had some time to fill, and with the aid of a map, we strolled north on the lively Avenida Central. The streets were humming with activity, yet Kathy kept her purse hanging in front of her neck while her hand remained half-submerged in my hip pocket, guarding my wallet.

"This isn't America—destitute people do crazy things," she whispered in my ear and her arm squeezed me next to her.

Her protective impulses toward me I treasured, and I planted my lips on her head. Even the sidewalk stones could taste the tenderness that flowed inside me for my wife.

"Since I look Nordic maybe we should say, if we need to say anything at all, that we are making an effort to trace one of my ancestors—a missing uncle," said Kathy and winked as she promptly endorsed her own plan of action.

We backtracked to the Spanish colonial square and there we marveled at the massive archways along the National Palace and post office, despite their cracked plaster and overlapping, fading paints of past decades.

By the entrance, a native leaned against the wall. His long white shirt was pulled down over his trousers in an effort to conceal a grand belly. He was well-fed and smiling.

"You are the Americans from the Central Hotel?"

Ricky Rodriquez seemed eager. He was in his late thirties and greeted us with courteous handshakes. With a convincing air, he wasted little time in telling us that his favorite aunt lived in Santa Fe, New Mexico, and that he loved Americans—although many of his compatriots were a bit hostile toward us at times because of the one-sided canal treaty, of course.

"Actually, we here in Panama live our lives very much like the American way of life. Maybe not so rich, but very similar. Although soccer is our main sport, we like baseball and football, and the movies—oh my God, yes. The movies we like here in Panama are American movies. Stars like Robert Mitchum and Humphrey Bogart are great heroes in Panama. Every Panamanian man is a tiny bit in love with Marilyn

Monroe, may she rest in peace, the poor soul now that she is dead. What an awful thing for such a pretty woman to end her life like that. A shame." His eyes fell on Kathy's chest and he added, with a spark of appreciation, "The lady here, Señora Kathy, she look like Marilyn Monroe a little bit, no?"

Kathy's vanity surfaced and with a smile she uttered a gracious thanks along with a feminine giggle as she squeezed my hand to show me that Ricky was no one's fool.

We passed through three levels of clerks before we were shown into the marble-walled office of Señor Hector Guerrero. He was tall and trim, serious, and gray-haired. He was also courteous but blunt, even with the amiable Ricky, who translated for us. Though the hotel manager had assured us his friend, the director, was bilingual, Señor Guerrero kept speaking in his native tongue. Maybe Ricky needed to earn his money and Guerrero was obliging, I thought.

"You have come a long way just to look at our records," Ricky said as he translated. Guerrero spoke rapidly in a monotone. His look jumped from Kathy to me and back to Kathy, who thought it appropriate to speak.

"We are only serving the will of my ailing, dear grandmother who hopes there may be a forwarding address on a registration card for a post office box that was rented by my Uncle Hayes. In 1947 he used Panama City as his address but has since vanished."

The director studied us.

"But Señora, you do not have official credentials. Obviously, you are not journalists or detectives or the FBI, and I do not see why I should be persuaded to offer you access to our files. They are not located in this building anyway, but far from the center of the city in a warehouse in a rather, ah, poor district, not very safe for . . . well, let us say, tourists such as you and your husband."

"Señor Guerrero, please hear me out. We know we lack the appropriate credentials and that our task is a very difficult one, but my grandmother has been a loving soul all her life and she hasn't much time left. My husband and I assured her that we would try to fulfill her last wish and make this effort to locate her lost son. All we can offer you for your cooperation and graciousness is our, and my grandmother's, gratitude for giving us this chance. You would be doing us a great favor by assisting us in this terribly frustrating situation." I saw Kathy studying the director's immobile face. "If you cannot gain any personal satisfaction from this, then perhaps a monetary contribution to the postal services is in order ..." She unclipped her purse and reached for her wallet, but Señor Guerrero stood as he gestured for her to stop. His bushy gray brows arched like a pelican's wings preparing for lift-off, and a benign, warm grin wrinkled his temple.

"Señora please," he said in accented but perfectly understandable English. He walked around his desk past Ricky and me, and reaching out he took Kathy's hand in his own. "Ricky here knows the way to the warehouse and he should be sufficient protection. I will provide you with an employee who will show you how and where to begin your search for whatever you are seeking. But I am afraid you are looking for a ... should I say, a needle in a haystack. Much time has passed since 1947 and our records have not been accurately reorganized since the fire. You see, an arsonist set the warehouse ablaze and many of our files were lost."

He spoke to Ricky and gave orders to a male assistant, and then took my hand.

"Why the charade of being strictly a Spanish speaker, Señor Guerrero?"

"People have a way of being more sincere when they are struggling to communicate. I apologize if I appeared deceitful." He turned to Kathy once more and said. "At any rate, good luck in your chase, Señora Barlow, and *buenas dias.*"

The landscape grew increasingly desolate and threatening. The taxi took a left turn off the paved road and drove over bumpy, dusty streets through the San Miguelito district. The postal employee sat in the front chatting with the driver while Kathy and Ricky were engaged in a lively discussion about film stars. I remained silent and amused at the cleverness with which my innocent-looking wife had coyly gotten Señor Guerrero to help.

We pulled up and stopped in front of a dilapidated structure made out of sheets of corrugated tin. For a brief paranoid instant I thought of Kathy's wild assumption and I worried that this was a trap, that Hans Tenner had infiltrated the local political system and like a god-father enjoyed firsthand knowledge of the intentions of all visitors to this small nation.

"Walk quickly and stay close to me," Ricky said after the taxi left us off.

The area resembled a bombed-out ghetto. A large rowdy group of ragged, dirty teenagers appeared to wonder why these tourists would want to penetrate the shadows of their world. Like awakened preda-tors they began to edge toward us, led by a tall, pimply-faced punk with a filthy baseball cap shoved down to his ears; the postal clerk sped to unlock a door while Ricky hustled us inside and bolted it.

The dark interior was musty and full of cobwebs and rows of boxes. The postal clerk pushed up on a large rusty breaker switch, and some bare light bulbs that dangled from the ceiling on long electrical cords suddenly illuminated what appeared to be a vampire's crypt. Not only were postal records buried there, but also newspapers and forgotten official-looking documents. Ricky translated for the postal man.

"I will show you where the post office boxes are kept, but I must inform you that it is against Panamanian law to inspect or remove any-thing unless you have been authorized to do so."

Kathy and I nodded. We were led to a section behind some parti-tions where bold black lettering scribbled on plywood indicated the years 1945 though 1950. The clerk handed the key to Ricky, told us *"Adios,"* and disappeared.

"Well, now, what is that name we will be looking for? Hayes?" Ricky sized up the boxes and scratched his chin. "This may be a difficult search, *amigos,"* he said with a broad smile.

Suddenly I realized that our hired hand Ricky, this total stranger who was a member of a culture about which we knew nothing, must be told our true mission. Kathy appeared preoccupied and silent.

"Ricky," I cleared my throat, "the man we are searching for was in this country in 1947, but we do not know his name. He fled Europe under an assumed name and we hope to discover his phony identity. The only information we have so far is that he may have been the renter of Box 47 in the year 1947."

Ricky gave us a puzzled look, his lips parting into a nervous grin of mistrust. Fear that he was getting involved in something more serious than he was willing to participate in for the agreed-upon daily wage of ten dollars was racing through his mind.

"Señor Yiannis, this man you are looking for . . . he . . . he owes you lots of money?" he asked suspiciously.

"No, Ricky. He was in trouble in Europe."

"*Que?*" Ricky seemed to flinch and he crossed himself. "This man is a very dangerous man then, no? A Nazi, maybe?" His eyes showed a lot of white.

"He left Panama long ago, Ricky," I said, hoping I was telling the truth.

We began the painstaking search through what seemed to be thousands of cards sprinkled with dust and soot. The arrangement was grouped neither by year nor by date.

After three hours of fruitless labor we all complained of hunger, and Ricky readily offered to go and fetch us some food.

"And a good bottle of vino," I added, handing him some money. He smirked and took off quickly. Kathy and I remained engrossed in our task. The time flew by until I glanced at my watch and realized that two hours had passed since Ricky left.

"Do you suppose Ricky . . . ?" asked Kathy. Had she sensed my alarm?

"He has been gone for some time," I replied calmly.

She turned and stared my direction.

"Stop and look at me for a moment," Kathy said coolly. "Maybe I can overlook, for a little while longer, the fact that I'm about to collapse from hunger. However, I'm beginning to believe that we have seen the last of Ricky we'll ever see. We need to begin to plan our escape from this tin pit right now."

"I'm starving too and I think you are right about Ricky, but I can't relax until we find that card."

"Tell me, Yiannis," she said wearily, letting her torso droop, "what good will the card be to us if we never get out of here in one piece?"

I stood up, stretched my arms to loosen the stiffness in my back, and bent to hug Kathy who was squatting, leaning over a long, weathered, and solidly packed box.

"At least if we go, we will go together," I murmured lightheartedly.

She gazed up tenderly. Her face had streaks of black soot painted under her eyes as if she had prepared for a football game.

I lifted her and held her in my arms, kissing her smudged face until she purred and sighed and made tiny blissful sounds, forgetting the danger and her hunger. Then I took her hand and led her toward the door of the building.

We peeked through the cracks and saw a darkening sky. The gang of unruly teenagers was still there. We were stranded in this decrepit, hostile part of the city, and our one link to safety had either been abducted or had abandoned us. I searched for a weapon and finally found a discarded, partly scorched two-by-four about two feet long. I told Kathy to stay inside the warehouse while I scouted around for a pay phone. My plan was to call the hotel and ask them to dispatch a taxi at once, but my idea didn't go over at all well with Kathy.

"I meant every word when I said I'm not letting you out of my sight. Besides, this doesn't seem like the kind of neighborhood that would have a pay phone."

My alarmed eyes fell on an old fire extinguisher propped by the door. I feared for Kathy's safety more than anything, but she was strong and she wouldn't hesitate to clobber a wrongdoer on the head. So I handed her the club and unfastened the extinguisher. I unlatched and kicked the door courageously and we marched out into curious, suspicious stares. The tall skinny punk with the baseball cap flicked his cigarette to the ground and motioned to the rest of the pack to follow him.

A humble abode stood across the way with a little girl at its lighted front. I pointed the muzzle of the weapon at the punks' faces and, sheltering Kathy from their reach, we advanced. The moment we reached the open door I shoved Kathy inside.

"*Señor! Señora! Por favor, me necesita un telefono!*" I shouted at the top of my lungs.

Instantly, a strong-looking man in a dirty T-shirt appeared, his mouth still chewing. He stared at us, with half bravado and half fear. "*No hay telefono,*" our stranger host answered while he viewed first Kathy with her blackened two-by-four in hand and then me, gripping the antiquated fire canister with one hand and its snout with the other.

The audacious young thugs remained outside looking through the opening, but were not brave enough to cross the man's threshold. Finally, our gestures of despair and my pantomime of our dilemma must have registered, and the man of the house shook his head up and down. He walked past us and commanded the menacing pack to disperse, then disappeared. A tense smile returned to Kathy's face when a reluctant *señora* came from behind a curtain with an infant child in her arms and a brood of three others, all pulling at her soiled gray dress.

In ten minutes our host returned with a taxi, and while we were muttering a million *muchas gracias,* Kathy emptied from her purse all her sweets and candies, everything shiny, even her lipsticks and creams, and gave it all to the children. Then we climbed into the sanctuary of the vehicle. As it sped away, the windows up, the doors locked, we sat close and agreed to forget the card for the night.

"Tonight let's celebrate love and life," said Kathy.

"Yes. Let's," I agreed.

By Cafe Jimmy, a casual restaurant near our hotel, we asked the driver to let us off. An outdoor patio with colorful tables between flowering hedges invited diners for an evening meal.

From some of the menu items we concluded that the proprietor had to be of Greek descent and the waiter verified our suspicion. After I revealed that I, too, had come from Greece, a handsome man with a generous mustache soon strolled by our table and, in Greek, welcomed us to Panama City. He told us that a small Greek community had settled there, mostly shrimp fishermen. Then Jimmy, the owner, served us the most delicious meal we had ever sampled. The grilled prawns were juicy and bigger than baby lobsters. We grew mellow over a bottle of local white, and holding hands we talked of our closeness.

"When we must part, I pray to be the one to go first. But if my plea is ignored, I assure you, my Sunflower, I will follow you soon, since you have given me everything I have ever hoped to get in this life. There is no stronger desire in me than to be with you, no matter where you may be." My mate's confession quickened my heartbeat and my eyes turned moist.

A tiny soft noise, a faint scratching, awoke me from a peaceful morning doze. I sat up. My vision rested on a white envelope as it was being pushed on the floor through the crack under the door. I sprang, picked it up, and speedily opened the door to catch a glimpse of the tail end of a skirt flying behind a wall of the corridor. I couldn't give chase; I was naked. I retreated, sat on a chair, and read a short, unsigned, typewritten note:

> *Señor, the only man who can help you is a dedicated reporter. His name is Emilio Medina. You should be able to contact him at* El Panama America.

Who could have drafted this note other than Ricky? He was the logical author, the only person suspecting our true reason for our visit to Panama City. I spread a bath towel on the tiled floor and began my morning routine, referred to as the four Ss—the daily ritual that had become part of me from my early army hitch in Idar-Oberstein.

Since Kathy still slept, when I finished my stretches I picked up a Panama travel guide, stuck the note inside the book, closed the bathroom door, and sat on the throne pursuing the second S. The stretching and mild calisthenics stimulated the digestive tract and served as a natural cathartic, as I told the world each chance I had and hoped they listened. I heard Kathy calling room service. After the delivery of her order she pushed against the bathroom door with her head while she held a tray with two steaming cups of coffee.

She kept her nostrils and lips compressed and made funny faces, so declaring her displeasure with the scent, but she reached down to give me her good morning *filaki* before she kneeled nearby. My objections to her intrusion she overruled, claiming that we had important matters to discuss and time was of the essence. I handed her the note and asked her who she suspected as the sender, expecting her reply to coincide with mine.

"I would say Ricky, of course," she readily replied. "There's no one else who knows what we are after."

"Yes," I puckered my lips to show her I was judging her speculation, "but he's dead or in hiding, frightened." I scratched my head in thought. "And there's something strange about Hector Guerrero's behavior. His comments have been bothering me, though I would like to believe that he fell for your fib about your lost uncle." Kathy stared at me blankly and I went on.

"If Panama City was used as a stepping stone by Nazi war criminals, Guerrero has seen plenty of survivors come asking to search the postal records."

"What are you trying to tell me, Sherlock?" Kathy asked in a defiant tone.

"That Señor Guerrero, since he has been with the postal service for a long time, knew all along what we are after. He did seem sympathetic toward you, didn't he? So, he may have sent this anonymous note to help us."

I began tearing squares of paper tissue from the roll and carefully folding them in twos until I had a total of four. Kathy, with the curiosity of a learning child, took in this tedious ritual without missing a trick. Unable to hide her disappointment as I was discrediting the impact of her convincingly-delivered lost-uncle story to Señor Guerrero on the previous day, my Louloudaki tossed her head up mutinously and tightened her lips.

"So Guerrero didn't fall for my story, hmmmm?" she snipped. "You think you are right—you think you are always right—Mr. Perfect. Even when you prepare your poop paper, you do it perfect. Look at you. You tear the poop paper into squares and wipe your little button like a nanny does the mouth of a prince after a meal." She stood up and stormed out of the bathroom, pretending to be upset.

When I emerged, showered and shaved, I found her curled up in bed with all the pillows propped behind her back, leafing through a magazine and acting indifferent—a standard scene each time she felt her efforts to help me went unappreciated. I bent over, took her face in my hands, stared at her lovingly, pecked her nose, her mouth, her hair, and her cheeks, then wildly, passionately, as if I had lost control of my senses, randomly, I planted a thousand rapid smooches on her soft skin and told her how precious she was to me until her eyes mellowed and we kissed and played.

Later, she rubbed my face with lotion, something she insisted on doing to prevent it from drying up, and I made my usual protesting grimaces and groans.

"The army tamed you some but didn't cure your cockiness completely. What you needed was a much longer hitch. But then it would have been pure hell for me."

She went about her toilet while I dressed quickly, took the stairs to the lobby, and walked directly to the manager's office.

He greeted me jovially.

"Any word from Ricky?" I asked with concern.

"Are you expecting him and he is late?"

I told how he had disappeared. Then I asked him to first call Ricky's home and, if there was no answer, to follow with a call to the police. Señor Pinero chuckled, which jarred me.

"No cause for alarm, Señor Yiannis. Ricky is, as we say, a character. Although an honest and capable man, he is a little absent-minded at times. He probably ran into a pretty señorita and neglected his duty toward you. When he turns up, he will be duly chastised by me, I assure you. It was regrettable and dangerous that he left you alone in such an unsafe place as you describe, but there is no cause to worry for his safety."

"I'm relieved you think he is all right," I said. "How well do you know a Señor Emilio Medina?"

He smirked and questioningly lifted his shoulders.

"But which of the many? Emilio Medina is a common name in Panama."

"The one who is a reporter for *El Panama America*."

"Oh him, the investigative reporter." The manager's standard grin left him and a trace of puzzlement hid behind his bushy mustache. "I know of him. He has been around forever, but I hear he is a strange man. Some Panamanians love him, but many hate his snoopy, persistent manners. A rumor has it that . . . ," he stopped abruptly and cleared his throat. "However, he is very good at what he does. May I place a call to the newspaper on your behalf?"

"Please. And whoever answers, will you mention that I need to get hold of this man—that it is urgent?"

"Should I ask for an English-speaking person so you can explain your wishes in private?"

I admired his tact and nodded my agreement; when he handed me the receiver with someone from the newspaper at the other end, he left and closed the door. A mature female voice told me Señor Medina was out. I gave her my name and explained that my wife and I were in Panama City for a few days, in search of some historical data, and that a serious source had told us Señor Medina could . . . . The woman interrupted to say that Señor Medina had just arrived and she would fetch him to the phone at once.

He was on the line seconds later, speaking fluent English in a voice with all the gruffness of a marinated reporter. I identified myself, told him about the note, and asked him if he could meet Kathy and me for lunch. After a brief vacillation, he agreed, then recommended the Blue Falcon Restaurant near our hotel, at one-thirty.

At long last it seemed things were coming together. I felt flushed with excitement. I went to the lobby and thanked the ever-smiling manager for his gracious assistance. Kathy was standing by the newsstand thumbing through local postcards. I gave her a quick rundown on developments. We decided to take a trip to the Miraflores Locks to view ships passing through the canal. Kathy suggested that we contact Chino to be our driver.

Chino showed up in half an hour, talkative and seemingly happy that he had made enough of a good impression that we hadn't forgotten him. We drove out of Casco Viejo across Panama City and after nearly a mile through a rundown district, neat tree-lined streets with whitewashed bungalows appeared.

"The Canal Zone," Chino explained, "Little America."

A small crowd carrying hand-lettered signs marched beside the Zone.

"You heard about our troubles?" Chino shouted.

"No," I said.

"Terrible—Americans and Panamanians fighting, like fathers and sons."

"Who do you think is more qualified to run the canal, Chino?" I asked.

"Americans maybe. Panamanians? They want more jobs, a little better pay, and a little more respect. We are simple people, we enjoy little things. We like to sing and dance, and play with our babies, but we are a country, too. A tiny country, but we have our pride. A little more respect from America is good."

We climbed a platform overlooking the canal where loudspeakers blared in Spanish and English. Huge ships crawled a few yards away from us, guided along by tiny locomotives, and carrying enormous cargoes—hundreds of cars from Europe, or tens of thousands of tons of crude oil from Middle East. Once a ship glided from the confines of one steel lock out into another, the lock emptied at an astonishing speed, only to refill as soon as another vessel slid into its belly.

We arrived at the Blue Falcon with time to spare. At that hour Panama City, its heat and humidity on full blast, seemed unbearable, but the restaurant was air-conditioned. A hodgepodge of memorabilia, from signed photos of personalities hanging on aging green-flowered wallpaper, to shelves of whiskey bottles of past vintages, decorated the large room. We asked for a private table and told the gracious fat lady who seated us that we expected to be joined by a Señor Emilio Medina.

"*Si, si,* Señor Medina the reporter. Of course. I will show him to your table as soon as he arrives," she assured us in English.

At one-thirty a wiry, short man with wild black eyes and limp, greasy gray hair, his frail body in a loosely fitted and soiled three-piece linen suit, with Panama hat in hand, was escorted to our table. The short man's face lit up and his thin lips parted in a grin to show one silver tooth and two missing.

"What a lovely lady you are, Señora Barlow," Emilio Medina said as he reached for Kathy's hand and kissed it. Then he turned, studied me carefully, and offered me a firm grip. His lips looked salty, his dark skin was moist and wrinkled, and his breath smelled of stale cigarette smoke and alcohol. He took a chair.

"And how can I be of help?" he asked, smiling flirtatiously at Kathy. His restless eyes zeroed in on our rum-and-cokes and he snatched the sleeve of a passing waiter and demanded straight rum over ice and pronto. Once we ordered lunch, I described our mission and concluded with the mysterious, unsigned note.

Medina smacked his lips and darted his bloodshot eyes back and forth at Kathy and me, and his empty glass. His voice was sober.

"Señor *y* Señora Barlow, I am a dedicated reporter and I deal with uncovering the truth. Truth is not a sprinkling of facts, but all the facts. Sadly, we Panamanians, like most all the underprivileged peoples of the world, would rather bury our faces in the sand than see the light. If the truth doesn't place an extra portion of beans or rice on the table, no one cares for it."

He caught the eye of the waiter by raising his finger, indicating his prompt need for one more rum. The small, unkempt man had said little so far, but my senses were keen with anticipation. An intuition inside me caused a tumult I could not justify with reason. He raised his index finger again, only this time to make his point.

"Truth is a goddess of unparalleled reverence. It is the established principle, the law, the agreement with correctness. It is the conscience of a society. The world belongs to humanities who respect and demand the absolute truth from their leaders. And when strong interests in a nation suppress or ignore the truth, the eagerness, dreams, and vivaciousness of its citizenry expire."

His drink arrived and he drained half of it with one gulp.

"Whoever wrote you the note was intuitive, I should say, a friend. Whoever this person is, Señora *y* Señor, he is your friend because he has referred you to the truth, the one source that can help you."

Neither Kathy nor I dared to interrupt this skinny little man as he reached into his past, sorting out memories filled with accomplishment and shattered aspirations. He polished off his drink, blinked his eyes, placed his Panama on his head, cocked it a trifle, and continued.

"On June seventeenth, 1947, Father Vincenzo Grandi was found murdered, stuffed inside a large garbage can at his home, his throat slashed from ear to ear. The coroner estimated the act had been committed forty to fifty hours earlier. I was put on the story.

"The Papal Nuncio claimed it was random violence, a robbery, but I didn't believe it, and neither did the police inspector nor the doctor who did the autopsy on Grandi. Whoever had committed this homicide needed time to escape—the body had been moved and concealed. Perhaps the perpetrator wished to break a chain by eliminating one link. For the past year or so, ever since the padre had arrived in Panama

City, he had been seen in the company of various non-natives, possibly Europeans. A very tall, blond man with cold, pale blue eyes was repeatedly mentioned as having been his frequent companion. The priest sometimes drank a beer at a cantina owned by an old German woman, but the tall man was a total mystery.

"My investigation led me to the post office where I discovered through an observant employee that, a few months before that June, the padre had chaperoned the tall blond man to the post office where the mysterious foreigner had rented a box under the name Alfredo Gregorio Giacominni."

The notion that this little man was fabricating a tale so he could justify his lunch and drinks shot through me but I dismissed it at once.

"Alfredo Gregorio Giacominni? But that is an Italian name!" Kathy looked to me for an explanation.

"Tenner was given an assumed name, remember?" I said mechanically.

"I phoned the local cathedral and the archbishop's assistant referred me to the Vatican Nunciature in Panama. I wanted to know why an Italian priest had been sent to our poor country, when there were plenty of native-born priests eager for positions. The nunciature's spokesman, a Father Russo, gave a standard response: Father Grandi had been sent to Panama for the propagation of the faith.

"But then, I started to think of the rumors I had heard of Nazis escaping from Europe and arriving in our own waters as disguised men. The Catholic Church had never condemned Mussolini, or Hitler for that matter, not even during the war. Was it neutrality as it claimed, or a secret endorsement of their fascist deeds? Since the murder of a priest is not an ordinary crime in our land, I became intrigued by the challenge and determined to dig in and uncover something of consequence.

"I started to hang around El Cantina d'Africa, the old German woman's place on Via España, and I befriended an American *comunista* who was writing a book on the Vatican and the Nazis. He told me why the Vatican had moved Nazi war criminals all over the world, to the Americas, Africa, and even Asia.

"'Oh, yes, our dear papa in Rome had a lot of sympathy for all the terrible Christian boys,' my *comunista* friend said to me. 'He issued orders to supply phony papers to thousands and provided them with asylum and money, transit, and temporary shelter, and they were accepted virtually wherever they went.'

"I went in person to the nunciature and was received by Father Russo. He was an old man, and he listened to my story with a serene face.

" 'As you have been told before, Señor Medina, Father Grandi was dispatched to Panama City for religious reasons. Unfortunately for you, the Vatican adheres to a policy of confidentiality. Revealing the nature of Vatican missions is forbidden, unless of course there is some problem with the law. It is very sad indeed that brother Grandi, such a gentle and devoted colleague, perished under grotesque circumstances. The whole nation mourned his loss and we pray for his soul daily, but we wish to bury the past and go forward into the future, my son.' Russo stood up to show me he intended to say no more—and I left."

"Well?" I asked, staring at the dark little man.

"Our prime suspect had vanished, the church did not wish to pursue the investigation, and my publisher lost interest. The police, wanting to forget the matter altogether, concluded that it looked more like a robbery after all. My editor insisted that any connection between the Papal Nuncio and Nazi-smuggling was just too farfetched, and when I pushed him he thought I was losing it and immediately transferred me to the society beat, covering weddings and baptisms for an entire year.

"I kept the investigation going in my spare time, for a short while thinking of doing a book, and, indeed, I discovered that the trafficking of Nazis from Europe to our hemisphere under the umbrella of innocence of the Catholic Church was hardly a fib, but instead very real, and very, very dangerous to expose. So I shelved the concept quickly, and the truth, my dear *amigos,* fell and sank into a deep hole here in Panama, where it is likely to remain in obscurity."

None of us had touched our lunches. Señor Medina drank his by ordering one more rum, and Kathy and I asked for sodas.

"So Alfredo Gregorio Giacominni was a tall blond man people knew little about, and he was the renter of Box 47 in 1947?" I asked.

"Kathy, Kathy! Oh dear, what a wonderful surprise. I can't believe you are here in the midst of the Americas!"

Ethel, Kathy's aunt who had played the piano at that first Thanksgiving, and who traveled extensively in Central America chasing archeological digs, was rushing toward our table at full gallop, dressed in white cotton voile and a wide beige sun hat with yellow ribbons.

"Aunt Ethel," shouted Kathy, springing up as they both laughed and embraced.

"Absolutely stunned with happiness!" Ethel burst out.

Señor Medina, like some flabbergasted soldier who suddenly from the corner of his eye caught sight of his general approaching, leapt to attention and stood dumbfounded and rigid until, realizing that an extra chair was needed, vaulted to fetch one.

Aunt Ethel seemed her usual self. A bit tipsy as always, she smooched me on the cheek while still holding Kathy around the waist. Then coyly she offered her bronzed hand to Señor Medina, who snatched it, bowed, sniffed it, and kissed it with reverence.

"My pleasure is indeed grand, Señorita." Suddenly his lips quivered as if he had stepped inside a minefield, and in a voice camouflaged by a harsh giggle he added, " . . . or is it Señora?"

Ethel's eyes shot the briefest dart of steel while the rest of her face smiled broadly.

"Still hoping for the right gentleman to cross my path, Señor." She seated herself regally, crossed her shapely tanned legs, and in a ceremony she had rehearsed a million times, took from her purse a packet of Marlboros and placed a cigarette between her lips. Then, as an afterthought, she passed the open box to us. The enigma I had detected in her eye when we first met long ago struck me once more.

With a smile that revealed his silver tooth, Medina snatched her offering arm and took a cigarette while with the skill of a pickpocket he produced a dilapidated Zippo, flicked it open, and offered its flame. Ethel daintily steadied his wrist with her long fingers and hungrily drew in the tobacco. He lit his, then both puffed clouds of smoke as if in a contest.

The waiter brought Ethel a scotch, and an additional rum was placed in front of our Señor, who sat glowing at Ethel with exaggerated admiration and suppressed discomfort. Was it a state forced upon him by masculine hormones bubbling within that decrepit little body of his, ablaze by the healthy dose of rum which now flowed inside his veins, or a badly performed play?

Medina appeared totally diverted from our previous conversation. Unwilling to accept that Aunt Ethel's emergence had brought a sudden devastating end to our pursuit of Tenner, I said hurriedly. "Ethel, Señor Medina was about to ...," but the little man brushed at the air with his arm to convey annoyance and the message that the subject should be dropped at once.

He sat up straight to increase his small size, retaining his silly courtly pose.

"Miss Ethel, are you on our humble soil on business or pleasure?"

"Oh, Señor, even though it's business, it's also pleasure." Ethel wore a forced smile. "The Mayan ruins of Petén, Tikal, Piedras Negras, Uaxactun have engrossed me for many, many years. Unraveling riddles of those extinct cultures has fascinated me since I was a little girl."

"How interesting," said the Señor, grinning and gulping down his rum in one slug.

"Unless one becomes directly involved with a project one can never fathom the thrill that exhilarates the soul when through a lot of painful efforts an entire court where ritual ball games were performed many centuries ago is unearthed, staring you in the face, as that in Tikal, for example."

"Oh, how exciting, Aunt Ethel," cried Kathy.

"Hieroglyphs, steles, magnificent sculptures, pyramids—all buried under the thick vegetation of the rain forest," she said, while tossing a passing glance at a table. I followed her eyes to three seated blond Slavic-looking men. "Did you know that the Mayans were the only civilization known to man who worshipped time? Just think, let your imaginations wander. Worship time as a deity! Captivating, isn't it."

As my brain labored to perceive the reverence of time, an alert man in his thirties with bulging muscles, tiny waist, and a crewcut wove through the seated crowd and tapped Ethel on the shoulder. She leaped like a greyhound out of the gate at a racing course. They talked in hushed tones. She kept her back to us, and in less than a moment the man left in the direction from which he had come. Ethel faced us, her lips split into a strained grin, and when she sat it was on the edge of her chair—signaling her stay would be short.

"This dig business . . . ," she shook her head, "so darn demanding." Her stare circled the room and halted briefly at the table with the three Slavic men.

"The two of you must come to our embassy's bash this evening." She tapped lightly at Kathy's thigh. "It'll be lots of fun; our ambassador is a darling man. All Americans are welcome, you know. Don't neglect to bring along your passports. The crowd gathers around ten— Central America functions on Mediterranean time."

"Very interesting, indeed," garbled Medina while a yawn shadowed briefly his stupid glow.

With a mixture of pity and disappointment Ethel tossed the Señor a shun. Then, in a pretentiously soothing voice she addressed him.

"Señor Medina, will you come to the embassy party too?" I picked up a trace of passion. "As my escort perhaps?"

The Señor seemed stunned and fought the dimness of his brain while his bloodshot eyes made a desperate effort to reignite.

"*Si, si. Si,* Señora . . . well . . . I mean Señorita, I'm honored," he muttered. "How? Where? When? Oh, yes, at the embassy. But, of course. The American or the Chinese? *Si, si,* I'm honored. I shall be there."

Ethel raised her eyebrows in a gesture of hopelessness. She rose, planted a motherly kiss on Kathy's cheek, and added affectionately, "I'll be expecting . . . ," she coughed away a tickle in her throat, "you two at the Embassy at ten. So long everyone." Her pace was hurried and while still waving good-bye, she vanished behind the green wall.

Relieved, I turned to Señor Medina.

"Finally. Now that our unexpected interruption has ended, can we . . . ?" I stopped. No reason to continue. Medina stared into space, wearing the same silly grin, his silver tooth in full view, mumbling incoherently in Spanish.

At ten o'clock sharp, we arrived at the embassy compound. The Marine guards scribbled our passport numbers on a guest list. Colored bulbs hung from strings wrapped around coconut trees, and floodlights cast shadows of intrigue on a diverse crowd scattered between hedges and flower beds. Two portable bars hummed with activity.

A familiar tango, badly performed by a sizable local orchestra, had tempted numerous couples onto a dance floor by the pool. Old men stiffly guided vibrant young women through the snappy steps, and aging ladies with tight wrinkle-less faces and stretched mouths glowed wishfully while tucked cozily inside the strong arms of clumsy younger officers.

Circles of groups with cocktails in hand and imposing airs offered their solutions to the pangs of the world. Glitter from jewels, joyful giggling, scents from perfumes and colognes, and constant nibbling from an ambrosial buffet composed a superficial tableau of grace with an underlying restrained rowdiness. We found a table on a tiny knoll overlooking the band and the dancers. Kathy watched with fascination.

"An amusing gathering," she commented. "It seems to me youth, looks, wealth, and influence are for sale, here."

"I wonder how many ...," I muffled the rest of my sentence and followed her eyes.

"You wonder about what?" asked Kathy alertly, still studying the festive scene.

"Well, how many of these people are spies, and counterspies. Who is chasing whom, and who is chasing the one who is chasing someone else?"

Kathy faced me, blinking her eyes in an awakening way.

"Oh, my Sunflower."

"What, my Louloudaki?"

"A thought just came back to me ..."

"What?"

"Things aren't always as they appear to be. Right?"

"Well, yes. In the Intelligence game at least."

"I remember a long time ago when my father casually mentioned to my mother his curiosity about Aunt Ethel."

"Come on, tell me. It may be what I've been suspecting all along."

"Okay. I've never mentioned this to anyone before and, needless to say, I don't wish it to go beyond you and me."

"I promise."

She bent toward me until her nose touched my face.

"Since Ethel's inheritance when my grandfather died was modest, and the only job she has ever held was her three-year hitch in the army at the tail end of the war, if you consider that a job, how could she afford to travel eleven months out of each year on digging expeditions?"

"Yes?"

"So he suggested that maybe Ethel was with . . ."

"The CIA, or a similar agency," I filled in quickly.

"But how did you guess?"

"Things have been swirling inside my head, too."

"Really? And what crazy things are jumping inside your little head this time, my lover?"

"Oh! Just a simple suspicion that someone knows of us being in Panama City. I can't believe that Ethel's bumping into us at the Blue Falcon Restaurant was a coincidence."

Kathy snatched my arm and squeezed it hard. I faced her.

"Gran. She knows."

"Knows what?"

"I told her we were on a important mission—looking for someone—and I believe I mentioned Panama City."

"And Ethel, a loving daughter concerned over her mother's failing health, telephones Gran often, I take it."

"Once or twice a week, Gran said."

"The note under our door. The flying skirt in the hallway. Señor Medina. Aunty Ethel in the Blue Falcon Restaurant." Kathy stared at me with serious eyes. "A captain with the Army Counter-Intelligence in Germany told me once that help may come our way without us knowing its source."

Suddenly Kathy shouted, "Señor Medina! I think I saw Señor Medina."

I followed her pointing finger. Through a sliver of unobstructed space between two bodies, half of the newspaperman came into view. I sprang after him.

Medina was bright-eyed and fresh, smelling of a strong spicy lotion and dressed in a suit similar to that worn at noon, only this garment was bright yellow and, though wrinkled, it appeared free of grease spots. The slacks broke noticeably over a pair of aged white buck shoes freshly sprayed with some sort of talc. A bright red handkerchief exaggeratedly overlapped his breast pocket.

"I've been looking for you," he announced with a spring in his speech, a total contrast to his wasted state of some hours ago. We joined radiant Kathy.

"Aunt Ethel! Have you run into her by any chance, Señor?" she inquired.

He reached into his coat pocket. "This note was delivered by taxi to the offices of our newspaper. I picked it up on my way here." He casually handed it to Kathy and politely asked her to read it out loud.

> *My dear Señor Medina:*
>
> *Please be advised that events beyond my control may force my absence from the embassy gathering this evening.*
>
> *Upon my failure to attend please extend my farewell to my favorite niece Kathy and her husband. I shied from telephoning their hotel because disrupting their valuable siesta seemed unnecessary, and messages often do not reach their destination on time.*
>
> *Your credentials have been left with the embassy guards for your admittance to the grounds.*
>
> *Señor Medina, my sources (and I assure you they are most reliable) have informed me that your reputation as a journalist is legendary. And since I admire rare men of courage and magnetism, such as yourself, if you are not already spoken for by a very fortunate lady please join me for a few days in Guatemala City and share with me a noble trek through the jungles of Petén, the lands of your ancestors.*
>
> *You may reach me through PO Box 1156, Guatemala City, Guatemala.*
>
> *So long until we meet again,*
>
> Ethel Freizer

"A most complimentary note, Señor Medina," observed Kathy.

"I hope you take her up on her offer, Señor," I added, hiding my mistrust of the note's intent.

"A most intriguing proposal—by a lovely and sensuous woman. Do you suppose she intends to recruit me?"

Kathy froze. I looked first at Señor Medina and then at my petrified Louloudaki.

"Recruit you? I don't follow you, Señor," I muttered.

He studied the dancing couples.

"You know, dedicated diggers such as Señorita Ethel are always on the lookout for recruits: volunteers for excavations and what have you," he said unaffectedly. Looking at the Señor sitting there calmly in his full wild splendor, the distrustful part of me kept sounding its alarm.

Kathy sneaked a glance full of relief in my direction, and I asked Señor Medina if he would like something from the bar, but he refused, claiming he had had more than his daily dose of alcohol at lunch.

"Then, may we continue our interrupted conversation, Señor?" I said with an eagerness I could no longer suppress.

He seemed completely composed.

"I have a photocopy of the postal registration card you are seeking; it's in the archives. If you wish to see it, Señor, you may stop by our offices tomorrow morning. I will have a copyboy fetch it for your review."

He smiled broadly and his silver tooth made its evening emergence.

"But please do not arrive earlier than ten. As you may have already suspected, the tropical climate forces us to be most productive during the coolness of the night. I retire rather late, often in the early morning hours. My schedule may appear a trifle lazy by North American standards, but I assure you that I remain resourcefully creative almost twenty hours a day."

"Señor Medina, please accept my deepest gratitude for your help. I've a photograph of the man we seek. Do you suppose any of the postal employees would recognize him if they were shown his picture?"

"It's worth a try. The man I contacted at that time ... let's see ... about fifteen years ago, is probably retired by now. However, we should be able to find his present address through the postal service's personnel records. They should have one where they mail him his pension check. That is, as a dear friend, an Englishman, used to say—if the jolly good fellow hasn't bitten the dust by now."

"Just one more question before we close the subject for the night, Señor Medina. In your profession you must have had the occasion to work with a reliable private detective agency. Is there one that can be trusted to search shipping records? I want to hire someone to look up Giacominni as a passenger or a crew member on ships that left Panama during the days immediately following Padre Grandi's murder. Airlines, too."

"The Moreno Detective Agency is the most reputable in Panama. Eustacio Moreno is an honorable, capable man. Tell him I sent you. His place is two blocks from our offices; I can direct you there in the morning after your visit to us."

A slow romantic tune urged me to reach for my Louloudaki's hand. We excused ourselves from the Señor and took the short stroll to the dance floor. Silently we shuffled our feet a few inches with each beat as we clutched each other's hand, serenely glued together.

When we returned to our table, Señor Medina had vanished.

That night, gunfire awakened me. Kathy slept through it, but I sneaked out of the room and took the stairs to the lobby. A crowd in nightclothes and slippers had gathered to ask what was going on. The night clerk assured everyone there was nothing to fear—no revolution or anything serious like that, just students with signs, protesting, and American soldiers firing up into the air.

The following morning Chino and his taxi were waiting out front. Anticipating some traveling, we had notified him that he should plan on being our chauffeur for most of this day. It was past ten when we arrived at the offices of *El Panama America,* a yellow colonial building with red trim.

A dark-haired woman told us to take a seat, pointing to a fraying black leather sofa. Señor Medina soon appeared, fresh-scrubbed, cologned, and smiling. He motioned us to follow him. In the depths of the decaying structure, we were ushered into a conference room; on the long table lay a withered manila envelope. He opened its flap, removed the contents and spread them out, arranging each document upright.

"Well, here it is—the entire investigation." We stared at the parade of discolored papers. Medina picked up a yellow card and, somewhat perplexed, handed it to me. "This is the card you have been looking for, Señor Barlow. I am somewhat mystified that the original is still in our files; I was almost certain I had returned it to the postal authorities."

I held it in my hands and stared at it intently. The dim but legible writing from an ink pen read: *Marzo* 17, 1947, Alfredo Gregorio Giacominni, and in the outlined box under *Signatura,* a faded, illegible scribble could be seen. Next to it I noticed the initials of the postal clerk on duty.

"May I have a copy of this card, Señor Medina?"

"Of course, here. Since we still have the original you can have this copy." He passed me an aged, off-center photostat of the card.

"Who was the postal employee you interviewed, do you recall?"

"It's here. His name should be here." He consulted a document. "Let's see . . . oh, here it is—José Eduardo Philipo."

I wrote down the name. We thanked Señor Medina and assured him we would contact him soon to arrange a social outing, perhaps dinner at his favorite spot, before we left Panama. He beamed and asked us to feel free to seek his further assistance if we needed it.

As we were being escorted to the exit, Kathy turned and asked, "Señor Medina, do you know a man named Ricardo Rodriquez? He is known around as Ricky."

"I am afraid I do not know this individual, Señora."

"How about the postal director, Señor Hector Guerrero? You must know of him, I'm sure."

"Hector Guerrero? Oh yes, very well. Hector and I have been friends since our youth when we attended university together. He has always been a very principled man. But why do you ask, Señora?"

"Oh, it's the note. I'm still wondering who the sender could be."

Chino drove two blocks, stopped, and pointed to a battered yellow house. A sign in brown lettering on a white wooden plank hanging over the door read "Moreno Detective Agency." I told Kathy I would only be a minute.

I greeted a young secretary in a tight flowered dress who appeared absorbed with banging the keys of a vintage typewriter.

"I'm here to see Señor Moreno," I said in English.

A corpulent man with piercing black eyes, a huge cigar hanging from the left side of his mouth and a gun stuffed in his waistband, came from a back room and studied me.

"*Si?* What can I do for you, Señor?" he asked while he chewed on the cigar.

"My name is Yiannis Barlow. I need a detective to search for a man. Señor Emilio Medina from the newspaper told me to look you up."

"You want to find someone in Panama?"

"Yes."

"When did you last hear from or see this man?"

"1947. Can you do it?"

"Well, of course I can conduct a search, but 1947 was a long time ago. What information can you give me?"

"A post office box and his name."

He waved me into a simple room with a small desk and three wooden chairs. He sat on the one behind his desk and picked up a pencil. "I'm listening."

"Alfredo Gregorio Giacominni. In 1947 he was the renter of Post Office Box 47 in the main post office. He vanished after the murder of a priest, Padre Grandi."

"I remember that murder—never solved. Buried, like so many things get buried here in Panama. How old is he, and what does he look like?"

"His description is of no importance." Moreno looked up, squinted his eyes, and rubbed his face.

"Let me explain. What I need from you is a search of the records of all shipping companies whose vessels departed Panama on the fourteenth, fifteenth, sixteenth, and seventeenth of June 1947, in the hope of finding either a passenger or a crew member under the name of Alfredo Gregorio Giacominni. If you fail there, we will talk about searching the airlines."

"What you are after then is the destination of the ship?"

"Exactly. Can you do it?"

"How much time have I got? Even in 1947 many ships passed through Panama, Señor. I need time and money for such a search."

"Time? You can send me a letter with the information. Money? How much?"

"For the initial search, two hundred up-front and one hundred upon finishing the job. If we have to go to the airline records, much more; maybe twice as much."

"Okay." I handed him two one-hundred-dollar bills along with my card, shook his hand, and left.

We drove to the post office and while Kathy waited inside the cab I rushed in, hoping to see the postal director and ask for his assistance in locating José Eduardo Philipo's address. Senior Guerrero was out for the day but his familiar aide, a young bearded man, courteously asked if he could help. When I explained what I was after, he promptly telephoned the Social Security office, and in a short time someone called back. The bearded assistant handed me a piece of paper with the information written on it in capital letters.

"I am delighted you are making some progress with your wife's uncle's whereabouts," he said, smiling when I thanked him.

Colón was our destination on that muggy, overcast afternoon and, as we stared at the jungle rolling by, the tall bridge of a freighter slowly moved above the terrain like a ghost ship in a dream, sailing through the land in the mist.

We reached a wild port city crowded with cheap shops, drunken sailors, and girls in short tight dresses stumbling out of bars and strip joints. Dangerous-looking men stood on every corner, and the over-painted faces of smiling women beckoned from dirty windows.

"This city, no good place to come in night," commented Chino as tiny handprints of begging children smudged the taxi windows. He turned left and drove past the port to a small hidden neighborhood near the water where a hard-won air of decency scented the Atlantic breeze. Small, freshly painted cottages with fences, tiny gardens and window boxes with flowering geraniums greeted us, a contrast to the chaos and ferociousness of Colón, infamous as the most free city in Latin America.

Chino stopped the taxi and asked a middle-aged woman directions to Señor José Eduardo Philipo's home. She pointed out a little white house with blue trim. Tending a small front yard was a man with thick black hair and dark skin who stared at us as we emptied out of the vehicle. Chino spoke to him in Spanish and the man's eyes brightened. He invited us into his orderly, modestly furnished front room.

"I speak pretty good English," he said, directing his eyes at me. He gestured toward the sofa and chairs and we settled in them.

"What do you need from me?"

"A man," I said, "who rented a post office box from you—Alfredo Gregorio Giacominni."

"When? I been retire for many years, Señor."

"In 1947."

"Oh," he sighed and smiled, "very long time ago. My memory still purty good but ..."

"Señor Philipo, *por favor,* it's very important to me. His box number was 47."

"Numero quarenta siete," Philipo repeated, searching his mind.

"Señor, many years ago the police interviewed you about this man; a reporter, Señor Medina, spoke to you too. The renter of this post-box had been seen in the company of Father Grandi before he was murdered."

Suddenly his eyes flashed and he smiled broadly.

"Oh, *si, si,* I remember well tall blond man. My coworkers and I give this man a name. We like to play games. We give names to our customers. Him, we name him El Nazi, because his eyes was the color and ... and temperature of two ice cubes."

I began to perspire from excitement. I took the photograph from my pocket and asked, "Señor Philipo, do any of the three men in this photo resemble Alfredo Giacominni, El Nazi?"

He took his glasses from his shirt pocket.

"I don't need too much time, Señor—the man in middle is the man. I am sure this is Giacominni. Yes, yes I am very, very sure."

In my exuberance I shook his callused hand again and again.

The next morning Kathy and I boarded the ferry to Isla Taboga. Our return flight had been arranged for the following morning, so on that last day we took our swimwear and headed for that island of flowers with its renowned white sand beaches.

When we reached the tiny paradise, fearless birds chirped their welcome and bougainvilleas and palm trees waved to us in the breeze. Lost among the cheerful natives, we held hands and strolled barefoot on the wet sand.

When we returned to our hotel, a messenger informed us that Detective Moreno would like to meet us in the bar at nine in the evening and that he had news to deliver. My efforts to reach Señor Medina to join us for dinner on this last night failed; I was told he was still on an important assignment.

At eight-thirty Kathy and I sat in the courtyard beneath palm trees sipping fruit drinks. The moon rays flickered through the quivering leaves and cast silvery shadows.

We were absorbed in our devotion fueled by the smells and sounds of this last tropical evening. An occasional sigh or word vowed for the millionth time that our romance would never end, not even beyond this life.

"Buenas tardes, Señor y Señora." Moreno appeared, biting on his cigar and smiling. He pulled up a seat. "I have excellent news for you. Perhaps we were a little lucky; detective work often needs a little luck, you know. First, we searched the records of Lineas Blanco. Nothing. Then Lineas Estella. Again nothing. On our third try, at Lineas Centro America, bingo!—like you Americans say! Our man Alfredo Gregorio Giacominni sailed on a Panamanian freighter named *Conquistador*. Destination?" His eyes played back and forth between us. "San Pedro, Port of Los Angeles!"

"Oh my God!" exclaimed Kathy and looked at me.

I tried to remain cool.

"Los Angeles," I said. "I never thought he might have ended up so close to home!"

"Giacominni left Panama City on June sixteenth, 1947, and arrived in San Pedro, California, on July second." Moreno presented me a sheet of paper with the information on it, and his eyes gleamed with accomplishment.

Feeling extremely generous, I peeled off two C-notes, instead of the one the detective had coming, and handed them to him.

He lit up from ear to ear. He stood up to leave, but then he hesitated and looked straight at me.

"Now that you have discovered what you wished to know, Señor, what do you intend to do?"

"Find him," I replied coolly.

"Yes, but if and when you find this man, whatever his real name may be, then you will have to decide."

"Decide?"

"Whether to kill him yourself, or turn him over to the police," Moreno said and walked away.

10

A TEAM OF THREE

We arrived at the Miami airport in the afternoon. A taxi took us directly to the Fontainebleau Hotel. The lobby hummed with guests and efficient personnel. Once Kathy and I were in our room, we edged out onto the balcony and gulped down deep breaths of the Atlantic. The color blue stretched infinite and powerful. I reached for her waist and brought her close to me.

"I feel good about what we've accomplished," I said cheerfully and kissed her. She looked lovingly at me, yet I detected a shred of uneasiness about her, and her lips seemed tense.

"Yiannis, last night the detective ... " Her simple words jolted a dormant anxiety in me.

"I love the sea. I must have been a walrus or something, some thousands of years back," I muttered hastily, lightheartedly, to mask the queasiness her forewarning sentence forced upon me. I squeezed her closer, wishing that our touching bodies could smother her forthcoming inquiry.

"Until last night I never thought about it," she said with a worried frown.

"About what?" I asked, pretending I didn't know.

"What we would do with Tenner if and when we find him." Kathy had never asked and I had never volunteered to tell her. She pushed me gently to arm's length. "But last night, Moreno asked you a question that awakened me. 'What do you intend to do when you find your man? Turn him over to the police or kill him yourself?'" She appeared dreadfully burdened with concern now. I kept facing the sea, determined to conceal from her the truth, for a little while longer.

"Well . . . don't you think I should know, Yiannis?" she persisted. I could feel the blood rushing to my neck and head.

"Aren't we putting the cart before the horse?" I gasped. "Let's first find the bastard, then we'll decide what we must do with him." I lied to my wife, and the instant I did it I sensed she knew.

"The answer is in your face. Don't try to pretend otherwise."

"I'd rather drop the subject for now, Kathy." I started to edge forward but she wedged herself between the railing and me.

"I am your wife. We have chosen to spend our lives together, remember? I need to know your plans, Yiannis," she said softly but sternly.

The time had come to tell my mate the secret I held back from her, and I was unprepared. I closed my eyes. Silently I bent my head and began to pace back and forth.

"Please, talk to me. I beg you." My heart picked up thrust to feed the demanding organs abruptly called to defend the vow I had made to my dead father.

"Kathy, a man who has committed crimes in other lands, someone like Tenner, cannot be prosecuted in our country." She stared at me in a most odd way.

"I don't follow you, Yiannis. I don't understand what you are trying to tell me."

"If we turn Tenner in to the authorities, the most our government will do is deport him back to West Germany, the country of his origin. You see, his only crime here is falsifying his naturalization application by using a fictitious name to gain entry."

"How do you know that?"

"I have done basic research in this matter."

"If it is as you claim, then, the government of West Germany will punish Tenner. Surely the Germans will find him guilty for all the atrocious crimes he has committed against civilians. They will put him to death or jail him for life, I'm sure."

"Oh, but you are so wrong, my Louloudaki. The Germans will do absolutely nothing to Tenner—or almost nothing."

"This man is a known war criminal!"

"Please, listen to me." I faced her. "When the United Nations War Crimes Commission closed its doors in '48, all the compiled dossiers of Nazi war criminals were turned over to the United Nations. Since that date, access to these files has been almost unattainable. My dear wife, do you know why that has been so?"

"No, but I would like to."

"Well, I'll tell you. Because both the English and the Americans, soon after the Big War, endorsed an attitude of leniency and forgiveness toward almost all former Nazis. Unfortunately, the Cold War forced our government to adapt this policy, in clandestine terms, of course. 'The enemy of our enemy is our friend' has been an unprincipled philosophy practiced by many nations, and now this same policy is polluting our own land. And so, ex-Nazis—not all scientists, I'm afraid—have immigrated to America using phony names—and no one cares about apprehending them."

"I don't want to believe that our own country has stooped this low—allowing these butchers to come and live among us. I just can't believe that someone like that could be our next-door neighbor."

"Because it is disturbing doesn't make it false. Now, if fair America has turned a blind eye to ex-Nazis, do you honestly believe West Germany—which incidentally, has a large number of ex-Nazis in prominent positions—will prosecute a deported Tenner? And even if public pressure demanded that Tenner stand trial, I assure you, it would be nothing more than a kangaroo court. His defense would be the same old recycled plea which has been used so successfully by war murderers in the past. 'Tenner,' they'll argue, 'was a soldier. All soldiers are trained to carry out the orders of their superiors. Hitler gave the orders and Tenner, a soldier, simply obeyed his Commander in Chief. Therefore Hitler is the guilty one. Tenner is innocent.'" Kathy bit her lips.

"It's hard for me to believe that an awful person like Tenner, who has committed heinous crimes, could be tried in a court of law and let go scot-free."

"Well, maybe the German judge, to appease world opinion, would slap Tenner with a few years' imprisonment. For good behavior, soon he'd be out, snickering at our foolish world with its retarded justice."

I took my wife's hands inside mine, lifted them to my lips, and kissed her palms. Looking intensely into her big eyes, I whispered, "Can you see, now, why in Tenner's case only an eye for an eye will do? And I'd rather take my chances and punish Tenner in this country, if he has made his home here, than have to chase him down in Germany or some other land. The ideal way of bringing Tenner to justice would be to kidnap him and take him to Greece. Do you remember in 1960 when a handful of Jews pulled off that gutsy abduction of Adolf Eichman from Argentina? Eichman was tried in Israel, found guilty for exterminating millions of Jews, and hanged. But Israel and Jews from around the world were together on that one. Do you suppose the two of us could ever amass the resources to snatch Tenner, smuggle him out of this land and take him all the way to Kalavryta to stand trial there?"

"What about the Greeks? Couldn't we get Greece and some Greeks to help us?"

"Greeks are war-weary. All they want is a cigarette and a glass of retsina to help numb the past."

Suddenly an honest tranquillity enveloped Kathy and she touched my nose with her finger.

"All right," she whispered and huddled inside my arms. "However you decide to handle this, I'm completely by your side."

I planted a fond smooch on my Louloudaki's fragrant hair and retreated to place a call to the law firm of Brown, Panza, and Pagalos. Stavros' excited voice came on immediately. He wanted to rush over, but I asked if we could meet later at the hotel for dinner. Eagerly, he agreed. Our date was set for seven. He mentioned he would bring along his fiancée, Lea.

A few minutes before seven Kathy and I took seats facing the entryway, my eyes glued to the large doorway, scrutinizing all the arriving men. I was anxious to learn whether I would recognize Stavros. We had not seen each other since the spring of 1944.

A bit after the hour, a trim man of medium height, wearing white slacks and black shirt and holding hands with a striking, younger, dark-haired woman appeared. I recognized him instantly. The same bright playful black eyes gave him away, and I sprang up and rushed to intercept him.

"Stavros," I shouted. We embraced and looked at each other's face. My lips quivered and I fought back tears. His laughter, his gestures, his gentle speech were the same. He was handsome with an easy smile, sleek black hair, and a mustache. We introduced our women and, while those two engaged in a lively conversation, the four of us advanced toward the restaurant, Stavros and I each with an arm over the other's shoulders.

Lea was a talkative sort and Kathy seemed at ease with her, so Stavros and I plunged into an orgy of recollection, updating our lives and exchanging news from home. At the conclusion of the meal, with our coffee cups steaming, I came to the Tenner affair. I told Stavros everything we had learned and ended with the most recent piece of news: Tenner had entered the country under a pseudonym at San Pedro, California, on the second of July in 1947.

"Alfredo Gregorio Giacominni," Stavros repeated as he scribbled the name on the back of one of his business cards. "We're associated with a firm in DC. I'll ask one of their guys to search the Immigration and Naturalization Service files—see if we can come up with something. Through the INS we should be able to find Giacominni's birthplace. It might be that the identity Tenner assumed was totally fictitious. But, he may have taken the name of a dead person. In any case we should be able to trace Giacominni's record by hiring someone to visit his claimed birthplace and check the register there."

"How long will that take? To check through the INS, I mean."

"No longer than a week. I'll get on it first thing in the morning. The moment something is relayed to me I will contact you."

On the first day back in my office, Maria handed me my mail. A brown manila envelope from AGG Enterprises caught my eye. I opened it first.

Dear Mr. Barlow:

This registered letter is intended to serve as our last effort to negotiate fairly with you. Please reconsider our original proposal and

*respond at once. If we do not hear from you shortly we will have
no other recourse but to pursue our position to the fullest extent of
the law.*

Sincerely,
Barry Boyette
General Legal Counsel
AGG Enterprises

This time I placed the letter back inside the envelope and set it aside
for further study. I skipped through the rest of the pile and tossed a
mountain of unopened solicitations, then called Maria in to bring me
up to date on things. Maria assured me that all had sailed smoothly and
nothing of consequence had developed while we were "in Europe." At
that point she gave a little cough and her smirking eyes rolled to make
me once again aware that she had never fallen for my dead aunt story.

"Bossman, can I please have the third week of July off?" she asked,
still grinning. "My only brother is arrivin' from Italy on the 18th. Charlie is an ex G-man, FBI, you know. Got himself early disability retirement and took off for *la bella Italia.* Here, the good doctors had pegged
him for dead but he didn't buy their story. Told 'em in so many words
to go to—you know where—and took off for Tolfa, a sleepy mountainous town near Roma, where our parents came from. So off he went
and got himself cured with a bunch of old-country remedies."

"What was wrong with him, Maria?"

"Developed some skin ailment—cancer, they called it."

"Melanoma?"

"No. Somethin' else. Mycosis somethin'. Pretty nasty stuff, they
claimed. A whole lot of bull those doctors dish out to you when they
get you inside their jaws. 'Lord have mercy on all the diseased and
spare them from havin' to visit medical people,' mama useta say in her
broken English. So poor Charlie went to hell and back, and all that for
nothin'. A nice boy Charlie is. Had lots of girlfriends. Never married
though—felt strongly that a law enforcement man mustn't take on
responsibilities. You know, wife, kids and the rest of the stuff that slows
a man down."

"Getting back to your request, Maria. Of course you can take that week off," I assured her. "But about your brother, Charlie—did he serve in the Bay Area?"

"Oh, he did his early duty in Washington, DC. Last ten years he served here in San Francisco—to be close to his lovin' sister, he said. Adores San Francisco. Asked him to come and live with me; the house empty as it is, why not use the darn thing? But no. Likes Italy. Be here for a couple-week visit—that's all. Who knows? Maybe he'll stick around longer. Hope so. Like to pick him up at the airport—spend a few full days visitin', catchin' up and all that, you understand."

"The workings of the bureau have always intrigued me, but I've never met an FBI man. Do you think I could meet your brother?"

"By gully, Bossman, Charlie knows about you. See no reason to deny you the pleasure of his acquaintance. Now, listen here, soon as my good brother gets over his jet lag he'll be in here shakin' your hand. Promise you that much. You'll love 'm. Filled with humility and a heart of gold."

I reached the house in low spirits. The evening was warm and in the kitchen Kathy was skewering marinated chunks of lamb between slices of onions and tomatoes. As soon as we kissed—a ritual between us when we parted even for the briefest of time—she tossed the kabobs on the gleaming coals. They sizzled, spreading aromatic fumes, and I sat watching the blinking beacon of Alcatraz Island brightening as the sunset gold faded into gray.

Then, Hans Tenner took over my being. His vague portrait slowly took shape before me and I began to wonder about the beast who passed himself off to the world as Alfredo Giacominni, and where he might be if he were still alive.

"Sunflower," Kathy called from the kitchen.

"Yah?" I replied absentmindedly. She came and slowly slid behind me and slipped her arms around my neck, bending over to kiss me.

"I can never get enough of your scent," she said. She dropped to her knees and placed her head on my lap and brushed it against me like a kitten. "A penny for your thoughts."

"How much I love you is in my mind." I stroked her hair, still looking off into the distance.

"I never tire of hearing your sweet thoughts, but I can feel your mind is far away."

"What right have I to drag you into this?"

"You mean about Tenner? Things will work out."

"It's a vast world out there. I don't know how we'll find him."

"We have done very well so far." She tapped her finger on my nose, stood up, and danced out of my grasp and away to check the smoking barbecue.

Saturday morning came crystal-clear, one of those rare summer days when one can see the Farallon Islands, a bunch of rocks twenty-some miles away, usually hidden in the fog of the Pacific.

"A great day for sailing," Kathy said.

We took provisions and headed for the marina. *El Greca,* our orange, 26-foot international folk boat, rocked as if smiling at our arrival. The moment we cleared the breakwater we hoisted her sails, and enraptured we listened to the hissing while her canvases split the fresh westerlies. Exhausted from a ten-hour-long labor of love, we buttoned her up and came home to a ringing phone. I picked it up.

"This is the great Stavros Pagalos speaking, defender of the criminal class. I hear you are searching for a fine lawyer," he giggled. He asked about Kathy, and after some trivial talk he shifted into a more formal tone.

"Are you sure about this, Yiannis?"

"Sure about what?"

"About finding Tenner."

"You've forgotten our vows, Stavros?"

"I remember them clearly."

"Then?"

"But we were young, and very angry."

"And what is that supposed to mean?"

"Surely you aren't considering taking this matter into your own hands. Or are you?"

"Fulfilling my vow to my father is very important to me."

"But Yiannis, my dearest friend, I deal with victims of revenge every day."

I chose to ignore his comment. "Did they find something in Washington?"

"Yiannis, as a rule I refrain from passing judgment on someone's actions, but you are like a brother to me and I need to warn you of the consequences—for Kathy's sake, if not yours, for crying out loud!"

"Kathy is with me all the way and I have thought of everything—many times over, actually!" The tone of my voice was cool. "What did you find out?"

"Your information checked out. Giacominni entered as an immigrant and was issued permanent resident status soon after his arrival."

"Any additional info?"

"His birthplace is listed as Civitavecchia, Italy, a coastal town near Rome. Rome's port city, actually. Year: 1916."

"Is that all? I mean, did your guy come up with anything else?"

"Giacominni's sponsor was Father Anthony Licavoli. Father Licavoli, an Italian Catholic priest, was with Saint Sebastian Church in Pasadena. We did a quick check and discovered the church has been demolished and the priest is dead."

"So, the only follow-up on this Giacominni is through the birth records back in Civitavecchia," I said, thinking out loud.

"I can start looking for an Italian detective agency. It should not be difficult to arrange."

"Oh, I can handle that from here, Stavros."

"Yiannis . . ."

"Yes."

"I may not be volunteering to become your co-conspirator in this thing, but I want you to know I will spend my whole life to vindicate you no matter what road you choose to follow."

On Monday, July first, I was in the office early. From my wallet I took out the crumpled piece of paper with Karl's phone number and asked a female operator to place the call. She let the bell ring longer than normal, but soon it became apparent there was no one at the other end. She asked me to try again later, and after fifteen minutes I made another attempt, but the results were the same.

Maria arrived at nine and peeked through the door. Surprised to see me behind my desk so early, she stammered a rushed greeting and at that instant, a flash came to me.

"Maria, your brother Charlie, he speaks Italian?" I asked.

"Does a duck swim? Like a native, Bossman. I barely recollect my papa, but our mama, an immigrant too, spoke English like a parrot. As youngsters the first language we learned was Italian."

"Can Charlie be reached by phone?" I asked.

"Well, he lives with our cousin Guiseppe, who is kinda well-to-do by Italian standards, got an import company of sorts, and yes, they got a telephone over there."

"Great! Do you suppose he would mind doing some snooping for me?"

"If I know anything about my brother, I can tell you flat out he'll love it."

"Can you give me his number?"

"Bet your boots." She glanced at her watch, "Let's see. Right now it's the tail end of their siesta. Italians aren't much different from the Greeks, you know. *Una facca una razza.*" ("One face one race.")

I remembered this expression from my earlier years. It was a common saying during the Italian occupation of Greece. Maria went on.

"Yah. At midday those Mediterranean tribes load up on pasta or whatever, get stiff on vino, and pass out for a coupla hours or more. Charlie loves that crawling pace, slower than a turtle dragging its ass across the sand—pardon my French—but then you know all that stuff yourself, right Bossman?"

"And how!"

"Charlie is probably bored to death waitin' for the next meal. I'll get him for you."

I overheard Maria shout. "How ya doin' big brother? How y'all down there in the land of sunshine, olive oil, and marble?" After a brief introduction Maria told me to pick up the receiver. Charlie had a strong, friendly voice with a slight Texas drawl similar to his sister's. It turned out that Civitavecchia was just a skip and a jump from Tolfa. He had absolutely no problem with taking a shot at a speck of investigative work to spice up the boredom of his small-town life. When I mentioned compensation, he rebuffed me, citing his gratitude for my patience with his beloved but complex sister.

"Sometimes such information is just not available, Yiannis. Lotsa things got tossed out or burned up during the war years. Maybe there's no water in the well. But if there's anything there, I'll have a copy of it for you by the time I leave here for Frisco. Okay?"

Some weeks later, Maria entered my office followed by a dapper, dark-complexioned, and tanned man in his sixties, with sharp brown eyes topped by bushy brows, a full head of gray hair, a pleasant smile, western boots, and a brown ten-gallon hat in hand over his heart.

"This is my brother, Charlie Santoni." His strong handshake belied his years.

"Good looks run in the family," I blurted lightheartedly.

Maria blushed as she withdrew.

"You know, we north Mediterranean tribes have the elegant features—like the chiseled noses and things," he chuckled with typical Texas-style bragging, a friendly way of sharing our old-world heritage.

Charlie was a jovial man, and we began a comfortable, lengthy dialogue. He talked about his father's family, which had been very poor. With his grandfather dead, his grandmother was essentially forced to sell her firstborn, Carlo—Charlie's father—to some Scots who were scouring Italy snatching up cheap child labor to man the mills in Scotland.

His father was strong and had survived the abuse, slaving fourteen hours a day seven days a week, until eventually he stowed away on a cargo ship headed for New York City. There, he married the daughter of a butcher and they had two kids, Charlie and, years later, Maria. The family picked up and moved to Lubbock, Texas, and opened an Italian deli. The lack of proper nutrients in Carlo's youth finally took its toll and he died a young man, a few days before he reached forty. Moisture came to Charlie's eyes and he looked away.

"So, you are making your permanent home in Italy?" I said, pretending I hadn't noticed his upheaval.

"Since I quit at the bureau, yeah. The land of my ancestors agrees with me. The sage, the rosemary, the olive trees, the grass, the soil; sharing the simple life of those plain, kind folk has rejuvenated me completely. Feel strong and peaceful since I moved there. As the sayin' goes, 'Italians, in a very loud way, are friendlier than normal folks,' and I love each and every one of them—except for a few old soreheads."

"You look great to me, Charlie!" I said brightly.

Suddenly his lips tightened and his eyes narrowed. "Yiannis, this thing you asked me to look into in Civitavecchia, it's legit, right? Been a clean FBI man all my life, and I don't want to get bogged down in anythin' illegal."

I sat up straighter in my chair as I felt myself blush.

"You be the judge, Charlie," I said, and my statement came out slowly and with emotion. "If trying to locate the Nazi who murdered my father along with a thousand other innocent souls is illegal, then you had better not share with me what you dug up."

Charlie studied me. His stare was professionally impassive. "Hmmm, you are a victim of the war, just like Maria."

"Maria?"

"Never mentioned it?" He appeared surprised. "Guess she figured no sense in advertisin' her troubles. No market for them."

"I would like to know," I insisted.

"Widowed by the war. Normandy. Johnny, her husband, was military—a lieutenant in the marines. Parachuted behind enemy lines, was captured by the Germans and shot. Johnny was a kindhearted kid. Maria loved him dearly. His pictures are all over the house. She lives with her memories. Refuses to tarnish them by considerin' another marriage."

My head bowed in honor of the dead soldier. Silent heartaches and undeclared sufferings surround us in abundance, I thought. Some mute moments passed. Then Charlie spoke.

"My buddy Giorgio, one of the two policemen in Tolfa—he's related to our family somehow—got a cousin that works in the registrar's office in Civitavecchia. So I go to the cousin. He gets me an okay from the higher-ups and some help to search the old files. A messy affair, but if you don't scale the mountain you can't see the view. We tracked the ledgers year by year. The only Alfredo Gregorio Giacominni registered in the Civitavecchia records is a poor *bambino* born in 1916. Died in 1919. Other Giacominnis registered? Well, yes, about half a dozen, born in different years, but Alfredo Giacominni—and specifically

Alfredo Gregorio Giacominni born in 1916? No. Only that one little person with such a name on the Civitavecchia birth registers."

"So Giacominni took on the identity of a dead child." My mind was racing. "How many Alfredo Gregorio Giacominnis exist in this world? And how can I begin to search for them all?" I muttered with resignation, expecting Charlie to toss me a sympathetic good-luck-kid look and graciously change the subject.

But instead, he remained silent. He paced back and forth with his head bent and his fists joined behind his back. Finally he stopped and peeped up at me in an absorbed way.

"Wanna give me the job? Need no pay. Just expenses. Love the stuff. Miss the bureau, darn it. Damn shame I had to leave it so early."

I looked up and closed my eyes in worshipful contemplation, even though the identity of the deity I was directing my adoration to seemed hazy. The telephone rang and Maria called in to me.

"Bossman, that sleazy, chubby, little lawyer Boyette from AGG Enterprises is on the line. Claims it's urgent."

"Tell him I'm busy; not available; out of the country," I shouted back.

I told Charlie all about AGG Enterprises' initial demand and its escalation into a threat of a lawsuit.

"How you intend to handle this?" asked Charlie with concern.

"Well, presently I'm ignoring them. But if they deliver on their threat I'll have no alternative but to fight them in court." My answer sounded strained, filled with anger.

Charlie chewed on his lips and ran his finger over the wide rim of his hat.

"Our judicial system may be the dandiest in the world but it's got holes in it. Big money is in control here. The good old boys in Washington see that the laws they pass reward their well-to-do friends. The rich can file their frivolous suits and time is on the side of deep pockets. Need big money to fight with the big dogs." Charlie's face grew tender as he reflected. "One day, after school, when I was in the first grade, I walked into our deli in Lubbock. My daddy was busy nailing a framed picture on the wall. 'What's that picture, papa?' I asked. 'My son,' he said with a very serious face and pointed to the picture, 'this ise the good Lady Justice. She ise a nice lady, *ma* ...' 'Why are the eyes of the good lady covered, papa?' I interrupted. 'Lady Justice, she ise a good lady *ma* her scale ise old and crooked. *Capisce?*' 'No, papa' I said. He looked compassionately at me. 'My son,' he put his arm around my shoulders 'she ise a good lady but she ise ashame to look at her cheatin' scale, and ... she ... she cover her eyes.' He pointed to his temple and winked. '*Capisce,* now?' he asked. Then he added, "My son, you go to schoole, and when you grow up you buy the nice lady a new scale. Okay?"

"Your father was a perceptive man."

"He was simple and honest. A goodhearted, hardworking man." Charlie added with admiration.

Charlie's comments along with his father's earthly interpretation of Justice and her blindfold rekindled the powerlessness and outrage I felt. Looking at the situation rationally, I knew that engaging AGG Enterprises in a legal battle would do me in financially.

"But most all my money is tied up here. I've paid cash for the darn thing. Besides, Kathy and I both love this building."

Charlie shrugged his shoulders.

"What do you suggest I do, Charlie? Let those asses walk all over me without a fight?"

"Askin' me for advice?"

"Please."

"Got to remember, when the shit flies, if you stand too close you're bound to get hit. So if I was you I would make a darn good effort to negotiate a better price for myself. Then I would let them have the blessed thing 'I love' and go on with my life. There's a belly-full of buildin's out there for sale, Yiannis, and some may even be better than the one you got here."

Half of the month went by and I had no word from Charlie. One evening when the air was cool and the fog spilled into the bay and over the city, the drizzle created an early, eerie darkness. While the foghorns bellowed their mournful sounds, Kathy kept close to me. She looked around with uneasy eyes. Finally she said, "I just can't rid myself of a weird feeling! Actually I'm scared." We held each other tight and just then the doorbell rang.

I rushed to the bedroom and stuffed the Luger into my belt. With Kathy dangling from my neck, we parted the curtain next to the entrance a sliver and peeked out. Charlie's sharp eye caught the faint movement and he waved to be let in. He approached the two of us with a solemn face.

"Brace yourselves!" he said the moment he stepped inside.

Kathy's eyes looked wild and I searched Charlie's face for a hint.

"A-G-G," Charlie said slowly, accentuating each letter as he took a chair. We both stared at him stupidly. "A-G-G! Does AGG ring a bell?" He gave us time to search our memories.

"Why should it?" I asked.

"Maybe AGG Enterprises will do it."

I was pouring him an ouzo. My back was turned and I shook my shoulders in ignorance.

"A-G-G—the principal owner and president of AGG Enterprises. A-G-G—the first letters of Alfredo Gregorio Giacominni."

The bottle of ouzo slipped from my grasp and shattered on the hardwood floor.

"Oh my God!" exclaimed Kathy and buried her face in her hands. Charlie leaned forward and talked in a near whisper.

"See, Europeans aren't like Americans who are cocksure they live in the best place and don't give a hoot about visitin' the world. Figured Giacominni might be naturalized by now—acquired an American passport and all that. I had this itch. Itchin' though, doesn't do much good till you scratch it. So I spent time in DC at the passport service. My hunch was right on target. Alfredo Gregorio Giacominni was issued his first passport in '52. The most recent renewal—July of last year. Through his fresh application I traced him to Palo Alto. Got his office listed as his permanent address."

"Do you think it's him?" I asked, almost timidly.

"That question I can't answer, but I can tell you, as milk makes butter, that the long, cold trail you've been following ends in Palo Alto."

Kathy was on her knees scooping up broken glass and mopping ouzo with a towel, while I stared at Charlie as if a doctor had shot my brain full of anesthetic.

"Are there any physical characteristics that could give him away?" Charlie asked.

"Yes," I said, still in my trance.

"Well, what?"

"His wrist. His right wrist juts out at an odd angle, a war injury from Russia."

"And you remember this from the time he spent in your parents' home?" Charlie uttered, perplexed.

"The SS sign, double thunderbolts tattooed on his left arm, and the dislocated right wrist were authenticated by his ex-sister-in-law. A German detective, Karl, and I had a chat with her only a few hours before she was murdered."

Shock parted Charlie's lips and he shook his head in disgust.

"Think this guy Giacominni, slash, Tenner had somethin' to do with her murder?"

"She was a harmless invalid who lived in seclusion on the outskirts of a remote Bavarian village, and probably the only living person who could identify Giacominni as Tenner."

"You've got to pay Mr. Giacominni a visit and soon. May discover you recognize more about him than you think. Eleven-year-old minds remember a whole lot, even when twenty years 've gone by."

Charlie stood up and patted me encouragingly on the back.

The moment he left, Kathy rushed over and threw her arms around me, and when she looked at me there were tears of anger, or joy or relief, I couldn't tell which, in her eyes.

"Yiannis," she said while I stared at her impassively, "as I have said before, this terrible man must be exposed. Whatever you decide, I'm with you, forever and ever."

Union Square was bright and hot since the usual breeze or fog had neglected to make its appearance that day. From my office window I could see the traffic edge sluggishly along; a cop dressed in a heavy blue uniform stood on the corner of Geary and Powell, stoically bearing his suffering as he pretended to scrutinize the passing crowd. My moist hand snatched at the phone receiver for the tenth time. Throughout a sleepless night I had rehearsed my short speech. My shaking index finger found the holes and dialed the numbers.

"Mr. Giacominni, please. I am John Barlow"—as a precaution I used my official first name—"owner of a building near Union Square. Mr. Giacominni has expressed an interest in purchasing my building and I need to speak to him." I repeated the same exact sentences to a female who claimed to be his personal secretary. At her request I spelled my last name before I was put on hold.

"Yah, yah, this is Alfredo Giacominni." The piercing voice struck me with horror; it was tinged with an accent and absolutely icy.

"I am the owner of the building on Powell Street."

"We have been anticipating your response." I took the deepest breath.

"Let me get right to the point. I may be prepared to sell you my building. However, I wish to deal exclusively and directly with you, and the transaction must be in cash." There was a pause.

"Your request sounds reasonable, Mr. Barlow." There was another, longer hesitation. "I see no sound objection to your conditions, whatever your reasons to demand a cash transaction may be. Would you prefer to meet here in our offices, or there in yours, to discuss the particulars?"

"I don't mind traveling to your office."

"Very well then, let me see . . . ," I could hear him fingering pages, "is Thursday at two o'clock agreeable?"

"I'll be there." My palms were wet with sweat, my throat felt dry, and my lips trembled. Had I been communicating with the vicious animal whose discovery had become my obsession? I glanced toward the corner. The cop was still there, mechanically studying the strolling crowd.

Charlie had responded to my urgent call, and when I arrived at my office on Thursday morning he was already waiting. His greeting was short and without sentiment, and he appeared fidgety. He paced back and forth with his arms laced behind his back. Then he stopped abruptly and faced me.

"No possibility that he might recognize you, Yiannis. You were a boy, and he a Nazi officer. Thousands of young faces must have passed through his eyes throughout his nasty hustles from Russia down to the Balkans." He resumed walking. "However, you gotta consider that this man, if he is that snake Tenner, will be flat-ass suspicious. Fugitives are acutely sensitive to deception because they've learned to master the art themselves. Always keep that thought in the background."

I was listening carefully.

"The good thing here is that you talk American like a lad who was brought up munchin' on granny's apple pie, because he would be alerted by a man who speaks English with an accent, maybe a European." Charlie's black eyes grew wider and more serious.

"You can't let your feelin's take over, you hear? You can't be yourself. You gotta be just a man who wants to transact the sale of his buildin'."

"Charlie, I'm not a man who hides his feelings well."

"When you negotiated the purchase of this buildin', did you lay all your cards on the table at once? Course not. Now, stop worryin'. You'll do just dandy. I bet you'll be cool as well water."

I chewed one side of my upper lip and listened while Charlie, like a dedicated coach, took me through a vigorous drill, working on how to exercise control over my emotions.

"Observe his mannerisms. Idiosyncrasies are deeply rooted parts of a man—remain embedded until he croaks. As we say down in Texas, 'You can't take the hog out of a ham.'"

Charlie kept pacing back and forth with his hands clasped behind his back. He reminded me of my father, who often strode back and forth in a similar stance when he was lost in thought.

"Detect, yes, but with subdued sharpness. You can do this thing real easy, Yiannis, I know you can. And because it's natural for all of us to want to hide our deformities, don't you go on and stare in the hope of catchin' a glimpse of that crooked wrist.

"However, not at the beginnin' when you first meet, but when you shake hands at the conclusion of your visit you must shine a smile and do it properly with lotsa warmth—you gotta force yourself to appear normal. Accept his hand inside both of yours in a kinda peasant-style salute and then let your left hand do the crawlin' around, feelin' for his bad wrist. You hear me, Yiannis? That way, at least you'll have the chance to turn and walk away and hide your face, and the bastard won't read in your eyes that you found out he's the Jack of Spades."

AGG Enterprises was a freestanding, flat-roofed concrete building on the edge of an office complex north of University Avenue on El Camino. Its one-story facade was white marble, and the recessed entrance looked impressive. I parked, approached the tinted mirrored-glass double doors and walked into a spacious lobby dotted with couches and chairs. A pleasant receptionist greeted me with a smile.

"Good afternoon," I said, hoping my voice wasn't wavering as much as I thought it was. "I'm John Barlow. Mr. Giacominni is expecting me."

"You must be his two o'clock."

I smiled and she asked me to take a seat, pointing to the sofa. A few minutes passed before a stocky man, about my age, in a gray suit and tinted glasses, gave me a careful scrutiny as he approached. His voice was coarse and heavy.

"Mr. Giacominni will see you now. Follow me."

We walked briskly down a long marble corridor that ended at a massive oak door with brass fittings which he pushed open, inviting me to enter a smartly decorated office where a robust woman in her forties sat. She sprang up and hurried ahead of us to fling open a second gigantic carved oak door.

"Sir, Mr. Barlow is here to see you," she announced in a subordinate voice.

Quickly she ushered us into a spacious room. A blond man sat regally behind a huge wooden desk.

In the middle of the oak-paneled space an ornate chandelier hung. Etchings and oil paintings, illuminated by indirect lighting as in a museum, garnished three walls. Beyond the heavily carved desk, a grand floor-to-ceiling case stuffed with books of all sizes stared at me.

The man stood and dispassionately came around his desk. He was tall and lanky and dressed in a black pinstriped suit and gray tie subtly patterned in red and silver. His long slender hand came up to meet mine, and I noticed his light blue eyes were almost gray, piercing and very cold. A chill crawled over my skin and I knew instantly that I had faced this man before.

"Have a seat." His request sounded like an order. I dropped his hand and slid onto a leather armchair while I tried to control my trembling. He returned to his throne. We stared at each other, but because the room was windowless, in the subdued lighting I found it difficult to read his face.

Charlie's instructions pounded my brain. "Don't panic, stay calm, you are only there to sell him your building!"

"So, we will make a transaction?" he asked, his stare remaining glued to me.

I put on what I thought to be an innocent smile and took another deep breath.

"That is why I am here," I said, regaining composure.

"What are your terms?"

I looked over my shoulder to view the husky man standing by the door like an obedient dog. Giacominni raised his brows in a signal and the man quickly withdrew.

"I want to deal exclusively with you, no intermediaries—because I wish to be paid in cash. I have my reasons. The entire amount must be in cash."

"Which amount?"

My gut feeling dictated that I should forget about entering into a bargaining debate.

"The three hundred and ninety thousand dollars you have offered."

He leaned slightly forward, his posture rigid and his face waxy. "I don't see a problem. When can you deliver us a notarized bill of sale? We have done a search and found the title clear."

"In one month, maybe a little longer. I'll have to vacate my office."

He remained stone-faced. "I must have a date. When you deliver the related documents you will expect me to hand you the cash, so I must know the specific date in advance."

"You, sir, just you—no other witnesses can be present. Otherwise the deal is off. Am I making myself clear?"

"I understand, but ... I must have a set date."

The wheels were turning in my head. Tenner had executed my father in Kalavryta on the thirteenth day of the month, a date I had learned to hate.

"September thirteenth, at five-thirty p.m. That will give me the time I need. On September thirteenth, at five-thirty p.m., I will be here with all the documents executed and signed, and the building will be yours."

He consulted his calendar. The light of his desk lamp reflected the shadows on his thin face, giving him a devilish semblance.

"Fine. Friday, the thirteenth of September, here in this office at five-thirty sharp." For the briefest moment his colorless eyes did a brisk jig then froze again.

He reached under his desk and a moment later the bully in the tinted glasses stuck his head through the oak door. Giacominni stood up, walked around his desk once again, and extended his hand to me. I gritted my teeth and pretended that our meeting had been a cordial one. I moved forward reaching out with both arms. While my right hand clasped his and shook it vigorously my left probed his wrist.

As if I had gripped a high-voltage wire, a violent impulse shot through me. A murderous flash commanded me to reach out and snatch him by the throat and choke him. Instead I let go his repulsive flesh and, fighting the bile rising in my throat, I turned, moved to the door, and, followed by his bodyguard, stalked down the corridor and through the front lobby until I reached the parking lot.

Outside, perspiration drenched me; it felt as if bugs were crawling down my back. Once in the car I turned the fan on full-blast and sat there willing my mind to think. Vague plans for torturous medieval killings skipped through my confused head. Heat radiated from my hyperventilating body and fogged the windows of the tiny roadster. I wiped them clean, while my eyes roved the parking lot searching for witnesses to my frantic state. But I saw nothing stirring and became convinced that no one had noticed my turmoil.

The moment Kathy laid her eyes on me she knew.

"It's him. Giacominni is Tenner," she said, taking my hand and holding it against her chest.

Her whole being radiated compassion.

"Let's go out. Let's stroll to Enrico's—people-watching is a soothing pastime. Let's relax over a glass of wine and you can tell me all about it."

A large red sun had begun to slide behind Mount Tam. Having my wife by my side holding my arm somewhat appeased the inflammation of my sour innards. When we reached Broadway, the bustling traffic and human presence calmed me.

Tiny, the seven-foot-tall maitre d', ushered us to the last vacant table, one against the brick wall. Luckily it offered us some privacy. I ordered a bottle of merlot and fried calamari, our favorites. The crowd was gay and loud and the promenaders colorful. Some of the patrons were familiar to us, and we were obligated to exchange greetings.

"There may be some drastic changes in our lives," I said.

"I'm prepared."

"We may have to leave America."

"I can live anywhere as long as we are together."

"Soon."

"Greece?"

"Crete."

"An eye for an eye, then."

"More like an eye for thousands of eyes."

"Well ... yes."

"And, those are just the dead. The living are owed, too, for their memories, their losses, their nightmares."

Kathy's face reflected my heartache and she looked at me as if she were ready to split her bosom and offer me her gut as a permanent sanctuary from my pain.

"Please Yiannis, don't do this to yourself."

"I fought a great war within me before I came to this conclusion."

"I can imagine."

"You must go to Crete and wait for me there."

Her whole being instantly distorted to a wrenching plea and her hand clenched mine like a vise.

"You aren't going to send me away. You need me. I can help you, my Sunflower. I can do lots of things to help. I will stay out of your way if you ask me to, but we must be together. You promised that we'd never part, ever, ever again."

"You must go. There is no other way."

Drained of all color, she stared at me as if I had plunged a dagger into her heart.

"I can't. I mustn't. I won't," she whispered, and her chest shook. The half-empty wine glass she held trembled. A teardrop fell into it.

She set the glass on the marble table and gripped my forearm with both hands, squeezing her nails into my flesh. "My duty is to be at your side, where I can give you support, aid and love," she proclaimed. "What purpose will I fulfill if I'm tucked away on a distant island, beyond danger? Can you imagine the maddening thoughts ... the torturous pain of not knowing whether you are dead ... or wounded, or ... or jailed? Each second, each minute, each hour of such uncertainty would drive me insane."

"You must go. I need the freedom to move and think clearly. I won't be able to do what I must if I have to worry about you. My sister and her husband will be good company for you. I'll take you there, but I must return alone."

Her eyes were red but the tears stopped. She managed a faint smile but she remained silent, staring at me, waiting, begging for a sign that I might yield.

"I'll do it," she finally said with resignation, "but we must work out a time frame for your return. And if I don't hear from you or see you within the prearranged period—I'll kill myself." She was cold, determined, and fearless. Selfishly, I realized that if I didn't survive my mission, I also wished my Louloudaki dead.

We lifted our glasses in a mute toast. Then we reached over the table and united our lips to seal our somber covenant.

The moment I entered the office the next morning, Maria said, "My brother is waitin' for you, Bossman." I rushed to meet him. Charlie's eyes searched mine with impatience. He sped toward me.

"Was callin' your house till ten last night," he said.

"Kathy and I were out. It was too late to call you when we got in."

"Well? Positive identification?" he whispered in an effort to muffle his words from reaching Maria. I closed the door for privacy.

"Yes, it's him," I replied casually, suppressing my excitement, all along thinking how much I would miss Charlie's valued guidance. For a time we drank our coffee in silence. "A thousand souls will always be grateful to you, Charlie," I said finally.

"What do you mean?" he asked and looked at me in a surprised way.

"You have helped me find Tenner. Your job is finished now. But I don't know how to thank you."

"Wait!" Charlie's eyes widened. "You firin' me? Worried about me becomin' an accessory?" Suddenly a flicker of hope ignited my insides.

"Well. You're a cop—you know the law."

"Oh! I know the law, all right." He paced slowly to the window and looked out somewhere far away and up into the gray sky. His words came low and slow, but very clear. "But I'm with you on this one . . . Doin' it for Maria's Johnny." He paused and turned to face me. "Or maybe because I feel it's the last run around the block for me. Need to stay on and see you get the son of a bitch."

We walked to the coffee shop at the Sir Francis Drake Hotel and worked most of the morning roughing out a plan. Charlie would handle all the logistics and do all the information gathering and surveillance of the location, its alarms, and guards. I would check his strategy, take Kathy to Crete, dispose of all real properties and belongings, and plan my escape.

"Need a breaker," Charlie said. I gave him a blank stare. "Someone trustworthy, who can knock off all the goons that guard Giacominni."

"Climpt will do it," I offered without hesitation.

"Who in hell is Climpt?"

"My army buddy. A karate expert. He's in the Far East, but he'll come over in a jiffy if I ask him to. We were very close in Germany." I added, "As an old Greek folk saying goes, Climpt and I were as close as my ass against my drawers."

From a seldom-used public phone, my first attempts to get through to the military overseas operator started at six-thirty a.m. and lasted until nine. The meager correspondence with Climpt had been funneled through the Military Assistance Group, Saigon. I gave Climpt's company to the young soldier at the other end, and he said it would take some effort to locate his outfit and then to get him to the telephone. All morning I baby-sat the phone. Finally, at around noon, the bell startled me. Climpt's company commander came on the fuzzy line to say he would pass on to his noncom the message to contact me immediately, and that I should expect a call in a few hours. I took a short walk to kill time and strolled back with a cup of coffee. It was almost six when the phone rang and jolted me once again. I snatched the receiver.

"Hello," I shouted. The line howled and echoed with overseas clutter.

"Hello, Sergeant Cook heah," a big Georgia voice hollered. It sounded even more drawn out with the time delay.

"Climpt, this is Yiannis."

"I read ya, Yiannis, what's up, ma pal?"

"I need you, Climpt—target date September thirteenth. Need you to be here a couple days ahead of the due date."

"Ya dug up tha yella fucker, hah?"

"It's been a long haul."

"Hot dog. I could pee down both legs."

"Can I count on you, friend?"

"Be in Frisco ifen I gotta swim."

"Great, call me when you get in."

"Target date Septembuh thuteen, right?"

"Roger."

"Okey-dokey; I gottsa, ma frien'. Ovah an' out."

On Monday, August fourth, Charlie and I met for lunch at Bardelli's. The place was my choice. The food was always good, the service excellent, and the stained glass entrance with its peacock displaying his tail in full bloom enhanced my appetite. Each time I ate there, I took a chair to face the foyer and gaze at the colored feathers amid the roses and tulips as the natural light filtered through the colored panes.

The restaurant was humming, and since we had failed to make reservations George the Greek, the hefty waiter who had been a fixture there for more than half a century, had to rearrange some tables to accommodate us in his station.

"Climpt is on board," I said in a low voice.

"Your buddy—he capable of takin' out two or three bullies at once?" Charlie asked and coughed while he toyed with his fork. "Could've done it myself thirty years ago with no sweat. Was tough as boot leather when I was younger."

"Climpt has been military all his adult life. He came out of the swamps of Georgia, lied about his age, and joined up—no family ties, little education, and a big heart. He knows about Kalavryta and Tenner. The man is stronger than a gorilla to start with, and then he took up Kempo Karate—black belt instructor now."

"And you trust this Climpt soldier won't tap dance when the action starts?"

"With my life."

Charlie studied my face and, seemingly satisfied, continued. "Showed my old badge, which I never turned in because I couldn't part with it, to the contractor and got us a set of plans for Giacominni's buildin.' Built with no windows. Two doors only—one up front and one in back—like a bunker! Pulled the same with the alarm outfit. The place is bugged like Tiffany's in New York." Sensing my question, he smirked, "When you mention FBI, everybody gets all flustered—no one ever gets the guts to ask your name and stuff like that."

"But they can give a description of you."

"Ah, don't you worry. In the bureau we know all the tricks. Besides, my flight is all arranged. Be returnin' to Italy on the mornin' of the due date."

"Charlie, I've been meaning to ask you."

"Go ahead and ask."

"Intelligence agencies like the FBI, CIA and others—do they cooperate with each other?"

"FBI has got jurisdiction inside the country and the CIA outside. Sometimes the CIA boys start messin' around here in our stompin' grounds. Then the shit begins to fly, because we don't want others clutterin' our turf. To answer your question, yes. We exchange information all the time. Even work with the military, like their Counter-Intelligence Corps and others."

We nibbled on fried zucchini sticks, a specialty of the house, washing them down with a decent zinfandel. Charlie casually asked, "Told Kathy yet?"

My stomach soured at once. I stopped eating.

"Yeah, last night."

"Well?" said Charlie.

"She didn't take it well; but she finally agreed. I'm taking her to Crete and returning alone."

"What about draftin' your escape route? You spent time comin' up with a disguise for yourself?"

I shook my head no and Charlie drummed his fingers on the table again. "Very little time left. Can't help you much in that part of the cow pasture, Yiannis. Devisin' your escape route is your responsibility. It'll have to be your own top secret, you hear. Nobody, not even Kathy, should know your plans. But you got to attend to it now and alone." Just then, simultaneously, we caught sight of Maria advancing toward our table.

"Sorry to interrupt, but this cable just came. It's from Heidelburg, Germany. Thought I should bring it over before I skeedaddle." She handed me a wire and walked away. A premonition shrank my throat. I opened the envelope.

> *Karl is missing. We fear the worst. Your identity may be in jeopardy. Take appropriate precautions at once. Baroness*

I handed the brief note to Charlie, sprang up, and raced to the phone booth. When Kathy answered I blurted, "Lock up the house and don't answer the phone or the door. Meanwhile, start packing essentials. I'll explain as soon as I get home."

"Okay, time for action. I'll be ready. Wow! Intrigue! Excitement! Should I stick the Luger inside my belt just in case?" Her spirits were up. I was surprised to discover her cheerfulness in the face of danger.

"Jiminee, Kathy, one minute you are completely insensitive to danger, the next you crawl to me like a frightened pussycat. Can you just do this for me, please?" I hung up and returned to the table.

"Charlie, I must run. Expect a call from me later."

I found Kathy sitting on an overstuffed suitcase, puffing and out of breath, trying to shove inside it all sorts of materials that protruded from around the edges. When she finally managed to force it shut, she gleamed in accomplishment, and as she caught my stare she exhaled with force, "Phew! I'm bushed!"

A number of suitcases and boxes were lined up by the entry door. I had no attachments to material possessions, but Kathy was different. Books, photographs and mementos, a clay head of an aborigine youth her mother had done in an art class, her favorite pillow, all these things meant a lot to her. Asking her to part with her treasures, perhaps forever, would be a heartless demand.

"I'm ready," she announced, speeding into my arms. I held her close, the only treasure that was immensely dear to me, and bestowed on her my *filaki*.

"The Baroness sent a cable; Karl is missing. We must assume the worst," I announced.

She looked shocked.

"How awful. Should we hole up at my parents' house in Berkeley for a little while?" She was trying to read me.

"We're heading for the East Coast. Then Crete."

"Right this minute? Today?"

"We have no choice. And no one must know our destination, not even God—not your parents, brothers, Gran, nobody. Do you understand, my Louloudaki?"

"And what am I supposed to tell them?"

"That we are going skiing, in Australia!" I snapped. "We'll phone them from the airport."

"What about LB? You don't expect me to abandon LB?" LB (for "little bitch") was our priceless cat, the third member of the family and one who enjoyed greater rights than most earthlings.

I took a deep breath.

"Your parents can look after her, I'm sure."

She stamped the floor with her foot.

"I'm not taking one step without LB! She is coming with us and that's final!"

We loaded her Chevy station wagon and left a house key under the doormat. At the airport, while I was arranging passage to Boston to confuse any tail, Kathy, her protective eyes never losing sight of LB's wicker pet basket, phoned her brother Michael. She explained that we were unexpectedly flying to Florida for a friend's wedding and had decided to stay there for a while, and she asked him to pick up the Chevy from the airport parking lot; the key would be tucked inside the rear bumper.

My call to Charlie was very brief. I assured him I would be back in a couple of weeks at the latest and emphasized that everything must continue to advance according to our original plan. I also asked him to tell Maria that we unexpectedly flew to Australia to go scuba diving at the Great Barrier Reef, or whatever excuse he could dream up.

We flew nonstop, rented a car at the airport, and began our drive south along the awesome New England coast. In Plymouth, we stayed overnight, and the following evening we checked into Manhattan's Plaza Hotel for three days. Without ever discussing the Tenner matter, we lived each day as if it were our last.

Through the concierge we secured tickets to see *My Fair Lady* and *Camelot,* we danced in the Rainbow Room above Rockefeller Center, and strolled through Central Park.

Browsing down lively Fifth Avenue, we came upon an enormous bookstore where my Louloudaki loaded up on reading material and I bought a copy of the Torah as well as a Yiddish phrase book. Later, while waiting to board our flight for Athens, I composed a brief note to Captain Rosenburg's father in Chicago.

> *Dear Mr. Rosenburg, Sr.:*
>
> *My name is Yiannis Barlow and I served in Germany with your son Herb. Herb has helped me trace and unearth a despised rat, the Nazi who executed my father during the mass murder of a thousand Greek civilians, some as young as eleven.*
>
> *After a lot of soul searching, I have concluded that the only way I can be sure this animal is punished properly is to do it myself.*
>
> *Your son Herb told me to contact you if ever I needed a favor. He said you were an influential citizen in the Chicago area, with numerous contacts.*
>
> *Our shared, deeply rooted hatred for all Nazis makes us brothers, so I appeal to you, sir, to assist me in securing a temporary shelter somewhere near Chicago so that under a Jewish disguise I may flee to Israel.*
>
> *Please mail your response to PO Box 53, Davis, California. The time is just one month away. I trust in your confidentiality.*
>
> *Forever grateful,*
Yiannis Barlow

I sealed the envelope, wrote out the address from memory—Winnetka, Illinois—and dropped it into a mailbox.

In the dirty, stuffy Hellinikon Airport in Athens, hot and miserable and exhausted, we hung around for three hours before catching what appeared to be a standing-room-only flight to Chania. The spaces between seats seemed ample only for midgets, and the smells of food and bodies permeated my nostrils as noisy conversations reawakened my subconscious. It seemed as if life had stood still and I had never escaped from Greek odors and disorder.

Kostas, the imposing colonel, and my sister Betty were at Chania to greet us with hugs and tears. Everybody cried, even my stone-faced brother-in-law.

When those two realized that all the suitcases and boxes and the wicker basket with a restless cat belonged to us, they crossed themselves in wonderment, as all Greeks tend to do when something seems beyond their comprehension. They asked me, facetiously of course, if our intent was to relocate and make our home in Crete; I told them, "Yes, those are our immediate plans."

They crossed themselves again, exclaiming, *"Doxa nachi o Theos"* ("God be praised"), and stared at each other, dumbfounded.

Kostas' tiny Fiat was too small to accommodate our gear, so we piled it into a taxi. When the driver heard Sfakia was our destination, he coughed and protested loudly—the difficult trek on an almost inaccessible road, the dangerous inhabitants notorious for their feuding, the time and distance involved—until the colonel's forbidding stare and the revelation of his credentials hushed him. Pretending that we never heard the cursing under his breath, the four of us hopped into the Fiat and took off. The taxi followed.

We traversed the eastern side of Acrotiri, and our gaze took in the magnificent natural harbor of Suda Bay below on our left. Two anchored frigates flew American flags. Around a trying curve along the innermost part of the bay, we came upon a cemetery and Kostas stopped.

Solemnly, we paid our brief respects to the heroic Australians, Britishers, and New Zealanders who had fallen while defending the island during the fierce battle in the Second World War when Cretans and Allies fought gallantly side by side against stubborn German parachute troops.

Soon we connected with a two-lane highway and headed east through lush groves of orange and other citrus trees. At a Y we turned south, and in the midst of the shady village of Vrisses we veered left and began to climb a frightening, winding, narrow road up and up to the top of the rugged White Mountains.

The soil was crumbling limestone. Goats took refuge from the blazing sun beneath atrophic oak trees while a few brazenly munched on thistle, thyme, and oregano, the only vegetation that dared grow on the desolate terrain. Loose boulders lay on the dirt road as it turned and twisted, and our vehicles seemed like two beetles traversing the flaky scales of a dead snake. Occasionally we passed what had been intended for a road sign but was now a purposeless, bullet-riddled piece of tin on a wooden pole.

We drove past tiny villages inside small valleys. An occasional roadside dwelling displayed a cardboard sign spelling out KAFENION, each coffee house sporting one or two tables and a few torn chairs out front.

Beyond the summit, at the beginning of Impros Ravine, Kostas pulled to the side again and stopped. We stretched our legs and edged near the craggy, wind-whipped, and treacherous ridge. From those dizzying heights our eyesight fell to the almost vertical drop down to the Libyan Sea.

After an hour's drive in first gear, which allowed the little engine's torque to choke the car's descent, we plunged into the pint-sized village of Chora in the Sfakia district, the most remote Cretan territory, where the statuesque residents are considered pure descendants of Hercules and Agamemnon.

Fair-eyed women and children peeked curiously from behind the semi-shut shutters of their stone houses. In the kafenion, shaded by three plane trees, sat a handful of old men. They wore the traditional long, dark, Turkish britches, wide scarves tied around their waists in lieu of belts, embroidered vests over black shirts with long sleeves, and black cavalry boots. *Krousalidatos* (bands of black beads and tiny dangling tassels) adorned their proud wrinkled foreheads.

"Yiassas, gerondes," shouted Kostas, saluting the health of the old gentlemen. Their arms took a momentary break from fiddling with their *kombolois* (strings of amber beads) and waved.

"And to your own health, General; and to your fine company's, too," came their gregarious reply—a gross overstatement, since Kostas' rank was colonel, and a lieutenant colonel at that. We smiled and signaled back our greetings while my brother-in-law zigzagged to avoid running over chickens pecking on seeds. Unattended goats and sheep grazing on the roadside kept tossing us scornful stares.

Around and about the grounds of a modest stone house we noticed frantic activity. Men and women were busy placing long boards on chiseled stones to serve as tables and benches. Betty excitedly told us that a wedding was to happen on the following day, Sunday, and the whole village would participate in the festivities. "The joyous affair should last three, four days, maybe longer."

Kostas brought the Fiat to a halt on a piece of flat ground next to a hill, and the taxi man edged his dusty machine behind. The cabbie glanced about suspiciously. He wiped his sweaty brow with his shirt sleeve, unloaded the cargo quickly, snatched his pay, and left in a hurry.

Kostas pointed up.

"This hill is called Tholos; its history goes way back to the Franks."

Up on Tholos' crest, amidst brown stone ruins of some bygone era, stood an imposing two-story house with small windows and an arched door. Built of rough stone, it was flat-roofed and graceless. The four of us loaded ourselves with belongings and climbed the fifty-odd stone steps to the entrance landing. Two red bougainvilleas growing out of the mouths of two enormous terra-cotta jars, one on each side of a metal-studded door, shaded the entry from the merciless sun. Kostas produced a medieval-looking key and unbolted the door that responded to his push with a cry for oil. Kostas' ancestral home was used as a summer retreat now that his widowed mother had moved to Athens to live with her younger sister.

Under the house, a tunnel led us to an airy, earthen courtyard, and in the center an olive tree older than Methuselah, its trunk marked with cracks and crevices, spread its branches to the four winds. Whitewashed stone banquettes and a long table of bleached wood nestled below the healthy leaves of a grapevine. Two lemon trees, clay pots filled with oregano and basil, and numerous ornately glazed oil vats splashed color against the high stone walls.

On the left side a chapel with its round dome painted pale blue to match the sky added orthodoxy to this heavily Christian region of wilderness. It had been erected in memory of Kostas' great-grandfather, a sea captain and founder of this rustic compound.

As if standing sentinel over the Libyan Sea, up ahead and south, a small, one-story structure of similar stone came into view. Betty led us through a blue wooden shutter that served as a door for an opening no larger than three by five feet but thicker than a fortress wall. Through tiny pigeon-hole windows light filtered into two rooms. We dropped our belongings onto the slate floor.

"You may stay here for as long as you wish," said Kostas, staring at both of us, studying us for a reaction.

A bentwood double bed, a mirrored armoire, and oil lamps converted to electricity furnished the bedroom. The space to the left served as a kitchen with a stone sink, a table, and two chairs. Behind a plaster partition a semi-private bathroom boasted a Turkish-style porcelain toilet, with an exposed hole in the middle. A shower head made of tin hung from the ceiling; water dripped when a handle on an exposed pipe on the wall was turned.

An opening, similar in dimension to the entry, led out onto a cliff-hanging terrace from where a brave eye dared look down along the vertical drop to the rocky shore below. The canvas of two chaises lounges and the leaves of two young olive trees flapped and whistled in the warm African wind.

"So ruggedly beautiful!" exclaimed Kathy.

We gazed from a spot where pirates, Franks, Venetians, and Turks had stood as conquerors. All had retreated, though, abandoning the meager soil of this barren spot on the island to the simple natives who revered its nakedness.

After we took a much-needed nap, Betty prepared sweet thick coffee and served it in tiny cups outdoors beneath the grapevine. We made chitchat in English, since both Betty and Kostas spoke the language fluently, until the gray-purple dusk came. We hiked down to the lonesome fish-taverna by the white pebble beach. The stars glittered like diamonds and the sea whispered. I asked the busboy to drag a table by the humming surf's edge, and Kathy and I took off our shoes and let the warm water kiss our feet.

The proprietor charbroiled four fresh perch for us and served them with healthy portions of boiled dandelion greens soaked in olive oil and lemon juice, along with large chunks of feta, crisp brown bread, and a glass vat full of local retsina.

As the alcohol gave her courage, Betty sheepishly asked our reason for such a sudden visit. I cleared my throat and told them that Kathy and I had agreed to divorce ourselves of all material possessions. That, for a while at least, we wanted to try to live our lives in a simple, humbler way, to cleanse both our spirits and bodies, and had concluded that six months to a year of basic existence in Chora should do the trick.

Once the retsina had numbed our reasoning even more, I announced that I would have to make one quick trip to San Francisco to finalize a couple of business transactions but would be back in less than a month. At the conclusion of my story, Betty and Kostas stared at each other, then at us, but suppressed any questioning.

"Tomorrow you must come to the wedding," popped Kostas.

"But ...," Kathy started to protest.

"No need for an invitation," Betty was quick to assure her. "The entire village will be there."

Sunday evening in the courtyard of the bride's parental home, under a lopsided trellis, a pompous priest read from his soiled little book, dragging out the vowels of each word beyond acceptable limits, as if he were determined to lengthen the ordeal of the perspiring youthful bride and groom, who stood stiff and green and about ready to pass out from fright. While the chanter did his Byzantine thing, accompanied by the crescendo of cackling chickens, barking dogs, and squealing piglets, the best man crisscrossed the nuptial crowns, and the instant the mystic matrimonial Isaiah dance came to completion, the throng scrambled to congratulate the newlyweds, offering their presents of live roosters, lambs, or goats in plain view of the appraising eyes of the relations.

When the crowd's obligations, so to speak, were fulfilled, the entire throng advanced about three blocks to the abode of the groom's parents, a steaming drummer's monotonous beat leading the parade. There the dowry was laid out on makeshift tables to be scrutinized by all. After the army of peasants offered their loud exclamations for the dexterity of the bride's golden hands, they rushed, pushed, and shoved to secure choice seats near the head table—next to the hired musician where the singing and dancing and all the hullabaloo would promptly commence, lasting until the entire village finally surrendered to fatigue from too much merriment.

Kostas, because of his revered status as a decorated hero of the war, and Betty as his wife, were regally seated next to the *koumbaria* (best man and family) at the head table.

Amid suspicious, somber inspection from the surrounding crowd, Kathy and I wedged ourselves in the middle of a long table made of boards laid flat on level stones. The patch of earth destined to be compressed by the stomping feet of the dancing assembly lay obliquely to our right with a fair view.

"Xeni!" ("Strangers!") whispered a gray-haired man in thick eyebrows, his sleeves rolled up on his crossed arms, the veins popping out, his wrinkled eyes squinting at Kathy.

"Americani," matter-of-factly replied a man of similar height and age, with dusty boots. He covered his mouth with a callused palm in a play at diverting the sound of his speech from reaching our ears.

Upon the appearance of the newlyweds with their colorful gay and noisy entourage, a big-bellied Cretan in full ceremonial regalia coughed, laid his *lyra* (fiddle) on his huge left thigh, and with his bow scratched the strings as if it were a miniature viola. A tune was born and to its rhythm the entertainer, in a coarse voice, began to spit out the lyrics of a treasured *mandinada* (rhyming couplet).

"Kori gaitani n' epleke chrono gke pende mines." ("The maiden in braids knitted one year and five months.") Before the bride had a chance to take her spot at the head table, among boisterous encouragement she was hoisted off her feet, hand-carried, and offered one end of a handkerchief to lead a circle of dancers in the traditional first jig.

At her first step, Brrrrrrrrrrrrrrrr! crackled a Tommy gun.

Bang! Bang! blasted a rifle.

Clap, clap, clap, whistled a Beretta.

Boom! Boom! blasted two shotguns, and the assemblage broke into wild shouting and whistling, their good wishes reverberating against the surrounding hills.

The young bride gave up her honored post and offered the hankie to the best man, who snatched it with fervor and jumped up high as if a trampoline were beneath his feet. He swirled around like a spinning top and with his free palm slapped loudly the heels of his boots; with each smack the dried dung caked upon them chipped and flew away.

Bang! Bang! blasted two rifles.

Brrrrrrrbrrrrrrrbrrrrrrr! crackled three Tommy guns.

Clap, clap, clap, clap, clap! shrilled two six-shooters, and the fiddler, inspired by the pandemonium, like the true *palikari* (warrior) he was, gulped down a water glass full of *chikoudia* (Cretan raki). Fired up by that potent drink, his playing and singing picked up steam.

"Ke dekapende Kyriakes k' ekosi dio Tetartes" ("and fifteen Sundays and twenty-two Wednesdays"), screamed the entertainer at the top of his lungs, all the time keeping up the beat with his fiddle.

Clay pitchers filled with chikoudia, flasks and tumblers with retsina, heaping platters of gluey matrimonial pilaf (a proud Cretan specialty prepared in gigantic copper pots), boiled kid, and large chunks of skewered lamb roasted over huge open fires all came our way.

An old priest in a gray collarless cassock and orthodox black stove hat sat across the table from us rubbing his tobacco-bleached mustache. With a devilish spark in his feisty black eyes, he raised his wine glass to an old maid roosting on our side whose appearance could have frightened a scarecrow. He hollered to attract the ridicule of the villagers within earshot.

"Aide mori Froso, ke sta dika sou!" ("You, old moron Froso, let's drink to your wedding, too!")

Coarse peasant laughter bellowed. The agitated old witch assumed the stance of a striking cobra.

"Ton kako sou to kero, PapaKosti" ("May your future be miserable, Father Kosti"), she hissed back, her mean, beady gray eyes peering out from under a black kerchief tightly tied around her wretched face.

While all the guests invaded the spread with gusto, diving into the offerings with their bare hands, imposing Kostas stood up, looked about with confidence, and presented a toast to the young couple.

"Na mas zisune," he shouted, wishing them a long life. At that very instant, as if that respected military leader had given the signal for a much-anticipated assault against some enemy on a battlefield, all hell broke loose! Machine guns, revolvers, automatic pistols, and shotguns spat fire, powder, and thick blue smoke. The old priest cupped his good ear and a bright smile stretched his wrinkled face as he took in the fiddling. He joined in the singing.

> *The maiden in braids, knitted one year and five months*
> *And fifteen Sundays and twenty-two Mondays.*
> *Indoors, she knitted the sky, the stars and the moon*
> *Indoors, she knitted her lover's face.*

Brrrrrrrrrrr, crackled a Tommy gun. Clap! Clap! Clap! whistled a six-shooter. Boooom! Brrrrr! Clap! Clap! Brrrrr! Booooom!

The following five days were among the best of our lives. We hitched a ride on a truck to Chania, the gem of all small Venetian cities in Europe, and took a hotel room by the harbor.

We strolled through the old Jewish section, a labyrinth of narrow cobblestone alleys filled with arts-and-crafts shops. The medieval harbor with its slender stone lighthouse lured us, and we promenaded on the quay alongside the colorful fishing skiffs. We exchanged greetings with native and visiting groups who sat about lazily at the outdoor tavernas and cafes, nestled cozily against the shelter of mammoth crumbling walls.

We enjoyed light shopping inside a boisterous cruciform glass-roofed market with countless stalls selling myriad tantalizing delectables produced by the fertile island. Then we scaled the hill to the tomb of Eleftherios Venizelos, the great statesman whom my father had worshipped as the sacred patriot of contemporary Greece.

Before daybreak on the fifth morning, supplied with water, bread, feta, and fruit, we took a taxi to the plateau of Omalos. From that lofty spot, Kathy and I descended on foot into the grandiose sixteen-kilometer gorge of Samaria, the longest in Europe. At "The Iron Gates," barely three meters in width, we gazed up between two perpendicular cliffs, six hundred meters high, and marveled at the tiny sliver of blue sky squeezed between the towering rocks.

By a murmuring creek which trickled throughout this deep and long mountain tear, a hundred yards from the shores of the Libyan Sea, we squatted fatigued on the dry grass, a patch of holy land believed to be the birthplace of Artemis, Goddess of Crete. Overwhelmed by such an unrivaled yet exhausting expedition, we patiently waited for the arrival of a boat which would sail east and return us to Chora.

Three fair men, all with muscular legs, alpine footwear, and walking sticks, appeared from around the gorge's bend, moving swiftly in our direction. When Kathy saw them, she grabbed and squeezed my calf, murmuring, "We have nothing to defend ourselves with, darn it."

The three men advanced rapidly toward the plain and us.

"A brave person dies once, a coward a thousand times," I spat out. Kathy stared at the alpiners piercingly, as if she were seeing strange men for the first time.

"These folks are here to enjoy the magnificence of this gorge, as you and I just did," I said calmly, hoping I was right. By now, they were upon us.

"Guten tag," I tossed out with a smile.

"Guten tag," three friendly voices replied, smiling as they passed us by. My flower let out a sigh and a "phew," her standard sounds of relief.

A caique came and picked us up. During the two-hour passage I became acquainted with the barefoot Captain Fokas and a tall, blue-eyed, strong lad, the captain's nephew, the sole crew member of the vessel *Agia Maria.*

The captain, erect and unsmiling with a kerchief tied around his thick gray hair, a thick mustache twisted on its drooping edges, didn't warm up to us, even though we greeted him in Greek, until I revealed that Kathy and I were Americans and the in-laws of Colonel Kostas.

At that, his solemn expression evaporated and he broke into a smile. I dared ask if he ever chartered beyond the local seas. The Cretan captain cast a contemptuous stare at me, flicked his eyes to the heavens in awe, and crossed himself, as seamen often do to appease and flatter the Almighty with their submissive reverence. Then he muttered an appeal to the Virgin Mary to grant him protection while at the mercy of the fickle *levendopnichtra* (drowner of courageous men) sea. Now, with his heart and soul at peace, he raised his head proudly, expanded his chest, and in a slow tempo declared, "You know who I am? I'm Captain Fokas. Everybody knows Captain Fokas is a skillful, fearless mariner. Why, with the guidance of the Divine creator and the Virgin Mary, Captain Fokas wouldn't hesitate to sail to Hades and back." In a flash he stuck his enormous palm with its calluses and crevices smack against my face, forcing me to study its intricate map. "Each cove and cape around the entire sea I know better than the palm of my hand, because friend, as the Lord up there is my witness, my caique and me have combed this sea more times than I've combed my own scalp."

"How much money and advance notice would you need to fetch a cargo from Ashdod, Israel, and deliver it to Chora, Captain Fokas?" I asked. His gaze drifted from the sea to the bow, and back to my face. He seemed suspicious. But then his leathery face relaxed and he made some quick calculations using his fingers.

"Such an undertaking is a demanding voyage. A voyage so lengthy could cost many, many thousands of drachmas." He studied me. "But since you are related to our hero Kostas, the proud warrior of Chora, I'll be honored to charge you half as much."

"And how much will the half as much be, captain?"

Whispering to himself he calculated one more time and quoted me an amount equal to six hundred dollars, adding that he needed at least two weeks' advance notice to prepare for such a long passage.

I took crisp Greek notes from my pocket, counted out the amount he had requested, handed them to him, and offered my hand to seal the deal. He grabbed and squeezed it with the grip of a Titan.

My calculations put me in Ashdod six days after the thirteenth, barring unexpected events. To play it safe, since it would be wiser to have the caique waiting for me than the other way around, I asked the captain to be in that port city on the eighteenth of September, and stressed that our arrangement should be kept totally confidential.

"The eighteenth of September Captain Fokas, with the blessing of the Virgin Mary, will be in Ashdod for you and your cargo. The cargo

... it's not too bulky, I hope? Often the winds are unpredictable; at times even traitorous."

I raised my head up indicating no, a common mute Greek gesture.

"Captain, you must write the date on paper so you won't forget," I insisted.

"Captain Fokas needs no pencil nor paper, because Captain Fokas never forgets."

We hopped off the bow and climbed up toward Tholos Hill. As we were passing by the young groom's house, we noticed a banner of sorts hanging from the balcony. We stopped to stare at the blood-stained sheet, signature of the bride's taken virginity—it was riddled with buckshot holes, the jubilant endorsement of the village folk for a proper union.

The following night Betty and Kathy helped each other with the cooking, and the four of us took our seats around a table on the terrace where a breeze fluttered through the flickering leaves of the olive trees. We gazed out at the Libyan Sea and up at the limitless bright stars, but our conversation seemed spiritless, as if all of us understood the danger inherent in my morning departure.

Kostas' and Betty's motions toward Kathy were filled with tenderness, and she, conscious of their warm feelings, suppressed her anguish and kept her eyes fixed on her plate, barely touching her food.

At last her inner turmoil won out and she broke into uncontrollable sobs. Confused and wide-eyed with sympathy, but unwilling to intrude into our affairs, Betty and Kostas excused themselves and quickly withdrew, leaving Kathy and me alone.

While she cried the poison of our impending separation, I took her by the arm and led her to a bench near the cliff's edge. Holding her in my lap, close against my heart, I hoped she would hear the strength of my love. Then I rocked her tenderly and softly sang her favorite lullaby.

Let me tell you sweetheart
I'm in love with you
Let me hear you whisper
That you love me too.

The splendor of the clear night eased my own pain. Gently, I kissed my wife's lips, moistened with tears.

"My spirit will be with you each second . . . and soon I'll return to you in the flesh."

Between choking sighs she reaffirmed her choice. "If you fail to come back to me within one month, I'll jump onto the rocks below."

Next morning I packed my knapsack and waved good-bye to Kostas, Betty, and Kathy, who all stood in somber silence. Kostas had arranged a military truck heading for Irakleon to take me along. I boarded a plane for Athens. From there I flew to New York and finally to Las Vegas.

A talkative cabbie dropped me off at Caesar's Palace, where I cashed two thousand dollars in traveler's checks and took a room for the night. Immediately I phoned Las Vegas Boris, whom I had met numerous times during his frequent visits to San Francisco.

Boris, the younger brother of my barber Tony, was a flashy hoodlum, con artist, and pimp with a gift for gab. He never stopped bragging about his abilities to deliver, and on time—just like Old Faithful in Yellowstone Park, he would say—whatever one wanted on God's little green earth, as long as the request was confined to the boundaries of his own glittering gameopolis. This man of flash and magic had often urged me to look him up if I needed anything—one or two or maybe three broads for the night or the week, or a couple of last-minute tickets to a popular show or boxing event, or an invite to a party with celebrities—because he, Las Vegas Boris, was the shaman who could deliver, for a reasonable fee, of course.

A woman with a smoky voice answered. When I asked to speak to Boris, she identified herself as his mother and asked if the call was urgent. Boris was still in the sack, since he worked the graveyard shift.

"My name is Yiannis; I'm from San Francisco and I know both your sons pretty well. When Boris wakes up, could you tell him that I'm here for the night and need to meet him for a drink at the corner bar at Caesar's at eight?" She assured me she would deliver the message when the prince rose from his sweet dreams.

Next I placed an overseas call to the post office of Chora and asked the postman to notify my relatives that I was okay. Refreshed after a long hot shower, I strolled through the gigantic casino, took a table by the bar, and waited for my contact to arrive.

Sure enough, at exactly eight, tall, muscular Las Vegas Boris strolled in with the stride and swing of Elvis, tanned, and dressed like him too, in a white shirt with long sleeves and pointed collar, open down to his belly button to display every hair on his chest. A twenty-dollar gold piece dangled from his neck on a thick chain, and his lower body was stuffed inside tight black trousers that pressed against his testicles so that they bulged out like two fair-size grapefruits. He caught my eye, and when I stood up he stretched out his arms like the wings of a guardian angel, snatched me, and lifted me into the air before he planted a wet kiss on each of my cheeks.

He reeked of cologne, and when he sat he crossed his legs, exaggeratedly lifting the cuffs of his trousers to reveal the full height of a pair of fine western boots.

"You like'm, hah?" he asked.

"Gorgeous," I replied.

"Horn-toed lizard—you can't get'm no more." He went on to explain that the horn-toed lizard was endangered and could no longer be slaughtered for its hide. "What brings you to my town, Yiannis?"

"Well, a buddy of mine has gotten into a bit of trouble and needs an alias—a social security number, a driver's license with a local address, you know—and I know you know how to get that stuff. He wants a Nevada address."

He grabbed his crotch with one hand and shuffled in his seat a little to ease his restricted balls.

"IDs are as easy to get as a piece of ass—and you know how easy that is around here. For a hundred bucks I can get you a professional job from a Spaniard. If you don't care about the quality I got a Mexican who can do it for half the price."

I peeled off a hundred-dollar note, handed him an extra fifty that he refused to take on the basis of our valued friendship, and was assured the stuff would be in my possession before morning.

"I got a couple of chorus girls—look like angels but kinkier than a nigger's pussy fuzz. I could meet you after the late show and we could all go out, have a coupla belts and horse around a little. What do you say, old buddy?" he said with a bright smile and smacked my thigh.

"Boris, thanks, but I'm happily married." He frowned, tossed me a scornful glance as if I had lost my marbles, and stood up.

"I hate to leave you, buddy boy, but I got urgent business to attend to. Rest assured what you ordered will be under your door before you get up in the morning. Have sweet dreams, Yiannis."

After another bear hug Las Vegas Boris hurried away waving, bowing, and throwing kisses to the slot-handle-pulling crowd as if he were the main hit on stage and the world lay under his fancy boots.

The fatigue of my lengthy travel caught up with me and I passed out like a light, but in the morning an envelope was under my door. Boris had delivered. The two cards enclosed were made out to Roy Harry Moses, as we had agreed.

After a hearty breakfast, I strolled to a nearby used-car lot. Using my new ID, I paid cash for a clean, inconspicuous, gray two-door '57 Ford coupe. Then, in sequence, I visited a theatrical costume shop, where I acquired two stiff clerical collars, two black shirts, a used black suit plus a black wig and a mustache; Library Books, where I purchased their entire stock of Bibles, about two dozen copies in all; the Goodwill Store, where I picked up an assortment of used men's clothing, size large, which I stuffed inside a battered suitcase; the restroom of a gas station, where I put on my reverend's attire; and finally a cheap residence hotel.

At the Rolling Sand Dunes Getaway, I listed myself as Reverend Roy Harry Moses, traveling Bible salesman, and with a broad smile handed the owner-clerk one of my Bibles. "A gift from God," I said piously before I paid up front one month's rent in cash. In the room I dumped out and scattered the used clothing, hung some in the closet, and finally yanked the covers off the bed to make it look used.

On my way out of town, a branch of the Bank of Nevada came into view. I made a brief stop to open a checking account under the name of Reverend Roy Harry Moses, listing the hotel's street and number as my address. Hours later, I pulled over at a roadside motel and spent the night.

Early the following afternoon, the sixth of September, I drove the Ford into the fenced long-term parking lot at the San Francisco airport. I parked and took an unhurried short walk to the terminal, carefully observing the crowd for any unusual reaction to my impersonation. No one seemed to notice me. I entered an isolated restroom. There I removed the collar, wig, and mustache, shoved them into my sack, and hitched a taxi home.

The driver dropped me off at Lombard and Kearny, from where I had an open view of our bungalow and garden. I checked intently for any suspicious activity.

Two men in gray suits stood chatting nearby, but in ten minutes they separated and disappeared. Since everything appeared normal, I walked once around the block, approached the front door, and went inside.

The interior showed no sign of entry and the Luger remained tucked under the right side of the mattress, where I had hidden it before our haphazard departure.

I breathed a sigh of relief and dialed Maria's number, anticipating that I could talk to Charlie. No one answered. I placed a call to the office out of habit, even though by three o'clock Maria was ordinarily long gone for the day since her short shift ended at one.

"Barlow Investments." Maria's voice came on sweet and mellow.

"Maria, is this you?" I asked, surprised.

"Who you expectin', Bossman, the good fairy or the yellow rose of Texas?"

"Yes, but ... what are you doing there at three o'clock?"

"Killin' time. Got a doctor appointment at four. Hangin' around til then. How was your trip—wherever you were this time?"

"Fine, the trip was fine. We did a lot of diving. Any calls? Any messages? Any correspondence of any importance?"

"Nope, it's borin' when a whippersnapper like you aren't around, Bossman. Some calls from friends. Many from peddlers. Must think you're very rich because, oh, *mama mia,* the darn phone never stops ringin' for handouts. Well, the usual stuff. But Charlie's been busy. Don't know what you two guys are up to but that brother of mine has been as busy as a one-armed paperhanger with the itch. Why, some nights he stayed out all darn night long. I don't mean to poke my nose in my Bossman's business, but you got to confess to me—you didn't turn my good brother on to some hot-blooded floozy, or have you?"

I broke up laughing.

"Will you have Charlie call me? I should be home for the rest of the evening."

"Will do." I started to hang up when I thought I heard her voice still chattering. "Bossman, are you there?"

"Yes, Maria?"

"Durn near slipped my mind. Your Uncle John from Davis came by yesterday lookin' for you. Told him you were out of town. Dropped off a letter mailed to his post box with your name on it. It's on your desk. From Illinois, or someplace like that."

"Great. I'll get it in the morning."

"Maybe you got your days all screwed up from flyin' them long trips. You see, tomorrow is Saturday all day. Comin' in on Saturday?"

"I need to—so much catching up to do."

"Hmmm, you want your one and only faithful secretary to show up and give you a hand? You know I wouldn't mind."

"Maria . . ."

"Yes, Bossman?"

"No. No. It's okay. I'll catch you Monday."

I stretched out on our comfortable bed and reprimanded myself for putting off the unpleasant business of telling Maria that by the end of next week she would be without a job—her Bossman would be in jail, or dead, or a fugitive from justice, and the building would be owned by other interests.

I was catnapping when the phone jangled me. Charlie asked if he could come over. Shortly he appeared, casually dressed in khakis and sneakers with briefcase in hand and a smile on his lips.

"Everythin' we need is here," he said, pounding the side of the case with his free fist. "Blueprints of the entire structure, alarms, exits, bugs, all the rooms, the hallways, the chamber where a goon sits in front of the surveillance screens. The locations of six hidden cameras! This operation is down cold like a well-digger's ass in January."

Charlie moved aside a coffee table and chair, sat on the carpet in the middle of the living room, and started thumbing through copies of plans.

"Schedules of the staff, comin' and goin' of Giacominni's private gal, the shifts of his bodyguards, overall security durin' and after office hours. Even jotted down the schedule of the garbage pickup." I sat on the carpet opposite him and stared at the pile of material.

"Looks like you've thought of everything."

"A job has got to be thought out. Planned right down to the minutest detail. No room for errors. Like a poker hand, you got to be able to figure what cards are out there. That's what makes the difference between winners and losers. Goof-ups aren't allowed in my profession. With Climpt showin' up in three days, time is tighter than old Dick's hatband, Yiannis."

We went over the entire plan five times. Charlie told me our precise course of action, and I parroted it back. Climpt would have to carry out his own assignment without a hitch in order for me to have the half hour I needed alone with Tenner.

I opened my last vintage bottle of cabernet, and as Charlie and I shared it, I said, "I don't know how this will all turn out but I want to drink to you and tell you now . . . I thank you, Charlie."

"Criminals must be brought to justice, Yiannis. When I was with the bureau, nothin' bugged me more than a killer who evaded the law enforcement agencies and stayed somewhere out there free as a mustang." His face showed honest strength. "When I was assigned to a case, days and nights were the same. Trackin' lead after lead, day in and day out, month in and month out, chasin' clues, prayin' for that one break; that was the constant energy that drove me."

He edged toward the large window and looked out. His stare seemed fixed on the flashing beacon of Alcatraz in the midst of the dark bay as if he hoped it could guide him through the sea of past memories.

"Maybe you can appreciate my unwillingness to marry—raise a family. I couldn't. Had no time to call my own. The duty of a lawman lasts twenty-four hours a day." He coughed and lifted his glass but stopped short of bringing it to his lips. He faced me.

"Had a gal once. Rita was her name. Was mad in love with Rita. Young, beautiful . . . ," his voice broke. "Ended up marryin' some doctor. Cost me plenty—the heartache was ... " He took a deep breath, and cracked a crooked smile. "But better to dream gentle thoughts of her than let my heart take over, plunge into a union that most likely would have turned unhappy. A good woman wants her husband at home at night." We didn't speak for a while. Charlie returned to staring out at the flashing beacon.

"You and Kathy are close." His voice was gentle.

"Two souls couldn't be closer," I said with pride.

"I've noticed."

"I'm fortunate to have found her."

"And you're gonna risk your life and her happiness to give this Tenner guy what's due'm?"

I wanted to explain. I took a slow sip of wine.

"Charlie, in a way, you, Kathy, and I come from the same mold. We aren't like most who are resigned to their own destiny. Somehow the three of us differ because ... we are ... because we have chosen to be the masters of our own fates." I took another sip. "Except for the Kalavryta experience, my life has been a good one. I've got a lot to be thankful for. A devoted wife with whom I'm madly in love, some money in the bank, and properties, thanks to a dear uncle who left me a starter, and above all, we both enjoy fine health.

"Destiny would have allowed a very complacent course for Kathy and me—cherish each other, multiply, amass possessions, accept God as our Lord, and die with a priest's assurance that we will end up in heaven. Yet the two of us are on the verge of squandering it all in order to bring a prick to justice for crimes he committed twenty years ago— crimes hardly anyone cares to remember.

"But, just as you did not give in to your heart's urgings to marry your Rita, but instead chose to bear the pangs of loneliness and heartache, so Kathy and I are committed to pursue this lofty goal, which society is unwilling to provide—the punishment of Tenner. With this choice of action, Kathy and I are carving out our own fates."

Charlie played with his glass.

"Yes, sir. 'Whoever has resigned himself to fate will find that fate accepts his resignation,' someone said once." Then with a sudden alarm he rubbed his face with both hands.

"You told Maria yet?" he asked.

I blushed with shame.

"No," I admitted with regret, "I just didn't have the heart. I'll tell her the first thing Monday morning."

As always, the wine did its miracle, and upon Charlie's departure sound sleep came to me. At dawn I rushed to the office. The contents of the letter from Illinois were my utmost preoccupation.

> *Dear Yiannis:*
>
> *My son has spoken to me about you. Be assured my house will be your sanctuary if you so desire. Indeed, I have many friends who can help. Good luck in your most noble pursuit.*
>
> *A friend*
>
> *PS: Please destroy this note immediately.*

Relief overtook me and with a smile I struck a match, burned the message, and flushed the ashes down the toilet. Then I sat at Maria's desk and began typing away.

First, I wrote our landlord that unexpected developments would prevent us from exercising our option to buy the bungalow.

Then I sent a letter to Stavros in Miami explaining that hopefully an anonymous courier would soon be delivering documents, tapes, and a case full of cash. The cash I wished to have deposited in a local bank and through a wire transaction transferred to my Swiss account. The documents and tapes I hoped he would use to reveal to the authorities and the world the true identity of Giacominni.

I handwrote a thank-you note to the Baroness for her help in unearthing Tenner and for her vigilance over Kathy's and my safety, and sent her my wishes for Karl's healthy reappearance.

Lastly, I wrote to my mate.

> *My Louloudaki,*
>
> *Last night I slept in our bed. The fragrance of your hair and the scent of your body are still in the sheets and my yearning for you drenched me with fantasies. I dreamed of you lying glued to my skin as we always sleep, and I'm still beaming with bliss.*

Here everything appears normal. Arrangements are progressing smoothly with the expert help of our valued friend. Six days remain until the delivery, and as you can imagine these last hours are bustling with buttoning-up operations. Our second friend will be arriving soon.

Anything valuable will be stored with your parents. Stavros will see that the funds from the sale of the building are forwarded to our Swiss account. Give my love to Betty and Kostas and all those hospitable, proud Cretans.

Even though the project is expertly planned and seems flawless, and we should be in each other's arms soon, don't neglect to toss a wreath of lavender petunias in the Libyan Sea and appeal to the benevolent spirit of Goddess Artemis to be with us.

The sun and the moon and the stars should be blitzing you with my ceaseless love and the winds should be delivering you a billion of my kisses.

> *Your lover,*
> *Yiannis*

Then I reached my lawyer at his home, explaining that only urgency had forced me to chase him down on a Saturday. I asked him to meet me for lunch at the Trident Restaurant in Sausalito.

When he agreed, I hunted through our files, placed in a manila envelope the deed of the Powell Street building and other pertinent papers for his review, and headed across the Golden Gate Bridge.

The fog withdrew and midday turned grand. We took a table on the bayfront deck. While the seagulls performed their acrobatic stunts I explained that I needed documents drafted since my intent was to transfer ownership of my building to AGG Enterprises for three hundred ninety thousand dollars.

"Which title company will be handling the escrow?"

Anticipating his question as I watched a bird's dexterous landing on the top of a nearby pole, I answered, "None." Naturally he questioned my sanity.

I replied that, for reasons I didn't care to discuss, I had elected to handle the transaction in an unorthodox fashion. He coughed, and swallowed hard.

"I'll do as you wish, of course; however, I wash my hands of all responsibility, my friend."

At the conclusion of our meeting, intoxicated by the freshness of the early afternoon wind and harboring an unmatched fondness for our little sailboat *El Greca,* I headed for the marina. This sailboat represented my only attachment to anything inanimate, and it seemed almost as if my soul were obsessed by her haunted call.

With both the jib and the mainsail full and hard against the wind we headed through the Golden Gate. The bay was emptying out rapidly, colliding with the strong westerlies; and the "potato patch," half-hidden in the fog, bubbled like a monstrous steaming kettle. Recklessly I guided *El Greca* toward the inferno. And while the waves broke over me, drenching me through and through, in the midst of this dark rage a mad howl heaved from the depths of my chest.

"Bastard Tenner, you killed my father. You robbed me of my youth. You've been soaking me with nightmares. Now it's your time to pay up. The time to face up to your deeds has come. Bastard Tenner, the time to pay up is here at last."

El Greca slapped and split the tall breakers fearlessly and with contempt, as if to reaffirm her brave talents and to reassure me that her spirit would remain my companion for all time, no matter who the master of her tiller would come to be.

In harbor, I buttoned her up with affection and gave her a farewell pat but left her unlocked. I had arranged to have a yacht broker sell her.

Next morning I took the Luger and headed for the shooting range at Sharp Park. The target's bull's-eye took the semblance of Tenner's face. I fired fifty rounds. Only half a dozen bullets went astray. Still from twenty yards my aim was deadly.

Climpt called from Travis Air Force Base and I raced to pick him up. "Good God, you look like a general!" I exclaimed when I recognized him leaning against a pole by the bus stop. He wore a khaki uniform, his broad chest filled with medals and his long, massive arms dangling inside sleeves adorned with colorful patches and stripes.

"Hey, ole buddy," he said as I snatched him and swung him around.

He didn't bolt, and I was delighted that he had learned to accept the hugging of another man. "Ya dressed up fit fer Sunday an' ya looks lak' a rich man," he said and his yellow eyes squinted with gladness.

While we drove toward San Francisco, Climpt told me how he had befriended an old Korean karate master, and as his student, he had conquered that art of self-defense. Now, a black belt master himself, he held classes for American soldiers and commanded respect among the men.

We recalled past times in Idar-Oberstein and laughed and cried. Climpt kept gazing about the landscape with fascination.

"Sure glad ta be back on tha good ole U.S. o' A. soil. Hope ta git ma ass outta gook rice paddies afore somebody tears up my ticket. Messy as a pigpen in tha rain ovah in Nam, Yiannis. Nobody's s'post ta know we got twelve, meebe fifteen thousan' Americans an' more comin'. A mean war befallin' on our hands with them Vietcongs."

"What in hell is going on over there, Climpt?"

"Well, Diem, he don' know whether ta shit er go blind since that ole monk sprayt hisself with gas an' torcht hisself ta death. An' this general Nku, Diem's brothah, he gone apeshit an' stirred up a hornet's nest when he killt lotsa monks 'nside theirn Temple, who done nutin' bad 'xept protest fer freedom ta pray ta theirn Buddha—an' now, tha shit's flyin' thick everwheres."

"What do you think is going to happen?"

"Well, ma appraisin' o' tha whole mess's mortifyin'. What I mean is—I be darn if tha boys reckon what fuckin' business we gots ta be in that gook-land in tha fist place—'xeptin' that them bible thumpers an' them do-gooders politicians, here at stateside, stir up all kinds o' fuss ba claimin' that them gook reds's ungodly, slimy sombitches, an' burnin' everone o' tha motherfuckers's a godly thin' ta do, on accoun' them commies's nutin' but a bunch o' motherfuckers an' bad ta ourn democracy an' tha more o' them we bump off tha more God's gonna love us. An' so, we dispatch them choppers an' bomb tha shit out o' towns we s'spect meebe a Vietcong er two been sneakin' 'bout hidin' somewheres, an' we commit offensive deeds ta children, an' butcher folks we surmise ta be tha enemy, but it turn out, them hain't tha enemy, 'acuze we don' know who tha fuck tha enemy s'pose ta be, 'acuze all them motherfuckers look alike an' talk alike." I studied my friend's agitated face more than the road up front with its thick traffic.

"Pretendin' we's thar t'advise Diem, we keep killin' them hard-up peasant bastards, an' in theirn own darn back yeard ta boot. An' all tha while, tha big brass been hollerin' frum behin'. 'Now, lisen here, boys,' they hue and cry. 'Ya been doin' just fine. But, fine, goddarn it, it hain't good enough. Ya gotta go out there an' kill, an' fuck some more o' them commie gooks. We gots us quotas ta fill. An' when ya's done doin' fuckin'em good an' ya git this here fight ovah with, an' ya come back hume lak' tha champs an' . . . an' heroes ya s'pose ta been, then, yern President's gonna pin a big shiny medal on yern chest, ya hear?'"

Suddenly, fury flashed through Climpt's small yellow eyes. He raised his arm and bashed his thigh with his fist.

"Got me a helluva time tryin' ta sort out thin's in ma head." He beat his chest and cried like a trapped animal. "Ya hear me, brothaaaah? I's all fuckt up 'nside acuse I fail ta comprehend what side tha fuckin' righteousness's on. Ma own country, er them gook peasant bastards." Climpt's torment stung my skin as if it were bursting out in hives. The need to add my two cents to Climpt's soulful protest of the Vietnam conflict drove me.

"Climpt," I said, glancing at the windswept clouds that raced above our heads traveling north, "there's this one tune I've been blowing through my harmonica since I was fifteen."

"Yeah?"

"It goes like this. 'Each generation that comes along spawns a handful of folks who are gifted to see through both their eyes. A few thousand, though they got two eyes, can see through just one, and the remaining millions have two eyes that are just a decorative ploy, since the poor bastards either are unable to see or don't want to see, yet they claim they see.'"

Climpt squinted and scratched the top of his head fiercely, as if stirring his brain to help it grasp what I said. Gradually a dreamlike serenity overtook him.

"Fine ta hear ya preach agin after all them years, ma frien'. Yern preachin' in Idar-Oberstein done me good. Help me see thin's clear 'bout them niggers an' other affairs." His nostrils kicked up a quivering jig and his utterances came out soft and with yearning. "Never figgert I'd evah git homesick, but I gotta admit, them Georgia swamps been heavy on ma min' lately."

"After our meeting with the Nazi on the thirteenth I hope you won't mind dropping off some stuff to an address in Miami for me."

"I'll do that much an' more fer ya, frien'."

"Once there you should take a day or two and visit the spot where you grew up, Climpt."

He leaned against the seat and looked to his right out to the distant gray San Pablo Bay. Slowly he mumbled, "Mebbe I will, mebbe I hain't."

"You got a girlfriend over there, Climpt?" I blurted. Startled, Climpt rested his long arms in his lap, sat up straight, and looked directly at me.

"I coulda. But Brenda hain't forgivin'."

"You still burn a torch for Brenda?" I was surprised. Climpt's close-set eyes strained but then his face became serene.

"Brenda, she hain't no easy ta forgit. Weird, meebe. Kinda spooky, ta put it plainly. Well, I reckon, when tha body's gone done an' quit ta function, tha spirit refuse ta go alon' fur tha ride, an' it strolls 'bout 'nside tha livin', kinda, in tha memories o' tha ones left behin'. Ya fallow me, frien'?" He sat stately, feeling gratified he had made his point in a clear, scholarly fashion. "When I git me a stiff dick an' I's 'bout ta stick it inta a Viet gal, ma Brenda pops up ta life in ma head, glarin' at me. Purty as she always been, an' believe ya me, Yiannis, ma dick faints faster thana yella weed in a blisterin' dog day's evenin'." He raised his brows and studied me with keen curiosity. "Now, I's axin' ya. Hain't that sometin' eerie ta reckon with?" Climpt sparkled with a strange thrill. "But I digs it. Yesirreee, ma frien'. Ma Brenda hain't let go o' ma heart yet, an' I digs it."

Climpt bent forward, shifted his feet nervously, rubbed his palms together, and examined his fingers peculiarly. His mouth twisted like he had munched on a handful of poisonous seeds and swallowed some. A low, shaky sigh and a whisper reached me. "Why she hadta go so soon?" His yellow eyes were watery now. He looked away from me. A muteness fell that neither one of us wished to disturb.

Finally Climpt's jaws parted and he yawned, his teeth showed, then his eyes closed.

"Boy, I's dog tired—plum wore out. That damn plane bounct lak' a goose feather 'nside a cyclone. Darn long haul, travlin' fer thirty-odd hours er more." He stretched his limbs. "Buddy, I shorely need ta hole up somewheres. Hain't gonna be worth a tinker's damn ta ya till I git me some rest." Soon his mouth fell open and he began to whistle like a locomotive engine climbing up a steep hill. I drove directly to Palo Alto. One block from a motel with a blinking neon sign, on El Camino Real, near Giacominni's office, I shook him hard to wake him.

"Go ahead and check in," I told him. Climpt crawled out with his duffel bag in hand. "Call me the first thing in the morning."

"Will do," he replied and wobbled away in a daze.

Before sunrise on Wednesday, Charlie and I sat sipping coffee in the Kearny Street bungalow when the phone jingled.

"Nutin' a dozen hours sleep won't cure, ole buddy." Climpt seemed in high spirits. "Ya gonna let me git a piece o' that motherfucker Nazi's balls, hain't ya frien'?"

"Get yourself something to eat at the corner coffee shop and wait for us. Charlie and I should be there in an hour."

"Charlie who?" His voice turned ice-cold.

"There's a third party in this, Climpt, an ex-FBI man."

Climpt paused.

"Ya trust this FBI dude, frien'?"

"He's okay. You'll have a chance to judge for yourself. We should be there shortly."

"Roger," uttered Climpt, but the reservation in his voice came through crystal-clear.

We traveled in separate cars. Charlie would spend some of the day and night with Climpt to brief him and familiarize him with the layout, and we had agreed that I shouldn't be seen in the area.

I arrived at the coffee shop first. Climpt looked remarkably civil in his dark sport shirt, black slacks, and boot-like shoes. From his shoulder hung a canvas satchel, and when I pointed to it and asked him if he had taken up photography, he patted it and referred to it as his SOG, short for "Special Operatin' Gear," offering no further explanation. Before Charlie appeared, I outlined his credentials and mentioned that his heritage was Italian.

"This eye-talyun FBI dude, he hain't some kinda fink, ya reckon?" Climpt stared at me queerly. "Lernt ta trust nobody. No motherfuckin' nobody, ya hear?" He leaned back and his yellow eyes drooped to cast a dreamlike smile. "Think lots 'bout us when ya an' me wuz in Kraut-land. Ya an' me. We wuz mighty close, remember? I coulda trust ya with ma life an' ya coulda trust yern life ta me." The reminiscing left him. He brightened and his face reflected a serious interrogation. "This here eye-talyun mother, he haint playin' no trick on ya—leadin' ya on, ta git all tha scoop an' turn inta a canary, Yiannis? Don' wan' nobody messin' ourn deal here."

"I trust Charlie as much as I trust you, Climpt."

At that moment Charlie appeared and hurried toward the booth where the two of us sat. Climpt wrinkled his narrow forehead and surveyed Charlie, and Charlie gauged Climpt as they shook hands. Charlie, to defuse Climpt's apparent mistrust, told us about his hitch in the service in the first big war fighting in the Rhine under MacArthur.

Climpt's tight thin lips soon started to thaw, and in time he recounted a couple of incidents involving fierce shutouts with Vietcong. An hour into the visit the ice melted completely and Charlie and Climpt spoke to each other with growing admiration. Charlie soon came to the point and asked Climpt how well he could manage at immobilizing two or three strong and perhaps armed guards.

Climpt's face squinted as if calling on a self-hypnosis technique. Then, with the assurance of a magician preparing to perform his most spectacular trick, he cracked his knuckles and sliced the air with his stretched, rigid palms.

"Ifen no more than a half-dozen o' them yella bastards, I hain't gonna even break sweat," replied our gorilla. Charlie, satisfied that his question had been adequately addressed, told me to take off—he and Climpt needed to do some cruising.

On Thursday morning, my last day at the office, Maria walked in with her head bowed to hide her emotions. Shyly she handed me a farewell card; she was fighting back tears. Three days earlier, with a cringing apology for having waited so long, I had told her I was selling the building and shutting down the office.

I sprang up and embraced her, assuring her that she would remain in my memory as the grandest secretary of all time. Then I asked her to confirm my appointment with Mr. Giacominni for five-thirty on the following evening, and while I was placing a few personal items in a bag she returned, composed, to say that Mr. Giacominni would be expecting me.

On my way out the door I handed her a sealed envelope with a thank-you note and a substantial bonus and told her to open it on Saturday morning. Outside, I crossed the street, and from the opposite sidewalk I gazed at my building for the last time.

The rest of the day I spent running last-minute errands, gathering documents and making phone calls. At seven, Charlie, Climpt, and I met in an obscure Italian restaurant on a side street in downtown Burlingame.

There we synchronized our watches and once again labored over the charted details of the "assault."

Four minutes after I entered the Giacominni building, Climpt would drive up in a gray van marked with lettering to match that of the Pacific Alarm fleet. He would be disguised in their uniform and carry a technician's ID from that firm, which had installed the entire security system and retained the maintenance contract. Claiming that he had been dispatched on an emergency call to investigate a malfunction in the surveillance wiring, he would secure access. Once inside, he would proceed first to neutralize the sentinel who manned the surveillance room, turn off the alarms and related switches, then go on to take out the two bodyguards plus anyone else who happened to be on the premises.

I gave Climpt Stavros' address in Miami, where all the documents and the attaché case with the cash should be delivered, and asked him to safeguard the address in his wallet.

The time came to say good-bye to Charlie and we stood up and hugged. In a choked whisper, I accepted his invitation for Kathy and me to call on him in Italy sometime in the future.

I mumbled something to Climpt indicating that he and I would be seeing each other the following evening at the conclusion of the attack, and I left the two together for their final rehearsal of Climpt's raid.

Before I exited the restaurant, I turned to look at my two friends. Charlie smiled in an encouraging fatherly way and Climpt gave me the thumbs-up sign.

11

THE DELIVERANCE

Sleep was hard to come by. I lay awake contemplating whether the spell of a goddess controlled my actions, like a puppeteer directing a marionette, or whether the impending deeds were my own choice. I listened to the articulate mockingbird, who with his lively chattering for the past nights had commiserated with the turmoil of my heart. I the judge? And I the executioner? Had my reasoning been warped by abysmal hatred?

I heard a thousand inner voices engaged in a tumultuous conflict, a merciless war of attrition where only one selection would prevail. The vow of my youth, the image of my hands soaked in my father's blood, savagely pounded my brain. "When I become a man, I will find Tenner and kill him. Kill him. Kill him. Kill him."

"Why not place this vengeance you have in your heart in God's hands and go on with your life?" the Baroness had asked me long ago. And Stavros' advice twisted my soul. "But we were very young then, and very angry—I deal with victims of revenge all the time—I warn you of the consequences—for Kathy's sake, listen to me."

When the first rays of sun sneaked through a crack in the heavy drapes, I arose. The open briefcase on the dresser caught my first glance. All the collected documents were tucked inside two folders and placed on top to conceal a ⅜" Dacron rope twelve feet long, a small Sony recorder, and a short length of steel-link chain with a strong combination lock. Everything I needed was there except the loaded Luger.

I took it from under the mattress, cocked it, and carefully placed it under the folders.

I showered and dressed in the black suit, less a tie. As I retreated, my gaze impassively took in the furnishings and collected trinkets that pleaded for some final regard. I exited through the front door and pulled it shut for the last time.

Out front, Kathy's favorite rosebush greeted me in full bloom. I plucked a bud and threaded it through my lapel buttonhole, then raised a hand in a gesture of *adieu* to the surroundings that had been our companions for the past years. I drove the Healey to Washington Square.

That early, parking was ample in front of the church of Saints Peter and Paul. At the corner, Mama's breakfast hangout spilled the aroma of strong coffee. I walked over and bought a cup to go.

The morning was bright. My senses suddenly reawakened to the marvels of life. I felt as a dying man must who, a short time before the clock of nature is about to strike the end of his earthly visit, perceives the splendor of the world with a new cognizance. I stretched and touched affectionately a red leaf of a maple tree.

A young man wearing a yellow bandanna around his head sat on the dewy green grass strumming his scratched-up guitar. Nearby on a wooden bench roosted three aging Asian women with wrinkled skins and playful eyes, and hair dyed black except for the neglected snow-white roots. They listened intently to the tune of the troubadour, and one clapped, badly off beat.

Leisurely I walked down Columbus Avenue to my cherished Fisherman's Wharf, drawn to the smell of the sea and the cooking crabs. I leaned against the wooden railing and took in the tiny harbor—the boisterous gulls that dove for stray anchovies among the colorful skiffs, and the leathery Italian fishermen with their tackle and bait, crab traps and fishnets, who communicated with each other by shouting at the top of their lungs.

At a loitering pace I followed my nose up to the Cannery, the Hyde Street Pier, on to Aquatic Park. At the Buena Vista Cafe, I shared a table with visitors from Belgium and South Africa and listened to them praise the virtues of my city above the fragrance of their Irish coffees.

The midday throng was out in full force now. I grabbed a pole on the Hyde Street cable car and smashed up against tourists and locals who dangled next to me like grapes from the vine. The rumbling car mounted Russian Hill, and at California Street I hopped off and hiked to the top of Nob Hill with its grand hotels and elegant houses.

There I slipped into secluded Huntington Park, an often-deserted patch of serene greenery, and sat alone facing the fountain with its marble figures of men lifting turtles into the water while jesting with kittenish dolphins.

Absent from these immortal forms were the destructive forces that lurk in real humans, whose impulses are to conquer or kill, to dominate and enslave. Two pigeons splashed, jumped, kissed and chased, and the harmony of simple life and stillness soothed my anxieties.

But soon age-old stirrings came to me again. War, murder, slavery, and hunger—peace and tolerance—life and death—crime and punishment, and Justice, the coy maiden with her fickle scale.

The big bell at Grace Cathedral rang twice. I walked the block and a half to the Powell Street cable car. Washington Square came up quickly and I sprang off while the car was still rolling. A parking citation decorated the windshield of the Healey. A sly grin twisted my lips as I tossed it aside.

I turned left on Broadway and darted glances at the strolling crowd. By Enrico's I waved back at two friends who recognized the roadster, then climbed the on-ramp which connected with Highway 101 South, and headed for the airport.

Near the long-term parking I slowed to make sure the gray Ford was still there and consulted my watch—one hour to go until five-thirty.

The southbound Friday commute traffic was heavy. I hugged the slow lane until I exited forty minutes later at University Avenue. At El Camino Real, I turned left. Three blocks south, Climpt sat behind the wheel of a parked, gray Dodge van. When I drove past him he grinned, raised his white-gloved hand, and gave me Churchill's victory sign.

The parking lot in front of Giacominni's building was almost empty. The day had turned dark. Heavy swirling fog spilled over the San Mateo mountains as if a flock of ghosts had traveled across oceans to witness the final judgment. I turned on the tape recorder and with my brief-case in hand I headed toward the entrance.

The instant I passed through the glass door, two muscular men blocked my advance.

"I'm John Barlow. Mr. Giacominni is expecting me."

One of them, the bully in the gray suit and tinted glasses, allowed me in. I breathed deeply to steady the shaking in my knees. He strut-ted toward the depths of the building, down the marbled hallway. With head held high, I followed a few paces behind. To my surprise, this time a third goon, tall, blond and athletic, stood by the first heavy oak door. But I was relieved to see that the secretary had left for the day. The man with the glasses ushered me through the second oak door and I heard it click shut as he withdrew.

Giacominni sat behind his huge desk. The ornate chandelier shed its yellow light on the dark oak panels. Without the slightest indica-tion of awareness of my arrival, cold and still like a crocodile in his pond, he stared at a thick stack of bound pages.

I took a seat and waited.

"Are the documents in order?" he barked without lifting his head.

"Of course," I replied with a touch of cynicism.

"And I have the cash. Very well then, let me see them. I must attend a very important function at seven."

I opened my briefcase, took out the top folder, walked toward him, laid it on the desk, and returned to the leather chair, placing the opened grip in my lap. I faced the despised man.

He studied the contract of sale and my notarized signature and, satisfied, he broke into a faint smirk. He picked up his fancy pen, signed the copy, and carefully placed it on the top of the credenza.

"All yours. The cash is in the case on the credenza there. You may start counting."

"That won't be necessary. I trust you are a principled man." I could not suppress a tint of sarcasm in my voice.

He retained his reptile-like posture.

My heart began to race. After twenty years, a clock was readying to strike its final bell and announce its retirement from service.

"Mr. Giacominni. You and I have met before." I took three hurried steps forward, placed the second folder on his desk, and retreated.

His eyes rose for the first time and looked at me sharply.

"Yes? I do not recall." Now he leaned forward and began to study me. "Unless you are referring to our brief encounter some months ago inside your building, or should I say my building now."

"I would not expect you to recall. It was in another world, another setting."

"What is that supposed to mean?"

A muffled noise reached us. His nostrils widened and twitched and his cold eyes focused on the oak door, the source of the unexpected sound. I continued.

"Simply that you and I have met, somewhere in Europe. You are European, are you not?"

His stare left the door and alertly focused on me.

"I was born in Italy, yes. In a town near Rome."

His answer came with the first trace of vacillation.

"Civitavecchia, isn't it?"

"As a matter of fact, Civitavecchia is where I was born." He bent over his desk stretching his neck toward me, scrutinizing me. "But how would you know?"

For the first time fear left me and appeared to enter this snake in human form who sat before me. I could feel his mind racing, galloping.

"Mr. Giacominni, it is all there, inside the second folder on your desk." I took my time. "One Alfredo Gregorio Giacominni was born in Civitavecchia in 1916." Keeping my eyes glued to his despised face, I noticed a twitch and loss of color. "According to the official town records there, the one and only Alfredo Gregorio Giacominni ever born in Civitavecchia was born in the year 1916, all right, but that unfortunate child died three years later. Is it possible then that you may be mistaken about your birthplace? And perhaps your heritage also?"

He raised his chin then settled his head down into his neck, appraising me. His eyes glowed piercingly, his upper lip jerked, and his speech was hoarse.

"What is this interrogation anyway? You came here to sell me your building."

It took an effort to make his voice commanding and unaffected.

My confidence grew. The long-awaited moment had finally arrived. The ghosts, my audience, stood invisible next to me, all listening. One thousand spirits had gathered to attend the finale of the twenty-year-old play. The clock's mechanism was raising the striker to pound the large bell, announcing the hour. My voice shook the room like thunder.

"I know who you are."

Flashes of confusion electrified his abhorrent face. His lip began to quiver uncontrollably.

"In another life you were known as Commandant Hans von Tenner—the feared Nazi SS commander. A vicious dog who obediently and efficiently carried out his master's barbarous wishes. The monster who committed savage brutalities against mankind. The beast who indiscriminately executed thousands of hostages and prisoners of war, and innocent civilians of both sexes and all ages as if they were so many sheep in a slaughterhouse."

Like an awakened hibernating bear, he sprang up, ready to strike.

"How dare you?" he screamed and pressed the alarm button on his desk. He shouted furiously for his guards, his repulsive face drained of blood.

I pulled the Luger out.

"This time I am your God, while you, the unarmed, are rendered my lowly, beggarly subject."

"Security! Guards! Guards!" he screamed in a frenzy.

"Sit down," I ordered. "Your thugs have been neutralized and your security alarms have been disarmed. And may I warn you that I know how to use this pistol as accurately as you did during your terrorist escapades throughout Russia and Europe down to the Balkans."

He gazed about, frantically searching for help to come. Suddenly, he collapsed into the cushioned chair as if all the air had escaped from his body.

"You are going to pay for this. I have friends in very high places. You won't get away with this abuse and accusation." His quaking voice was barely audible and his shoulders sagged.

"Documents before you contain historical data detailing your infamous past. Enormous time and effort has been spent to collect this material but, at long last, through them we have found you."

He kept staring at the muzzle of the gun.

"You are wasting your time. My name is Alfredo Gregorio Giacominni and you can go to hell—along with your commandant . . . whoever . . . hallucination."

His voice sounded subdued. Slowly I raised the Luger until it was level with his head.

"On page two of the second packet of documents you can read about certain war injuries that left irreparable marks on you, such as the badly deformed right wrist which was severely broken and never healed properly during your ferocious military adventures at the Russian front."

He seemed muddled, but made no attempt to search the folder.

"Lift your sleeve so I can see your right wrist," I commanded.

The gun clearly frightened him, and his bid to renounce his hidden identity was wavering.

"My wrist was broken when . . . when I was a child and I fell into a ditch in Civitavecchia." His faint protest lacked persuasion.

I took my time studying this man who once took the lives of fellow humans as if they were annoying ants.

"What about the praiseworthy lightning bolt tattoo? Your left arm must still bear that esteemed emblem—or did you dishonor yourself and have it removed, Commander?"

Suddenly, he bared his teeth and growled. "Who in hell are you? How did I miss blowing out your fucking brains?"

I took a slow deep breath and began.

"You took our home and slept in our beds. You stole our food and what little we had left after three years of misery and hunger. You set our town on fire. Then you killed my father and the fathers of my friends. You killed many of my friends too, students, blameless children, unarmed civilians. You cut them down with machine guns and then you, with your Luger, blew out the brains of each and every one who breathed, smirking at their cries and pleas. I was only eleven but your evil eyes are imprinted in my memory." My voice vibrated with emotion.

He looked wilder, and he seemed to sink behind his desk.

"And when you were done with your abominable deed, all along deaf to the screams of the universal sense of right and wrong, you led your men away from your grotesque act, singing and in proud step."

A hard lump formed in my throat but I struggled on.

"When I found my father with a hole through his head, I made him the promise that someday, you, his murderer, would be looking down the barrel of a similar gun, frightened and begging for your miserable life."

At that, I fired a bullet that shattered a crystal vase filled with pink roses sitting on the top of his desk. While glass and water and flowers flew through the air, I moved the muzzle to zero in on his forehead.

Instead of fear, a conceited sneer played over his thin lips. He sat up straighter and arrogantly raised his head.

"As a soldier, I never tarnished my oath to my Fuehrer and Reichsfuehrer. I upheld the ideology and obeyed the orders of my commanders with honor. The extermination of barbaric races who polluted our streams, mountains, and valleys was justifiable. When scum and parasites became obstacles to our cause we dealt with them with fierce force. It was wartime. I only wish we had won."

I felt my anger rising and my finger tightening against the trigger. A strong urge tempted me to squeeze it, but shooting him was not in the script.

I shook my head in disbelief.

"Repentance has apparently never crossed your mind. You claim it was your duty as a soldier to uphold the ideology and obey the orders of your commanders, Hitler and his partner in horror Himmler, mad gangsters who robbed and killed innocent, defenseless people. May I remind you that Himmler's, your Reichsfuehrer's, last words before he bit the phial of cyanide to end his despicable life were, 'Am I accountable for the excesses of my subordinates?' So, where does the responsibility for your grotesque actions lay?" I needed no answer. "You have made a mockery of an honorable soldier's pledge. Your warped code of patriotism has betrayed the values and ethics of all decent men. Your horrid deeds defied the universal morality of mankind." I stood up and spat on the carpet with abhorrence. "Therefore, Commandant Hans Tenner, you are condemned to die the same way some of your disgraceful leaders did. You must die by hanging."

I took out the rope and tossed it onto his desk.

"Pick it up and tie the end around the chandelier, or I'll shoot."

He half-snickered. "You appear too chivalrous to shoot an unarmed man."

"Honor and valor are performances between men. There is only one man in this room and that man isn't you."

"How dare . . ." he started to protest and I fired a second round that scraped his left ear. I pointed to an upright chair.

"Place that chair under the chandelier and bring several thick books to provide you the needed height."

Stunned, grasping his bleeding face with his hand, he performed his chores like a coolie. When he had completed rigging the heavy line I ordered him to put the loop around his neck. While he stood there high above me his face grew pathetic. To my surprise this former demi-god of Hades began to weep and utter mutterings which seemed directed toward his own conscience.

He looked meekly down at me.

"I'm very rich. I can pay you for my life. I'll pay you more for your building."

"How much more are you willing to pay, Tenner?"

"One million. Two. Even three or four," he cried out, hope flickering in his begging eyes.

"Ten, twenty, maybe one hundred dollars for each man, woman, and child you have murdered. Is that what they are worth to you?"

"Please let me live to see my children grow up."

I thought of this monster's audacity to bear descendants so that his beastly genes would be guaranteed immortality.

"Children? The world needs children from the likes of you?"

I sensed my heart softening. Then my mind raced. I saw the faces of my father and the thousand innocent men and boys, all lying mutilated on the hill, their spirits still asking, "WHY?" I saw Veronika, the kindhearted invalid who was snuffed out because she knew this beast's secrets.

"Turn me over to the police. When you kill me you'll become a fugitive. Am I worth additional grief to you?" He kept weeping, hoping.

Urgency crawled inside my gut. Suddenly I knew Tenner had made his last appeal.

"Taking your dirty life is no compensation for the pain you have inflicted on the town of Kalavryta, Tenner." I allowed him a minute to recollect his crime and calculate his punishment. Then swallowing my growing pity and ignoring the consequences awaiting me, I kicked the chair from under him and watched him dangle, shaking and choking for air, his arms reaching for his throat and his legs fluttering in convulsions.

As the blood in his hated face turned from red to gray-blue and he quivered no more, a serene relief flooded every inch of my being, like an orgasm that had been building up for twenty years.

I turned off the recorder, took the steel chain and the lock and hung them around my neck, collected the two folders and my copy of the bill of sale with his signature, and laid them all inside the satchel. Carrying it and the attaché case full of cash in one hand and the loaded Luger cocked and ready in the other, I advanced toward the oak doors.

The corridor was deserted. When I exited I wrapped the chain around the door handles, threaded the lock through two links and snapped it shut.

The gray van with its black letters discarded pulled up. Hurriedly I climbed inside. Climpt's soldier's uniform complete with all its decorations peeked from under the draped white coat of the Pacific Alarm outfit. His white-gloved hands grabbed the wheel tensely.

"Let's get the hell out of here, Climpt."

"Yesireeee," he said, and gunned the engine. Soon we were traveling north on El Camino Real.

"How much time have we got?" I asked.

"Plenty. Them purty boys 's peaceful as they can be. Hog-tied an' lockt up 'nside a closet. Quackin' like a bunch o' ducks on a gook bus, so I hadta use ma special tape ta hush 'm up."

I looked at my watch. Barely six-twenty and yet a blackness hung below the thick fog.

"The door shaker won't show up 'til seven," I commented, meaning the special cop who shakes the front door to see if it has been left unlocked through neglect.

"Tha stinkin' Nazi. Danglin' frum tha end o' tha rope lak' he s'pose ta?" asked Climpt looking ahead, minding his driving.

"Yap," I replied somberly.

"Hard ta kill a feller, even ifen tha sorry bastard need killin' acuse he's that Nazi devil Tenner," he said.

Now that my climax had subsided, my mind seemed strangely muddied. I didn't answer.

After a few miles Climpt turned right into a side street and stopped where it dead ended at the railroad tracks. He emptied the contents of the two briefcases into his duffel bag. We both sprang out and faced each other. Climpt started scratching the asphalt with his boot and pretended to make a design.

"Friend, we'll have to make this good-bye last us," I muttered. Climpt kept studying the ground.

"Hope somebody got a streak o' goodness ta stan' up ta righteousness, fer a change."

I shrugged my shoulders.

Now, he edged near me like a shy boy on his first date. Softly he placed his long arms over my shoulders and gave me a hug.

"Made me real proud I coulda did sometin' fer ya acuze I . . . I . . ." he stuttered, "I luvs ya betterer thana real brothah," he said and choked.

To dilute some of the acid that soured my gut I added rapidly, "By the way, take some bread from the bag. Whatever, it's okay by me." My breathing was heavy and my voice vibrated uncontrollably. "So long, friend."

He kicked the dark air, tossed his bag over his shoulder, and started to edge toward El Camino to flag a cab. Maybe he sensed my stare on his back because he stopped and turned, a silhouette in the darkness.

"Hell, I got me a bitch o' a time spendin' tha bread I got me. Don' need no more bread. I got me plenty o' bread."

I stood briefly, watching Climpt, hunched and bent in the waist, disappear inside the fog. Then I climbed into the van and headed for the airport.

At the lot I parked three cars away from the gray Ford. When nothing was moving I abandoned the van and crawled inside the sedan, dragging along a small suitcase packed with the reverend's belongings. In the blackness of the night I fished out the clerical collar, a black shirt, the wig and the mustache and, so disguised, I lit out for Chicago.

12

A TRIBE OF NEW FRIENDS

I drove for three nights and two days with only intermittent rest, usually in church parking lots, until, senses and limbs debilitated, I arrived in front of the Rosenburg home on Sheridan Road in Winnetka, an affluent suburb a few miles north of Chicago. A very large antebellum-style white villa with manicured lawns, hedges, and flower beds stood before me.

I stared blankly at the offered refuge while a barrage of feelings did a macabre dance inside me. Insecurity and fear fought with relief, fulfillment, and pride for dominance. I climbed out of the Ford.

The late evening sun shot scorching rays through my black suit. I vaulted the stairs three steps at a time and rang the bell. It was humid and the wig on my head was driving me mad. I longed to shed every bit of cumbersome clothing and dive naked into a pool of ice water.

At long last, the door was opened by a barefoot, handsome woman in her twenties who was startled enough to recoil slightly. Her long red hair was pushed back under a headband. She stood in the center of the doorway dressed in black chiffon over a white bikini and smelling strongly of perfume. She swayed her wide hips, shifting her weight from one shapely tanned leg to the other.

"*Shalom,*" she said, staring at me curiously, as if she were facing someone who had just crawled out of a sewer.

"*Shalom.* I am looking for Mr. Herb Rosenburg, Senior," I said, forcing a grin. "I'm Reverend Roy Harry Moses. Mr. Rosenburg is expecting me." She hesitated.

"Sure, sure. Come on in, Reverend Roy. I'm Anna. The whole *mishpocheh* is in the back by the pool. You just missed little Simon's *bris*. The cute little guy is still wailing up a storm—maybe the *mohel* chopped too much off his tiny dick—pardon my disrespectful tongue, Reverend."

I followed her along a corridor, and although totally exhausted, I could not help but notice her expertise in the art of swinging her hips— like a professional model parading for a designer fashion show.

An archway gave out into a portico with gray pillars, and sounds of shouting, playing, splashing, and crying reached me. An Olympic-size pool full of brawling children came into view. Men and women of all ages and shapes lay scattered about, lounging in chairs and on chaises beneath colorful umbrellas. Beyond them I could see an endless Lake Michigan, stretching its gray waters.

A woman dressed in a loose-fitting cotton shift paced back and forth, tenderly holding against her breasts a crying infant, whispering comfortingly while occasionally reaching out to whack at a naked, shrieking, and demanding boy who pulled on her skirt.

To the left, under a trellis overhung with trailing large brown grape leaves, half a dozen perspiring men sat around a huge circular table, most dressed in stiff street clothing and all puffing on long cigars. Swinging their arms wildly, they were speaking in loud voices. The sight of Anna brought the conversation to an abrupt halt.

"Is this *eppes* a beauty!" exclaimed a bare-chested man in bright-colored Bermuda shorts. All sets of eyes embraced Anna. Then the men, nudging one another, focused on me. My cadaverous appearance and out-of-place apparel clouded their faces with confusion.

Only the man in the shorts, who bore a strong resemblance to Captain Herb Rosenburg, remained unruffled. His green eyes gave me a contemptuous glance. Then his attention returned to Anna and with a twinkle he said, "Now, Anna here, she is a true specimen of God's chosen people." Strong sounds of approval filled the air. "As for the rest of us, sitting around this table, God be blessed, I see no reason to be making similar claims."

Protesting boos and sputters of cigar smoke caused the still grape leaves above to quiver. Anna giggled and her white teeth sparkled. She addressed the jester.

"Mr. Rosenburg, this Reverend Roy, he says you've been expecting him."

The assembly's attention jumped from me to Rosenburg. The bare-chested man gave me a closer scrutiny.

An ugly old fellow who resembled Rasputin kept blinking his eyes. He spoke in a heavy accent. "Reverent insite Jewish home? Now, I see everyting, no?"

"And what is so terrible about a reverend visiting a Jewish home, Albert?" asked the bare-chested man. "A man is a dirty dog when he is a reverend? I agree that this gentleman, whoever he is, belongs to the wrong religion, but there are reverends who do some good deeds."

"Noting against zem, Got forbit, I vas trying to say zat . . . "

Rosenburg scratched the thick hair on his chest and interrupted. "Don't you mind him, Reverend Roy." He pointed with his hand. "Our Albert, here, has his own way with words. When he speaks, expressions that should be sugar-coated . . . well . . . they usually turn up coated with horse manure."

"May the One above protect us from our Albert's tongue," remarked another man. He had the aura of a pious Jew and sat sweating inside a black three-piece suit.

"What brings you to our home, Rever . . . " Rosenburg stopped abruptly. His green eyes flashed. He sprang up and with his long arms pulled me against his hairy chest, gave me a hug and kissed my cheeks.

"Blessed be He. *Shalom. Shalom.* Welcome, Reverend Roy." He winked at me. "I failed to recognize you. God almighty, you have lost a lot of weight! Why, the last time I saw you, you were playing tackle for your high school football team, and you were a lot bigger then. How's mom and dad?"

He was quick and witty and I liked him already.

"They send their greetings," I answered, playing along.

He kept his left arm braced around my neck.

"Let me introduce you to my family and friends."

Being inspected by that mute, inquisitive assembly felt like standing in front of a somber jury for judgment. Rosenburg sensed my discomfort and, aware of my exhaustion, dropped his arm, placed his palm against my back, and gave me a gentle shove toward the house, away from the solemn council.

"You look awful, Reverend. You are coming down with a virus, maybe? You should get some rest before you join us for the evening meal. You can meet everyone then."

He pushed me away. As we edged toward the archway I heard the cigar-smokers sing in chorus.

"Yah, yah, sure."

"Coming down with a virus, maybe," uttered one voice.

"He deserves some rest," said another.

"A nice man, the reverend!" said a third.

"Yah," most voices agreed.

"Maybe a *shnorer,* a bum, looking for handout, I tink," murmured Rasputin with contempt.

Rosenburg led me in silence up a back stairway and ushered me into a spacious bedroom. When the thick door shut behind us he faced me, his eyes searching mine.

"You fooled all of us." His large hands gripped my shoulders. "So, justice has been done, my son."

"Yes," I whispered.

"The papers have gone crazy with the news—the usual half-truths, all the distorted garbage reporters write and expect us feebleminded readers to accept as the gospel. Wild theories. They claim robbery was the motive for the hanging—that the killer robbed him of his cash. Have you listened to the news?"

"I had the radio on the whole way."

"Then you've heard it all." He dropped his voice a few notes. "Things need time to cool off. All the documents are in order. The only holdup with your passport is your picture. We can attend to the photos the first thing tomorrow morning." He smiled. "Your disguise is most astonishing."

I started to thank him for allowing me the sanctuary of his home, and he placed his palm to seal my lips.

"Shhhh . . . no need for that. We are simply helping a friend in need."

He looked me over again and smote his forehead, and his grin returned. "So help me God, you had me fooled too. We have been expecting your arrival and yet no one realized you were the one, not even I." He shook his head. "A bunch of shmucks, all six of us!"

I flung my coat on the big bed, impatiently peeled off the wig and the mustache, and tossed them on the chair with a great sigh of relief. Rosenburg scratched his head and his mischievous green eyes lit up.

"Maybe we should put the exhausted Reverend Roy to sleep. Maybe we should have you reappear as . . . ," he stared at the ceiling thinking, "as Sam Cohen—Sam Cohen is a peculiar Jewish name, ha, ha, ha— dressed in your regular clothes. No one will make the connection that the Reverend Roy they saw and Sam Cohen, the guy they'll meet later, are one and the same fellow." To reassure himself of his plot, he added, "Yes. Yes. That'll work better for the women and the kids too. We won't have to explain what in God's green earth a reverend is doing in a Jewish home." He rubbed his palms. "Keep mysteries to a minimum. Just wear the mustache and you'll be just fine. And more comfortable without that . . . that wig, for damn sure."

Rosenburg picked up the pile of black hair from the chair with the tips of his fingers and examined it, sniffed it, plugged his nostrils, and let it drop as if it were a dead skunk.

"Phew! This thing needs disinfecting! What kind of hair do you suppose they use to make these ugly things nowadays—porcupine?" He burst into a loud laughter. "Ai, ai, ai—a monk disguise! What did you do, rob a priest?" He headed for the door. "I'll take care of your belongings personally—park the car far away from here. Go ahead and freshen up. In an hour I'll come up to get you and we'll join the others. They are all very anxious to meet you. And son—you can relax now. Trust this house as your very own. You are among close friends."

Rosenburg slipped through the door chuckling, tossed me a wink, and disappeared. I stood feeling fortunate to have been taken in by this Jewish tribe.

When the two of us approached the massive table, all the men were smiling. Though they sat in silence, it seemed apparent they knew who I was and what I had done.

Rosenburg first presented me to a stout, middle-aged, blond man with a powerful chin and blue eyes. "Our rabbi, Aaron Yannoff—Russian heritage—our spiritual leader and, ah, what a scholar he is! A family man with a big heart and virtuous convictions. And gifted with a grand baritone voice."

With an aura of authority, the rabbi hummed an inaudible comment and shook my hand with a steel grip.

Then I met Emmett Friedman, a dignified, gray-haired engineer of advanced age who had survived Buchenwald, immigrated to the States, settled in Chicago, and worked for the Illinois Utilities Company until his recent retirement.

"Very much respected, first as a man and second as a leader in our Jewish community—not only here in Chicago but all over the world. A man of myriad contacts, a *macher*, a real operator. Every day I ask God to give me long life so when I grow up I can be a man of worth like my good friend Emmett," Rosenburg concluded, and they all chuckled in unison, like wind-up dolls.

The frail man of medium height with the sympathetic face came around the table and embraced me.

"That vas a very courageous thing you did. Vonderrful to have von less pig on the loose, yah?" he said in a heavy accent.

"Yaaaaah . . . ," sounded all the cigar-chewing men in spontaneous agreement.

Next came Abe Rabinovitz. Short and chubby, he sat regally in his black suit, sweltering gallantly in the scalding air.

"My son-in-law, the religious pillar of the family," announced Rosenburg with a touch of irony, "who lives in accordance with our God's teachings and believes in reincarnation when the Messiah returns—even though many professed dates for such a holy event have already come only to pass. Abe is a good provider for my daughter and my five grandchildren, four rambunctious ones, and the little one that just came, bringing added joy to our hearts."

Showing a bit of displeasure for the tone of his father-in-law's prologue, Abe stood up and offered me his plump moist hand.

"May the Almighty be with you, my friend."

A spectacled, bald, older man with a long thin face and large lips sat wedged deep inside his chair cracking his knuckles and yanking on his slender fingers while he stared at me.

"My beloved brother-in-law, Professor Mark Lefkowitz. Teaches economics at the university. A good head on his shoulders. A respected scientist. Mark has been expertly forecasting the economic retrenchments and expansions over the years—except for last April's disaster where Professor Lefkowitz was quoted by the press, 'The U.S. stock markets will crash before the summer.'"

"*Oy!* A man must be always right, just like the weatherman and Herb Rosenburg, Senior," said the professor, looking to the heavens and raising his hands in prayer. "So what if I were wrong once? My models had been tampered with, Herb. I've told you many times three of my models had been interfered with." Calmly and unhurriedly he extended his hand across the huge table.

"Welcome to my *kibitzer,* my teasing brother Rosenburg's *haimish* (warm, unpretentious) home," he said with a wink and a smile.

Finally I met the thin, dark-skinned, old man who didn't like reverends. With an enormous humped nose and beady, shifty black eyes under bushy brows, a goatee and hairy hands, hunched over and dressed in an ill-fitting, somber black outfit, he appeared to be a ghost from a past era.

"My adopted son, Albert Zimmerman, a Hungarian Jew. Smart man, because he lived through the war in neutral Sweden. An *oyrech auf Shabbes* (a guest for the Sabbath), Albert has refused to abandon us for better offers," said Rosenburg, smirking. "A great fiddler, Albert has played with the Stockholm and Chicago Philharmonics. Now, during his golden years, his sole passion in life is to save two bucks from his retirement check and wager them on the horse races at Arlington Park. But he entertains us with his fiddle now and then, when he has a winning day, though, *ai, ai, ai,* such a day seldom ever comes!" Everyone chuckled and an ugly grin cracked Albert's lips.

"Aha. So, Rosenburg, you tink always I lose? Vell, now zat you mention it, yestertay I hat a vinning day. Zis horse pait me very vell. Unt because frient Sam arrive from mission, I vill play ze fittle tonight, yah?" He took my hand limply and pumped it once as his eyes briefly brushed mine.

"Honor to shake your hand."

A younger man with sparkling green eyes and an honest smile, not much older than I, tall and broad-shouldered and a bit pudgy in the middle, approached the table dripping wet in swim trunks and extended his arm, anxious to greet me.

"My younger son, David—a very good boy," said Rosenburg affectionately. He just returned from two months at a fat farm in Florida; they took thirty pounds off him down there. Corned beef, pastrami, lox, and cream cheese are David's favored nourishment. That beautiful filly Anna, she is David's fiancée, and she hosts in a high-class deli where big-shots congregate—you know, theater and movie directors and producers. Anna never gives up hope. She wants to be discovered. Become a big star. And my David—he spends his evenings in the place and he *fresses,* he eats, God bless 'im, like . . . well . . . like a kosher rhino, ha, ha, ha."

David brushed the air with his arm to hush his father, an outgoing man who loved to tease a crowd.

"Stop *utzing* me, Papa," he said, and directed his warm eyes to me. "My brother told us about you. Glad you're here with us." His voice was deep and sincere, and he excused himself to join his Anna.

I was offered an empty chair while six distinctly different shapes of mouths puffed clouds of thick cigar smoke into the Chicago air.

"Vell, did the pig scream for mercy? Did he crawl on his belly for forgiveness? Vat he did ven you vere about to hang him?" demanded Emmett Friedman, his eyes flashing the ferocity of a predator when staking his prey.

I took time to respond but when I spoke, I tried to sound composed and restrained.

"He asked to be given a chance to see his children grow up, and he tried to bribe me. He offered me millions."

"Good we have a mighty God," said the rabbi.

"Finally the devil took him," added Friedman.

"Amen," symphonized the gathering.

"Tell us your story, my friend," asked Rosenburg and his green eyes showed a genuine interest in sharing my past grief.

A formidable silence fell around the table.

I began by describing Kalavryta as a tranquil, picturesque mountainous village in northern Peloponnesus and spoke of the closeness of my God-loving family during the pre-war years, of the famine and deprivation and misery during the occupation, the looting, the torching, and the massacre of almost all the male civilians by Tenner.

Friedman blew his nose loudly, greatly moved by the tragedy.

"Good God in heaven," Rosenburg said, his face aflame with anger, "why can't You put an end to this madness?"

I continued my narrative with my vow as a lad to avenge my dead father and all those slaughtered, and my lifelong obsession to track down the criminal. Finally I described the chase, the identification of Tenner, and his hanging.

Rabbi Yannoff stood up and asked the rest of us to rise because he wished to offer a prayer. We all bowed our heads and he began.

"*Elokim*. Blessed You oh Holy One, who with Your redemptive powers brought Your people from bondage to freedom, and from mourning to festivity, and from darkness to great light. And blessed be this gentle courageous young man ...," he coughed, undecided as to what name to use and then settled for, " ... Samuel, who even though he shares not our faith, through his heavenly deliverance, in Your name and the name of Israel and all the decent human races, has brought some solace to the restless and wandering ghosts, all those millions of innocent men, women and children who were slaughtered by the most heinous savages of all time. Amen."

"Amen," voiced the small crowd.

A refreshing breeze sneaked in from the lake. As women and children in groups approached, Rosenburg introduced me as Sam Cohen from Worcester, the son of an old friend.

While the ladies assembled a sumptuous buffet, bottles of brandy and red wine and glasses were fetched to our table, and the rabbi coughed and cleared his throat.

"As I was about to explain earlier, spiritual search and fulfillment is the prerogative of each and every living soul." He cleared the frog from his windpipe once more. "However, we Jews should not and must not tolerate *apikorus,* must not allow heresy."

"Amen," shouted Rabinovitz, clutching his hands in agreement.

"Dedication to the teachings of the Torah is the solemn duty of all Jews." He, too, cleared his throat. "A man without God is a lost man. A man with God in his heart is a good and hopeful man. We must insist that God is instilled in the hearts of our young. You must have heard the story of the bright student who came to the rabbi and with a defiant eye, he declared. 'I must tell you the truth; I no longer believe in God.'"

"Noooooo!" cried the crowd.

"Yes, yes," affirmed Rabinovitz. "'And how long have you been studying Talmud?' asked the learned rabbi.

"'Five years,' replied the student.

"'Only five years,' exclaimed the rabbi, 'and you have the nerve to call yourself a skeptic?'"

"Good story," voiced Friedman. "Our young must be shown road to Got so they vill become good Jews and they vill remain good Jews throughout their entire lives."

"And raise worthy Jewish children," added Professor Lefkowitz proudly.

"Amen," affixed Rabinovitz.

"Let's toast to that," said Rosenburg. He raised his brandy glass, and the party began.

When the stars came out for their nightly assembly in the dome of our world, Zimmerman fetched his fiddle. He placed his crumpled handkerchief under his chin, and notes of popular Hungarian czardas spilled about on the fragrant wind—those slow, sad folk melodies with arrangements that sound like voices crying, followed by the rapid, festive second parts, unique to gypsy tunes.

Then, as if his playing so far had been only an exercise to loosen up his stiff and tired limbs, the old man's shoulders hunched some more, his gaunt features tightened, and in the semi-darkness he took on a devil-like stance. His eyes glowed and his long, hairy, bony fingers started to move up and down the neck of his weathered instrument with the rapidity of a tarantula's legs in flight. Paganini's masterpiece, "Variazioni di Bravura," one of the most astonishing feats in violin virtuosity, filled the courtyard. All stood enchanted and bewitched, even the boisterous children.

The sky was cloudless and the stars hung low, gleaming like gigantic pearls. Awakened from its long siesta, the full moon shyly slid up from the mysterious depths of the dark lake to join us. Now, with a heavenly tableau assembled, a mood was set. Rabbi Yannoff stood up, puffed his chest like a peacock, cleared his throat, and in his baritone voice began to hum the melody of "Vu Is dus Gesele?" ("Where Is the Little Street?")—one of the most haunting songs of the Russian Jews, Rosenburg explained.

With yearning and ache in his face, he sang the pangs of total helplessness and loss.

> *Where is the little street,*
> *Where is the house,*
> *Where is the maiden who stole my heart?*
> *Alas, it is all gone . . .*

All the men, women, and children joined into a magnificent and heartwarming chorus. So breathtaking was the blend of sounds in the ethereal scene that my heart swelled with profound emotions.

Then the rebbitsin, the wife of Rabbi Yannoff, from the distance vocalized softly "Tumba, Tumba," another tale from Russia, about a young girl sitting by an oven in a hut sewing and a young man teasingly pulling at her thread. Again the chorus followed, with the refrain:

> *Now upon the oven we have two people and they are not sewing,*
> *Tumba, tumba . . .*

It was magical.

The night went on affably. With the help of the good wine, abundance of hearty food, and the security offered by my trusted new friends, my anxieties diminished so that, wearied as I was from three near-sleepless nights, the moment I slid between the clean sheets my mind drifted to my Kathy. Her comforting face stood smiling before me and her skin touched mine, and a sweet, deep sleep came to me.

A commotion awakened me. Hurried footsteps and men's urgent voices reached me. The door was flung open. Rosenburg appeared, along with Rabbi Yannoff and Friedman, all wild-eyed and shouting.

Half-awake, the only sense I could make from the three agitated men was that unexpected events had made the shelter of Rosenburg's home no longer safe, and I should leave there at once.

Still dazed, I was dragged down the stairs and soon found myself, along with the three men, in a large automobile, speeding away toward an unknown destination in the semi-darkness of the dawn.

As I sat in the back seat next to Friedman, I began to pull myself together, buttoning my trousers and my shirt, while he, his hair disorganized, violently waved a newspaper.

"Have been betrayed! No all Jews are honorable! No! Have always known that! But to be betrayed by von of our very trusted friends is most shocking!"

"A *dybbuk* has entered into him," declared Rosenburg.

"Mr. Friedman, what happened? Who betrayed us?" I asked in absolute confusion.

"The revard—von-hundred-thousand-dollar revard is on your head, my friend! All here—on front page of *Chicago Times*. The Giacominni family offer von hundred thousand dollar for your apprehension!"

I snatched the newspaper from his waving hand and began to read.

$100,000 Reward for Accused Murderer
The Giacominni family of Palo Alto, California, today offered $100,000 for information leading to the apprehension of John Barlow, principal suspect in the death of influential businessman Alfredo Giacominni, chairman of the financially powerful conglomerate A.G.G. Enterprises. Three days ago, Mr. Giacominni was found hanging from a chandelier in his office in Palo Alto.

Barlow, a San Francisco real-estate investor, was scheduled to finalize a pending sale with Giacominni on the evening of the murder. According to sources close to the victim, Barlow was the last person to visit Giacominni's offices, in order to complete the sale to A.G.G. Enterprises of a building Barlow owned in downtown San Francisco.

On the evening of September 13, the three employees at the premises of A.G.G. Enterprises were tied and gagged by a powerful accomplice. Giacominni's body was discovered by the janitor.

A briefcase containing $390,000 in cash vanished along with the suspect.

The rabbi's driving was fast and erratic. Rosenburg urged him to slow down else the cops would soon be on our trail, then he turned and faced Friedman and me.

"My fault for having trusted the *kaporeh* (good for nothing). One should never trust gamblers—they are vulnerable like dope addicts. They'd sell their own ass for a fix! Oh, *zeeser Gottenyn* (sweet God) in heaven, I have offered him my home. He lived with us as a member of my family for more than two years! Do I feel betrayed? Do I feel like buying a pistol and shooting dead the ungrateful bastard?"

"Traitors, Herb. I see many Jew traitors in my life; have lived vit them in camps. They vere all over camps. They betrayed our race to save their own dirty skin. But Zimmerman? Vould never, never think him a traitor. My heart very sad, Herb, because . . . because I love the man and . . . and his fiddle playing."

He moved swiftly to brush moisture from his eyes.

I was starting to get the picture, to piece the puzzle together. But how had the fiddler's squealing been discovered to allow us time to flee? Friedman must have read my bafflement.

"Phone volk me up this morning. Vell, I vas sleeping like a baby after the good party last night and, brrrrrrrr the phone ring and the police captain, my good friend Michael—very good Jewish boy Michael he is—say to me. 'Friedman,' he say, 'this is Michael the policeman.' 'I robbed a bank? My house on fire? Got forbid,' I say and vaited. 'Zimmerman . . . Albert, the fiddler in my office.' 'Yah?' I say. 'Tell him hello from Friedman.'

"And I ask, 'You call me in middle of night to tell me fiddler Albert is in your office, Michael?' And he say, 'I'm calling from room next door because I don't vant fiddler to know I calling you.' 'Yah? And?' I ask, and the policeman say, 'Albert got the late edition of newspaper and he claim he legally entitled to von-hundred-thousand-dollar revard.' So, I say to Michael, 'You have von hundred thousand dollar laying around vit no purpose? Give to poor fiddler. He can use to bet the horses vit it. But ask Zimmerman to play something on fiddle for you before you give him the whole shebang.'

"And then, good Michael say, 'Friedman, this is serious police business. Important man vos murdered by hanging, near San Francisco three days ago. The family of victim offering von hundred thousand dollar for apprehension of murderer, and Zimmerman, he vant to collect revard. He say he know vere killer hiding and he hiding in Rosenburg's place.' And Michael . . . "

"May beets grow inside his ugly belly," Rosenburg interrupted angrily.

" . . . And he, Michael say to me, 'Friedman, I know Herb Rosenburg is very good friend. I don't know vat is going on down there, and if you have something to do vit it or not, but because I know you stick your nose in many things, I give you one hour head-start. I vill take my time asking judge for search varant for Rosenburg's place. One hour. No more. So run Friedman, run!' my good friend Michael say. My heart stop beating but somehow already my feet vas inside my shoe and I run like rabbit."

Rosenburg looked me square in the eye.

"Our plans have changed. We can't afford to keep you in Chicago. You won't be safe here, not now. The police captain must investigate Zimmerman's claim. *Oy!* After all, it is his duty—above all else he is a cop. By the time the good captain gets a search warrant and drives to my house, you must be out of the Chicago area and on your way to New York."

"For sure," added Friedman.

"You must be on the nonstop flight to Tel Aviv that takes off at nine-thirty this evening."

"No choice," said Friedman, shaking his head.

"My son David is booking your tickets right now. The manager at El Al, the Israeli airline, is his very good friend; they grew up together."

"No problem getting tickets. Manager vill see to that," interjected Friedman confidently.

"Even if he has to bump two passengers and take their seats, he'll do it. Right now we are heading directly to the forger's office. We need your documents at once."

Can a forger be trusted? I thought. And why two seats?

Friedman, who was observing me, spoke again. "No vory. Kol the forger perfectly trustworthy—most honorable man. Von of us. Survivor of Auschwitz. Entire family perish in that awful place. Kol principled man. Anyvay, Kol vill take photograph and complete passport in short time. And vile friends occupy traitor Zimmerman, ve vill go to airport and Rabbi Yannoff vill come vit you to Israel. Rabbi Yannoff brave and dedicated man. Rabbi vill be very good companion."

The rabbi, who had not uttered a single sound until then, half-turned his head and shouted, "Incidentally, your new name is Theodor Elias. Memorize it. Theodor, without an 'e' at the end."

Grim realization sped through me. My heart was too small to store the admiration I felt for these men, and although my survival depended almost totally on their selfless aid, the decency learned from my two very moral parents protested.

"The rabbi is a married man—coming along as my companion will be dangerous! All of you have taken extraordinary risks to help me. You will be in my heart no matter what happens, but enough is enough. You can't jeopardize your lives and families any more than you already have. As soon as my new identity is secured, you must drop me off by some car rental agency. Then I'll drive to the airport alone and take my chances."

"No. No. Out of question," said Friedman, pointing his finger at me like a scolding teacher. "Ve know the vay and ve have no time to spare."

"When we volunteered to give you a hand we knew there were going to be risks," Rosenburg agreed.

"Jews are commanded to obey the will of God. God wants us to help you. His will must be carried out," declared the rabbi.

The car slowed and edged against a curb, where it stopped. Deadness had taken over this district. Rows of abandoned brick industrial buildings faced each other in disrepair and silence. A sultry wind scattered garbage along and around the gutter, and the sidewalks and pavement were dotted with potholes. The area had seen its industrial renaissance come and go.

We walked briskly to an old metal door surprisingly painted bright blue, and Friedman tapped it four times with his fist. Anxiously we waited. At last the door separated narrowly from its frame with a loud squeak, and a wrinkled, spectacled, gray-eyed man with wild white hair peered from behind. One by one we sneaked inside a huge dark room. Antiquated machinery, gadgets, trinkets, and spare parts lay about as if dumped there by some careless and confused collector. The place and the barefoot proprietor smelled foul. After the traditional hugs and greetings in Yiddish and Hebrew, Friedman raised both arms.

"Kol, my friend, von of greatest brains to immigrate to Chicago from old vorld. A genius. But in haste to escape extinction, *ai, ai,* he forgot deodorant in Auschwitz."

All giggled and Kol laughed goodheartedly at his friend's snipe.

"Come, come, my Emmett. Visiting perfumed whorehouse? Nooo. Kol's vorkshop maybe stink like shithouse but do good vork. Best vork, yaah?"

"The best work," agreed the rabbi.

"Yaah," exclaimed Friedman.

"Kol, we must hurry. Our friend must catch the nine-thirty plane to Israel from New York tonight," warned Rosenburg. "It could be deadly if he misses that flight!"

"Vere is vig?" asked Friedman, staring about in alarm.

"Vig and Hasidic decorations hanging there on hanger," said Kol pointing to an old broken-down armoire.

"Vat ve vaiting for? Dress him up. Ve must take photos right avay," urged Friedman.

They brought me a wrinkled coat and seized a wig with side curls and a beard, and the four started to fuss over me like mothers assembling a bride. They talked in Yiddish, Hebrew, and English, smacking each other's hands in disapproval, and back-slapping each other in endorsement.

When the masquerade was complete, they all walked some paces back and away from me to view their accomplishment, and all exclaimed, "Aaaah, yaaah," as they chatted like a bunch of happy children playing games of pretend, elated to have created the perfect disguise.

Then mild panic struck.

"Streimel," shouted Friedman and brought his hands to his face admitting to his goof about overlooking the final touch.

"Streimel!" echoed Kol, pointing to a black broad-brimmed hat worn by Orthodox Jews, hanging from a nail flat against the wall.

"My Lord, we almost overlooked the final touch," commented Rosenburg with scornful resignation. Shaking his head, he dashed over to fetch it. "We forgot the awful hat," he mumbled. He reached for the old streimel and dusted it off by slapping it against his right thigh.

They laid it on my head and Kol stared at me with warm speculation before he exclaimed, *"Riboyne shel o'lem!"* ("Just look at you!") He brought out a camera of primeval vintage, adjusted the tripod, and shoved his entire head inside a long, frayed hood of dark cloth. As if the spooky contraption were a talking machine too, Kol's voice shot through it, commanding me to stand still, and two flashes jolted the room. His ugly head reappeared. With negatives in hand, his lanky frame in its dirty coveralls sped toward the darkness at the rear of the messy space.

In half an hour I possessed an American passport. I was now Theodor Elias, born in Salonika (Thessaloniki), Greece, in 1932 to Hyman and Sheila Elias. If I needed to explain further to anyone of authority, I was to claim that my parents were Orthodox Jews of Greek nationality who had died in unknown Nazi concentration camps, and that a sympathetic Greek family had raised me as one of their own until 1951, when I immigrated to the U.S.

Viewing myself in the passport picture as a Hasidic Jew normally would have tickled my insides, forcing me to burst into wild laughter. But these were not ordinary times and my innards remained numb.

Rosenburg advised me that I should refrain from speaking, but if I got in a jam I should mix English with Greek, the basic Yiddish I had learned studying my phrasebook, and my hands. The combination of those four plus my attire should be sufficient to make me sound and look authentic to any gentile interrogator.

Kol handed me a New York driver's license, a number of documents such as letters and receipts in various states of wear and age, all displaying the name Theodor Elias, plus a Bank of Credit checkbook with some checks missing. I was asked by Kol to fill out the stubs and deposit slips in my own handwriting.

Kol performed his last inspection and, finally satisfied, he smiled and smacked me on the back. His teeth were missing, and his rotten aging gums gave his colorless hard-featured face a mask of dread.

Just then, we heard the sound of a motor vehicle rolling by at a slow speed. Wild looks flashed about. Kol rushed to the one small filthy window, barely lit by the bashful dawn. With a waving arm he stripped away the cobwebs, spat on the glass, and rubbed it with his palm before he peeked through.

"Unmarked car vit two *schvarrzerrs* (black men) in front seat. No good. Come, come." His large palm motioned us to follow him at once.

We crawled like rodents in a sewer under brick archways lined with busted pipes, weaving through discarded furniture and around rusted abandoned appliances. Finally we climbed a stone stairway and landed inside the remnants of an abandoned laundry facility. A dusty white truck bearing large black letters reading "Abe Frank's Laundry" was parked facing a large dilapidated steel gate.

Kol tossed a white coverall and hat to Friedman, asked him to put them on, and told him to drive since he was familiar with the operation of the machine, then yanked open the rear door, motioned to the rest of us to hop inside, and slapped it closed. We scrambled between stale-smelling bundles of linen and cardboard boxes. The squeaky gate opened, and Kol shouted, *"Shalom!"* Friedman started the engine, engaged the gearbox, let the clutch out fast, and the truck vaulted onto the street.

Soon we could hear around us the hum of traffic and all the sounds and vibrations of urban awakening.

The rabbi carved a hole in the midst of the piles of linen, and he and Rosenburg and I faced each other in a circle. We sat in introspective silence, each alone with his inner fears.

I felt my blood pumping, as fleeting, scrambled images hurtled through my mind. I saw Kathy's brightness and beauty in a haze, like abstract reflections of Monet's water lilies, then her loving eyes growing restless, drenched with agony and distress, and my tongue tasted her bitter torment.

My fatigued mind lacked the competence to assess what rewards there might be, if any, of having delivered justice.

We were traveling fast at an even speed and the motor purred like a well-oiled compressor. Rosenburg looked at his watch and broke the drone of the road hum.

"Fourteen hours for the drive to Idlewild Airport. With some luck we'll be there on time."

Inside our cavern Rabbi Yannoff had perched with his hands clasped in his lap and eyes lowered but now, as if a divine inspiration had commanded his spirit, he lifted his arms skyward.

"God bless Kol and his bright ingenious mind. Between Kol's resourcefulness and God's grace, Theodor and I will soon be on the revered soil of the Holy Land and among Israelite friends."

Rosenburg rocked on his box seat.

"My good rabbi, may God bless you, please repeat that inspired wish just once more, to give my fainting heart a tiny shot of that much-craved courage," said he, while his green eyes flashed, showing the fire and playfulness of his mischievous mind.

The rabbi threw Rosenburg a contemptuous glance and looked away, but Rosenburg who, I suspected, was determined to bring a touch of levity to the gravity of the scene, insisted. "Please, my dedicated rabbi, do it just for me."

"I said, 'Between Kol's resourcefulness and God's grace, soon we shall be on the soil of the Holy Land among our people.'"

Rosenburg's face took on a shine and his lips cracked into a most prankish twist.

"Oh yes, yes. That is what I thought you said, which reminded me of the *bummerkeh* (lady of the night) who tap-danced with her right leg and toe-danced with her left leg and ... between her two legs she made a darn good living."

Rosenburg broke into a noisy laughter and was still chuckling when shrieking from a siren reached us. Abruptly the three of us stared at each other in dismay.

The laundry truck slowed and eased to a halt. The siren became deafening then stopped. I could hear my heart thumping like a giant drum. Crazy thoughts invaded my reason.

"May I see your license, please," a powerful voice commanded.

"Sure, sure. Vat I did so terrible, mister nice policeman?" we heard Friedman ask.

"Your foot is a little heavy on the gas, gramps. This old wreck of a van wasn't meant to fly, you know. The speed limit is sixty-five miles an hour and I clocked you going over seventy-five."

"Customer need laundry right avay. *Ai, ai.* Seventy-five? Maybe I vas going a little fast, mister nice policeman, but no seventy-five, God forbid. But if you say so, mister nice policeman, vat am I to argue. I promise you, as Almighty is my vitness, now that you told me, I'll vatch it."

"Well, listen. Because you remind me a little of my grandfather, and because I hate to see an old man like you still working to scrape a living, I'll let you go this time. But be careful. Don't you let me catch you speeding again. Okay mister . . . Friedman?"

"Thank you, thank you, mister nice policeman."

"What are you delivering, anyway? Don't tell me. Let me guess. Let's see. From the overall looks of the van I'll guess . . . diapers to a pig farm. Ha, ha, ha."

"Ha, ha, ha. Thank you, mister nice policeman. Ha, ha, ha."

Gears shifted, the truck was coaxed into motion again, and the rabbi breathed, *"Ai,"* and wiped his sweaty forehead.

Rosenburg looked about, making his voice tremble a bit on purpose. He caught my eye.

"Theodor, Rabbi Yannoff here has a very special relationship with God," he stated solemnly.

I took his comment seriously.

"I believe so, Mr. Rosenburg."

Rosenburg's twinkle reignited. He pointed at the rabbi. "I believe inside this ordinary mortal is the much-anticipated Messiah we Jews have been awaiting for millennia." He raised his arms, lifted his head, and stared up at the heavens. "If not the real chief himself, maybe his brother or his cousin. Because suddenly, after this close call with the authorities, I feel free of fear. A divine assurance has convinced me that our mission will not fail because of our rabbi Yannoff's special connections."

His voice became livelier.

"Aah, can't you feel a guardian shield around this humble van? Can't you sense, because of our beloved Rabbi's company, a lofty spirit is guaranteeing us imperishability?"

"For God's sake, Rosenburg, you should have been a *badchen* (clown). Can't you be serious for once in your life?" exclaimed the rabbi.

Rosenburg's eyes lost their jocularity and in a switch of moods he announced that he wished to make an important statement.

"When the human soul is burdened with puzzling riddles, one gram of humor melts wretchedness, and just as a shot of morphine numbs the aches of the dying, a dose of witticism yields mad hope and lifts the spirits of the woeful to tolerance and faith."

He scratched his head to harvest additional wisdom.

"My learned teacher, let modest Rosenburg add a speck of insight to your book of knowledge." He pointed his finger. "A stroke of satire is a shot of morphine. And since the three of us here could use a dose of that fine medicine right now, I'm going to tell you a story—if it's all right with you, my respected master."

"Only if you must, Rosenburg," the rabbi grumbled and frowned. In a show of exaggerated patience he shook his shoulders and motioned Mr. Rosenburg to proceed.

Anew, Rosenburg's face sparkled like a child's whose mother had chosen him, from a brood of five, to receive her last piece of candy.

"Marsha and Aaron, an older couple, are in bed for the night.

"Marsha asks Aaron. 'If I die will you get married again?' Aaron looks at his wife of fifty years and says, 'I probably would.'

" 'You mean, after fifty years with me you would marry someone else?'

" 'I probably would.'

" 'Will you bring your new wife to this house?—our house?' asks Marsha with displeasure in her tongue.

" 'I probably would,' says Aaron.

" 'You mean after fifty years of marriage to me you would bring into my home a strange woman?' asks Marsha, obviously perturbed.

" 'I probably would,' says Aaron.

" 'And what about our bed? Will you bring this woman into our own bedroom and let her sleep on the bed which you and I have shared for fifty years?' asked Marsha, hoping Aaron would show some fidelity to her.

"'I probably would,' says Aaron without the slightest remorse.

Exasperated, Marsha finally snaps at her husband. "'What about my golf clubs? Are you going to let her use my golf clubs too?'

"'No,' replies Aaron with a somber face.

"'And why not?' asks Marsha, spitting sarcastic venom through her old lips.

"'She is a left-hander.'"

All reservations and fear deserted me and I broke into giddy laughter. The rabbi remained unmoved, though, so the bellowing Rosenburg gave him a whack. Finally the rabbi joined the two of us, and we kept guffawing, oblivious of the van's slowing to a stop. Friedman peered through the back door of the truck.

"Ai, ai, ai! You gone crazy in head from heat?" he asked, bewildered. "Think this is some foolish game?" Quickly he told us he was making a stop for gas and that this would be our last chance to use a restroom.

We plunged into the humid dusk and stretched our limbs at a forgotten gas station sitting deserted in the midst of pines. I was the last to use the facility. When I came out, the laundry truck with my protectors had vanished. I slipped back into the bathroom and stood hidden, my panicky mind racing over my choices of possible escapes. I decided to run for the woods.

I slowly eased the door open and took a peek around outside before I began slinking along the wall toward the rear of the dimly lit station. In the shadows I saw three figures standing next to a white police van. The forest was my only chance.

"Rosenburg, go get him—tell him to hurry!" I heard a voice say.

Was it a cop's calculated trick to flush me out? I stared intently until my bleary vision penetrated the dark. What looked like three policemen standing next to their van was really Rosenburg, Friedman, and the rabbi waiting for me by our own vehicle.

I sneaked up from the shadows.

"Oh blessed Holy Jerusalem! Friend Theodor give me heart attack!" said Friedman, bringing his hand up to his chest.

"When the truck was gone from the pumps I thought something terrible had happened," I explained.

"We found it safer to wait in the unlit part of the station," said the rabbi. Hurriedly we climbed into the truck and continued traveling toward New York. Only two hours 'til nine-thirty!

With his lively talk, Rosenburg had numbed my heart to danger, and the lullaby of the purring engine drugged me. I leaned against a stack of laundry bundles and stared at the steel ceiling. Kathy was there fondly embracing me, her perfect teeth shining behind her delectable lips. I licked them with hunger and told her how much I loved her, and she whispered she loved me more, much, much more. Good things passed through my head now. Pleasant things rolled by my eyes as their lids felt heavy.

A strong pull on my sleeve awakened me. "We must hurry!" a voice urged. The rabbi stood by the open rear door. I jumped off, still groggy from sleep.

"Is this the airport?" I asked.

"Yes!"

I blinked and viewed a remote corner of a parking garage, devoid of activity.

"No vaist time vit prolong good-byes, my friends!" said Emmett Friedman with a nervous grin on his tired face, and when he extended his wrinkled hand, I took it inside both of mine and was reluctant to let go.

Then Herbert Rosenburg, Senior, came forward and we snatched at each other and exchanged kisses on the cheeks.

"Son, we'll meet again, soon." His jaw trembled. The separation wasn't easy for either of us. Stirrings of suppressed emotions seemed to want to surface, but instead moisture appeared at the edges of his green eyes. He let go of me, heaved a deep sigh, and said, "Maybe one day men will learn to be kinder to each other."

A million thanks were on the tip of my tongue. The rabbi pulled my arm and placed a bag in my hand. We sped toward the terminal.

"Shalom," the two shouted from behind.

We turned and saw them standing by the van, waving, beaming encouraging smiles.

"Shalom," the rabbi and I yelled in return.

We trotted to the ticket counter and to our surprise found only one last-minute passenger scrambling for her ticket and seat assignment.

David Rosenburg's efficient connection had not let us down. Upon presenting our passports to a smiling clerk she gave us our boarding passes, with only ten minutes left.

In our haste, we took a wrong turn and got lost, but a big porter told us to backtrack. Frantically we cleared the baggage check and rushed forward.

Uniformed and plainclothes personnel loitered everywhere. No matter how I tried to remain calm and indifferent, I felt the perspiration pouring from under my wig, mustache, and beard.

A second security checkpoint came up—cordoned-off aisles leading to two tables manned by trained officers. Rabbi Yannoff headed for the first aisle while I made a dash for the second, but to my astonishment the rabbi blocked my advance and motioned me to precede him into his aisle. A dark, middle-aged man with sharp brown eyes asked for my passport, and with a trembling hand, I offered it to him. He casually leafed through the document and, with a suppressed indifference, as if he had been planted there to see me through, stamped it and allowed me to proceed.

I rushed forward. My eyes fell on a tall man in trench coat and fedora, with broad shoulders and icy stare. He kept scrutinizing the rabbi and I, the last two boarding passengers. I sensed he glared more inquisitively at me. Had he detected that I was a fraud and was readying to intercept me? I hurried past him, with my heart between my rattling teeth.

Briskly we made our way the short distance across the tarmac, up the steel steps of the ramp, and into the airplane. The rabbi urged me to take the window seat. The time clicked away in seconds that seemed like years. We sat in total silence. A flight attendant passed by with newspapers and magazines and I reached for one. She handed me the *Times*. I began to thumb through it, pretending to read though my mind was frozen, incapable of focusing on even the largest print or the pictures. At last, two male stewards shut the door. The engines whined. A female voice gave the aircraft's emergency orientation, and the cabin personnel were instructed to take their seats. The rabbi poked me.

"We are on our way. God has been with us," he whispered somberly.

"*Sholem aleichem* (Peace unto you), ladies and gentlemen," a deep voice came through the loudspeakers, "this is your captain speaking. There will be a slight administrative delay. Please make yourselves comfortable. God willing, we should be in the air soon. Thank you."

Groans of protest erupted from all directions while the staff leaped into action. Two attendants rushed to open the aircraft door, and as my eyes followed the returning ramp gliding back to fit against the fuselage once again, my heart sank. The end of the masquerade was surely near—I had fooled no one! My whole life passed rapidly before me. My Kathy waiting for me. A flash shot me like lightning. Is it in moments of such despair that a trapped man acknowledges his helplessness, creates deities, and begs for help?

The silhouette of the very tall, wide-shouldered man appeared in the cabin. Grim and forbidding, he inspected the seated crowd. I glanced at the rabbi but his face seemed peaceful, as if no fear had invaded his heart, while mine pounded like a gong at a Tibetan monastery. Moments passed before a furtive peek from under the lashes of my lowered eyes showed me the big man standing next to the rabbi. From inside my coat pocket I snatched the *Siddur,* the book of prayer, and clutching it between my perspiring palms, I closed my eyes and began rocking back and forth.

"*Shalom,* Rabbi Yannoff."

The stranger's voice stirred foggy memories. I kept up the rocking motion, pretending deep invocation.

"*Shalom aleichem,*" replied the rabbi coolly.

There was a pause and I could feel the man's steely eyes shooting through my Hasidic garb. Even had I been a devout man, calls for God's intervention were surely futile now—peril was real, discovery imminent.

"Greek," a voice whispered, "go on with your silly act and don't look up."

Captain Herb Rosenburg! I wanted to explode, to spring up and kiss him! I sneaked another peek, a longer one this time around.

Older and slightly heavier, probably a full bird colonel by now, my past CIC contact in Heidelberg stood hunched over the rabbi. He placed a finger on his lips to indicate restraint, and he went on speaking to Yannoff, although his words were meant for me.

"Remember the note under your hotel room door in Panama City?" He paused to give me time to recollect. "Our people delivered it. I've been with you all along, and I'll be with you in the future. Job well done . . . Rabbi." I peeked again and saw his brown eyes winking, smiling at my deception. He stood erect and authoritative. *"Shalom,"* he said, and with an assured step he walked up the aisle, bent to clear the cabin door, and disappeared.

13

THE END ...
AND A NEW BEGINNING

D espite days of sleeplessness, adrenaline flowed inside me and I felt pumped up as if I had swallowed a handful of uppers. Rabbi Yannoff seemed in high spirits, and he initiated an extensive discussion on religion and God.

"Christians and Moslems—in fact all Western religions—believe in the God of the Jews," he declared.

"Yes, but Christians accept Christ as the Son of God, therefore for them Christ is a God also."

"Christ was a wise teacher who preached to the impoverished of salvation from worldly misery through God, but he was not the son of God. Who would be in a better position to have knowledge against such a claim than the Jews and the Arabs, the natives of those lands where Jesus was born, grew up, and spread his gospel?"

"Christ was merely the founder of a ministry," I agreed.

"I'm sure you're familiar with Constantine. Constantine the Great was ruthless, courageous, ingenious, and responsible for Christianity's accomplishments."

"Christ was the founder of a religion and Constantine, three hundred years later, became Christianity's avid promoter. Correct?"

"Precisely. Constantine believed that a vast empire's cohesiveness depended on a strong religious foundation and uniformity. Mithraism was an inherently pagan sect of Persian origin for men only; its practitioners worshipped Mithra, the Unconquered Sun, as the most important of all gods. The religion was carried out in caves throughout the Byzantine Empire mostly by the military elite and the imperial nobility. Christianity, on the other hand, was a monotheistic religion that included both sexes as well as the poor and the underprivileged, a faith of comfort and mysticism, of hope and equality, of brotherly love and fellowship. Having to choose between his inherited Mithraism and Christianity, Constantine cleverly settled for the latter. Christianity, with its strong assurance that upon death one ascends to the heavens for an everlasting life, harvests brave soldiers, so Constantine shrewdly professed to a vision of a shining cross in the sky and claimed to have been visited in his dreams by Christ.

"He embraced Christianity, adopted the cross as his emblem, and led his armies victoriously, first against Maxentium in the battle at the Milvian Bridge near Rome, and second against Licinius at Chrysopolis. Since Christianity had served him well, helping him become the sole ruler of the vast Byzantine Empire, he proclaimed Christianity the legal religion of the land. Because of its appeal to the masses and its protection under Constantine, Christianity (an insignificant religious group then) was immune from civic burdens and legally privileged, so it gradually fortified its foundation to expand and prosper and finally dominate the Western world."

Not wanting to be overheard I lowered my voice a few notes. "But Christianity is an oriental religion and Semitic in concept. Since by your own admission Christians worship your God, why are you, Jews, considered so different from Christians, aside from your refusal to recognize Christ as God?"

"Religions, for their self-preservation and perpetuation, are forced to be unkind to each other. Even today the dominant faith of a region discredits all others as reactionary, strange, and unacceptable. And although the Jewish God is the God of all Western lands, all the Jews of the world are often looked down upon because we believe we are God's special people. Jews teach their children that the love of their God toward them will never end, that He is the only God of Heaven and earth, and His affection for them is eternal. 'A people that dwells alone, not reckoning itself among the Nations' is an excerpt from the

Hebrew scriptures. And because we believe we are so privileged in this respect, others view us as different and set us apart as strange."

"But, honestly, Rabbi Yannoff, do you truly believe, deep down in your heart, after all the hardships your tribes have suffered across the millennia, that you are indeed God's chosen people?"

"I would not be a Jew if I believed differently; and certainly not a rabbi."

"But isn't this claim of the Jews as elitist as that of the Christians who assert that only devout Christians are entitled to God's favors?"

The good rabbi played with his beard as his eyes jumped in thought, but he remained silent.

I pursued my point. "Here we have three religions worshipping the same God, yet each is at the throat of the other two. Judaism and Islam do not accept Christ as the Son of God. Christianity and Islam do not accept the Jews as God's chosen people. And Christianity and Judaism repudiate Mohammed as a prophet and renounce the Koran as a divinely-inspired scripture. To go one step further, Judaism is divided into Orthodox, Hasidic, Reformed, Conservative, Reconstructionist, and more. Christians are split among Orthodox, Catholic, Protestant, Lutheran, Mormon, and only God knows how many other groups. Islam is divided into the die-hard Fundamentalists, Moderates, and Sufis. Of all these dissimilar religious assemblages that give credence to the same God, which one is right?"

"Only He knows the answer," said the rabbi and pointed to the heavens.

"But who is God? Are the accounts of the Old Testament worthy of reverence? Those claims that God created the sky and the earth in six days and nights, that He molded Adam and Eve out of clay, and that mankind is descended from those two? And even if it were so, isn't it unjust and ungodly that devoted simpletons and flimflam evangelists who have adhered blindly to God enjoy privileged seating in the heavenly arena while superior minds that have inspired and shaped our world are spitefully forbidden admittance to the eternal show? Minds such as the free thinkers Confucius and Gautama Buddha, wavering pagans (shy monotheists, actually) like Plato and Aristotle, or the atheists Machiavelli and Voltaire, and agnostics Huxley and Kazantzakis?"

"The Jews don't believe in heavenly redemption. We believe in laboring to create a just society through the guidance of God, who rewards obedience and punishes rebelliousness."

"I take it by rebelliousness you mean evil."

"Well, yes."

"Here is where I come against a stone wall. If I were a Jew, accepting that life after death is a Christian aberration, and that God punishes evil here on earth, why ...?"

"Why the holocaust? the murder of your father?" the rabbi filled in. As if peeking through a confused mask he shook his head and scratched his golden beard. "Those are disturbing questions, Yiannis, for which no one has an answer."

"Is it possible then that God doesn't exist?"

"Man without God is aimless. Man needs God."

"Maybe God exists in the minds of those who need him," I said.

"A divine sovereignty over all mankind is as normal as the sunshine. God is the Creator of order. Without God and his teachings there would be chaos in the world."

I pondered the God of the Jews and my father, the very same God who, according to Rabbi Yannoff, was now guiding me to freedom, and I felt a powerful urge to state my convictions.

"I'm a bit of a Jaina myself," I said gently. "Actually, I believe the world was never created. I perceive the universe as infinite and eternal. Matter is indestructible. Only its condition changes. Space is formless—endless—as is time. Assertions to anything contrary are manifestations of man—his efforts to explain the incomprehensible. Also, I believe that soon, modern man will accept his mortality as his total end. Then he will sit down to formulate his own moral rules and ethical doctrines, shed borders and prejudices, and will go on to construct a fairer, nobler world for himself, here on Earth, because Gods, angels, messiahs, and prophets have failed him."

The good rabbi started to leaf through a glossy magazine, his blue eyes darting from picture to picture. He chose to remain mute and I returned to the *Times*.

Upon our arrival at Lod Airport on the outskirts of Tel Aviv, we rented a jeep. In a few hours of easy driving through a desert transformed into fertile fields, we reached the harbor of the port city of Ashdod and located the caique *Agia Maria*. Captain Fokas and his strong nephew were diligently awaiting my appearance.

"Where is the cargo?" shouted the captain, leaning against the tiller with concern when he saw the two of us alone in the jeep.

"I am the cargo, Captain Fokas," I shouted back.

The captain and his nephew looked at each other in a dumbfounded way, crossed themselves three times, and together said, "God be praised." Then the righteous, skillful captain turned his perplexed head, spat over his shoulder into the sea to ward off all evil spirits and added, "Get thee behind me Satan, for sure."

After choking shaloms and tight hugs with Yannoff, I climbed on the wooden vessel. Captain Fokas started the engine and we slowly motored into the waters of the Mediterranean Sea. In three nights and three days of drafty sailing we reached the tiny harbor of Chora in Sfakia.

Kathy, the most beautiful soul of my world, stood on the cliff like some majestic goddess of the Libyan Sea. Shading her eyes from the glare of the setting sun she discerned the markings of the boat. Strong wind pressed her clothing against her torso while her long skirt flapped in the breeze like a welcoming banner. Suddenly she broke into a frantic waving. As Captain Fokas was preparing to kill the trusted engine, I watched my life's mate race down the hillside, shouting and calling out to me. She jumped the rocks and boulders and sped across the white beach pebbles and into the sea, submerged up to her waist and crying out my name. I plunged into the water clothed, yearning to breathe her scent, and met her halfway.

Betty and Kostas had returned to their home in Athens. In confidence, over the phone, I told them of my completed mission. Then I explained that Kathy and I had chosen to remain in hiding since we could not trust the Greek authorities to protect us if and when the U.S. Justice Department demanded my extradition.

Two months after my return, my mother's fragile heart gave out.

She went to her grave unaware that her son had collected the revenge due her. Kathy and I attended her funeral from a distance and wept.

The February following the Kennedy assassination in Texas, a brown manila envelope arrived in the mail. The sender had used a typewriter to address it, and the postal markings appeared military.

The winter sun stood bright but the temperature in the shade was cool. Like a cat who finds a sheltered spot to soak up the precious rays, I took a seat on a stone bench and faced the eternal light.

I tore open the envelope's edge, careful to avoid destroying any contents and, as my fingers reached inside, a bent piece of metal fell out onto the compacted earth. Panic instantly overcame me and with trembling hands I picked it up. Part of it was missing but I could still read: CLIMPT COOK.

Tears poured out of me as if my inner being had turned into a swollen waterfall. I hugged what was left of my buddy's dog tag and between sighs asked over and over again the same dumb, unanswerable questions.

Before my bleary eyes a giant butterfly, black and lavender with yellow spots, wobbled in the sunlight. It flew up and down shyly deciding the safest place to land, fatigued after a long voyage. It fluttered its wings, almost tickled my face, and gently dropped on my hand and delicately kissed it. I reached to touch it but it reticently flapped its wings, became airborne, flirted with me a bit longer, and flew away.

Finally, feeble courage roused me and I shook the envelope to rob it of its remaining secrets. A crumpled, bloodstained notebook slid into my hand. On a lined muddy page scribbled in pencil over many erasures I faced a letter meant for me. I read it many times to grasp its meaning and added some punctuation as I went along.

my Pal yiannis, Must knowed by now Kennedy is a goner with a shot in the head an' Johnson flip about winnin this dam fite, an' our almighty God, bless his obsession, got numb on moonshine, all while snickerin' at the mess, careles about who die down here in Nam. Acuz I got me confusin' thoughts about fitin' fer my country, an' all that stuff, an' acuz I been a witness ta a beliful o' kilin', I done some o' that mself, they be no more renlistments fer me. I gets my ass out in july. Sides, as o' late, a spooky feelin' been creepin' up an' down ma spine ticklin' me here an' there, so I left word with ma CO to sen' ya my dog tags if I gits it in the bely or gits blowd up by a dam mine like some o' us gone done an' git blowd up an' fertilizet them here gook rice fields. Admittin' my dog tags hain't much gift ta sen' to ya to keep frum me, but its somethin o' yar old pal who love ya lak' a . . .

In memory of my "brother" Climpt I began to write the story of *Just Another Man.*

Sunny weeks passed and rainy months came. Kathy and I exchanged a hundred smooches and licks each day while we murmured assuringly that our devotion packed enough energy to propel a space ship to the most distant galaxies.

One evening the two of us stood embraced on the terrace of our eagle's nest. Fierce south winds, preceding heavy, black clouds charged with electricity, whipped our faces. Lightning and thunder broadcast the intimidating course of the rapidly rolling storm. "My love for you is boundless," I shouted and pulled Kathy tighter against me. Bewitched by the might in the sky, the stirring in the sea, and my fondness for my mate I went on.

"Thirty-one years ago, up in the rugged Kalavryta, a tiny seed was snatched by a blizzard like this one coming, smashed against a rock, and split in two. One half got buried there in the mud and germinated into a man—the other flew a five-year voyage across the world—it landed far, far away in California and there it grew into a most beautiful young woman. After time, the man miraculously sniffed the young woman out. And here we are, my Louloudaki, you and me, one soul with two hearts—two lovers with one spirit."

Better than a year and a half trickled by. I woke up before dawn one morning, my heart powerful and my mind fresh. A million thoughts danced inside my head. Obedient to inscrutable urges, I grabbed my writing pad and pencil and sneaked out, walked the length of the courtyard, and under the main house, I opened the massive front door and crouched on the first stone step. The earth smelled of chamomile. From a distance two roosters crowed in contest, a dog barked, and a lonesome goat bell spilled its dim ding-ding. The village below had begun its shadowy stirring. In the semidarkness, a priest, resting a pickax on his shoulder, like a phantom hurried across the wide triangle of compacted earth, the bottom end of his frock flowing one step behind his boots. The simple notes of a bamboo flute tickled the earthly setting. Frantically I scribbled down thoughts, capturing them before they had a chance to flee. As if in a dream I heard Kathy say, "Oh here you are; I have been looking for you everywhere." Vaguely, I remember her peck on my lips when she dropped off my morning coffee. Time passed by rapidly and now the sun stared down on me, as if wishing to read my scribbling.

At last, my bent head rose to face the most glorious spring morning. The salty air scented with the sweetness of the potted marjoram, oregano, and basil delighted my lungs. Vasilis, the postman, shouted from below, a white envelope in his waving arm.

"Mr. American, a letter. It's from America." He climbed some steps and I walked down to meet him.

"Good morning," he said with his usual broad smile.

"Good morning, indeed."

"A letter from America," he glowed and passed the envelope over to me in a most delicate fashion, as if it were stuffed with pearls.

"What an important job you have, Vasilis," I announced brightly.

"Hmm. You think so, Mr. American?"

"Yes. Of course."

"But how so?" he asked suspiciously and tossed me a bemused look.

"Oh! Think, my good man. Just think of the myriad surprises you bring along with your short visits."

"Yah?"

"Laughter, love, hope, memories, introspection, preparations, anticipation, along with some disappointments and tears. You are the bearer of all those significant things, Vasilis, and many, many more."

He shook his shoulders, cocked his hat up, and marched away whistling a Cretan tune.

The letter came from Miami; Stavros broke his news in a brief note. I searched for Kathy and found her stooping behind a crumbling brown stone wall of the Frank ruins where in a patch of rocky earth, sheltered from the winds that blow from the African plains, my Louloudaki had planted her garden. When I approached, she was in deep dialogue with the iris and her spring rosebushes. LB, stretched nearby, pricked up her ears to the sound of my approach.

"We can return home," I murmured calmly, barely suppressing my urge to demonstrate my rapture. Startled, she straightened up, brushed her soiled hands against her prairie dress that stuck out noticeably — she was six months along with our first child — then ran them through her ruffled hair and came to me. Her eyes fell on the piece of paper I held, then darted up in appeal and focused on mine.

"Stavros writes that Fox, the District Attorney, is a veteran of the Second World War — served in Europe — and has no sympathy for ex-Nazis. If we return home and I surrender, Fox has guaranteed my freedom, on a token bail, until the trial is over. Stavros adds that some great legal minds are offering to help with my defense."

She didn't jump with elation nor did she shriek with joy. She tenderly took my hand, kissed it and sighed, and her voice trembled like the petal of a pansy in a faint breeze.

"I love you, my Sunflower," she whispered and turned to hide her tears.

We stood gazing at her mute companions, admiring their splendor. Kathy wove her fingers through mine and murmured.

"I'll miss all my friends here, Yiannis."

NOTES

Readers interested in further information on these topics might want to seek out one or more of the following books, which were of assistance in writing this volume:

The Rise and Fall of Nazi Germany by T. L. Jarman

The Inner Nazi by Hans Staudinger

Fascism in Western Europe 1900–1945 by H. R. Kedward

The Pledge Betrayed by Tom Bower

Knights of the Black Cross by Bran Perrett

The Nuremberg Mind: The Psychology of Nazi Leaders by Florence Miale

The Architect of Genocide by Richard Breitman

Conquest of the Balkans by the editors of Time-Life Books

The Drama of Kalavryta by Dimitzi Kaldizi (in Greek)

Greece in the '40s: A Nation in Crisis edited by John O. Iatrides

Himmler by Peter Padfield

Inside Hitler's Greece: The Experience of Occupation 1941–44
   by Mark Mazower

The Joys of Yiddish by Leo Rosten

The Story of the Occupation by Dimitrios Gatopoulos (in Greek)

Unholy Trinity: The Vatican, the Nazis, and Soviet Intelligence by Mark
   Aarons and John Loftus

The Wiesenthal File by Alan Levy

I am also indebted to my family for their encouragement and suggestions, and in particular to my "Louloudaki" Kathy, who has shared every bit of my frustration throughout my four-year labor to complete this book.

My gratitude goes to Virginia Ferguson, who with patience deciphered my original scribblings. Also, my deep thanks go to Johnnie H. Langley for his southern quips and folk expressions, Eduardo Jimenez for his assistance in research, my editor Jean Arnold for her invaluable advice, Paula Morrison for her sensitive and creative book design, and Kathy Glass, my final editor, whose skills are golden.

I would like to acknowledge my friends Nadine Breed, Shimon Van Collie, Larry Hatfield, Hal Lauritzen, Violetta and Greg Nikolas, Susan Stack, and Christopher Uphan for their input after they graciously agreed to read unedited versions of the manuscript.

Lastly I extend my everlasting thanks to Kitty and Michael Dukakis for being so gracious to read a nearly final version of this manuscript and pass on to me their valued comments.

THE PHOTOS